Cristofo
Wizard of Earth

Cristofo
Wizard of Earth

Dino Pietrobon

Print information available on the last page.

Rev. date: 04/18/2019

To order additional copies of this book, contact:
Xlibris
1-888-795-4274
www.Xlibris.com
Orders@Xlibris.com
790501

CONTENTS

PROLOGUE

For no less than four thousand million years, a great and renowned mother of creation has been spinning around and flying in the vast starry abundance of space, turning and constantly working as creature upon creature spawned from her. They would ooze into existence, willed astir through her essence and molded into form by use of the necessary ingredients that were rife and abundant within. Eons and ages of creature and beings would be nurtured in all of their multitudinous and varied forms, each remaining free to reap the benefit of an ever-giving soul; to live, to die, to survive, or to become extinct, the paths are there for all to choose as they set sail their course. Entrapped and cemented in her course, she remains with the sole purpose of existing and providing life for those who favor her warm embrace.

Born an incomprehensible birth, this mother was the mother that is sometimes so cordially and commonly called Earth. Spontaneously expulsed by an immeasurable force, she raced at incredible speed for time and distance that is not of our faculties to comprehend substantially. Suffice it to compare that generations of man and beasts would come and go as in the blink of an eye and through it all she would fly tirelessly and without fail. But alas, as with all things to which there is no exception, time is a force that will ultimately take its toll. Eventually and inevitably, she tired and slowed, and as if by some divine decree, she reluctantly yet deliberately fell prey to a massive and fiery star that skillfully drew her in with its spell. She of such mighty determination was captured, trapped as a mere fly in the web of an ever-so-powerful spider, yielding to a preeminent foe against whom she was no match; beyond her great will, she was forced to acquiesce.

Around and around she would fly, unable to escape but nonetheless struggling and fighting with all her strength, refusing to succumb to the overpowering magnetic charm that the omnipotent fiery spider seemed to wield so easily. For ages, she would battle steadfast, standing her ground while stubbornly maintaining her distance and all the while helplessly watching countless other fragments of similarly entranced conquests and victims submit to the powers of her incredible captor's charm. One by one, they would fall and become lured into the beast's fiery bowels, filling its belly and feeding the flame of her enemy, and as her foe's allure strengthened, so too did her resolve.

For countless centuries, this eloquent ballet of sorts continued as predator and prey danced and swayed in battle, until wisdom forced its imperious hand toward compromise. Finally, the great mother that so many now know and love made herself comfortable in her forced confinement, spinning and flying around her subduer in a trancelike state while occasionally relishing the companionship of other resilient yet similarly trapped kin. She was indeed trapped—jailed to a degree— but also free. Eventually, she would come to embrace the strength and warmth that her great captor undoubtedly provided, and a symbiotic relationship ensued, which evolved into one that would suit her just fine. She did well to flourish and nurture life of all kinds for millennia and millennia to come.

For the sake of clarity, it must be mentioned that the audience toward which these words are intended cannot easily understand the spans of time about which I speak. A million years' passing cannot truly be fathomed, let alone thousands of millions. Just know this: all or most of the earth's countless creatures and abundance of life can at any time be lost in one fell swoop. Any number of times in the course of a million years can life be erased in whole or in part, and in fact it has. Each time, however, it eventually prevails, returning for better or worse, in greater or weaker numbers, and in the same or variant forms. Some elements seem to resurrect with regularity, while others spawn anew and are unique. Overall, one thing has been certain to date: life has triumphed.

Moreover, throughout the course of time and throughout the various epochs of existence on Earth, many tales have somehow endured—tales of simplicity and greatness, tales of timeless spirit and will, tales that bring excitement and fire to the souls of its audience, tales that reach out and touch the hearts of its listeners, wherever and whenever they may exist. Such a tale as I will now have the pleasure to purvey ...

I am Altarius the Prime, holder of the unique position of lead wizard for the animus realm of existence. Now what does that mean exactly, you might ask? I will answer and attempt to clarify in simplistic terms and in words that will not reveal secrets and truths that are not yet sanctioned for your ears to hear and your minds to comprehend. In all, there are five who hold the unique rank of wizard in this realm of which I speak, this realm in which both you and I are found to reside. As lead, I hold the highest position of the group, and while I do not argue against the rationale for my honorable rank, it is not one that has been self-imposed. No, indeed. Conversely, it is an honor I was blessed with long ago. By whom? you may wonder. Well, suffice it to say that it is a privilege bestowed upon me by the overseers of all realms, a group of seventeen metaphysical beings charged with the task of bringing order and regularity to a chaotically churning omniverse, a place about which you would have little to no understanding. Suffice it to say that these overseers charge themselves with the task of creating balance and harmony over all known planes of existence and realms that subsist in great numbers throughout the unconfined infinity of time and space. Now, while I will not be as bold as to charge that my position implies power and abilities greater than that of my four cohorts, neither will I deny it. Let it be sufficient to say that while it has never been proved that I am the most powerful of the five, neither has it been rebuffed. To say that we are all powerful and impressive in our own right goes without question.

Malthazar is another of the five wizards of the animus realm, a comrade in arms and one with whom many of my journeys have been intertwined. He is regularly my pairing on the odd occasion when a task requires a combined wizardly effort. By way of stature, he stands quite unimposing in physicality, a facade made real and shaped of his own design and choice, but be not fooled by appearances, for he possesses abilities that tower above the imagination. Mysterious spells and powers abound in the crafty little rascal's arsenal, incantations that always stand at the ready to bring him the advantage of surprise. Stealth is the skill for which Malthazar is best known; invisible as the wind, he flies in an out and all around anywhere, gathering information and garnering advantage in the most slippery of ways. I, on the other hand, prefer a more direct and confrontational approach—to each their preference, I suppose. True as the dawn, he stays on task, and with an unfailing statuesque resolve, he endures time and time again.

Bellatrix is our one compatriot of female form. Rest assured that a more worthy ally would be near impossible to ascertain. Holder of the mystic rock of Tempestas and purveyor of the formidable power that it beholds, she wields its omnipotence with the skill and grace of one who has mastered the taming of otherwise savage and untamable beasts. Time and persistence have afforded her the luxury of breaking the wild stallion that she so proudly displays atop her staff. No other touch or sound will bring this mysterious rock to life, and rest assured that it can wake with a fury that cannot justifiably be described by words. Its powers can calm the stormiest of seas or quench the thirst of the most barren deserts. Indeed, it is with a mere whim that she manipulates a planet's entire atmospheric phenomenon, any planet that is, or at least any upon which she has attempted the task to date. No, this mysterious crystal is not of your world, nor was it any small undertaking to procure. How she managed to garner this treasure and master its mysterious power is an exhilarating tale, but alas, it is a tale for another place and time.

Veneficus is my old friend and a wizard of great esteem. Long has he held rank and ventured to task, jaunting throughout the realms with unmatched skill and ferocity. He is favored for appointments of an expeditious nature, where his mercurial qualities thrive. By far, he is the busiest of us, to say the least, but while his efficiency and quick purpose make him a most formidable force, he lacks the strength of wisdom and resolve that can only grow through seasons of water and passing sun. For this reason, I venture to surmise that he was overlooked as Prime, even though he bragged the longest existence and age of us all. On many occasions in my passing adventures, I would hope, call, and pray for his resounding presence. And on many occasions in my passing adventures, he would appear as though in a dream and just in time to salvage the portentous situation at hand. What a great friend and stalwart soul upon which one can always rely. Too few are the occasions of late when our paths come to be crossed and adventure is found to be shared.

Finally, as last but certainly not least, we have Cristofo—a being of your world nonetheless and the first and only wizard spawned of the earth. Discovered as a boy and skillfully guided toward his correct path in life, his burgeoning soul was accordingly bolstered and extolled with the intention of expediting the inevitable. Well, in all fairness, his guidance was also to serve as a test to ascertain with certainty that which, at least in my mind, was there all along. Yes, as you may have now surmised, I was the one who initially discovered the great light in this young boy oh so long ago, and it was I who was charged with the task of guiding his course. You see, it is quite simple, really; a wizard's power and skill of observation is quite strong relative to that of most all other known creatures and kinds. Whereas one of your species may see a simple tree, I would instead see a majestic imposing colossus with cavernous veins pumping water and nutritious food from the soil and groundwork below. Long-tentacled and bristly arms burrow into the ground, sucking the milk of the earth in an enduring drive to reach out its flowers and touch the sun. Survival and proliferation is the ultimate goal, as is the case for most all life. A thick crusty armor of bark covers and protects her from harm, while a great number of animals and insects alike make home in and around the great umbrella that she so willingly provides. I hear her leaves chiming in the wind, conducting music like an orchestra of finely tuned instruments. They chatter among themselves in this manner, speaking of things of forest-ly importance. And let us not forget to mention their smell; sweet delicious essence of the land emitted robustly and with an enchanting ease. Ah yes, trees, the great and majestic extensions of the earth that flourish widespread to cover vast expanses of her surface, but I digress. You must forgive an old wizard of age, for I do sometimes lose myself in the details of thought.

Now, to return to my point, I will explain about the spark of life. It exists in all, it exists with differing magnitudes, and it exists in opposing spectra. These three truths remain and consistently endure. The first truth is absolute and easily understood. The second is understandable but deciphering the degree of spark is no simple earthly task; instead, it remains the skill of wizards and of few other creatures of advanced and uncanny abilities. The third truth is also quite comprehensible. In all life there exists good, and in all life there exists evil; it is the great universal divide that exists from necessity. Like opposing magnetic poles, these great forces keep each other in check and allow for robust growth through a creation of purpose and an inception of resolve. The extreme sides of the spectrum are relatively easy to recognize, but as you approach the middle of the multitudinous array, it gets extremely complex to decipher. Only with many years of scrutiny and thought can the art be mastered, and mastered it must be for any who act in a wizardly capacity. I myself am known to be particularly gifted in this arduous craft, which is why my behest to make wizard of the boy was met with such an open mind. Seldom does the opportunity present itself to witness one of such exceptional spark, let alone one who is deemed to be destined for a wizardly calling, and so when such occasion does present itself, action is certainly required.

There you have it, a foreshadowing of the substance and meat of this impending tale, but let it not be thought of Altarius the Prime to jump into story without the proper serving of hors d'oeuvres for the mind and so first some background and atmosphere to whet the palate.

CHAPTER 1

The Alchemist

Many generations ago, in the land then known as Nephesh, just north of the equatorial plains and six days' march from the tempestuous seas, there existed an exceptional man—an alchemist by trade who made his mark on the world with a great discovery. Seldom would he allow the day to pass without excursion. Out he ventured from a very early age, trekking farther and farther as time passed and daylight allowed. All the while, he scoured, looking for any anomalies in the nature and land that were his environs. Trees, plants, stones, pebbles, insects, and rodents alike fell under the scope of his rigorous scrutiny. However, caves, caverns, holes, and subterranes were his most precious hosts. Rocks, minerals, and metals in like manner did he relish and look to the most for his precious ingredients.

A hunger for answers fueled the exceptional explorer as he continued in his quest to solve the myriad riddles of nature and life. He hungered for discovery of an extraordinary kind, discovery that he knew was forthcoming if not imminent. He felt it in every dream and in every essence of his being, and he knew beyond any shadow of doubt that it was destined to befall. But when? The timing was uncertain, but not the eventuality. Patience was not lacking, and the resolve was strong as by day he ventured out and harnessed his materials. By night, he toiled with his catch, using a makeshift laboratory rife with tools and chemicals. Indeed, he busied himself with experiments: trial and error, concoctions of all kinds, medicines, and elixirs. Ravenous was his appetite to spell out and invent.

Above all, fire presented his greatest fascination. Long did he hold the desire to master this wondrous element; to facilitate its creation was foremost on his mind. It was most incomprehensible to him that a valuable and necessary tool of culture would require such effort to inflame. Throughout the land, people in shops and households worked steadfastly to keep their fires roaring, purposely exaggerating their longevity, fuel of trees needlessly wasted for the mere purpose of avoiding a difficult rekindling. Blacksmith and baker in kind catered to their precious fires throughout the long day, preserving the fires' lives in desperate attempts to avoid resurrecting them anew. Households similarly gorged this warm and trusted companion, basking in the convenience of the fire's enduring flame. Friction of wood to the point of ignition was such a surprisingly arduous task, requiring much skill and patience. Many would have to toil long and hard to achieve smolder. And what alternative—the smashing together of two rocks or of rock against alloy of iron to create a spark with the desperate objective of catching itself upon a waiting bed of dry leaves, plant down, and string of wood so as to take firm hold and germinate into flame? It seemed such a barbaric means to achieving the desired result. The alchemist could not fathom this in a town of such size and bustle. Indeed, he would not have it so. Indeed, he would not allow it to continue.

Therefore, we arrive to his principal concern at the time, the project boasting the lion's share of his valuable efforts. Several months prior, on a particularly memorable spelunking excursion, a discovery was made wherein an intriguing reddish-brown vein of rock was uncovered on the walls of his favorite cave. He made quick work of garnering samples with his trusted explorer's hammer, noting the brittle and crumbly composition and feel. Without further thought, he continued with his usual task of searching and gathering specimens for experimentation and study. Then, later that evening, as was his usual practice, he settled in comfort at a grandiose worktable and began to toil with the day's findings and facts. The brownish-red rock was first to draw his attention, even though its sedimentary nature was interesting to a degree but not overly noteworthy. The alchemist shaped it quite easily with an iron rasp and hastily scrutinized the powdery residue under his magnifying lens. However, interest quickly faded, and focus turned away from the ground granules of rock, as nothing of a particularly fascinating determination was observed. Aimlessly he stared at his dependable magnifying glass until his mind wandered to thoughts of fire, as it so often did.

While he was known to be quite resourceful and skilled in all means of starting fires, directing the hot day's sun through his lens and into a pile of tinder was his method of favor. Unfortunately, it was also the method to which the night and clouds would boundlessly force surrender. So, there he sat in lost thought, staring at the fading fire beside him in the room, while the smell of the night's roasted meal still lingered. Then a new and totally unrelated manner of experimentation came to mind and awakened him from his languor. He sat up abruptly from his chair in anticipation of his next procedure. He whisked the overflowed sandy residue from the table and placed it in his hand. Then he walked to the dwindling fire and let fly the debris. Shocking eruption ensued as the fire was instantaneously reinvigorated. Equal was the eruption in the alchemist's eyes as his great mind quickly perused the next options for experimentation while he stared in awe at the newly enlivened fire. And in a matter of seconds, he laid out his work for the next number of moments as well as for the upcoming days.

Days passed, the moons faded and reappeared, the seasons changed, and the alchemist continued along with his tireless ritual. Progress was made on his foremost of inventions, as it was on other considerations as well. However, the main task was no easy one and was made more difficult still because of his rigorous perfectionism. This was to be his paramount contribution to the world, and he calculated for it to leave an enduring mark for generations to come. Yes, he had come to some success, but painstaking was the process. Long indeed did it take to find the proper breed of wood to host such a dry manner of flame. Just the right combination of porosity and rigidity were required, and the variety must consist of a grain that ran straight and true. Just the right mix of chemical and ground rock was required prior to mixing it with animal glue to bind and set the powder true to the tip. In the end, it was remarkable indeed, but not enough to satisfy the alchemist. The combustion was rewarding every time the fire stick was successfully abraded against a rudimentary band of crushed glass or any such abrasive surface, but alas, it still lacked consistency. It lacked proper magnitude and rate of burn. The tip of the fire stick often broke off without burning. Other times, burn would occur, but irksome small fireballs scattered about. Much work was needed still; the creation was not yet to be extolled.

Now, as it happened, one time while on crusade on a particularly lively and nimble Nepheshan spring day, the alchemist's feet brought him to the edge of a mountainous ridge some two hours' pace or so from his home. Something here fascinated him in a peculiar way. Numerous nooks, crannies, and caverns of various sizes and shapes riddled the facade of this mysterious and massive outcropping of stone, which was embedded into the earth in a most nonsensical way, he thought. It was akin to a monolithic mass of great proportion that fell from the sky and forced itself deep into her encrustation of skin. How strange the composition as well, he reasoned, sedimentary in nature and somewhat comparable to his prior discovery of a flammable persuasion. It was curious how the fractures and markings of stone played such stark contrast to the relatively sandy and barren clay of its surroundings. And the coloration was varied but tended toward a grayish brown, while the surrounding plains were more brownish beige. It was a subtle contrast to most but was flagrantly perceived by the alchemist. While countless others before him may have passed the great ridge in a comfortable aura of cluelessness, he was struck with awe. An uncanny island in a sea of land is what he saw. The urge to explore was overwhelming. Nary had a force so strong affected him, and nary had he experienced such difficulty in resisting the urge to hastily delve into the closest nook and explore relentlessly. Yet resist he did. The alchemist's wisdom prevailed, and sensibly he surmised that the proper course entailed surveying the prospective targets today in preparation of tomorrow's more thorough examination of choice.

So ahead he forged, with eyes wide and an excited spirit, peering into each and every nook and cavern, rudimentarily sketching his progress on a crude but innately correct map. Hours passed, and numerous similarly laid-out targets were surveyed, all of which possessed the noteworthy criteria—namely that both size and ease of access were suitable enough to host the alchemist's lanky frame. Sun languished, hunger and fatigue grew, and a mere shred of the monolithic ridge was properly explored. Homeward he bound with thoughts of tomorrow's more meticulous pursuits. Excitement prevailed through the long journey home and throughout that evening and night. What little sleep managed to befall his excited soul brought dreams of similar elation. *Where to begin? Which paths lead to wonder and bewilderment? What mysteries lie deep within, waiting for discovery?* Such thoughts simmered in his mind throughout and beyond the darkness of twilight and ripened as the rising sun forced his eyelids to crack open in anticipation of the oncoming day.

The necessary preparations were completed well in advance. A hearty breakfast of egg and bread would give him proper constitution, and a light cargo of necessities would hasten his pace. A small torch with cloth soaked in his own oily concoction would provide needed light in the dark Cimmerian caverns, which were to be his ambition. A few sticks of dry flame, as imperfect as he deemed them, presented a valuable substitute for his magnifying lens should a sunless ignition be required. His trusted explorer's hammer, of course, was carried in its usual station, and his small sketch pad and charcoal stick would fit just right in his carry bag. Faded from the sun of countless excursions, the alchemist's carry bag was an agreeable companion. It was worn to a perfect comfort and carefully crafted in quality by his own hands, using the most resilient of animal hides. It was customized with pockets and sheaths to suit his purpose, with ample room for samples and specimens being no small consideration. A thin belt-like strap fastened to the edges of the bag was designed to wrap around the waist, keeping it steady during stride or during awkward maneuvers and securing its precious cargo.

Next was a bladder of drink and a small quantity of dried meat to bridge the hunger until his return at dusk. Finally, he garnered his favorite blade for such an occasion, a modest length of sword made of a remarkable alloy of his own design and representing the perfect unification of strength and sharpness with an ethereal feel. It was crowned with an intricately carved handle of hollowed bone and sheathed in a scabbard of hide, the inside of which was ingeniously lined with a hardened powdery aggregate. This contrivance served a twofold purpose. Firstly, it protected the nimble but vulnerable hide from the sharpness of blade; secondly, it wrought an unmatched incisiveness. It dangled inconspicuously and unnoticed around his waist, camouflaged against his legging. About the length of a man's forearm it lay, unintimidating but always at the ready should the situation arise. An agile and skilled combatant the alchemist was, as witnessed by my own eyes on more than one occasion and surprisingly so for a mind of such scientific persuasion. Off he went to discovery and adventure.

His pace was brisk, as it usually was, and all the while, his mind calculated the quandary of the moment—namely, which of the many targets of note he would first choose to exploit. One by one, he perused his options, infiltrating the details of his memory and on occasion referencing the replete pages of his sketch pad in an effort to reinforce his conclusions, and so the decision was made. His first target of choice exhibited a tunnel-like opening near perfectly round in shape and design—quite peculiar, to say the least. It was not very large in size but just enough so that a man could waddle his way through in relative comfort. What struck him most was the consistent nature of the formation and how it seemed to travel straight and true like a borehole made by some inexplicably large mechanical tool. Level was its incline and strangely smooth was its side, or at least insofar as he could tell from his initial brief analysis of yesterday. A more thorough examination was definitely in order. The second target of choice also boasted a most noteworthy aperture. It stood as a tall vertical opening barely wide enough for a man to squeeze through. Slightly offset and overlapping lip-shaped sides camouflaged the opening from the ground below. A mildly difficult climb was required to reach its threshold, and upon peering inside, it seemed to open into a vast cavern of great breadth and size. It was spacious and expansive, or so it conveyed, but one could not be sure, as the certainty was basked in a darkness so absolute as though never before pierced by sun or eyes.

Time seemed to fly by quickly, as the mind was occupied in detailed thought, and so in what seemed to be relatively quick order, the alchemist stood fast before his purpose. Once again, he was struck with awe. A full day and night's contemplation of the mysterious range did little to wash away his astonishment. He recomposed himself and continued his pace straight toward his first target. Upon arrival to the juncture where the ridge's face met the dissimilar floor of sandy clay, he could effortlessly discern the round outline of his objective. Quick work would be made of his climb, as there were countless jagged edges and footholds of all sorts and kinds. A small flat landing adjacent to the entry conveniently welcomed him as he kneeled down and prepared himself for entry. His magnifying lens drew in the hot sun, and quick work was made in lighting his torch. The flame burned low and steady as a soft smile invaded the adventurer's otherwise inexorable visage. He allowed himself the brief pleasure of basking in self-pride while celebrating his handiwork—the perfect flame to suit his purpose—and then off he scurried into the unknown tunnel with caution to the wind and torch held outright.

The first ten strides or so revealed the same characteristics as the immediate area of entry surveyed in haste by the brief exploration of the previous day. The circular wall on the inside of the tunnel was relatively smooth and eerily consistent in circumference. If only he had brought rope, he thought, he would take some measurements to see just how true the diameter was in actuality. Next time, he concluded, but if not for the slight flattening at the tunnel's base, his judgment asserted circularity very near to perfection. Years of gravity taking its toll on the brittle sediment may have been cause for the modest interruption in curve, he thought, or a number of other reasons may be blamed for the linearity underfoot. Nevertheless, and whatever the cause, one thing became more and more certain: it augmented as he advanced. Now thirty strides in or so, the base formed a near comfortable ground, as a soft but granular residue seemed to have accumulated. The alchemist's hammer made quick work of the sample, and his fingers discerned a texture of hardened sandy ash. He made note of the coloration on the wall, which now seemed to have softened, tending toward a more grayish white, with a slight yellowing becoming apparent as well. He sat down for a moment and made a comfortable effort to recompose; the awkward contortion of his march was made necessary by the tunnel's inadequate breadth, and it began to take its toll.

Resourcefully, his torch was crafted with a small inconspicuous stand that could be pulled from the handle and positioned for repose on any decently flat surface, an invention necessitated from countless excursions of a similar nature. He turned around to face his point of entry and was met head-on with a small but bright round circular light, reconfirming his bearing and attesting to the undeviating precision of his situation. A wispy but intrusive air of smoke accumulated along the ceiling of the tunnel—but not so much as to deter him from continuing forward. The early morning sun was now encroaching into alignment with the symmetrical tunnel, allowing daylight to intrude on the solitude of the standpoint. It brought welcome companionship and comfort to the alchemist, who at that moment was coincidently weighing the astuteness of further advancement. He did not like the sensation brought about by increasing the distance between him and the only known point of exit. A more analytical scrutiny brought light to the fact that the wispy smoke from the torch migrated on the ceiling in both directions, bringing confidence that the tunnel sucked breath from a farther ahead source. Then, all at once, with a surreal flash of blinding sun, the infiltrating rays blew through the tunnel and the alchemist followed along with the impetus by spontaneously whisking himself forward.

With reinvigorated eagerness, he advanced, resuming his awkward stride and leaving his torch as it lay. His vision could now manage without, and his equilibrium was much better for it. The reflected light broadcast a faint glow on the tunnel wall, a yellowish white hew that magnified the intensity of the invading rays. Two score or so more paces in now and another brief repose was in order. Sweat from his brow was becoming bothersome, and thirst could no longer be ignored. The alchemist would certainly not consider himself a claustrophobe, but enclosures of this nature would dictate the occasional interlude to breathe and compose oneself. A sample from the glowing rock wall and some quick entries into his notepad served to distract his mind from the distress at hand. *Small increments of advancement,* he told himself, *are ideal in situations such as this, situations when the mind has doubt and the body begins to quiver in unison communicating discomfort.* He forged ahead ten more paces.

Finally, a change in the symmetry of the passage came into view. In the distance, he could see the tunnel transforming into an altered configuration of sorts, arming him with a goal and heightened curiosity. He trudged forward, the funneled light now clearly making visible the point of discontinuation where the passageway altered, and he perceived the floor abruptly ending. Now awash in vivid and bright daylight, he reveled in the amplitude of the massive cavernous opening that lay almost immediately at hand. He dropped to his knees, crawling, approaching the termination with caution while protruding his head out beyond the tunnel's resolute floor in order to survey his surround with careful consternation and with a childlike expression of bewilderment. Above him, a great dome-shaped ceiling of massive proportion hung there magnificently. Unlike the tunnel, it was not perfectly symmetrical, nor did it seem to have been somehow manufactured to serve some specific purpose; rather, it seemed to have been conveniently stationed and naturally occurring within its great mountainous habitation. Still, curiously it displayed a rough symmetry that made the alchemist question its naturality. Round symmetrical openings sporadically riddled the vaulting canopy, each sized consistently with the alchemist's current roost. *What could explain such a phenomenon?* he wondered. *A burrowing creature of giant proportion making various tunnels toward the comfort of its den as would various rodents of a more realistic earthly size?* It wasn't a likely explanation but still one that brought description to the appearance at hand.

The sun behind him now brought a miraculous beam that traveled directly across his alignment, hitting a slightly convex target some distance away on the exact opposite end of the cavern. This contrivance was definitely crafted and intentionally honed with some breed of reflective material. The sunlight continued off this mark and raced downward with a conical diffusion, bathing the enormous chamber in heavenly luminosity and furnishing brilliance to the distant floor below, where drumlin-shaped mounds of indiscernible material lay motionless but clearly visible, as though a school of oceanic beasts had hoisted themselves, breaching the water all at once and then suddenly becoming petrified. The alchemist lay there, perfectly still of body but head swiveling about and surveying the surround while making mental notes of methodical persuasion, and then suddenly it occurred to him. It was a marvel indeed to deliver light to the temporal darkness below in such a fashion. It was bewildering. Each tunnel was deliberately burrowed to align with the ascending and waning sun—and each with a precisely situated reflective mark to capture and deflect the full day's illuminating wonder. *What manner of being would be capable of ingenuity and advancement to this degree?* he thought. He could not even begin to fathom how any creature of earthly persuasion could have ever undertaken such an endeavor. *And what lies below? Is this an abandoned establishment? Or one still actively inhabited?* It certainly had the air of a habitat long forgotten.

Unable to advance, he began to scrutinize the surroundings, and what he saw continued to feed his scientific mind and nurture the imagination. What were those mysterious piles on the floor below? They were numerous in quantity and decently sized, it seemed, about as large as a baker's oven and similarly shaped with a narrower, almost pointy tail. *A function of dump piling as if with a cart or barrow,* he surmised. Yes, he now definitely understood that this was a factory of some strange kind, but what was being harvested? The stockpiles were evenly distributed, with substantial distance between. He estimated the piles to be nearly two hundred in number, and curiously, a half dozen or so of the perfectly aligned mounds seemed to have been intermittently absent, a strange darkened crater-like void in their place. *If only I could steal away a sample for study,* he thought, *but the distant floor is unattainable.* Even with rope of sufficient length, had he brought some, he would not attempt such a hazardous descent. The walls of the great cavern were comparable to the tunnel wall in composition and color, it seemed, except that they were more course and irregular, but by no means were they scalable, to the dismay of the alchemist. He would somehow have to find another way to access the factory floor.

Thirty-two boreholes were tallied in all, including the one where the alchemist lay. They undulated in an alluring pattern around the enormous walls, following with an uncanny precision that aligned with the sun's daily path. His perch began the wave where daylight would first invade, and upward it ran, until it approached the pinnacle of the great domed peak at the height of the midday sun. From there, the wave cascaded downward to a point about three quarters around the facade, where it ended at an equal line to where it began. *A source of radiance as well as an indicator of time,* thought the alchemist. *What an ingenious contrivance indeed.*

Abruptly, he perceived that the light behind him was now fading. For twenty minutes, give or take, he lay in observation, mathematically calculated based on the number of boreholes and approximate duration of sun, and true to his hypothesis, darkness now returned as his pupils swelled to adjust. He retreated slightly and turned to face his bearing, only to find his torchlight flickering in the distance and a small circle of daylight remaining beyond as a mark of his entry. He would retreat, but not for a few moments yet, until his theory was proved, and sure enough, as he turned to face his reassurance, that heavenly beam of soft light was once again seen infiltrating the awesome cavern from the borehole of the next angle and direction.

Reluctantly, the alchemist began his withdrawal, as he had absorbed all that the perspective at hand would allow and there was no longer any need to linger. He would somehow have to find a convenient passage to the chamber floor, where he could explore in more detail and collect samples. Quick work was made of retreat, stopping only momentarily to retrieve his torch. A sense of relief and accomplishment overcame him as he exited the rotund opening and felt the full unencumbered brilliance of sun bathing his outstretched frame. After taking a few moments to enjoy his unrestricted posture, he stifled his torch, retrieved his bladder of drink and some dry meat from his carry bag, and sat himself comfortably upon the edge of the flattened landing at the tunnel's mouth, where he proceeded to repose and collect his thoughts. At first, he entertained the idea of searching out the point of entry for the next borehole. He knew the approximate bearing and direction, after all, but as he glanced at the course, he realized that the climb would not be an easy one. The ridge was relatively maneuverable around its lower perimeter but appeared increasingly unmanageable to ascend. *Furthermore,* he thought, *such an endeavor would serve little to augment insight.* He would instead keep steadfast his initial plan and seek out the mountainous outcropping's second entry point of interest.

So there he remained, slightly flabbergasted and struggling to fashion a conclusion from what he had just recently observed. Since yesterday's initial bewildering glance upon the uncanny ridge, he had sensed a commanding impulse toward discovery of some wondrous kind; indeed, it seemed that he had been readily rewarded in that regard, but still the mystery of the stockpiled material eluded him. *Some form of creature or being went to a magnificent effort to orchestrate the light-bringing boreholes of recent determination, but for what purpose? Surely, the factory's product would be of an essential nature or perhaps a material of invaluable worth, but in any event such great effort would certainly not be expended on triviality. And why extend to such extravagant lengths to illuminate a cavern when simple torch light would seem to provide a more practical and logical solution? Perhaps the samples from the tunnel floor and wall would* provide insight he thought as he hastily extracted them from his bag.

The sample from the tunnel floor was ashy grey in color and texture, hardened but brittle, so much so that it crumbled under pressure from his rugged fingers and left them tarnished with soot. The whitish grey and yellow fragment from the tunnel wall seemed curiously familiar. It shared texture and feel with the mineralization discovered months prior in his distant cave of choice, and it was similarly odorless and brittle as well. Only coloration was notably different, as far as he could surmise. *Perhaps this mysterious ridge lies as an enormous stony mass of flammable persuasion?* he wondered. It made sense—the granular piles of material incumbent on the factory floor, the distance between them, the sporadic crater-like voids, and the imperative need to avoid torchlight or fire of any kind, necessitating a more creative conveyance of light.

Surely his conjecture was valid; the extraneous factory produced a fiery or explosive substance of sorts, and an unbelievably potent variety at that, judging from the hardened residue accumulated on the faraway tunnel floor above, the logical aftermath of enormous explosions long ago erupted and carrying smoky ash and cinder to lofty heights. The urge to substantiate was strong, but how to proceed? *A torch dropped from the tunnel's end down to the floor below would likely force ignition*, he thought. However, he didn't currently feel eager to repeat the vexatious journey. Furthermore, he had only the single torch. The ill-lighted return to daylight would be most unpleasant indeed. Perhaps a fire stick would serve the purpose of ignition. No, too inconsistent to rely upon, and the fire would almost certainly dissipate well short of achieving its distant target. An alternative method would have to be devised, or maybe a return trip with a second torch, or perhaps a few similar but smaller and more convenient ignitable projectiles would prove superior. A single toss may not suffice after all, should it by chance land between mounds or on a void.

In any event, he would calculate his method later. He decided to proceed to his second exploration point as planned, so up he sprang, with eyes and mind searching the direction of his next target. As he peered down the flank of the ridge and along the barren and plain surround, he noticed a faraway figure. It was a distant presence, a mere speck in the vista, but not one that formed part of the natural landscape. The alchemist was a man of keen eye and mind, and he knew how to recognize when man or creature was approaching. There was no immediate cause for concern, as many travelers or wandering creatures regularly crossed the barren plain. Relatively remote as it may have been, it was still decently traveled; however, the seasoned journeyer was perpetually cautious and on alert for precarious encounters, so he remained still for a moment and surveyed the approach while weighing the potential scenarios and his corresponding action.

It did not take long for him to actuate that there was indeed more than one form, at least two and possibly three or four. And the brisk pace with which they neared demonstrated that they were not likely traveling afoot. With heightened caution, he began to descend to the flat land adjacent to the ridge. He chose to distance himself from the tunnel's opening, not wanting to trap himself within its confining wall, nor did he want to bring attention to it. He would instead hasten pace toward the peculiar lip-shaped opening some five hundred paces or so ahead. This direction would provide him with the luxury of facing those who were approaching; furthermore, escape into the cavernous opening would be an option should the necessity arise. He did hold an advantage after all, in that he knew something of what was within, as per yesterday's quick examination, and he could only hope that his intuition was correct when he apperceived a vast cavity of enormous proportion.

So now halfway or so toward his mark, the alchemist could discern added detail of the nearing journeyers. There were three figures exactly, and each was on a sizable mount of indiscernible specimen. They were too far away. In size and framework, the riders resembled humans, and their carriers were perhaps colossal hounds or Accarnanian steeds. Either way, the situation left him feeling increasingly uneasy. He continued headlong toward the location where he could begin his climb toward the sought-after objective, continuing to observe but perceiving with certainty that he too was being observed. He placed his hand on his outer thigh and ascertained the reassurance that only the hard strength of his blade could furnish. When holding the blade, the alchemist felt a confidence that was perhaps alarming to a degree in that he became imprudent; he wasn't exactly careless, but suffice it to say that he donned a sense of false invincibility.

Now fifty paces or so from his mark, and the oncomers thrice that distance, the alchemist's pace of heart quickened and adrenaline began to percolate. The three riders were cloaked and hooded in robes of black, with faces not nearly visible. Each shouldered a razor-clawed hawk, statuesque and in a trancelike perch. And as far as their mounts were concerned, an incredible spectacle was revealed; wingless reptilians with limbs held in sprawling position, shuffling outward as they scampered forth. They were abhorrent creatures, ravenous and fierce in their habitual pursuit of a meal, never before seen by the alchemist but many times described to him in tale.

The alchemist's father held rank in the king's guard, a respectable vocation in Nephesh, one that brought much adventure. How he used to revel as a starry-eyed child at his father's countless tales of exploit and danger. He could vividly recall pleasant childhood memories of sitting in comfort as the great room fire burgeoned. He would incessantly urge to hear more and more until the late hours of night, when his eyelids would grow heavy and he would be carried off to dream of things fantastic. Therefore, he knew details about the advancers, even though he had never before laid eyes upon their breed. They were warlocks from the land of Atra, a foul but powerful species of man who immersed themselves in the dark arts; not unlike the alchemist, they favored a scientific persuasion, but unlike him, they held spark of a dark variety. They favored wingless reptilians for transport through the barren plains, creatures nearly impossible to saddle and qualify yet somehow mastered by the warlocks. Their insatiable appetites were satisfied only through tidbits and morsels encountered upon travel, such fare as the alchemist now presented. A razor-clawed hawk was a trademark upon the warlocks' shoulders—hunters of great skill trained to first assail the eyes of their mark. The alchemist began to run.

As he ran, he heard voices calling out but inferred no meaning; he was solely preoccupied, knowing that he had to begin his ascent to higher ground and to the advantage of the narrow opening. Within that vantage point, he would at least be guarded from the reptilians' broad and substantial masses. While they appeared bulky and awkward in movement, the alchemist knew that they were quite capable of climbing and clinging using sharp, powerful claws and multitudinous suction cup–like hairs on the undersides of their feet. He reached the juncture where his vertical ascent was to begin and urgently began to scamper up the ridge. Those who were approaching were now fifty paces or so away and continuing to bellow out some greetings or reassurances of sorts, innocuous to the alchemist's planned evasiveness. After all, a mountainous ridge would prove no obstacle to the brand of animalia to which the warlocks were master. Little did they know of their "powerless" victim.

Now within moments of his goal, the alchemist was curiously satisfied to recall that this entryway also commanded a comfortable flat landing as a threshold. He turned as he reached the refreshing plateau and stood fast toward his adversaries. Two of the warlocks were now dismounting and slowly approaching on foot. Readying himself to enter yet realizing that resilient torchlight would serve to betray his position in the consummate darkness within, the alchemist instead considered a more temporary method of viewing the cave's geography: ignition of a fire stick. This would afford him a moment to survey the surround and set his ambition to memory before strategically positioning himself in the dark. He placed hand in his carry bag, eager to put good use to his outstanding creation, but at that exact moment, he perceived shrill cries, commands bellowing from the depths of the warlocks' nefarious souls, resounding and tumultuous. Two razor-clawed hawks took to flight, and two wingless reptilians began their ravenous upward scamper. The alchemist's eyes narrowed, and his nerves steadied. Impulsively, his hand retreated from within the carry bag and grasped the invigorating bone handle waiting snug at his flank.

The overpowering screech of the hawks' approaching fury would have preempted most to flight, but not the alchemist. He stood fast his ground and readied, scrutinizing their parabolic approach as each hawk veered off in an opposing direction, aiming to converge in unison upon target. He maintained his sight forward, surveying the more moderate reptilian advancement and all the while considering the hawks in his periphery. The speed at which they sailed through the air was brisk, but not enough so to cause the alchemist to lose sight of his purpose. And knowing full well that the foray would be at eye level, he was well prepared when the moment came. With a deadly precise swipe of his blade, he halved the first assailant. At the same instant, he raised his non-sword-swinging arm in defense of his eyes, sacrificing skin and sinewy muscle in favor of more valuable ocular matter as the second aerial threat was fiercely upon him. Skillfully and instinctively, he recoiled the sword from his initial strike and swatted away the predator with great force and precision, leaving it with breath but clearly damaged and recumbent several paces away on the stony surface of the ridge. In turn, he was left with a cumbersome wound, one of little consequence for the moment but one whose ferocity would certainly bring permanence of a resounding scar. He now turned attention to the reptilians that were hastily on approach, the first of which was conveniently distracting itself with the easy meal of a damaged hawk that lay in wait. However, the second monstrosity did not waver and instead continued pursuit steadfastly toward more hearty prey. The alchemist nimbly clutched the severed portions of his fallen mark and then squeezed between the stony lip-shaped portal, entering the inside of the desolate cave.

Instant blackness greeted the alchemist, accompanied by an eerie but welcoming silence and the burn of his fresh wound, which was now stark in his mind. He reluctantly sheathed his blade and swiftly set fingers to search within his carry bag, where a small number of fire sticks lay in hiding within the comfort of resilient hide. He made quick work of apprehending his prize, along with the abraded band that would give purpose to quick ignition, and in a moment, there was the glorious sound of flare, followed by a soft incandescent glow. The darkness guarding the cavern's curious secrets was no more. In haste, the alchemist surveyed his surround. He knew that the warlocks were likely halfway up the ridge by now as they gave chase. The cavern was indeed vast and spread to a great expanse. The floor was flat and of barren earth, not at all wavy and turbulent like most naturally occurring caves of his experience. Like an abandoned arena or great hall, it lay in waiting, forever anticipating a monumental event or performance that seemed to have never come to pass. In the distance, he detected a wide doorway or perhaps a staircase of sorts, and instinctively he advanced to clarify his view. All of a sudden, he was startled by the sound of impact against brittle stone and the resounding hiss of hungry reptilian.

Behind him, the ravenous beast was furiously grinding horny skull against rock in a desperate attempt to press through the narrow opening. The half-spent fire stick was dropped to the floor and extinguished as the alchemist once again set hand to hilt of bone and turned to face the aperture. His previous and briefly postponed intention now returned to the forefront of action as he retrieved the bisected portions of hawk that lay at his feet and nonchalantly tossed them a few paces forward, where the opening began and the reptilian snout eagerly bore. True to character, the brute intuitively began to devour the morsels, and in quick advantage of opportunity, the alchemist leaped upon the beast. With force of both hands, he rammed his precious sword straight through the center of the creature's hard thorn-encrusted skull and frantically continued to apply pressure downward until he felt the blade's lethal point clang on the hard-stone surface of floor. With that, he was flung back into the darkness of the cave with enormous force as the monstrous reptile exerted its last rambunctious thrust before recoiling and withering lifelessly upon the rocky threshold, its steely downfall remaining completely wedged through its skull in effigy.

It took a few moments for the alchemist to reclaim his faculties. He was jolted with decent force and landed rather uncomfortably on the hard and unyielding floor. The darkness provided little help as he struggled to reclaim his balance, and just as he managed to recapture his posture, he heard the enraged song of approaching warlocks. This was indeed good medicine for recovery, and as he glanced upon their dull silhouettes maneuvering about the dimly lit portal, he quickly distanced himself a good number of paces.

"Vagabond!" A menacing voice had roared out the word, and it reverberated in a bone-chilling chorus within the great cavernous hall. "Come face your retribution for crime against the indomitable impetus of the warlocks of Atra!"

"Vagabond!" cried a different but equally disturbing voice. "Yield at once and we may consider a less tortuous prelude to your oblivion." The tone was sternly hostile now, as they had utterly abandoned their previously false persuasive air. Curiously, this genuine display pleased the alchemist; in fact, he much preferred it to its deceitful counterpart. He did not break his silence, for he held advantage in the darkness, and he now advanced slowly in the direction of the wide archway that was laid out quite accurately like a blueprint in his mind.

He heard softer mumblings now as the warlocks strategized among themselves, and as he turned to face their direction, he saw a modest glow, a faint illumination brought about by agitation of liquid contained in a vial, and then it was repeated. He beheld their forms, compromised by the convenience of their own luminous concoctions. The alchemist himself had experimented with such a chemical glow but had found the results consistently disappointing. The shine was poor and the radiance insufficient; he was relieved to learn that the warlocks had entered the cave bereft of torch. *Surely, they would have carried one in travel,* he thought. *Perhaps their rage from lost pet had brought impetuousness or perhaps the mysterious effect of the glowing solution intended to awe and intimidate.* In any event, it did not matter; this occurrence brought convenience to the alchemist, an advantage for which he was sorely in need since he was outnumbered. He could espy their position while remaining distant enough to evade their meager light. The warlocks placed their respective luminescent vials on clasps atop their staffs, holding them like desolate beacons, while they, like appointed reapers of the nether, advanced with caution and care.

The warlocks' weapon of choice was the staff. With it, they feigned wizardly talent, a pretense at best serving to add a convincing aura to their makeshift magic. Within the stitching of their intimidating robes, they concealed a number of devious devices and contrivances, the grand design intending to create awe and gain advantage over those with weaker minds and spirits. But the alchemist was not to be fooled, nor was he to underestimate. Indeed, he was sharply aware of what lay beyond the veil of deceit: hard dedication and training. Their mastery of weapon and mastery of mind would present him with a significant obstacle to overcome should he encounter their capable staffs, especially when absent of his own reassuring blade. And so now, as the warlocks advanced, the alchemist also advanced slowly and with caution, quietly placing each foot so as to not betray his position. He expected to reach the onset of the archway soon and preferred to do so without tumbling should the footing all of a sudden change in the pitch-black vicinity. He turned once again to observe his pursuers, who were still a good distance away, and he visualized them rummaging their hands within the draping robes.

What deviance do they aim to practice? he wondered, and within moments he had his answer, as he heard the soft whistle of a projectile flying through the still air and saw the smoky glow of light erupting some paces away as glass crashed upon the rigid floor of stone. Darkness was swept away in the moderate radius of the blast, which was thankfully not near enough to betray the alchemist's position, and then another blast came, then another, each one advancing nearer and nearer toward his whereabouts. The alchemist fell to his knees and began crawling in a quick effort to realize the passageway. Meanwhile, the warlocks intermittently launched their vials of illuminating liquid and quietly surveyed the area of each burst. The eighth catapult whistled dangerously near as the alchemist tensed in anticipation of being struck, and mere paces ahead, glass shred and smoky glow discharged, revealing a masterful stairway some ten paces wide and cascading downward for quite a distance beyond the faint reach of the light.

The steps had a majestic aura about them, not fabricated with blocks or pieces of stone but rather carved precisely and true, etched from the canvas that lay within the ground. While seeming to lack elaborate detail, a systematic consistency still spoke to the masterpiece of some extraordinary sculptor. The staircase was shouldered on one side with an astute angled stringer of large proportion, ascending a pace or so upward and beyond the steps until meeting a perpendicular wall, which was also sculpted to a precise flatness. The wall extended upward some distance before elegantly curving into formation of a perfect arch. The arch continued to meet the wall on the opposite side, which in turn extended down directly to each step without interruption of a stringer. Every edge and angle was perfectly square and intact, strangely enough displaying no symptoms of wear or use. The ramp-like pitch of the wide shoulder was wholly scattered with a powdery substance, likely comparable to the material stored in mounds on the factory floor, a small quantity of which lay littered at the abutted edge of each step. On the opposite side wall, torch holders lay in wait, or so it seemed, evenly spaced and blatantly visible, accompanying the steps as they descended into the dark.

The alchemist, his position now compromised by the faint glowing light of the barrage's successful charge, scampered to his feet and began to maneuver forward precisely at the same time as he was struck with the numbing burn of pain on his right hind leg, just below his haunch. A small and dense steely orb the size of a man's eyeball thudded to the ground; he took hold of it and desperately began his descent with no mind to the throbbing discomfort that ushered every step. Another small dense globe whizzed overhead and thwacked the expansive wall, dropping to the shoulder beside the steps and cushioning itself on the bed of powdery residue. The alchemist snatched it as well and placed both in his carry bag, scooping up a good quantity of the residue in the process, and all the while, he journeyed swiftly downward toward the stairway's dark and unknown conclusion. With hand in bag, he groped in search of another fire stick and the abraded band as light swiftly diminishing with his descent.

"Stand fast, vagabond, and face your slayers with dignity," bellowed an ominous voice, fading yet still profound. The alchemist's fingers uncovered their mark, and in singular motion, he pulled the fire stick from his bag and abraded it, fashioning a gratifying flare and a much-needed outburst of light. More of the same backdrop became clearly visible, namely the consistent craftsmanship of stone and the seemingly endless multitude of steps. Downward he trudged, sheltering the small flame with his cupped hand as the draft of his descent threatened to smother it. This forced a lessened pace and a diminished view, much to his disdain, and he reasoned that there was no other option but to reignite the torch, keeping in mind that only a few fire sticks remained on hand and that a quickened pace was still an absolute necessity. He turned about and saw the warlocks' presence as they began their decline at the head of the stairwell with faint glowing lights still perched upon their staffs. Without delay, he resumed his pace, employing what little flame remained on the wooden fuel of his nearly exhausted fire stick to relight the oily cloth of his torch.

Now refreshed with augmented clarity bestowed by veritable torchlight, the alchemist quickened his pace and continued his plunge, feeling invigorated on the one hand but experiencing heightened vulnerability to attack on the other. One hundred steps down or so, he continued forth, swiveling his head to survey his pursuers some fifty steps behind him. He quickened his step once more, striving to increase his advantage, and at once, he saw an anomaly on the consistently flat-shouldered wall. It was a hole—or tunnel, more precisely—measuring more or less the exact shape and size as the recently explored light-bringing borehole. Would the tunnel extricate him from the dangerous situation at hand? It may very well have led to an exit somewhere upon the widespread mountainous ridge, but then again, perhaps not. There was no justification to think that he could properly evaluate the tunnel's end, and so with precious little time to contemplate, he continued down into the unknown.

Thirty steps or so farther, another tunnel-shaped opening was espied; he turned once again and saw that he had indeed made some progress on augmenting his lead. Reverting his attention to his descent, he continued to strive down, the same scene reiterating without fail. The unwavering perspective entranced him and lured him away from focus, his mind drawing near entrapment of reverie, his consciousness veiled in a delusional cloud. His movement resembled a descent, but he became unsure, wondering if he was not in fact stifled, as though on a never-ending plane of reality where he would remain eternally striving downward, only to realize that no advancement was made. His fleeting pace of breath and resounding beat of heart served as the only anchor to the reality at hand, and as he hastily passed yet another tunnel opening, he desperately increased his speed of descent once again, throwing himself dangerously into threat of misstep and fall. It was merely a matter of time before his pace would be his ruin as the alchemist strode perilously down into the depths, but he didn't care. At that moment, he was electrified, replete of adrenaline and rushing downward two steps at once, challenging the monotonous obstacle to battle. Only one of two possible eventualities would cause discontinuation of pace; he would reach the stairway's enduring termination or he would falter upon her profound run of stone, cascading down with broken body and bone.

As it turned out in this particular battle, the alchemist proved himself the victor, and within moments, he caught sight of the long-anticipated end: a great landing that opened up into a circular area of sizable breadth, perhaps thirty paces or so in diameter. The landing's floor was fully coated with the powdery residue, and the alchemist was relieved to conclude his descent and set foot on its beach-like sandy texture. Five arched passages presented themselves, equally spaced along the circular walls of the grandiose lobby, one directly affronting the stairwell and two on either side. These pathways were narrower and more stout relative to the surround but were still of decent size and presence so as to allow comfortable and unrestricted access. As the alchemist turned and looked up to catch site of the warlocks, he saw the distant oscillating glimmer of their vials. Content with the lead his quick pace had garnered, he turned and headed to the straightaway passage without hesitation, plodding through the granular terrain in quick fashion, knowing that the warlocks would make quick work of discerning his footsteps and pursuing the proper avenue of chase.

The alchemist grew tired of flight and now focused his intellect on tactic and strategy of fray, wholly committing himself to whatever consequence the passage's uncertainty would provide. A number of schemes were concocted and weighed, analyzed in thought, and quickly arranged, a commonplace task for his exceptional mind. As he sprinted through the gritty residue, approaching the end of the adroit passageway a mere twenty paces or so in length, no less than three scenarios of encounter were fully rehearsed and apprized. The short jaunt through the passageway rapidly drew to an end, and as the alchemist came to an opening of sorts, he maintained his considerable stride, thrusting himself through its mouth in a brave yet jeopardous maneuver, rejoicing in his own uproarious bravado. Then he was suddenly aghast. The factory floor stood before him, presenting a momentous vision, dreamlike and formidable, an unearthly phenomenon basking in the heavenly glow of the sun's brilliant capture. The alchemist mustered a devious grin, flanked the wall adjacent to the passage, peered down its darkened path, and lay in wait.

Moments passed and the alchemist alternated view at intervals, peering down the passageway in search of glowing vial, then marveling at the awesome yet intimidating strangeness of the vast cavern. It was approaching the height of day in that seemingly distant and foreign world of sky and sun as the alchemist took note of the light's pathway through a borehole near the apex of the vaulted canopy. For some distance, fifty paces or so from the edge of the area's scabrous boundary wall to the start of the stockpiled mounds of material, the floor lay flat, level, and clean of residue as it circumvented the diameter of the expanse. It was crafted with a preciseness of equal stature to the enduring staircase, flowing throughout the space like the still water of an eerie and exotic lake, interrupted only by the scattering cover of the large and multitudinous heaps of inventory evenly spaced and isolated, twenty-odd paces of clean floor betwixt. The imposing walls of the factory were rugged and unrefined, flagrantly contrasting against the smooth and even floor. Evenly spaced openings were observed along the curved boundary of the wall, few in number but massive and arched, dignifying the area and bestowing an exalting air.

The alchemist turned his attention now, peering down the dark and confined pathway from which he came, listening for any hint of the warlocks' approach. He sensed them scurrying about in the rotund lobby at the foot of the persistent staircase, applauding themselves for tracking the course of their target, discussing the direction and desperation made obvious by the nature of the footprints observed. They, rationalizing themselves as superior and confident masters of the domain and the alchemist thinking them as rodents, eagerly pursuing a scent and all the while effortlessly being led into a trap. He now spotted their glowing vials as they began the short trek through the passage; he turned away and backed himself against the adjacent wall, hiding from sight, torch outstretched away from the opening. Blind to their approach, he counted pace.

"Vagabond!" bellowed a nefarious voice echoing out into the great expanse. "We have a proposal for you." The voice paused as though awaiting a response. "My brother and I have discussed your agile and capable evasion of chase. We agree that the fellowship of warlocks could use a man of such talent." There was a pause again to present opportunity of reply. "You would be well trained in the art of war and magic, learning great secrets and powers reserved only for the most exceptional among men ..."

"Together we will rule and conquer, living a life unrivalled by others," a second raspier and less convincing voice rang out. "What say you, vagabond?" With that, the alchemist leaped into view several paces beyond the opening.

"I say to the netherworld with the two of you—and likewise to your entire vile breed!" retorted the alchemist in a commanding but relatively calm voice as he lightly tossed his torch into the hallway and turned, sprinting away in anticipation of a blast. The warlocks were hardly startled by the display, and in unison they fluently raised up their pointed staffs, dexterously hurling them at the alchemist with deadly accuracy. The torch landed on the powdery residue of the floor, instantly detonating an obliterating charge, incinerating the unsuspecting warlocks and at the same time catapulting the alchemist with enormous force. He was sent sailing through the air, projected a good distance. Two pointed staffs cut through the fiery explosion with speed, one narrowly missing the alchemist and the other catching flesh of his ear as he senselessly drifted, coming to rest on the edge of a stockpiled mound just where it met the hard-resolute floor, his body blackened and inanimate.

The smoldered scent of cinder and smell of residual burn was the first recognizable sense that greeted the alchemist and hinted toward continuance of breath. Throbbing pain welcomed him to consciousness; it was an overall encompassing sensation as opposed to one that could be specifically attributed. He felt the texture of residue about his neck and face and apperceived a dull monotone ringing within his head, where it remained for a while, unwavering and true. A reverberating overtone imposed its clang like a distant and resounding tower of worship bell. His eyelids struggled to unlock themselves, fixed in place and inert like the weathered and rust-infused iron doors of a long-abandoned castle. He managed to force them ajar for an instant before they snapped back together with elastic force. What did he see in that quick clouded instance of vision? An apparition of sorts? A sparkle of small blue flame immediately before him and at rest upon the stockpiled residue?

Impossible, of course, for he had certainly ascertained the volatility of the material; his eyesight was surely clouded and mind unclear.

He took a few moments to solidify his consciousness, shaking his head clear and raising his neck to improve his viewpoint, and then he sprang open his eyes with vigor and caught full sight of the illusion. Indeed, it was a strange and minuscule flame sitting atop the mound of residue, resting there as if it belonged, at home and cozy. It was a clear vision now, primarily bluish in hue, with a slight tinge of orange glow in its center mass, a small quantity of the powder lying within it and stirring about. The alchemist stared with eyes fixated in disbelief, wondering if he still suffered delusion from the blast. A face of sorts began to take form, or so he perceived, the flame seeming to return the stare with an obscure outline of eyes. It was a strange exchange between the man and the flame, each seemingly mesmerized by the other. Recognizing life and character, the alchemist instantly sensed a presence of soul; the flame in turn flickered ever so slightly, wavering and oscillating about. The alchemist made a slight movement to rise, and the flame receded to a safe distance farther away on the grainy mound. He then scrambled to his knees and looked on in disbelief as the creature scurried away in haste, traversing over the surface of a number of mounds until it was no longer in sight.

Still suffering the consequence of the blast and perplexed by the creature he had just envisioned, the alchemist dazedly peered up toward the vaulted ceiling of the cavern in an effort to regain his bearing. He noted that the boreholes within view were all dull and that the illumination was now entering the area from behind his position, indicating that he had lost consciousness for a number of hours. Aiming to quantify more precisely the length of his absence, he turned in search of the light's location within the momentous time marker, and suddenly, without warning, he was bewildered in the face of an approaching staff brought down with force by an outraged warlock. Until now, the third warlock of the pack had evaded consideration, forcing the alchemist to outstretch his lacerated arm desperately in defense of the intended target of skull, and the arm's fore-bone cracked, yielding linearity as it absorbed the full brunt of impact from the hard and inflexible rod.

Pain was no longer a concern as continuance of life took priority; a second swipe came down and narrowly missed as the alchemist managed a vigilant turn. On the third swipe, the alchemist deftly turned his body once again, and at the same time, he ensnarled the staff between his legs while wrenching it sharply, managing to jolt it from the warlock's grasp and fling it away from reach. A thunderous fist came crashing down, bludgeoning the alchemist's cheek and shattering the delicate cartilage of his prevalent nose. Blood poured down, spilling into the alchemist's mouth, and the salty metallic taste of it, mixed with sweat, triggered a furious howl as he lunged headfirst into the warlock's abdomen. The attacker was taken aback by this, and the alchemist found an opportunity to scamper up onto the top of the sandy mound. Here he held the advantage of higher ground, albeit at the expense of firm footing. As he faced him now, the warlock presented himself much less rambunctiously. His hunched frame hobbled over to retrieve his fallen staff.

"You, sir, have cost me grievous expense of lost animal and man," muttered the tall and stately built adversary as he struggled to suck wind. The comment was a mere tactic, allowing proper time for him to recover lung capacity. The alchemist knew this and was glad for the opportunity, as he too was in desperate need of composure. "And for that you shall dearly pay!" The warlock now held his staff in hand once again, and with it, he managed to stand erect.

"And you, sir," retorted the alchemist, "have caused me much discomfort. I did not seek out you or your kind, nor did I interfere in your concerns. I am in fact the damaged party, standing here bloodied and burned with broken bone and a hazy, ambiguous mind. Take a thorough look around and familiarize yourself with your surroundings, for it will serve as the most wonderful of backdrops to what is certain to be your imminent and impending tomb; indeed, it is a magnificent one, with beauty well beyond that which you deserve. You, foul sir, will not leave this place with breath!" The alchemist's good hand was rummaging in his carry bag as he uttered those words, and with the last word, he pulled out one of the two dense and steely orbs previously collected, launching it with force. The warlock swiped at it with his staff, deftly deflecting it from harm's way. The second projectile quickly followed to flight; that one was swatted away with relative ease as well.

"Ha ha!" the warlock taunted with a maniacal and calculated laugh. "And with this, you aim to deliver my demise?" His face became stern in preparation for a counterattack, but the alchemist was not yet spent of projectile. A third bulbous vial of thick glass now lay in his hand, slightly larger and less dense than its steely counterparts; it was a container, in fact, one that resided in a customized pocket within his trusted carry bag. He let fly the object with immense vigor, hurling it with all his might, and this time, as the warlock skillfully whacked it with his rigid, unyielding staff, it shattered, spattering glass and liquid content about the assailant's face and eyes. A ferocious shriek permeated throughout the great domain as the warlock dropped his staff and clenched hands to face in a frantic but futile effort to mitigate the contamination. Blotches appeared, sporadically invading the skin around his face and neck as a soft and hazy vapor carelessly rose, distorting the reflected light that shone from above and behind the warlock's position. The vial contained an etching acid used by the alchemist to scrub clean some stones or minerals uncovered during his exploits; it was an effective concoction, quite corrosive indeed.

Now the disfigured opponent was no longer within the grasp of sanity; he placed his hand within his robe and withdrew a stout dagger, lackluster and curved like the enormous fang of some indeterminate beast. He lunged forth onto the pile of residue and began clawing his way to the top, where the alchemist was still perched, swimming through the material with reckless abandon and all the while swatting with the dagger in hope of piercing meat.

The sudden maneuver startled the alchemist, and he stumbled as he recoiled, falling back onto the forgiving granules and onto a hard object that stabbed at his lower back; it was his trusted explorer's hammer, still in its usual station. He had all but forgotten about it amidst the turmoil of recent events, but now he grappled for it eagerly with the hand of his good strong arm, all the while kicking frantically in an attempt to stave off his relentless attacker.

Just as he solidified his hold on the braided leather handle, a sharp pain materialized as the warlock's blade pierced clean through his foot and the aggressor continued his stride, dragging the alchemist closer as he heaved on the handle, dislodging the blade and swatting down again in continued fury. The alchemist let fly a tumultuous cry, enraged and now equally as incoherent as his foe, bringing down the pointed end of his hammer repeatedly. The cavern echoed with redundant screams, each man howling and swinging incessantly, pounding away in desperate fray until only one voice remained bellowing; it was that of the alchemist. He delivered two additional blows to the shattered warlock skull before realizing that the encounter had ended and that his nemesis now lay smote in a pile of bloodstained residue, hand still grasping the handle of a blade now wedged deeply within the alchemist's muscular thigh.

The alchemist lay there for a while, bruised and battered, burned, leg slashed about with steely blade still lodged, arm lacerated and broke, and strangely enough, a gentle smile meandered its way to his blood-encrusted lips. He had survived to roam again, to explore and learn, to discover and invent, to revel in all of the worldly glories that lay rampant in his glorious time. The path of the righteous had prevailed, and he knew at that moment that he was to be blessed with a destiny beyond what he could imagine.

He wriggled himself free and withdrew from the current encumbrance while turning his thoughts toward a most unpleasant retracement home. As he managed to kneel beside the pile of curious stockpiled material, pitching some into his carry bag for future examination, his little blue creature appeared once again, scurrying along the substance. The creature traversed the alchemist's steady hand and rode its way along the arc of flung material and right into the comfort of the reliable carry bag. The alchemist stood upright, accommodated his bag to its usual comfortable station, and peered within, gently placing his hand in and under the being and bringing it up on a gentle bed of the residue, lifting it toward his face for closer observation. Mystified, he placed it back within the comfort of the satchel and shuffled off with his newfound companion in tow.

CHAPTER 2

Cristofo

Nestled comfortably on top of an inviting branch in a majestic trident chestnut tree, a young man pondered life and the many other quintessential concerns that would be typically thought of by most humans on the cusp of entering adulthood. It was a pleasant night; the sky was unclouded and luminous as it basked in the delightful light of reflected sun that bounced off the earth's endearing twain moons, Tiburon and Tamar, both near full and aglow in the crisp canvas of night, center stage to a backdrop of the myriad trifling sparkles of far-off starlight. They were named for the ancient brothers from Nepheshan lore who shared an unyielding togetherness as flourishing children of regal descent; unshakable was their bond. Later on divided as each matured of their own separate ideals and ways, they came to compromise in lieu of blows, and each capable prince engaged his own following when the time of succession arose. The dominion transformed into twin fiefdoms, each individual state lesser in breadth but existing together in the same common lands and enjoying greater overall stature as independent yet harmonious bevies. Long did the populace prosper and thrive under the wisdom and good judgment of their great enduring leaders and their offspring for generations to come.

Thoughts of the distant stars, faraway worlds, and boundless adventure filled the young man's spirit. A clear starry sky with imposing moons would always bring about a unique sensation of mind, a delightful one that the youth dearly enjoyed. It was a difficult sensation to describe, as it brought forth invigorating hope of bold and daring endeavors, saddled in unison with the realization of the insignificance of individual life, forever dwarfed by the incomprehensible infinity of the beyond. But this awareness fueled the adolescent's character, leading him to conclude that he would make the most of his precious gift and that in all possible unfolding storylines in the performance that was to be his life, he would star, insignificant though he may well be. The boundless reach of his mind's perception would be his playground, where he would run the course and set the tone. He would command the stage, cast in place for his amusement and set to accommodate his great will.

The boy was named Cristofo, and this night he came to the wooded forest of Bornea, a small but vivacious timberland adjacent and to the north of the bustling town of Nephesh. It was a relatively tame domain but still filled with its share of strange and wild creatures, and although it was not a dreaded destination, it was certainly one that most would choose to avoid amid the darkness of night—but not Cristofo. Confidently he would approach all of his ventures with cool determination. Where others would show angst and fear, he would shine. On this occasion, he ventured out under the guise of hunt but with equal intent of gazing upon thought under rarity of a clear sky with a double full moon. His grandfather was soon to entertain a visit from a noteworthy old friend—a wizard in fact, and might I say one of great esteem! Cristofo relished the curiosity and could not wait for the affair. Oh, the questions he had, the enquiries he would make … He would not let such an opportunity pass without exhaustive inquisition. So he aimed to make an impression outright by capturing the main course for the ordeal. His grandfather had mentioned the favored course of his admirable acquaintance, wild barb-fanged boar, a delicacy that Cristofo intended to deliver, a prize for which he sat patiently in wait on that rugged and tolerant limb of trident chestnut.

His family held residence in a stately manor of excessive caliber on the far outskirts of Nephesh, which lacked little of the conveniences available at the time. His grandfather was the patriarch, spending a good portion of his comfortable years maintaining the acreage and toiling among the sizable estate, where a grand library of enormous breadth was his favored hangout, a spacious refuge of rectangular shape a good fifteen by twenty paces in size. A breathtaking fireplace overpowered the space, centered on the shorter wall and extending precisely one-third of its length. His grandfather would pace back and forth in front of the burgeoning flame, deep in thought and as though hypnotized by the crackling sound of spent wood and by the comfortable warmth of its outreaching aura. Like the steadfast and unfaltering swing of a pendulum, he would routinely march, wearing a pattern onto the extravagant floor of crafted marble. An ornately sculpted stone surround bordered the oversized opening, proudly displaying ominous faces: gargoyle, griffin, dragon, felid, and monsters of other variegated origins and sorts, both earthly and not. They were commanding beings that would typically be pictured emerging from the blaze with vigor and ferocity, but not so with this illustrious masterpiece. The vibrant flame encompassed the creatures, each one displaying lamenting eyes filled with languishment as though overpowered and drawn in by an omnipotent master, absorbing them into its essence. Fire was the force to be feared and respected or it would have its way.

The stolid walls of cobalt blue limestone were barely visible, veiled by a multitude of crowded shelves. Volumes lay scattered about the ledges, where they mingled with canisters, beakers, carafes, and other containers in no discernable pattern or order, seemingly in disarray to all but the grandfather, who could at once pinpoint his required ambition. A grandiose worktable sat stoically in a corner, littered with components of trials and procedures. Notes and papers, vials and vessels, and samples and ingredients alike lay strewn about the table, waiting in patient turn for the chance to find contented pride as part of some wondrous creation. A number of comfortable chairs were strategically placed within the library, staged to facilitate agreeable conversation or relaxed reading by candlelight, whatever the occasion would demand. A wide glass-like doorway invited the sunlight, enticing the occupants of the room and drawing them hypnotically out onto a glorious patio that overlooked the vast and beautiful acreage at the rear of the estate. The grandfather's personal garden was paces away, a small patch of nursery with produce intended not for consumption but rather to serve as ingredients and subject matter for his experimentation and study. Alongside the patio, an exaggerated amount of wood lay in wait, required nourishment for the voracious appetite of the grand fireplace.

"What do you think, Iggy? Any barb-fanged boar sauntering about this night?" The boy was speaking to an intricately crafted gold locket that hung affectionately around his thin yet muscular neck. A meager blue haze of flame that resided within the pendant answered through intensification of glow, partially showing itself through small carved perforations. The locket was actually quite large, more comparable to a hollowed-out pocket watchcase. It dangled on an equally elaborate burly chain crafted not of gold but of a less valuable and more durable alloy. The creature was a curious being of unknown origin, essentially comparable to the earthly element of fire except for a few substantial differences. First off, it was cognizant and conscious and could perceive thoughts, particularly those of humans with whom it was most familiar, signaling response through an increase or decrease in glow and with color variations in the range of blue, orange, and yellow. It could regulate the dissipation of heat, choosing to rest coolly on a friendly palm or within its comfortable carriage of gold, a metal for which it had an unusual affinity; conversely, it could inflame with searing heat scorching to the touch. It required neither fuel of wood nor breath of air to subsist, but without either, it stood meager and unimpressive, unable to enliven or wander about. A strange granular powder empowered the creature, a substance with which you are all too familiar with at this point in the tale, a substance that Cristofo would carry about in a satchel draped around his waist and always at the ready for his trusted companion. The entity was a treasure gifted to him by his grandfather on his eleventh year, just over four summer seasons past.

"I sense some creatures sniffing about. Roast me some more chestnuts." With that, the boy placed fruit of the stalwart tree onto the golden case, waiting briefly as his companion obediently singed it full through until he felt the scalding heat on his fingertips. One by one, he cooked a number of them in this manner and threw them down as bait around the rustic trunk of his perch; a warm and inviting smell lingered and permeated throughout the densely wooded vicinity.

"You hear that, Iggy?" the boy whispered quietly, not expecting a word in return. He nimbly poised himself, crouching on the rigid limb with remarkable balance while grasping his metal-tipped hunting spear that had been patiently waiting at his side, the opportune tool for this night's objective.

A stout wooden handle was expertly married to a long and steely conical point. Shorter and thicker than a traditional throwing spear, the handle facilitated mobility in the densely wooded surround, and the thicker rugged wood shaft would ensure resilience enough to penetrate hard target of bone or skull. Four sharp triangular wing-tipped edges circled the point, striated and barbed in order to ensure ease of penetration and hindrance of withdrawal. A modest grunting sound suddenly became apparent although camouflaged within the resonating ruffle of leaf and underbrush prevalent on the forest floor. Cristofo made quick work of pinpointing the large beast as it rummaged its way toward the fragrant temptation of bait. Indeed, it was a wild barb-fanged boar and a robust one at that, just perfect for its intended purpose. An arousing energy overtook the boy as he braced himself and patiently held ready. He abruptly sensed another presence and perceived movement of a different kind, stealthier and more cautious. It seemed that he was not the only one with the motive of hunt on that energizing, lustrous night, as a pair of eyes reflecting the moonlight was espied in the not too distant range. An enormous carnivorous feline was on the cusp of a deathly pounce; the striped Smilodon was a formidable and grossly muscled predator with preposterously long and scimitar-shaped front teeth.

Knowing that hesitation would cost him his prize, Cristofo sprung to performance more prematurely than would have been ideal. A few more moments would have drawn his prey closer, but he was without the advantage of such luxury, for the ferocious Smilodon concurrently darted in attack. With spear fastidiously held, he leaped upon his target some paces away, firmly and accurately thrusting steel into the broad neck of the unsuspecting boar just at the base of its skull, impaling it clean through and ending its existence straightaway and painlessly. A bloodthirsty roar commanded awe as it riddled through the air with thunderous might, and a massive bestial face presented itself with savage intent, openmouthed and flaunting a formidable arrangement of tooth; the Smilodon would not be robbed of its catch.

"Now, Iggy!" the boy proclaimed as he delved into his satchel, pulling out a heap of the explosive powder and hurling it toward the approaching menace. Wondrously, a blaze of blue flame flew from its golden lair, whizzing through the airborne powder like a racing comet and spreading flame upon the advancing mark. The Smilodon was instantaneously startled and taken aback. The flame lingered for a few moments, searing whiskers and fur as though to make its position clearly understood. Then it moderated heat and retracted as the subdued adversary whimpered and withdrew. The flame then scurried along the forest floor and up the leg and stomach of its trusted young master before reentering its comfortable carriage of gold. "Sorry, my saber-toothed friend, there will be no spoils for you this night," the boy bantered, "but be glad that you persist to hunt again." With that, Cristofo contentedly prepared to mobilize his prize.

Idly standing by was a lightweight wooden shield that he had brought to aid transport in the event of a successful hunt. It was the type of shield used for training of the king's guard, a large rectangular apparatus ample enough to conceal a man in his entirety. It lay slightly curvilinear in shape, crafted of joined thin wooden strips three layers thick and oriented differently for strength. Dyed strips of hide and an emblazoned mark in the center were absent, differentiating it from the standard shields used in battle. The boy placed the shield alongside the carcass and struggled to pry the husky framework with a fallen branch as he worked to shimmy the shield underneath.

"Whew. She's a hefty one all right, Iggy, a good fifteen to twenty stones for sure. Grandfather will certainly be impressed—and his friend as well. A real-life wizard ... Can you believe it? I cannot wait for the visit. I'm sure there will be wondrous stories, Iggy, filled with formidable and inconceivable adventure." He continued to ramble on incessantly. "I have so many questions—so much to ask—that I won't know where to begin. I hope he stays for a while." Now with his load well positioned on the makeshift gurney, he fastened it with rope through premade holes along the shield's edges, constricting and securing the creature like a foreleg laced up in a snug knee-high boot. He then firmly grasped the handle of the hunting spear, still solidly and purposely embedded with a comfortable orientation for pulling, and hoisted with effort as his muscular calves dug into the soil and advanced.

Several moments passed, and the boy emerged from the thicket with his deserved conquest, sighing with relief and applauding himself for having had the foresight to hunt along the edge of the woods, where he would have a more feasible task of transport. He paused briefly to recompose himself and took a well-deserved drink from a bladder that lay waiting, hanging on the saddlebag of his mount, which was resting carelessly and nibbling on the foliage of a nearby tree where it was fettered.

"We've returned, Brunella, and look at our trophy!" Cristofo caressed the horse-like snout of his ride as he watched her pebbled teeth grind away at the leafy vegetation she had gathered. "And look, girl, we've brought you something as well." He pulled a number of chestnuts from his pocket and held them up high in his palm to allow the creature to gnaw away at them, and she did, slobbering and salivating while nibbling contentedly. She was a gorallion, a fantastic and rare four-limbed plant eater one and a half times the height and four times the weight of the average adult man.

Gorallions were magnificent gigantic mammals with clawed feet and hands and long clumsy human-like fingers that allowed them to climb trees and grasp or manipulate objects to a degree. Their most notable attribute was their stance, with front limbs significantly longer than hind, so much so that they brushed the knuckles of their hands along the ground as they walked or ran on all fours. These powerful and muscular creatures were the preferred use during treks requiring strength and resilience in lieu of endurance and speed. A short but thick layer of fur surfaced the docile creature, white and tan in coloration, with a banded pattern on this particular favored choice of Cristofo.

Three others of the breed were kept in the sizable stables adjacent to the great estate.

"That's a good girl, Brunella," he continued. He placed the remaining chestnuts on the ground in front of her and persisted with the task of tethering his precious cargo to the harness of the ample beast, leaving her to grapple with the treats at her leisure as she clawed at the rugged shells and brought them up to her mouth for further processing. Then, as the load was fully secured, a sharp commanding whistle departed the boy's lips. Brunella crouched down to invite a more manageable saddling, holding the prepared stance as though in wait for the signal of some consequential race.

"Take us home, girl," the boy proclaimed as he held tightly the reins and nudged her strategically with his heel, bracing himself for the short but choppy and rough ride home.

As Cristofo approached the familiar lands of the imposing manor, he became excited with the thought of presenting his catch to his grandfather. They shared a special bond, the two of them, and held great admiration toward one another, rightly so considering their likeness of mind and manner. Both the old man and the boy would strive for excellence, inspiring each other with the nature of their personalities. The grandfather's son, Cristofo's father, was a remarkable man as well, solidifying a lineage truly fit for a wizard. The boy's destiny had long ago been rooted, but of course, he had no idea. And so now he rode up onto the cobblestone lane that seemed to forever roll down the gentle slope of frontage as it left the striking entry doorway and unraveled itself like the imaginary tongue of the monumental stone abode. It reached its end at the front of the tree-lined property, where it was flanked by twin huts of dignified stature, each occupied by a pair of men from the king's guard. Brunella kept pace, continuing through as Cristofo nonchalantly nodded as the guards exited and stood at the ready. The boy and his majestic ride then continued along toward the rear of the structure, where they assumed they would find the grandfather in his usual whereabouts, the grand library.

Brunella quickly abated pace as she arrived at the library's familiar stone patio and approached the oversized doors of glass, hunching down to grant a more comfortable dismount. The darker background of night facilitated the view into the library, which was modestly illuminated by the incandescent glow of the persistent fire. Peculiarly, as Cristofo sprang off his mount, two figures were spotted within the lofty room, sitting on comfortable chairs in front of the fireplace and sharing drink. The small wooden table between the figures accommodated glasses and a uniquely shaped bottle that the boy instantly recognized from the grandfather's favored stock of spirits. One of the figures displayed the obviously familiar tall and lanky outline of the grandfather, while the other exposed a more profound and imposing silhouette, one that seemed to emit an aura of splendor, an almost magnetic allure, you could say, or so I have been told on more than one occasion.

"Who could that be with Grandfather at this hour, Iggy?" Cristofo remarked while inattentively stroking the soft fleecy fur on Brunella's broad flank as it heaved and undulated, gasping to retain pace of breath lost from the short but demanding trek with the heavy load. "That's a good girl." He would repeat the words unwittingly, with attention mostly focused on the interior of the library and its occupants, who had both risen from their seats, presumably being startled by the intense scraping sound of wooden shield abrading against the coarse stone surface of the patio.

"Cristofo, my boy!" gloated the grandfather proudly as he slid open the surprisingly maneuverable oversized glass door. "You have brought us home a prize after all! I should know better by now than to doubt you. Well done, boy!" The grandfather turned to his companion immediately. He had anticipated this moment with enthusiasm and eagerness— the opportunity to proudly showcase his distinguished friend to his markedly impressed grandson and at the same time impressing his guest as well with the presentation of his extraordinary kin. "It is with pleasure that I introduce you to an old and dear acquaintance of mine, Altarius the Prime, wizard of acclaim! Altarius, I present my grandson Cristofo."

The boy's wide and astounded eyes stared at an imposing figure that stood a hand taller than his lengthy grandfather and boasted a poise which was much more statuesque. Long wispy gray hair and beard lay well kempt and aback as though perpetually manicured by a gentle but constant wind. A stolid face contradictorily manifested great age as well as strength, with dark piercing eyes commanding respect and implying wisdom, adorned with blackened brows and long elegant lashes. Modest wrinkles at the corners meandered like the tributaries of an opulent river, irrigating the skin as they approached the pulsating veins of temple. A sturdy and angular nose canopied a dignified gray mustache, blackened in the midportion as though by fire breathed through vigorous nostrils.

Earth-brown cloth of fine quality enrobed the figure, with an excessively long gray and black belt looping around the midsection, securing the garment and complementing the coloration of hair. A powerful red cloak, also accented with a few vertical stripes of gray and black, was draped over wide shoulders leaving strong and powerful arms exposed. The tanned forearms were roughened with age but muscular and coated with long curled hairs of black that grew shorter and less dense as they made their way past large weathered hands and crept between sturdy and unshakeable knuckles. Yes, indeed, the boy was taken aback. And I, strangely enough, was taken aback as well! The boy was a striking figure, to say the least, but his dark brown eyes simply mesmerized me. I peered within and lost myself for a moment, swirling into the jet-black pupils of his soul and allowing them to absorb my alertness as I was drawn in with the vacuous pull of a black hole.

You see, it is the eyes, for those creatures that have them, that serve as a portal to the soul, and there within is revealed the essence, or spark of life. And with absolute clarity on that memorable Nepheshan spring night of a double full moon, I witnessed a blazing spark like none ever before seen in all of my abounding long years. And like none seen ever since as well, I might add. I immediately shook myself free of abstraction, managing to veil my succinct trancelike state to all but the grandfather. No, the gesture did not evade the scrutiny of my old friend the alchemist, whose quizzical gaze at once quashed my intention to keep the observation a secret. A subtle nod of acknowledgment served as agreement that an explanatory discussion would soon have to follow. Yes, indeed, it was the alchemist of old who happened to be the boy's esteemed grandfather and an exalted countryman of high regard, now more commonly referred to by all as the magister, a title bestowed by the revered king of Nephesh himself, who had long ago officially inducted him into the regal conglomerate under the title of Magister Elementi. It was a reward for work of his great discovery, one that empowered and enriched the city of Nephesh to an extravagant degree.

"Well now, what have we here? What a striking young man you present to me, magister, a striking young man indeed! Hello, Cristofo, it's a rare pleasure for an old wizard of age such as myself to meet such a finely fashioned specimen of youth." I could not resist the embellished and uproarious tone, as I was well informed on the boy's enthusiasm. "Is that a barb-fanged boar I see, all laced up any ready for the chef?"

"Yes, it is, Altarius … Wizard, I mean … I mean … sir?" The boy was experiencing a rare lack for words. "Grandfather mentioned that it was a favorite course of yours, so I was hoping to surprise you. You're arrived rather early?"

"And so I have, son, so I have. Your thoughtful efforts are well received. Please refer to me as Altarius. Well, hello there, Ignatius. I see that you have found a comfortable new carriage and friend!" The boy looked on with astonishment as his faithful companion beamed and shifted to a bright yellow hue. "I have brought something for you, my brilliant little creature." And at that moment, I reached into the pocket of my robe, withdrawing a small quantity of a mysterious dusty gold powder. Holding it in my palm, I gently blew at the material, which curiously glided through the air in a thin straight line as it made its way into the golden case through the tiny but intricately carved perforations. The creature was overjoyed, zooming into the air and flying erratically all about my face and body as I laughed emphatically, and then finally it went to rest on the shoulder of its master, the still astounded and equally overjoyed boy.

"And what magnificent manner of beast do we have here, a gorallion? I had thought them all but extinct … My, what a noble and towering creature."

"Her name is Brunella," the boy interjected, "and you will not find a finer specimen in any place."

"Well, that's not hard to believe, young Cristofo," I replied, making contact with the animal's mind and compelling her to hunch down before my face to facilitate a curious examination of the essence of her nature. While peering within the dull and aloof eyes, I happily ascertained a simplistic yet good-natured and loyal being, one which felt great admiration and devotedness toward her young master, who had always gotten good use of her while maintaining respect and genuine care.

"Yes, Brunella, you are indeed a good girl," I said, attentively stroking the underside of her neck while reaching into the pocket of my robe, intending to bedazzle my exuberant audience yet again. "Let's see if I can find a treat lingering here in my robe for a good girl such as yourself..." With that, I pulled out an unusually large bunch of bright red leafy fruits, such a large amount as would logically have no business residing within such a standardized pocket, much to the delight of all present, especially Brunella.

These succulent and irresistible morsels were not of earthly extraction, resembling large translucent rubies and about the size of cherries, with long crunchy white stems progressing to thick and juicy fan-shaped green leaves. Brunella took hold of the offering, slowly at first, analyzing and sniffing the strange fare, and then tried some. Almost unnaturally, she let fly a resonant grunt as though calling out to the heavens in rejoice, and then she began devouring the snack with a calculated and intense pace, appreciating each and every morsel like nothing she had ever experienced before.

"Ha ha, I think you have secured a new best friend, Altarius," interjected the magister with an abrupt but genuine chuckle. "Come!" he sternly beckoned an approaching stable hand. "Retrieve the kitchen staff and have them fashion this fine boar properly; then see Brunella to the stable and ensure that she is well handled! My dear friend, shall we return to drink and discussion?"

"Why, yes, I believe that we shall," was my reply as we reentered the comfort of the library, followed by the still-amazed and awestruck boy.

The magister and I reestablished our positions in the commodious chairs and watched while Cristofo catered to the smoldering centerpiece, poking and readjusting the charred half-spent logs and then nourishing them with additional fuel brought in from the massive stockpile that sat in wait outside, adjacent to the patio. When his tinkering was complete, a marvelous fire declared itself, not intensely ablaze but rather moderate and consistent. A soft heat dissipated, bathing us in a soothing atmosphere of warm comfort. And visually the flame was pleasant, long and rectangular, with an uncanny symmetry in both shape and color. The soft crackling sound of it subdued the mind, and the amplifying characteristic of the vaulted room exaggerated it, evoking the sensation of being surrounded by the fire, sitting comfortably in the midst of its reassuring omnipotence. I glanced over to my friend the magister and found him proudly smiling and nodding, silently acknowledging the boy's skill and implying credit for his own impeccable guidance. I returned the succinct nod, concurrently communicating approval of the boy's prowess as well as applause for the master's good tutelage.

"Well, I see that you've inherited your grandfather's aptitude toward the elements, young Cristofo. I must say that you conduct that fire masterfully, arranging each instrument harmoniously and executing a melodious performance worthy of the greatest of orchestras."

"Why, thank you, sir … Altarius, I mean." The boy was beaming with delight at the compliment.

"And now, gentlemen, as a special treat for our magnanimous guest," he bellowed as he glanced into the curious and intrigued eyes of both myself and the magister, "I present to you the debut performance of 'The Wizard and the Dragon.'" The boy then invited Ignatius, his unique fiery little pet, onto his extended palm. "All right then, Iggy, just like we practiced," and with a tossing motion, the creature was flung into the camouflaging blaze, where he disappeared from sight while amalgamating with the fellow flame, and Cristofo stepped back a few paces joining myself and the magister in curious audience.

At once, a brilliant orange glow spread infectiously, encompassing the fire in its entirety and bestowing a most unnatural appearance. A blast of flame unexpectedly erupted, flying out from its guarded enclosure and encompassing its modest but startled audience. Flame as cool as a gentle wind magically embraced and massaged us and then quickly receded, morphing into the form of a tall enrobed figure. It was an obscure shape but obviously outlining a longish beard and hair topped with an exceptionally familiar tall and conically shaped hat. Both the magister and Cristofo peered in my direction, intending to observe and compare—and to gauge my reaction to the mimicry at hand.

"My word, Ignatius, that is quite a brilliant figure you present before us!" I pronounced in jest but with an air of approval.

"Yes, Ignatius, but be careful, for there is not room enough in this grand library of ours for two such exorbitant egos!" interjected the magister with an amicable tone. A playful scowl responded in reluctant acceptance of the friendly wisecrack. He did know me quite well after all.

Without warning, the roaring sound of intense flame materialized behind our position, and a moderate heat caught my attention, kissing the side of my face as a burst of dragon's fire thundered betwixt the magister and me, directed at the blazing wizardly figure in our foreground. I turned to find a wondrously imposing brilliant orange figure of a dragon hovering in the air near the library's ceiling, at full wingspan and repeatedly discharging vigorous bursts of flame. The flaming wizard then held out a long, thin smoldering framework of staff, mimicking the infamous weapon of choice. The staff was at all times held forward, positioned strategically to receive each blast of fireball, and as each blast connected, the figure recoiled slightly and magnified in glow. Then, after taking in a dozen or so blasts, it stood tall and intensified, transforming color into a brilliant white and outstretching its arms as though to implore the gods.

All at once, the staff was relinquished and the lustrous arms converged. A small but brilliant blue ball of flame emanated from the figure's hands, flying out from them and quietly thumping into the dragon's fiery center. The flaming dragon's mouth opened wide to let fly a thunderous bellow of crackling inferno. The blue matter then grew infectiously, systematically overtaking the imposing figure of radiant orange and altering its composition to one which was no longer aflame; instead, it now took on a glassy blue appearance, crystal-like and fragile, and when replete, it would shatter into pieces, littering the floor. Each fragment then broke down further into flickering particles resembling sand, and as they traveled along the massive slabs of marble floor, they converged with the idly glowing fallen staff. The triumphant wizardly impostor subsequently hoisted the now glassy blue crystallized staff and victoriously bowed to its good audience before collapsing to the floor and retreating into the fireplace where flame reestablished its previous magnificence. Iggy then tacitly emerged and remained quite still, a relatively meager presence seeming to bask in delight as the three of us stood in astonishment and cheered with enthusiasm.

"Well now, magister, you certainly are pampering me with fine amusement on this delightful visit, and I have only just arrived. I can only imagine what lies in store for the remainder of my stay."

"No, not I, Altarius. I had planned only fine drink and finer conversation," acknowledged the magister. "Cristofo and Ignatius are to be thanked for the evening's entertainment."

"Indeed, well done, young Cristofo," I replied. "And, Ignatius, you are full of surprises, you wondrous little creature. What other talents do you have hiding in that tiny little arsenal of yours?"

The creature's glare dulled slightly, taking on an almost bashful tone, and then it scurried along the floor and up the leg and body of Cristofo, reentering the comfort of its golden abode. In the meantime, Cristofo was nonchalantly pulling over a third chair and positioning it strategically between the magister and myself. He then proceeded to a modest cupboard that lay camouflaged against the stone wall of the library, surrounded by bookcases with brimming shelves. He took hold of a short-stemmed drinking glass and proceeded to sit with the intention of joining us in conversation. The magister and I sat silently and observed the production without much word or action until the boy took hold of the extravagant bottle and then the magister took hold of the boy's arm.

"A tad presumptuous, my boy, wouldn't you say?"

"But, Grandfather, I have so many questions … Altarius, how old are you? Are you immortal? And how did you do that trick with the golden powder … and with the bunch of radishes for Brunella? Can you fly? Have you ever fought a dragon? Have you ever been to another place among the stars?"

"Come now, boy, you embarrass me with your ill-mannered demeanor," the magister finally interrupted. "Please have some respect for our guest; he is not here to be barraged with questions!"

"I apologize, Grandfather. And, Altarius, I know I can be carelessly overzealous at times," replied the boy with eyes of chagrin.

"An outstanding quality that will serve you well, Cristofo!" I interjected in an attempt to appease the boy. I gently took hold of the magister's arm, calming him, and in turn he released his sturdy grasp on his grandson.

"Young Cristofo," I began as I calmly poured a small quantity of the exquisite spirit into the boy's eager glass, "your grandfather and I have some catching up to do, mostly pertaining to boring matters—you know, chatter of old acquaintances and such. I do, however, require a tour of the celebrated stables about which I have heard such great things; perhaps you would care to be my guide in that regard?"

"Of course, Altarius. It would be a pleasure," he responded with joy, raising the glass to his lips and shooting down the entire small yet potent concoction as though acknowledging a formality to the affair.

"Cristofo," added the magister, "it will have to be in the evening tomorrow; have you forgotten that you have lessons with Myrina at the king's palace early in the morning? Off to bed with you now, son. Get some good rest. I gave instructions for Brunella to be saddled and ready for just after dawn."

"Yes, of course, Grandfather. Goodnight, and goodnight to you, Altarius."

"Good night," echoed in response.

"Oh, and by the way, Cristofo," I added before the boy could get very far, "they were rapinnae!"

"I beg your pardon, Altarius?" the boy replied confusedly.

"They were not radishes; they were rapinnae from the world of Quinar, a distant place 'among the stars,' as you would so eloquently put it." The boy's jaw dropped. Silence was his response. The magister also displayed silent astonishment.

"Oh, and I almost forgot," I added with a casual rapport, "I have brought a gift for you as well. Do a tired old wizard a favor and go fetch it, please. It's over there on your grandfather's worktable, under my hat."

The boy, still startled and silent, began to move toward the table in the corner of the room. Once there, eyes were fixated on the tallish conical headgear, which was weathered but of the finest-quality hide. It complemented the robe with predictable earth-tone coloration and presented a simple rustic charm. A moderate brim graced the circumference of the accessory and helped to shelter the face from sun or rain. A bent peak with a blunt point topped the hat, and as the boy clutched it in his hand, its feel noticeably took him aback; a comfortable suppleness somehow meshed with course firmness. He jolted it upward with considerable anticipation, and I watched intently as his face dropped and eyes became blank and befuddled.

"It's … a tooth?" the boy exclaimed in a disbelieving manner. The magister also looked on with dumbfounded perplexity.

"Not just any tooth, young Cristofo!" I blurted out dramatically as I rose to approach the boy. I encroached upon his personal space as my eyes drew dangerously close to his, but he did not blink or recoil. "That is a wizard's tooth," I offered with quiet seriousness as I took hold of the unappealing molar, a ghostly and mineral-like object, to say the least, and I placed it in the boy's outstretched palm. Then, with a most serious gaze and tone of voice, I instructed, "One wish … any wish … anytime." The boy quietly stared at the suddenly magnificent prize, momentarily entranced. Then his hand clutched at it tightly, enlivening the musculature of his forearm and the tautness of the tendons in his wrist.

"Wow! Are you serious, Altarius? I … I don't know what to say; it's amazing! Thank you so much. I promise that I will use it wisely."

"Of course you will, young Cristofo. I wouldn't have given it to you otherwise. Now do as your grandfather says, boy, and off to bed with you—to fantastic dreams and thoughts of tomorrow's rewards!"

The boy shuffled off quite distractedly, struggling to concentrate on the task at hand, namely to prepare for a comfortable and good night's rest. His mind was otherwise preoccupied with the remarkable article held tightly in his cozy palm. *What to wish for?* he wondered. The possibilities were exciting. Fortune was the obvious choice, treasure and gold enough to last a thousand lifetimes, but he already had more than enough. He lacked for nothing, really. Fame and glory, perhaps; no, these were not his ambitions. Longevity of life or the gift of immortality? That was indeed a compelling thought, one that he would have to consider as a possibility. Wondrous thoughts abounded: super strength, divine intelligence, the ability to read thoughts, magic powers, spells, teleportation, impervious skin that would wholly protect the body. Now that would indeed be a miraculous endowment, weightless and more resilient than the best of the time's available armor and yet another idea that made his list for future consideration. The power of flight, perhaps? All-seeing eyes, mastery of creatures, perpetual lungs circumventing the need for air? Time-traveling abilities? The possibilities were as limitless as the imagination. And then there was love. Ah yes, the all-powerful human emotion brewing within the bosom of the maturing boy, burgeoning. A flower in bloom sprouting with an exuberance equal to that of his exquisitely evolving physicality, a wish for her to be forever his; that would definitely be worth considering. But alas, the boy immediately realized that a conjured love was no love at all.

Princess Myrina was the sole offspring of King Reuel, the long incumbent, fair and just ruler of Nephesh. She was the embodiment of perfection, a striking young female of exemplary body and mind. Born on an illustrious summer's morn, she entered the world with a resplendence that bathed her onlookers with radiance akin to a morsel of sun. A fortnight prior, a kindred young Cristofo similarly entered into the world, ratifying his meaningful albeit modest seniority. From an early age, the two like-spirited individuals shared close association—an enterprising collaboration for which the queen and Cristofo's mother can be applauded. A joining of royalty with the progeny of Nephesh's most reputable family would do well to ensure a worthy lineage for the next generation's reign. Indeed, the two had shared closeness for the entirety of their young but fulfilling lives. Together they had been mentored, lessons shared and lessons learned by the finest of experts in the widest array of subjects.

Fencing and swordplay, archery, chemistry, geography, literature, sporting activities of all sorts and kinds, culinary arts, spelunking, falconry, mathematics, astronomy, hand-to-hand combat, etiquette and formalities, alchemy of course, and countless other activities for the body and mind were all taught in a seemingly endless series of private lessons taking place in rotation and expertly managed by the rigorous tutelage of Lady Valencia, an impeccable and meticulous servant to the king. A diminutive dwarfling, the king's most trustworthy governess was captured years ago during a raid in the faraway land of Asinor, where a general of the king's great-great-grandfather took pity on the then-infant and chaperoned her back to Nephesh, where she was raised in relative affluence. She appeared meager in size but was vigorous in personality, a wrinkle-free visage and raven-black hair adorning this sprite creature of considerable age. Thoughts of tomorrow's lessons at the palace overtook Cristofo's mind, with his favored activity on the agenda: dragon riding. Myrina's sweet bosom comforted him in slumber, and her familiar yet alluring smell came to mind, fashioning a smile onto the boy's face as he drifted off to sleep.

Meanwhile, in the grand library, the magister attentively gave audience, as I explained, in what manner I could, about my reaction when first placing eyes upon young Cristofo. The spark of life was well understood by the discerning, erudite mind of my old friend, but the degree to which it possessed the boy was well beyond his true comprehension. A stern and uneasy gaze was the product of my explanation, and the angry scowl of a protective guardian surfaced with an instinctive reaction.

"No, Altarius, I absolutely forbid it! That is not the destiny set out for my grandson! A wizard's life is not for him, forever elsewhere, venturing off to tinker with the course of existences distant and remote, forever encumbered with complications not of his own undertaking! No, I forbid that life for him! No offense to you, Altarius, but tinker with another's soul, not with that of my cherished kin!"

"Magister," I calmly responded when opportune silence allowed, "precious few are those which may boast the genuine honor of referring to me as friend; you unequivocally stand among them. The destiny of young Cristofo is not yours to adjudge, nor is it mine. It is simply predetermined and inevitable by definition," I continued with an increasingly emphatic and more strictly placid tone. "He is wizard! Of this, there can be no doubt. Fledgling as though he may well be, it is done! It exists within him. It is the fate conjoined with his soul, and neither you, nor I, nor any powers that be can alter this simple truth. And fate, my good friend, as I am sure you are quite well aware, is simply a force with which there is no reckoning." At once, the magister's disposition changed. He of scientific mind understood the inevitability of it all and conceded the fact that it was to remain unyielding in the face of an emotional outburst. The true purpose of the boy's exceptionality came to reason.

"But what will I tell his parents, Altarius? What of his presumed supposition as prince consort? Is he not destined to sire the future king? His mother will be overwrought, not to mention the queen! All that time spent in preparation, devising and planning in anticipation, has it all been for naught?"

"You have a good soul, my dear magister, for if you did not, I would be unable to call you a true friend," I began in an attempt to appease the concerns of the proud patriarch. "A great spark resides within you, of that I believe you are aware. The shepherds of fortuity have smiled upon you. They have bestowed the enduring gift of excellence upon your bloodline, and that is the ultimate bequest for which any mortal man can hope. Cristofo's destiny may very well include a royal coupling, just as it may include a number of other substantial events. Becoming wizard does not stifle the boy; quite contradictorily, it frees him. There are no restrictions or constraints, no rules or guidelines to follow, and nor are there any set routines or laws. There is simply the following of one's own axiom and the understanding that all actions result in meaningful consequence.

"The boy will live as his own stupendous mind dictates, as would be the case, wizard or not. No precedent stands as guidance, for he is the first of your kind to bear such advancement. Do not dwell on the title imposed; focus rather on the true meaning of the appointment. Greatness of unimaginable magnitude awaits the boy's course! In the morning, send rock doves to the factory with a message for his parents, a simple word about my visit and about my determination regarding their son. Under no circumstances are they to return home; instead, assure them that Cristofo shall soon attend to the factory under my accompaniment."

"And what of Cristofo, Altarius? How will the boy be informed of this surprising imposition?"

"The boy will dream of it this night. He will feel the incipient presence of the overseers in his mind's eye. In the morning, he will sense that a change is amiss, and the rest will come from me in due course. Now, let us speak no more of this for the moment, old friend. We have stories to share and this fine bottle to empty; a substantial enough task for this exceptional and resplendent night!"

CHAPTER 3

Dragon Riding

A startling sensation woke the boy as he sprung up from the comfort of his pleasantly firm and oversized bedding. Wide and alert eyes stared beyond the room's magnificent window, where a crack of sunlight forced itself upon the darkness, breaking its dreary spirit and forcing ephemeral exile, an innumerous routine concocted by the heavens, wherein a shift of the earth's diverse beings ensue. Creatures of the night retreat to slumber, passing the torch of vitality on to those who favor the warm and revealing light of day. Remnants of strange dreams lingered in his mind, fragments of things too outrageous to be real. Then consciousness ushered more sober thoughts for the moment, until the boy slowly opened his still tightly clenched fist and unraveled an unattractively tainted decaying gray tooth.

"Altarius," he whispered to himself ever so softly, recognizing a foreign sensation embedded somehow deep within his persona. It was a satisfying sensation, not at all bothersome or troubling, but what was its nature? the boy wondered, if only for an instant, until abruptly turning his head toward the chamber's ornately carved, solid wood door. Several awkward moments passed before he heard the reverberant clang of iron against the strike plate.

"Good morning, young master!" bellowed a familiar voice as a trusted servant entered the room carrying garments, a washbasin, and a grooming apparatus of sorts. "Well, what have we here? Already up and at 'em, eh master?" quipped the jovial attendant. "That's a surprising turn of events, I must say; I had brought extra water to splatter upon your face to ensure arousal, as per the magister's strict instruction, of course."

"Ha ha, very amusing, Timalty. That will be all, thank you," retorted the boy as he instinctively concealed the tooth in the pocket of his sleeping trousers.

"'Sire,'" was offered with an acknowledging bow as the slender well-dressed steward exited forthwith. Cristofo remained, contemplative and attempting to rationalize how he had seemed to perceive Timalty's arrival well before its occurrence. He shook his head confusedly in an attempt to clear it of overanalyzing thought and then continued the effort by cupping his hands and bringing fresh cool water from the washbasin up to his face, revitalizing himself as he forged ahead with his morning routine.

With his preparation complete, the boy hurriedly scurried down the narrower but still impressively spacious servant's staircase, leading him directly into the bustling locality that was the hub of the good estate's diligent attendants. Small industrious fires danced sporadically about the cookery, some heating kettles and pots of various size and content, while others cooked or seared a variety of meats and other food things. All in all, the boy was quite impressed with the kerfuffle as he absorbed the performance for a few brief moments, watching the various staff members scuttling about; a well-oiled mechanism churning in a seemingly synchronous operation. The blunt chime of knives against chopping block, the sharp sound of utensils of all sorts clanging in the background, and the resounding clamor of spoon against bowls, both steel and glass, served as a chorus to the ballad, while whistles and hums fluttered through the air, voices sang, and instructions were bellowed. Much preparation was afoot, as the magister had commanded their best culinary efforts during the visitation of his exalted guest, culminating with that night's feast and featuring the wild barb-fanged boar proffered by Cristofo's own capable hand.

"Enjoying the production, young master?" intruded a pleasant voice as a buoyant young kitchen hand approached Cristofo with an outstretched arm, offering a cold glass of his favorite morning beverage, chilled nectar of fruit. "What can I prepare for you this fine morning, sire?" She curtsied as he accepted the glass.

"Good morning, Magdalene," responded the boy, not at all annoyed by the interruption. "Nothing elaborate for the moment—perhaps a sample of that savory sweet roll; the lingering smell of it is quite seductive. And a handful of figs for Brunella as well."

"Very good, master. It'll be out of the oven and ready in a moment," responded the maiden as she scampered off in short order. Cristofo, in the meantime, took a hearty swig of his cool fruit drink and placed it down on a small dining table that rested against a wall adjacent to the staircase. Then he turned his mind to his fiery little companion, Iggy, and just as he turned the corner to begin his search for the pet, the tiny blaze of a creature appeared scurrying down the hallway and racing forth, springing up in a flash and entering its comfortable station within the pendant that swayed patiently as it hung around the boy's sturdy neck.

"There you are, Iggy. You seem quite excited this morning." A pulsating glow responded with enthusiasm. "I know you are, and I am too. I can't wait to see Cimtar. I hope he's in a pleasant mood today; it has been far too long since our last riding lesson. A fortnight or so has passed since last we soared through the air in wild unabated abandon. He needs that, Iggy. He needs it more frequently than it occurs. I know because I dreamed of it last night. I felt his anguish; I felt his pain. I felt it as clear as day; a creature of such majesty must feel the rush of air and the pounding sun against its mass as it soars through the skies. It needs to experience the fervor of power and the true worth of its innate right to dominate a territory or realm. And Somnia as well ... Obviously, she too is deserved of the same right. Neither can be stabled for much longer at this point. They need open space and freedom in order to properly mature. I will appeal to the good sense of Lady Valencia and ask her to triple the frequentness of our lessons. That will suffice for the time being."

With that, the boy proceeded with his departure, making short work of his breakfast and rushing out through the imposing front entry doors of the manor. Brunella stood saddled and ready just beyond the steps at the head of the cobblestone lane; she hunched down in acknowledgment of the boy's presence and with invitation for him to get astride.

"Good morning, girl." Cristofo took a moment to affectionately stroke the broad side of the gentle beast. Her fur conveyed a distinct feel for some reason on this particular morning; the sensation was not necessarily different but more acute than the norm. The boy relished it as each individual bristle tickled his hand, and underneath the short thick glossy coating, he felt pulsating flows, a resounding beat, and various other growls and churns all working in unison within the embodiment of the animal. He offered up the snack of figs and instantly deciphered a change in the creature's constitution as the machinery within altered; he was taken aback as a resonating growl emanated, and he felt its full course as it came to fruition, echoing through the beast's large and cavernous belly and out through its mouth. Otherwise, the air was crisp, the morning dew obediently moistened the stately lawn, flowers stretched out to reach the rising sun, in turn inviting bees and other inconspicuous insects to attend. Tree leaves danced in the revitalizing wind, and various Rodentia scurried about. Cristofo absorbed it all in a few brief moments, and in short words, he felt great!

"You know where we're going, don't you, girl? You seem as excited as I am to see Princess Myrina," he offered as he positioned a waiting satchel full of powder over his shoulder and Iggy quickly scurried into it. Then he mounted his magnificent gorallion and gently nudged her with his heel. They were off. "To the palace, girl, and make haste, for a glorious day awaits!"

The stunning palace of Nephesh was strategically situated in the exact center of the bustling metropolis, and it stood mostly unaltered from its inception some half millennium afore. A monumental wall of great breadth circled the castle, shielding it from all undesirables. Oh, but this was not just any wall; it was a massive structure two stories high and wide enough to provide a comfortable abode for a majority of those who held the honor of brotherhood in the loyal and long-standing king's guard. Their families as well were housed within the walls of thick and well-carved rectangular blocks of solid igneous rock, an impenetrable fortress rife with life and cheer. There was no lack of decently sized windows on the outward-facing facade of the complex, but the interior wall of each individual quarters permitted only one heavily laden door allowing access inward toward its royal protectorate. Heavy wooden planks lay in wait, ready to be placed firmly against thick iron brackets embedded deep within the mass of stone should the need to barricade arise. The top of the wall—or rooftop, as it were—was constructed of thick watertight timbers cemented together with a tar-like substance, slightly sloped toward the occasion scupper hole strategically placed to allow rainwater to escape.

Stockpiles of armaments were by no means lacking, aptly stored in rugged chests methodically placed adjacent to the walls of the hearty parapet. Lofty flagpoles and chimney stacks sprouted in turn out from above the summit, dressing up the structure like so many candles atop a celebratory cake. A constant and heavy contingency of guardsman would patrol the wide-ranging expanse, with extra fortification at the circuit's four evenly spaced entrance points; the main gate, which was northerly facing, happened to be the one presently on approach by young Cristofo.

A moderate lineup of merchants, townsfolk, and various other travelers of sorts stood in wait at the active entrance point, with each individual person and beast subjected to thorough inspection and scrutiny prior to being granted access to the royal grounds. Brunella slowed as she scampered by the arrangement, bypassing all and coming to rest at the edge of a small edifice, where a well-armed officer of the guard stood in a supervisory role. A tall, strong, and handsome clean-shaven man with wavy brown hair and a stolid but scarred face greeted the boy.

"Good morning, Master Cristofo," bellowed out a rustic monotone voice.

"Good morning to you as well, Paladin," retorted the boy unfamiliarly. He peered into the man's eyes and at once deciphered a noble and sturdy soul, experienced of battle and loyal beyond question. "I'm off to the dragon's terrain; send for the keeper and have him bring a key and some morning fare."

"At once, young master. Shall I send a stable hand as well for this gentle beast of yours?"

"No, I will ride her to the stables and proceed on foot from there."

A bow of acknowledgment ensued and Cristofo was off, traversing the vast domain that was the royal premises.

The dragon's terrain was a relatively large and fabricated habitat nestled against the southeasterly wall of the estate's massive stone enclosure. A rugged and rocky domicile, it boasted decently manufactured mountainous hills complete with sheltering cave and three modestly sized lakes, which were also man-made and generously stocked with robust and nourishing fish of various species. A thin, meandering moat delineated the territory, where a single narrow and arched access bridge constructed of stone was conveniently located to facilitate pedestrian entry. The moat, of course, was there to prevent wanderers from entering the grounds, as were numerous blatantly posted signs and placards of warning and caution. Chains of immense proportion lay haphazardly strewn about the landscape, steely symbols representing the massiveness of undertaking required to confine such powerful beasts. A multitude of links were as thick as a man's finger, unified in length and forming sufficient slack to grant access up to the edge of the monolithic castle wall on one tangent and up to the boundary of the pacific moat on the other.

There were two such chains per dragon, four in all required; one end was tethered to colossal spikes cemented deep within the bedrock and the other to thick and rugged collars. A generous lining of hide softened the collars, one of which had been designed for the ankle, while the other was for the hulking neck. Several persons were kept in employ, catering to the formidable creatures: two keepers, two grounds persons, a purveyor of foods charged with accommodating the appetites of the voracious carnivores, with sheep, goats, pigs, chickens, calves, lambs, and the like devoured in short order and with no lack of barbarity. Well-stocked and always attainable lakes of fish would placate the underlying possibility of turning toward a more human type of fare. Two blacksmiths as well were at the ready, constantly tending to the immeasurable length of sturdy chain, sometimes knotted and intertwined and oftentimes charred to a fragile blackened state in need of quick repair, a function of the creatures' grievance toward encumbrance of any manner or kind.

Yes, the keeping of dragons was an undertaking of exorbitant expense, not to mention the sizable fortune paid by King Rueul to procure the mystic beasts at the onset. One thousand times their weight in gold was reluctantly purveyed to the esoteric breeder who mysteriously appeared at the palace entry gate on the eve of Princess Myrina's ten-year celebration of birth with two nursling dragons in tow, magnificent and vibrant as they rode in the back of a simple wagon, where they were contained in modest wooden cages. The man spoke of an arcane land far north, from which he had traveled a long and arduous journey, knowing that his nonnegotiable price would be met without fail. One creature was male with scales of royal blue and deep green, the other a female with a consistent hue of yellow gold. They were siblings and of the rarest breed of dragon, feroxellae—a ferocious but diminutive variety and the only known form small enough to potentially be ridden by man. When fully grown, they would approach a stature similar to that of the boy's trusted gorallion.

The traveler was welcomed to stay for the night, and the next day a private yet cryptic bonding ceremony was performed wherein strange chants and wordage were uttered in an unfamiliar tongue. A small vial of blood was drawn from the princess and gracelessly poured down the throat of the female dragon with one hand, while the other pressured open its jaws and mouth. Similarly, the young boy Cristofo was also unified with the male of the pair in presence of his grandfather—a great gift bestowed in reward for the substantial undertaking responsible for ushering wealth of enormous magnitude into the city coffers, the very coffers that then lay considerably emptier as the traveler departed in a rickety wagon overloaded with weight of gold. It was a paradoxical sight, but it occurred nonetheless, as he was expeditiously on his way, adamantly refusing accompaniment or aid of any kind. Left behind were two mesmerizing creatures adorned in shimmering and radiant scales—one glistening of golden sheen forever bonded to the illustrious princess, the other beaming and brilliant as though covered in a coat of emerald and sapphire, forever bonded to the exemplary boy.

A healthy wisp of smoke gently permeated along the roof of the man-made cave, rising out into the freedom of the expansive sky and signaling to Cristofo that his presence was detected. Within, robust nostrils smoldered and sprightly lids unlocked to reveal magnificent yellow-gold eyes and thin parabolic pupils of jet black, vertical and swelling to focus in the dimly lit comfort of the adequate abode. The boy accelerated pace while traversing the simple bridge and cheered out in delight as he set foot on the bouldered and rock-ribbed territory.

"Cimtar!" he shouted with enthusiasm. "Come spread your wings, boy, and prepare to be liberated from your shackles!" A profound roar echoed in response as the glorious beast shot out of the cave's mouth, vigorously thrashing its wings and blasting fire of ominous proportion. The sturdy chains held taut, and the resolute anchor wavered, struggling to hold fast. Cristofo observed from below and was overwhelmed by the creature's magnificence as the sun gave life to the shimmering coat of callous scales and sent down a bright and blinding reflection. There was a sense of strengthened bond on this particular morn, more tenacious and intimate than that of previous ceremonial root. He turned to observe the keeper on approach, and with his mind, he beckoned the formidable dragon. At once, heavy steel chain crashed upon the rock and Cimtar's mass thudded to the ground, which in turn reverberated softly under the boy's feet.

"Well, hello to you, you magnificent creature!" an overjoyed voice blurted out genuinely as Cristofo took hold of the long brawny neck and gave embrace. The imposing brute succumbed, emitting hollow grunting sounds while billows of smoke exited its nostrils in intermittent bursts. The boy then took hold of the dragon's ferocious snout and stared into its eyes as his fingers slowly caressed the scabrous covering of scales. The two beings exchanged a silent sense of affinity and understanding, excitedly anticipating the imminent jaunt through the sky. In the meantime, Iggy was overzealously brilliant throughout the encounter, careening about the glittering scales, while Cimtar basked in delight; a unique affinity existed between the two creatures, both of fiery persuasion.

"At once with those keys!" shouted the boy as the keeper hurried forth, awkwardly shuffling through his pocket as two turbulent carry bags writhed and squawked as they hung off his shoulders and crossed onto either side of his hip.

"Hello there, Master Cristofo," imposed the keeper's ruffled voice. "Would you like the key, sire, or shall I unchain our excellent beast?"

"Unchain him and pass one carry bag to me. Go tend to Somnia at once, for she will soon be likewise aroused."

Collars were unclasped in turn, and the dragon's magnificent wings outstretched to full span as the creature basked in euphoric delight, relishing its blissful, albeit temporary, freedom. The boy stepped back several paces as he carefully reached into the sack and took hold of a sinewy neck. A rigorous toss then ensued, followed by the clamping of savage jaws as sharp-edged teeth made quick work of the slaughter; a quick gobble completed the task. A second snack was similarly proffered, as Cimtar's breakfast concluded rather quickly, quickly enough that soft feathers of poultry still glided carelessly and oscillated in the wind on their course to the as-of-yet unattained ground.

"Go on, boy, fly! But do not cross beyond the great walls; be free yet restricted for the time being," Cristofo proclaimed loudly and quite unnecessarily, as the dragon knew full well not to break such a boundary without his master in tow. And meanwhile, near the mouth of the cave, a second creature of beauty emerged amid the fervor, shiny and gold and excitedly roused as the keeper finalized his approach.

Then, abruptly, a change occurred in the boy. His pace of heart quickened, and a blushful red tone invaded his cheeks and face. Strangely, he perceived the pounding rush of blood as it coursed through his veins, culminating in resounding throbs to both of his temples. A shiver emanated from his spine and traveled a circuit through his limbs and body until discharged through scintillating fingers and toes. A welcoming scent materialized, causing the boy to close his eyes and inhale long and hard. He aimed to savor the moment with desperate tenacity as though it were his last opportunity to accurately emblazon it to memory. He qualified the vision in his mind before turning to behold the exquisite sight on approach, yet somehow surprise prevailed as he laid eyes upon the princess just as she dismounted her steed and tethered it to the post rail at the head of the simple bridge. Myrina's coy smile entranced the boy as he stood motionless, admiring the stream of her lavish dark hair as she dashed forward in her close-fitting and padded riding suit, a flattering outfit that encased her supple yet firm body and sturdied her ample bosom.

"Well, good morning to you, my alluring and stunning boy!" blurted out the princess, now just paces away, much to the satisfaction of young Cristofo. "You are simply a magnificent sight, my sweet ...," she continued, and just then Cristofo came to realize that her glance was not directed on an even plain; indeed, it was more upwardly aimed. "Cimtar!"

"Why, you little agitator!" retorted the dapper young Cristofo with a personable smile of contentedness etched onto his face.

"Ha ha," the princess chuckled in a fun and amicable tone. "Oh, and good morning to you as well, Cris. I must confess that you also present a most pleasant sight."

"Why, thank you, my beautiful princess, and might I return the same compliment with the utmost sincerity!" responded the boy playfully as he corralled her in his arms with outstretching fingers to maximize the sensation of her curvaceous waist. She reciprocated the embrace, placing hands upon his young broad shoulders and drawing him near; their eyes met and distance between converged as they enjoyed a penetrating gaze. And then it was she who broke the short-lived trance, thwarting the magnetic allure of inviting lips and withdrawing just as they approached a tender touch.

"Come. Let us go to my wonderful dragon so that she may join yours in liberating flight, and we can talk for a while before saddling our pets and riding them hard and fast to our hearts' content."

"You've cleared it with Lady Valencia?" interjected an excited young Cristofo.

"Of course I have, on the promise that we would return to hard study by late morning. And don't act so surprised, Cris. Were you expecting to put Cimtar back in chains while we departed to carry on with our studies? Your impudent act all but forced my hand in the matter," responded the princess with a firm but approving glance.

The two young nobles carried on in such manner, awkwardly balancing a relationship that had evolved over the years from that of childhood friends and peers to that of pubescent paramours promised to each other since birth and imminently to be betrothed. Indeed, they longed for each other at this point, but still they were expected to maintain a respectable innocence. They both struggled with equal frustration and with an equal commitment to the responsibility of duty. A degree of detachment from the commonality and isolation of sorts befell the pair, an unfortunate price paid for a luxurious and noble life with private learning and activities reserved for those of loftier status. In all fairness, it did do well to reinforce their closeness and to strengthen trust and appreciation in each other's talents and attributes. Neither had ever questioned or repudiated the prearranged pairing, nor had they strayed in thought toward any other possible coupling instead. While the saying insists that there are plenty of fish in the sea, why cast another line when the choicest catch is already securely on hook?

And so the sky above the sizable castle grounds feigned a grand arena where two wondrous creatures whizzed about spontaneously, soaring at will and with no discernible pattern. Bursts of flame danced about intermittently, blazing against the already bright and sun-filled sky. The guardsmen on patrol atop the expansive wall took pause to observe, as did most of the nearby populace, giving audience to the unique and bewildering performance. King Rueul himself stood in surveyance, resting his hands on the ornate and monolithic stone balustrade that enclosed the comfortable personal balcony that overlooked the beauteous property. The spectacle presented a soothing comfort, a reprieve from the norm, allowing healthy abstraction from the usual affairs of the mind—reflections, ponderings of burdens and hardships, and similar kingly thoughts that are incomprehensible to all but other kings. The wind ruffled his lightly grayed locks as he straightened, standing statuesque with crossed arms as rugged fingers gently stroked the short thick fur of his bearded chin. He watched as his treasured offspring frolicked playfully in the distance, enamored with an excellent and most worthy boy—a boy on the cusp of manhood nonetheless— one that he admired and cherished as if his own. For lack of better words, he was pleased.

Yes, the two enamored adolescents frisked and rollicked for a short while until finding a relatively comfortable seat of sorts among the scattered boulders, where they proceeded to engage in idle conversation as their incomparable pets took the opportunity to spread their wings in healthful flight. Cristofo explained all regarding his great wizardly encounter, of course, leaving out only the part about the incredulous gift of a wizard's tooth. An odd and instinctive sensation compelled him to omit this substantial detail for some reason, instilling secrecy— an admirable development bringing cause to the significance of the offering and denoting good wisdom.

Myrina listened attentively in wonderment, enthralled throughout the recounting. "That's fantastic, Cris; I hope I get to meet him as well. Surely he will call upon Father at some point during his visit. You know that he has held an honorary seat on the royal advisory council for generations; I am certain that he would not journey through Nephesh without calling upon the king. Did he or the magister mention anything to that effect?"

"No, nothing was mentioned, but he arrived just last night. I am certain that he will want to visit the palace and see his precious carnivoran trees. He has requested my company on a tour of our stables this evening," offered Cristofo proudly. "I will find out what I can during our time together there."

"Humph! I will tell Father that he is attending at the magister's, and he will surely send word requesting his presence for counsel, or supper, or both," returned the princess with a noticeably uppity air.

And so conversation advanced, with discussion mostly directed toward wizardly considerations and such. Cristofo recapitulated his recollection of the story of my first encounter with his grandfather during the early days of the factory's inception, a story whose details will remain unspoken for the time being. The princess told what she recalled about her great-great-great-grandfather king, who was presented a simple gift from a mysterious robed stranger long ago, a substantial basket of sprouts to be planted with precise spacing and distance, encircling the palace as a last line of defense. A precise sketch was included, and instructions were presented for planting and maintenance of the extraordinary timbers. Recipes that were secret to all but the king and his gardeners were left, outlining secret ingredients. One powdery concoction was to be sprinkled weekly, serving to keep the timbers fed a basal meal and leaving them placated and subdued; another formulation was to be applied in the event of attack, shocking the creatures astir and awakening the primordial hunger within their feral essence. Of course, the king was skeptical, but he somehow felt coerced to give credence to the strange ramblings of the elegantly bearded and cloaked foreigner with a curious and unusual shape of hat.

"One day in the not-so-near future, when these saplings grow into powerful and resolute trees, they will save the kingdom; indeed, they will defend an onslaught of the palace and safeguard the continuance of the royal bloodline!" touted the stranger with staff in hand, quite animated in gesture and loud in words. Yes, that was quite some time ago, and the wise king took heed of my forewarning, having gardeners tend to the trees with diligent adherence to instruction and with no regard for the passage of time. The stolid king's term in this realm passed as he departed the way of his forefathers, and as the years wore on and as his sons' and daughters' sons and daughters laughed, played, and cavorted among the unsightly and morbid trees, his resolute insistence for their care endured. Leafless and stout, with bare and skeletal limbs sprawling rampantly in all directions, the grayish wood stood testament to a monarch's hardened will and steely resolve—until one day when the unsullied palace suddenly came under siege.

Barbarian hordes loomed. From the far west land of Venarium, beyond the multitudinous lakes and just on the edge of the Caspian woodland, they came in full droves. They were searching for a more comfortable and prosperous homestead that they could simply overtake without regard for the endless seasons of hard work expended by the

bona fide incumbents, thick sweat and labor spent nourishing lands and
building infrastructure. Generations of harsh savagery precipitated the
transformation of the entire line into creatures awash of an extremely
dark spark. They thrashed and cleaved their way through the guarded
city and fought long and hard to overcome the impenetrable fortress
wall. Throngs of fallen comrades were gathered up and tossed in a pile
like so many sacks of worthless skin and bone, creating a buttress for
all to clamber up and scale. In this manner, the ruthless barbarians
gained distinction, infamously claiming the inaugural overcoming of
the celebrated palace wall. However, success came at great cost. Corpses
abounded on both sides of the skirmish, and the few dozen scores of
voracious barbarian warriors who persevered and continued steadfast
toward the vulnerable palace doors met with a sudden and shocking end
in the relentless and brutal line of the stalwart and enduring carnivoran
trees.

Yes, as the name implies, these foreign creatures of wood fancied
a heartier type of sustenance, not at all keen on drink of water and
nutrients of the soil like their rampant and widespread counterparts.
Flesh, bone, muscle, and organ tantalized these outrageous beasts as
shallow roots snapped out of the ground with the aggressive fury of a
large and heavy steel-jaw leghold trap. Their victims found themselves
instantaneously jailed within the callous bars of root. Ensnared and
helpless, they screamed with the unabated ferocity of those unfortunate
souls unsuspectingly presented with imminent death. Outstretched
arms desperately grasped, reaching for the life-giving freedom of air—
that freedom so often taken for granted yet at once unattainable beyond
the stony pickets they faced as the tenacious limbs curled inward and
begin to re-submerge. Relentless fear exacerbated as the roots gradually
enclosed, forcing the captives to feel the hard resilience of ground
and the immoveable pressure of tentacles crushing wind and breaking
body until the minds were no longer aware. Then the roots ruthlessly
continued downward, returning to their subterranean roost, where
other smaller and more bristly appendages worked hard to soak up
the spoils and absorb the precious nutriments. When the performance

came to an end, all was as it was before, save for the churned and fluid-soaked soil beneath the now blood-spattered and thick rustic trunks of carnivoran.

An advancing keeper awkwardly toting harnesses and riding gear detached the young couple from the fantastic imagery of the grisly daydream. Cristofo in particular was wholly enthralled in the princess's words, seeing the vivid gruesomeness as she recounted the tale, feeling utterly immersed in the moment as if it transpired then and there, just before his widened eyes. Buckles loudly clanged against the rock as heavy saddles of hide were dropped from the caretaker's overburdened shoulders.

"Shall we proceed with the saddling, your highness?" inquired the younger, more strapping dragon keeper as his older and more experienced counterpart drew near. A simple glance toward each other sufficed to ascertain agreement as the noble twosome erected themselves at once. Myrina nodded in acknowledgment and then cupped her hands in an effort to magnify a rudimentary yet surprisingly shrill whistle, while Cristofo smugly beckoned his dragon with silent thought alone, completely abandoning his previous more primitive holler. He could not wholly comprehend this newfound connection with Cimtar, but he understood that it was intact; he understood the creature like never before, and the creature in turn obeyed as the ground once more fell prey to the resounding thud of the two dense masses of dragon.

Several moments passed as the keepers endeavored with the task of fastening the bulky harnesses to the mighty beasts. No standard technique facilitated such a singular task; dragons themselves were rare enough creatures, let alone those which could be seated. The royal tailor spent many hard and laborious hours fashioning the apparatuses, customized for each dragon and always under advisement of the palace's head of corporeal affairs, a well-aged, meticulous, and experienced physician who held reputation of the utmost regard. There were a dozen trials or so during the initial ridings, with adjustments and alterations performed as per feedback received, and the devices evolved into their manageably functioning, current, and cumbersome state. The result boasted a succession of circled collars that clambered up the animal's long and beefy neck, clutching and securing it like so many lengths of butcher's twine tied around an enormous roast. Three hearty and evenly spaced lines of material ran up and down the length, spacing the series and adding reinforcement. Holsters placed for ankle, calf, and thigh were securely integrated using belt-like straps to accommodate a snug and secure fit. Short, sturdy handles of ivory graced the front of the unique garment, jutting out like an awkward set of antennae just at the onset of the creatures' bony skulls. These handles came equipped with comfortable supports for the forearm and were grasped for sturdiness. Additionally, they served the alternative purpose of facilitating the all-important function of steering and maneuvering the surprisingly speedy and agile brutes. Overall, at the end of the process, the riders were fundamentally strapped along the long and powerful necks of the mystical creatures, symbiotic passengers riding along safely and securely as they vaulted through the air. Oftentimes goggles were also sported in order to shelter the eyes from the relentless and sheer force of pounding wind.

Out of respectful courtesy, the princess was first to be strapped in, and off she flew as Somnia thrashed her wings in a fury, quickly dissipating from sight until a mere speck in the distance remained, barely visible to Cristofo as he looked on while eagerly awaiting the conclusion of his saddling and anticipating his turn to take flight. A quick burst of adrenaline invaded the boy just as he took hold of the rigid alabaster handles, and Cimtar shot into the air excitedly and sped off straight and true, as would an arrow launched by the gentle squeeze of trigger on a crossbow, anticipating yet foregoing an imminent command from the boy who had just at that moment readied himself. The harshness of rushing wind encompassed the able rider, and he embraced the sensation as the powerful force pressed against the tight skin of his face, causing his cheeks to undulate and thick mid-length locks of rich brown hair to flatten as they aerodynamically flowed. A deafening sound imposed itself as the sheer curtain of airflow passed by, and the boy relished it. He knew that Cimtar aimed to catch up to his magnificent sibling, exulting in the fact that he would not be outdone. Cristofo shared the sentiment.

The boy immersed himself in the moment, relinquishing all control as he lay upon the ominous dragon while allowing it to set course and speed as it sailed through the air. He remained peaceful of mind as he basked in the glorious morning sunlight, a mere shimmering scale among the legions of other scales that lay there patiently, making up the creature's glistening coat of armor. In this state, time seemed almost frozen to the exceptional boy, lingering as does the happy moment of a simple dream. While it felt like a lengthy, fulfilling journey, in reality only a brief period had transpired until speed was slackened, wind abated, and senses returned to their previous alertness just as the ostentatious males overtook their female counterparts. Cimtar careened as though leading the way, and Somnia followed suit as they soared upward now, aiming for a place high in the heavens but reaching a plateau at a more moderate altitude, where the air grew thin and the details of earth were nary visible. Here at this lofty venue, all four spirits seemed to coalesce—human, dragon, male, female; irrelevant differentiae—in this heavenly corner where all likeminded spirits were humbled and awe-inspired by the great equalizing vastness of the beyond.

There they sailed for a while, mingling with the clouds and absorbing the healthy phenomenon until all were fully reinvigorated of mind and soul. Then, and only then, Cristofo looked back and to the side, where his eyes met those of his cherished companion and a devious grin took form. In unison, they both tensed their bodies and fortified their grips on the inflexible handles of ivory, pressing forward and pressing hard. Stomachs lightened, seeming to float, and inner ears tickled as fluid within tiny passages danced to and fro while the magnificent beasts nose-dived, rocketing down with accelerating speed of free fall. Myrina embraced the thrill with rational nervousness and at the same time was thankful for the exceptionally solid workmanship executed by the tailor in fashioning the reassuringly snug leg straps. Cristofo, on the other hand, experienced no apprehension at all, feeling resolute comfort equal to that of his outstanding ride, relinquishing grip and closing his eyes as he dangled from the unshakable harness. He held confident advantage since his mind was somewhat melded to the splendid creature at hand. As the length of descent increased, so too did his excitement, until a level plane and equilibrium suddenly returned. He opened his eyes just as the tickle of leaves invaded his immoveable legs and Cimtar's underside brushed across the crown of a tall leafy deciduous grove of trees.

At this vantage point, they remained, gliding across the sizable coppice. The dragon seemed to delight in the titillating stimulus of spindly branch and leaf, while Cristofo scrutinized the surround, orienting himself and taking note of the landscape, the direction of the sun, and the variety of creatures scurrying, flying, and jumping about. He did not fully recognize the vicinity but did ascertain that the location was slightly askew from the path to the factory, about half the distance or one hour's march or so away. Up ahead, as they crossed the end of the thickly forested area, it opened up into a serene meadow, where a pleasant and sizable rivulet dominated, hastily running through and blatant like a broad throbbing vein on delicate alabaster skin. And there Myrina and Somnia were espied, having previously pulled out of a nosedive at a more conservative height and succumbing to the allure of the beauteous vista as it drew them in for a closer look.

Somnia touched ground just on the edge of the rocky riverbed and stared enthusiastically into the rushing onslaught of water. There the creature waited patiently while her mistress unbuckled herself from the cumbersome leg hold straps. The beautiful princess Myrina dismounted, giving her ride the opportunity to wallow in the clear stream, where it took refreshing drink and perused the shallow habitat for a snack of fish. She, on the other hand, stretched her legs and pranced contentedly along the bordering grassy meadow. The princess felt comfortably immersed in the serene and picturesque countryside, exploring the grassy knolls and giving particular attention to the various outcroppings of colorful and fragrant blossoms. Cristofo observed contentedly from his lofty vantage point, not at all in a hurry to set down. Instead, he reached back and unbuckled some of the sturdy straps, leaving only ankles secured as he righted himself while continuing to unrelentingly ride his outstanding pet as it surfed the sky, enjoying the sport of it as he worked to balance himself through the various turns and pivots.

Cimtar also partook in the amusement, humoring the insatiable boy with accentuated movement and flow. The delightful banter continued for a number of moments, until Iggy entered the fray as well, careening out and whirling about the mouth and face of the magnificent beast, taunting and teasing as the dragon twisted, turned, and snapped its jaws in an effort to stifle the fiery creature and imprison it temporarily within its mighty chops. The skillful young Cristofo struggled and stretched his abilities as he balanced himself with incredulous agility while remaining thoroughly immersed and enthralled in the moment, until he was suddenly distracted by an awkward and unanticipated diminishing of light.

Strange darkness invaded the surround as the boy looked up to discover that a solitary cloud had materialized and stifled the ever-present sun. Ominous and opaque, more black than gray it lay, completely out of place in the bright and clear backdrop of day. Seriousness took command of the boy as he reestablished his grip on the harness handles and steadied his ride while veering around to face the irregularity. Iggy returned to the comfort of his pendant, absorbing the powder within until sufficiently stocked and then proceeding to take perch upon his master's shoulder, where the creature remained, anchored and alert and sensing that something was amiss. Silent flashes emanated from the cloud as small bits of fire flew about sporadically and with vigorous flair, like sparks forced astray of malleable steel upon the blacksmith's mighty stroke of hammer. Just then, three blinding cracks of lightning burst into the air, imposing wide gaping gashes upon the cloud, where a profound darkness was realized, prominent and absolute. Cristofo maintained his stature as a trio of demonic creatures emerged, grotesque and beastly winged things completely foreign to the eyes and mind of the remarkable boy. And moments following and good distance beyond, the waning roar of thunder caught the ears and attention of an astute and perceptive wizard of age who had been casually strolling about a small garden and interacting with an old acquaintance as they lightened themselves from an overly abundant breakfast.

"What is it, Altarius?" questioned the magister with an ill-at-ease tone as a strange sense of worry overtook him. "Why the troubled look, my old friend? Is it Cristofo?" he inquired fearfully, noticing a disconcerting, distracted, and pensive gaze on a stolid wizardly visage.

"He's in danger, isn't he? Please tell me, Altarius!" imposed the now-distraught grandfather, expecting at some point to hear words.

"To the stables! Two of the fastest steeds in the land to be readied at once!" commanded the magister as he pressed forward, only to be firmly stifled by the muted barricade of an outstretched arm.

"No man or steed will suffice, old friend," I finally replied to the worry-filled patriarch while extending my other arm to receive my nearby staff as it hastily flew to command. And I set her blunt end down hard to the ground with force, concurrently shooting skyward a resounding burst of shock wave—a far-reaching beacon indiscernible to all but its intended beneficiary.

"The boy is in danger, magister. I will not mire our bond with falsehoods. Vescolumen, scouts from the abyss, have infiltrated our realm. The foul stench of them besmirches my wizardly nostrils. They are vile, vaporous, wispy wraiths that can morph at will before resolidifying into their more common and most off-putting monstrous arrangements. Their scraggy skeletal frames are wrapped in a thick elastic coat of charcoal-colored skin with clawed extremities dominating, seven of them in all, disproportionately large and obvious. Twin bony arms emanate from either flank, impelling small negligible hands that serve mainly to anchor six long scraggly fingers, each capped with nails of dagger. Three dangling legs reach down with the steely strength of a trident's teeth, ideal tools for capture as the beasts swoop down with large ribbed and bat-like wings to clutch their targets with a skill and accuracy akin to deadly birds of prey. Elongated and pointed ears crown a vacuous face and skull, with mouth and nose apparent yet sheathed of the same rubbery skin as though asphyxiated by it and struggling for unneeded air. Fiery red sockets provide stark contrast, craters brimming of lava in lieu of eyes, windows from which their master can espy. Noxerus, my nemesis, my counterpart of the nether, how did the cursed scoundrel learn so quickly of the boy?"

"Enough with words," interjected the magister. "Grant me a moment to quickly fetch my sword and let us fly."

I could not bear to argue with my well-intentioned companion, nor could I afford the luxury of time, so I remained silent as he ran off, advancing myself to a more appropriate location of breadth at the open field near the property's edge. There I readied myself and stood by while a deep and profound rumbling growl grew more and more boisterous as my gargantuan ride speedily neared. Yes, as you may have well imagined by now, the fine princess and boy were not the only souls fortuitous enough to command a mythical and marvelous beast; Candilux was now on approach. A magnificent and mammoth dragon of the *gigantae* species, boasting a bright and shiny white thick and impenetrable incrustation of scales, she has endured for ages, this fantastical beast of mine, roaming free yet at hand upon my summons.

Massive flaps of far-reaching wings made quick work of distance, much to the convenience of our young and imperiled protagonist at that moment. As the wondrous creature swooped down to approach a more manageable altitude, an opportune beam of luminous blue light was conjured from my staff, up surging and lassoing around the spiny and prominent scales that ran in parallel rows along Candilux's backside from neck to mighty tail. I hoisted myself through the air, avoiding a tedious landing and finding a seat at the base of a strapping neck, where thick plating had been meticulously carved to form the suitable comfort of a saddle and where customized holes were arranged in the sides of the finlike runs of scale, perfectly sized to receive my staff as it inserted itself into place to form the pretense of sturdy handlebars. Off we sped to the aid of our precious fledgling wizard.

Fleeting though the time and distance to reach the boy may have been, he still faced an enormous challenge in opposing the vescolumen attack. Unbeknownst to him at the time, their command was to capture, not kill, although killing represented work of much gratification to the monstrous, soulless fiends. Tempting as it may well have been, they wouldn't have dared contravene an order from their master, an order, mind you, that did not apply to the princess, Cimtar, Somnia, Iggy, or anyone else, for that matter. As they emerged from the tumultuous cloud in the sky, high above the serene meadow, the lead brute quickly advanced, wasting no time in sailing toward Cristofo direct and true, while its two wretched compatriots lingered to a degree, reluctantly staying behind and seeming dissatisfied as though forced to be mere spectators in the gloriousness of the assignment's principal task. Cristofo remained poised and confident, embracing the approaching danger as adrenaline flowed and senses intensified. He steered Cimtar astray of the advancing demons and veered in the direction opposite to where the princess and Somnia had touched ground. Light did he travel while dragon riding, bereft of sword or satchel but armed as always with his great mind and skilled body, which were adequate enough weapons for most any adversary—any with skills of this realm, perhaps. But these creatures were not of this realm, and their skills and abilities were an outright mystery to the boy, as he would come to learn in short order.

Cimtar was pressed forward at moderate speed, slowly enough to allow the attackers gradual advancement yet with sufficient pace to allow for preparation before the anticipated convergence. As a point of fact, young Cristofo was not completely absent of blade; four modestly sized razor-sharp throwing knives were always present and readily concealed in his footwear, where customized sheaths anchored them, snug and indistinct as they reposed on either side of his strapping calves. They were unused, forged of the best-quality steel, and identical to the variety regularly used by the boy as he practiced the precise art. Two were of the half-pound class for use at shorter distances where precision was a more pressing concern, and two were three-quarter weight for occasions demanding more power and girth. He grasped the handle of the three-quarter blade and with it made quick work of freeing himself from the cumbersome ankle straps. A strip of hide was then fashioned from the cumbrous collar and fastened to devise a rein of sorts, a lariat for him to clutch and wrap around his wrist securely with one hand as he balanced himself comfortably atop his formidable ride, throwing knife held at the ready in the other.

Flapping bat-like wings proved no match for a dragon's mighty although slackened pace, and Cristofo led the demonic beasts along, feeling more than content in portraying the bait for the time being, drawing the obvious menace far afield of the princess. He turned frequently to observe the attackers, and on one such occasion, he was astonished at what his eyes beheld. First the lead and then the other two in turn vanished, puffed away in an instant, gone without a trace. The boy felt ill at ease with this occurrence, preferring to keep sight of his pursuers, and he tensed his body and sharpened his mind as he sensed the looming company of danger.

All of a sudden, a devilish and smoky haze materialized just ahead, ghostly and indiscernible, and at once the demonic lead resolidified into its prior hideous state, presenting no surprise to the boy as he pulled back on the makeshift rein, stopping his ride and positioning for battle. There our bold young wizard patiently held, steadying both his dragon and his fiery pet by use of his communicative mind since the two of them were overly tense and eager to engage. The malevolent attacker slowly approached the midair hover, bringing deep red eyes ever so close as it stared upon the boy, peering with a fiery glow that gave view to its master, who studiously observed from the beyond. Two more foggy bursts of haze then manifested, morphing into position at the rear of the lead just as it lunged three sinewy legs forward and down with the force of razor-sharp and grappling claws.

Cristofo deftly leaped aside, swaying on the sturdy rein and coming down with feet striking hard on Cimtar's side, veering the creature astray just as the aggressor's claws lunged forth with piercing intent. A ferocious outcry then ensued, a function of the freshly inflicted injury, as razor- sharp implements managed to slash across the side of the boy's majestic ride. The outburst was rooted more from anger than pain as sparks flew off Cimtar's shimmering coating and the capable dragon welcomed its inaugural battle scar. Resilient scales forever blemished with only minor damage to tissue below as the rare sight of gold-colored dragon's blood oozed to the surface along a number of substantial lacerations. Cristofo wasted no time in lunging off the side of his dragon, propelling himself with feet and legs thrust forth as he vaulted back to position and launched his ample blade with hard and deadly force. Before he could nimbly touch back down onto Cimtar's sturdy neck, three-quarter steel lay embedded handle deep and precisely betwixt the monster's round and flaring eyes. The demonic being faltered, head whiplashing back with solid force of impact, and then it fell, inert and stagnant, plummeting.

The other two brutes then advanced, jockeying for lead position of attack and eager to take control and gain commendation for the successful completion of task. Cimtar responded straightaway as a wide gush of flame was breathed with a menacing roar, encompassing both of the dastardly creatures. The mighty dragon maintained its blast for what seemed like a preposterous length of time as burgeoning fire perpetuated until the beastly outlines glowed distinctively and became brilliantly distinguishable within the inferno. Any being of flesh and bone would have long since been reduced to ash, dispersing feebly at the hand of gust and wind, but not so for these otherworldly abominations, for as the dragon's enduring attack finally extinguished of breath, they remained steadfast and unshaken, albeit aglow. Like blazing ingots freshly removed from a scorching blast furnace, they hovered, quickly thereafter dulling until reestablishing their naturally morbid and deathly gray tones. Fiery eyes once again became flagrant, no longer lost in the camouflage of blaze as narrow and concentrated beams discharged from them. Four robust lasers shot out and struck Cimtar's glittering incrustation of armor, biting through and singeing underneath as the foul stench of charred, scaly flesh radiated; the alarming sound of the agonized dragon filled the surround.

Cristofo at once stifled two of the deadly beams as a previously readied throwing knife once again found the mark of a hideous skull. Iggy flew to response concurrently, zooming headlong into the path of one destructive beam, overtaking it and becoming as one with the virulent ray, effectively changing its direction to cause it to veer into the path of the other. Both beams were now under control of the remarkable creature, which wasted no time in doubling back and reversing the course of the deadly, laser-like ray. The attacking brute recoiled upon impact of the powerful weapon of its own device, unable to cease the emission and unable to flee from its damaging force. And Iggy maintained the barrage, seeming to make headway in weakening the creature's diabolical resolve until all at once, when the beams halted. Iggy reappeared in their absence, flickering meagerly for an instant before fluttering downward, devoid of powder and powerless. Thereupon the boy reached to his footwear with the intention of finishing off the reeling brute by using a trusted throwing knife. But just as his hand made comfortable contact with the handle of steel, a devilish haze once again appeared before him. Shockingly, it was none other than the initial brute that had solidified once again and remained unscathed and appearing no worse for wear.

You see, traditional weaponry had no lasting effect on the vescolumen swine as they simply morphed into their wispy wraithlike states, wherein all damaged parts and wounds and all implanted devices, such as blades, arrows, axes and the like, simply dropped to the ground while the beings reassembled their figures back into their previous intact and heinous states. The dispirited young Cristofo could not help but feel unclear; it was a foreign sensation for the boy, who had always known his next moves with strict confidence. In this instance, with lack of better design, he reluctantly steered his vulnerable dragon away. Warily indeed, he commanded it to flee. Overall, it was not a terrible strategy considering the most recent turn of events, and although the boy would not have minded the challenge of outpacing the attackers with the aid of his astounding ride, one consideration persisted, blatant and crucial in his mind: the fair princess. She and Somnia must assuredly remain unharmed.

Within moments, the able rider sharply turned about, and as he did so, he instantaneously became faced with one, then two, and then three emulsified and suddenly solidified dark and dismal beasts. The original lead brute once again assumed the seat of command, and with an almost discernable faceless stare, he scowled at the boy, keeping devilish eyes fixated and intensified while motioning to his underlings, who in turn flew off immediately, heading precisely in the direction of the princess and Somnia.

At once, Cristofo dropped himself down, securely clutching the neck and collar of his ride as a sharp burst of laser narrowly missed its target, singeing strands of hair and backside before glancing across Cimtar's hefty tail. Both the boy and his noble pet were unequivocally of the same mind, and both had suffered their fill of distress as the mighty dragon shot forward incautiously, roaring furiously and conceding to the destructive beams as it swiveled its formidable head and snapped jaws shut with a raving fury. The foul taste of lifeless bilge was strangely satisfying as Cimtar summarily dispatched of the bestial midriff, swallowing it as the monstrous head and hind dropped off, severed fragments lost to battle and unable to reestablish absent its primary connective mass.

"Let's see you come back from that, you cursed horror!" The boy concurrently let fly with the facetious remark upon completion of a celebratory outcry as both he and Cimtar basked in the glorious sensation of victory—that of the preeminent kind, where survival is the precious trophy and hopelessness is all of a sudden overturned. But the jubilation was short-lived as they focused course and mind toward the other two pursuers, who were now dangerously afar and targeting their prey with murderous intent.

The boy leaped up straightaway, reestablishing a position of comfort as he held the makeshift rein and surfed atop his mighty beast, invigorated and calling for utmost speed. The encounter left him unscathed for the most part, but not so for his downtrodden ride, and although Cimtar put forth best effort, the pace was noticeably sluggish and far from its usual vitality. Nevertheless, they did manage to make some headway in narrowing the gap of pursuit, and as their female companions came into view, they too were already airborne and breaking away from the oncoming threat. However, panic struck the boy as he observed the brutes dematerialize, for he knew that they would reestablish themselves near at hand to Myrina's still far from proximate range. His innate sense conveyed the unnerving truth; they would not transverse the distance in time, leaving the princess and Somnia defenseless and vulnerable to the impending attack.

"Come on, Cimtar. Come on, boy. Give it your all. They're doomed if we don't make it there now. Quickly, boy, quickly!" shrieked Cristofo, desperately urging his noble pet on as he conveyed thoughts of encouragement and support with his mind. And indeed, the wieldy dragon gave his best effort to accelerate as the boy arranged his last two throwing knives, placing the half-pounder securely between his teeth and holding the three-quarter ready in hand.

In a flash, the demonic beasts presented themselves upon the unsuspecting pair. Concentrated beams flared as one beast let fly an incinerating blast that struck Somnia's nigh side wing, searing it and inflicting meaningful damage. The other brute swooped down upon the princess, clutching with inexorable firmness as sharp rapier claws dug into virtuous flesh. Up she went skyward, dangling and helpless, unable to move arms but still aware with legs writhing frantically and lungs shrieking with deafening intensity. Cristofo and Cimtar could do naught but bear audience to the crushing spectacle, observing in horror as the boy's precious heartthrob was clumsily carried away. The dragon's wondrous sister faltered, discharging desperate bursts of fire as she struggled to remain adrift while the monstrous attacker continued with its savage barrage until Cristofo and Cimtar began to arrive within range.

Cristofo stood well balanced, with hand firmly clutching his rein; patiently and painfully, he held position as he watched the magnificent dragon suffer relentless attack. Then finally certainty set in as he reached his maximal range, bringing much consolation, and steel was let fly from afar but with undeniable conclusion, soon lodging into the beastly backside with clout and putting an end to the blasts of laser as the inert brute slumped and hurtled earthward. However, the monstrous creature did not plummet for long, as a murky haze befell. The boy watched with discouragement as the lethal blade dislodged and proceeded to fall fruitlessly while absent of host and tumbling uselessly down to the ground. Thoughts of his fair princess added to the despair as he looked on with a broken spirit, while distance consumed the seemingly final vision of her exquisite form. Then it came to him: the wizard's tooth! Quietly it sat there lurking in a tiny pocket at the waist of his trousers, folded inward and inconspicuous. He reached for it. A day had not yet passed since acquiring the incredulous gift, and he aimed to expend it, for he could not fathom a more worthy cause with which to substantiate its power.

But lo and behold, a most marvelous sight zoomed into eyeshot. A massive white creature of awe presented itself formidably as Candilux entered the stage, thrashing gargantuan wings as an ear-splitting uproar echoed overpoweringly throughout the expanse, swooning straight and true in the direction of the carried-off princess. Atop the gargantuan beast, a modest-sized rider caught the eye, draped in earth-tone garb and erect as he clambered up the animal's towering neck with staff in hand and while displaying a most uncanny agility. A ferocious battle cry vociferated, blending harmoniously with the resounding roar of his ride as the commanding staff was placed in the path of the dragon's breath, miraculously transforming the creature's fusillade of fire into a narrow stream of water and ice. The slushy projectile flew precisely to mark, impacting the vescolumen scoundrel dead-on as it froze solid, crystallizing the beast and ending it. Its hardened icy corpse plunged downward, narrowly missing the princess as she too plummeted headlong, no longer secured by unyielding brutish claws.

Cristofo looked on, relieved and delighted by the performance, as Candilux and I swooped down to retrieve the shrieking princess. In the meantime, Somnia awkwardly fluttered, struggling with effort to touch down. Mighty Cimtar began to waver as both exhaustion and injury forced their unanimous hands. All at once, a stinging pain came down upon the boy, catching him wholly unawares as the remaining brute materialized behind him and immediately clamped down with jagged claws. A tenacious limb took hold of each shoulder, piercing deep and hard into muscle and nerve, paralyzing arms as they hung off the courageous young wizard, who dangled lifelessly and ineffectually while the third brawny appendage firmly clenched itself onto his bony skull. Curved and razor-like claws entrenched themselves into the boy's crown, forcing generous trickles of blood to precipitate as he was hoisted into the air. His brutish abductor ascended frantically, heading toward the dark and unearthly obscurity from whence it had recently disembarked.

The boy swallowed awkwardly as dribbling blood forced its way beyond clenched lips and into his mouth, where the precious throwing knife still lay reassuringly wedged. The maddening taste of the red fluid invigorated him as he bided time patiently, knowing that another opportunity for fray would present itself in due course as he acquiesced to the heartless, devilish creature, listening reluctantly as it emitted vexatious squealing shrieks of triumphant victory. Then they were upon the cloud, where the demon crossed the threshold into the dense black portal, leading the way into the very bowels of the sinister manifestation. And darkness supervened.

CHAPTER 4

The Netherworld, You Say?

An unfamiliar awareness presented itself upon our fledgling young wizard as reality transformed. A sweltering, murky haziness smothered his body and mind, incapacitating him and rendering him sluggish and disengaged. Heat permeated into every orifice and pore as he gasped for breath, drawing in the discomfort until it saturated his lungs and percolated throughout the entirety of his being. His eyes were of little use—blurry windows with little to reveal—and his ears became unwilling funnels that guided the sensation through tiny canals and channels until it reached his exceptional brain. It too became impregnated with the mugginess, rendering it dank and discombobulated as it struggled to maintain command at the helm of the magnificent boy, and although a deathly impression presented itself, consciousness invariably remained, albeit shaky at first but slowly steadying with each desperate gasp of unearthly breath. Then pain reappeared, this time portraying a welcome companion who brought the gift of assurance to Cristofo that he yet lived. However, the joyfulness was cut short as lungs quivered and burned in response to the infiltration of foreign air. The agonizing onslaught continued as the unfamiliar influx permeated, infusing blood and bones, innards and entrails, and organs following in turn as a hard all-encompassing suffering took hold.

Unexpectedly, a sharp and thin glittering blue streak of light came into his view, shooting ahead and beyond his position and presenting itself as though in a dream: a mirage, a hallucination, perhaps, a miraculous beacon of hope materializing before an unfocused mind. Excruciating delirium prevailed, yet nonetheless, the boy took notice of this incandescent beam as it lit up the surround and made visible a cloudy haze of an atmosphere, hazy and shadowy indeed, but not entirely black and absolute. The vision restored credibility to his eyes and gave much-needed distraction to the pain as the inspiring ray curved and looped back, lassoing itself several times around Cristofo's midsection, where it took hold of him stringently and firm, creating a distinct and physical awareness that invariably strengthened his presence of mind.

"Altarius," the boy muttered to himself obscurely as he felt my presence nearby, and it was a comforting realization, one that calmed him and helped to facilitate his recuperation. At once, cold and hard shattered fragments rained down upon the boy as the center limb of his malevolent captor crumbled under the crisp strike of my staff, thus alleviating the digging pain of its pressured grasp. Mindfulness was thereupon further improved as our young wizard now mustered a look up and overhead, where he saw his admired rescuer riding on the back of his foe, clutching a steely rod coiled around an emaciated and discomforted neck, a sturdy noose securing it rigidly and tight. It was ropelike but smooth, metallic and shiny, glittering ever so slightly of its own accord as it caught the boy's eye in the dark and gloomy surround.

Coldness then entrenched itself into the boy's broad and sturdy shoulders. It was a freezing cold, icy and relentless, and it caused him to actualize that his assaulter had been crystallized from the midsection down. Sinewy wings flapped desperately in an effort to mitigate an unavoidable descent as the weighted-down vescolumen swine struggled. Frozen and inert claws were rendered immovable, thereby preventing them from a convenient unloading of heavy cargo. Furthermore, the burden of a robust wizardly frame riding upon the beast's hind served to further intensify its discomfort and duress. Whatever sensation the foul creature endured, whatever it felt that likened to pain, it was not sufficient penance for the darkness of spirit and spark that was existent within the monster at hand. The same would apply to all of its wretched kind, yet even so, I could not find myself altogether devoid of mercifulness, for the brute could do little to contravene its true nature. Nor could I go against my natural instincts, for that matter. As we neared our approach upon the exotic and unearthly surface of land, I tightened and heaved upon my precious Maleabar forcefully and with vigor, decapitating the grossly outmatched miscreation and leaving it to drop down—a lifeless mass smashing against the hot, hard, and smooth extraneous terrain.

Cristofo came down hard and awkwardly as well, and as his abductor's two remaining frozen legs and claws shattered upon impact, he managed to right himself forthwith, satisfied to be free from capture at last. Strangeness of air still affected him, and he gasped and wheezed frantically while still managing to liberate the tenaciously clamped throwing knife from his mouth before returning it to the comfort of its snug sheath within the lining of his boot. "Welcome to the netherworld, young Cristofo! Breathe, my boy. Breathe generously. Fill yourself with the surround; embrace it. Be not afraid of the foreignness. Succumb to it and let it bring you strength," I instructed the boy reassuringly, and he took solace in my words, working hard to breathe as instructed, and in due course, he steadied himself. Regularity of breath was restored, and a reddish hue flooded his entire covering of skin, providing a camouflage-like appearance that blended with the backdrop of the newly landed upon hot and scorching, albeit dim and dreary, domain.

"Am I dead?" the boy managed to mutter in a serious and confused tone.

"Dead? Such a mundane human word, one that I prefer you not use again now that you are elevated among your breed." My words fell upon puzzled ears and a disoriented mind, one that still strived to right itself from trauma, so I grasped the boy solidly and stared deeply into his salient newborn wizardly eyes. He became enlivened, reinvigorated, and completely restored to his usual exuberance. He understood. Vaguely, perhaps, but also unequivocally, he understood that a change had occurred, a profound and wondrous change, a change that would be a part of him forever and one that would alter his existence in a most meaningful way. "From this moment forth, my good Cristofo, born of the fructiferous Mother Earth, you may refer to yourself as *wizard!* A simple word, but one with boundless meaning. I have peered into your soul, and an enormous spirit returned the gaze, one of unmatched radiance and brilliance and of clarity well beyond anything I have ever observed afore. It is with tremendous pleasure that I welcome you as the newest member of our selective band. And as lead among us, I will take you under my far-reaching wing. I will be your guide and your mentor and your confidant for many adventures to come!"

"Wizard!" The boy cast out the word with confidence and pride. He stared into the foreign and unnatural sky, blankly and with no particular audience, as though onstage and at the onset of a grand soliloquy. "It is shocking to hear your words and yet so fantastic as well, Altarius. I have felt something brewing within me of late, a difference in perception, a keener view on the world and of my surround, a more intense understanding of things and of the ways of creation. And my dreams have reflected similarly as well. Last night they were of unprecedented design, fantastic things revealed so implicitly and clearly that the boundary with reality became a mere shadow. I woke with fresh eyes and an enlightened mind as though an unknown impetus of sorts took hold, coincidentally synchronous with your eagerly anticipated visit. And so it is with a surprised yet cognizant mind that I accept your words, Altarius the Prime, great wizard of wisdom and age. Lead forth and instruct as you see fit, for I vow to you that an apprentice like none before now stands ready to be shaped and guided. Explain to me all that you can until your voice has no more strength. But first, what of Myrina, Cimtar, and Somnia?"

"Worry not about them, dear boy, for they have been left safe from harm's way. You and I, on the other hand, well, we seem to have fallen into a more precarious circumstance, one that may require a great deal of effort to remedy."

"The netherworld, you say? What a strange and eerie place. For what purpose am I brought here?" The boy looked around eagerly as he said the words, examining the environ and gathering his bearing. "What an odd formation of ground, smooth and steely yet rippled like the water of a lake pushed forth by a mediocre breeze and then all at once solidified. And such a deathly and dull color, gray as coal and inconsistent with the reddish nuance of sky and surround. You seem to have adopted a reddish hue as well, Altarius. And your staff … Why, it seems to be reveling in its vibrant and crimson tone. Look, it appears that I too have fallen prey to a similar invasion of color." The boy stated the obvious as he studied his hands and arms, twisting them several times as he examined the backs and palms in turn. "And over there in the distance, Altarius, that rushing waterway bears an uncanny resemblance to the flagrant rivulet that ran course amid the peaceful meadow of recent uncovering."

"So much to explain, my zealous young apprentice!" A sincere smile accompanied my words as I affectionately swatted the broad shoulder of my companion. I must confess that the association brought much excitement at the time; the onslaught of years tends to wash away passion to a degree; however, inspiration invariably returns on certain occasions, and this new acquaintanceship happened to be one of them. "Come, we must make toward the river. I will make things clear as we advance."

Onward we marched, employing a moderately quickened pace, an abrupt jaunt as opposed to a frantic sprint. I recognized that our solitude was soon to be disrupted, as Noxerus would certainly dispatch commandeering forces, but I favored a momentum that facilitated conversation since there was much to expound to our inspired young wizard, many details to explain and topics to cover. Moreover, it would take a sizable threat indeed to invoke breakaway speed upon this spirited wizard of age!

"You are correct, my perceptive young Cristofo, in recognizing the similarity between the rushing stream in the foreground and the vibrant waterway that beckoned the fair princess as it intersected the obscure earthly meadow. You see, several gateways exist sporadically dispersed among the totality. Portals, each and every one disguised and cloaked to blend into the scene, crossover points to numberless localities and places of unimaginable distance and diversity, a variety of destinations conveniently accessible to precious few of select status. Worlds and realms, sectors and zones, realities and existences like none you could imagine. In due time, you will learn more of this, but for now know that it lies within your power to utilize these transcendental modes of travel. Seeking out and identifying their innumerate gateways will form part of your lessons over the next number of years; the centuries will concede to mastery of this exclusionary skill, but for the moment, let it suffice to say that the estuary before us makes way toward a gateway that will escort us back to Earth. Deep down in the dark, below the magnificent factory of your grandfather's finding, an aperture resides wherein the border between worlds can be traversed. Yes, indeed young Cristofo, therein it lies within the bowels of the monumental domain, where oftentimes you would explore and survey as an inquisitive child. But never did you venture near the depths of which I speak; never did you realize what curiosities lie there rooted in the distant underground beneath the busyness of your prosperous family enterprise."

"But those nasty demonic assailants emerged from a cloud, one that materialized out of the blue as though conjured with malevolent intent. Would we not strive skyward in search of this cross-boundary aperture of sorts?" the boy inquired with a logical yet uncertain tonality. I, of course, proceeded to make it plain.

"A man would think that, my worthy apprentice, but not so for a wizard. You must think beyond the norm, think more widely than the obvious. There is great leeway among the manner in which we all operate; many variables are to be weighed, and many unknowns prevail. If not for this, the regularity of it all would make for a most uninteresting harmony. Noxerus is the name of your abductor. No, not the uncomplicated beast with plunging claws that lifted you from your dragon and carried you off into this hellish land, but its commander, a formidable wizard in his own right, a capable adversary with whom I have wrangled numerous times in battle. He is the lead wizard for this realm of existence, a realm that is not similar to ours. Somehow, he caught wind of your wizardly inception and curiosity took hold. He would discern a portal in another manner than would I, but always within the vicinity, always within the boundary of a certain range. Telltale signs of similarity in the respective landscapes will offer clues as to their whereabouts, hence the blatantly comparable waterways about which you refer. Yes, very crafty indeed that rival of mine, very crafty indeed. He will be anxious for our encounter; he will be relishing the opportunity for revenge."

"And the river? Will we be safe within its rushing flow? I must say that I yearn for its refreshing embrace, for the climate of this forsaken land brings a sweltering aura, most uncomfortable!"

"Safety presents a relative impression in this unnatural place," I reciprocated. "Yes, we would be safe to a degree, for water in this part would be as lava to these unearthly dwellers, as lava would be akin to water. Yes, you heard correctly—lava. The dastardly creatures bath in it, take in its molten sludge, and harvest from its bountiful fare. Diametrically characterized are the two substances between worlds, in proportion, in importance, and in most other classifications as well. It is merely one of many nuances for you to take in, one of many that will be learned over the coming centuries."

"Centuries?" the boy abruptly interjected, eagerly anticipating a repeat sounding of the word as though at first mention he held the term at bay, refusing to expound upon it for fear that it would be proven impalpable and be stolen away. "For a second time, you mention the interval. I take it as no coincidence or sleight of tongue. Am I to assume that longevity has been bestowed? A welcome accompaniment to a wizardly vocation, perhaps?"

"Aye, a welcome accompaniment, my young fellow, and one that grows more burdensome with the passage of time." I de-emphasized the significance of the endowment in an effort to moderate the boy. In due time, he would learn to appreciate the qualification, but in short order, his sense of invincibility could assuredly do harm.

"So just to confirm that I understand correctly, Altarius, do you mean to imply that I cannot die?" presented the boy with hopeful enthusiasm.

"Die?" I blared forth with a consternating clamor, reinforcing my emphasis by halting my pace and affixing my gaze upon the startled lad. "Again a variation of the term that brings discouragement to my qualified ears! Well, so be it, then. Let us address this matter at once. Yes, you can 'die,' as you insist on putting it, but the meaning is misrepresented in the context of your tongue. Thrice afore have I met with the foul occurrence, and thrice have I been restored. Think it not as an end but rather an interlude, a displacement to a singular realm wherein one cannot cross bearing physicality. It is a place with only one universal passageway, which is eternally at the ready to usher an entity's spirit in. Herein one faces a paramount challenge as one is heedlessly tossed to the feet of one's most formidable enemy, namely oneself. It is a monumental task indeed to overthrow the illusion and to return to form. It is a happenstance that will invariably occur but one that you should certainly make best efforts to avoid."

The boy stood there donning a mystified look, taking a short moment to ingest the notion. "Just how old are you, Altarius?"

"Two score and fifteen times have I endured to witness the passage of the great comet, my boy, a spectacle that you will not be privy to observe for a number of years to come! Now, let us resume pace and stand yourself ready for Maleabar signals that danger is on approach."

The boy gazed attentively at my precious staff and took notice of its curious disposition.

"Maleabar is the name of your staff? I must say that it is quite unique in its aspect. I have seen staffs before; in fact, I have trained with many varieties as part of my weapons and armaments sessions— all very resilient and firm and of various texture, length, and density, but all comprised of wood, various types of wood, perhaps, but wood nonetheless. Now that I get a good look at it, this staff of yours intrigues me. It's so smooth and uniform, almost metallic in appearance but much too light in color to have been forged. And you seem to wield it so effortlessly. Is that a function of your strength or is it simply extraordinarily airy? It is remarkably unscathed for an instrument that you seem to use regularly and for one that I assume you have used for quite a number of years. At first, when I took notice of it, just after regaining my bearing in this outlandish world, it seemed to glow with a soft reddish hue and vibrate ever so subtly. Now it has enlivened, augmenting in radiance, deepening in color, and vibrating more vigorously. It lengthens, Altarius; it lengthens as we speak. And it sings as well. Like a tuning fork, it hums with a consistent and increasing tone. Is this how it indicates that danger is near? Fascinating!"

"A wizard requires a staff, my boy. It is our weapon of choice, as you are likely already aware," I nonchalantly explained to the boy, once again halting pace as though emphasizing the importance of the subsequent words. "But 'weapon' is a word that brings injustice to the device. It is an arsenal, a depository, a beacon, and a harvester. It is a lifter, an intensifier, a gatherer, and a deflector. It is a detector, a supporter, an impaler, and a conveyor, but most of all it is a companion, a loyal accomplice that stands as a comfortable reassurance for those long and lonely wizardly occasions. Believe me, my good Cristofo, a wizard's life is replete with excitement and adventure, but also it is awash of loneliness and solitude."

The boy found occasion to retaliate. "Well, a staff may be all of those things, Altarius, but it is not my first choice and preference. It is not a sword!"

"Mine is!" was my abrupt response, and with a quick wallop to the ground, I exposed the true magnificence of my treasured apparatus as Maleabar transfigured into the form of a long, broad, and fabulously sharp sword. It was a weapon of stature and of imposing presence, a blade worthy of a king or similarly exalted being. In one harmonious and adeptly orchestrated pivot, I swiped while turning half circle, narrowly missing my dexterous apprentice as he ducked down, intent on keeping his head, while my swing continued to meet dead-on with its intended target as a devilish miscreant of an entity found an instantaneous means to its end.

We found ourselves nearly overrun as a legion of winged beasts swooped headlong about our position. They were vile and repugnant critters, a characterization that could apply to mostly all occupants of this foul world. Snakelike bodies with the consistency of hardened slag and with a scarlet glow displayed a short and stout stature that carelessly bolstered a rather large and spherical curiosity of head. A scattering of beady eyes and a slit of a nose lay there nonchalantly imposed upon the scaly reptilian-like faces of the vermin, faces that stood much overpowered by a pair of disproportionate fangs of considerable length.

The two proficient injectors tapered as they urged forward, curving with a faultless arc, ideally engineered for grappling onto a form and subsequently imbuing a generous quantity of noxious venom. Most inhabitants of the nether would instantaneously fall lifeless upon yielding to the virulent and tenacious bite, but the effect was less severe for us favorable beings of the animus realm. A few distasteful hours of paralysis would represent the entirety of what we would have to endure. Nonetheless, that very occurrence is what snared me into capture on one regrettable occasion many, many years afore. Since then, I have accustomed myself to the approaching whizzing sound of the vigorously fluttering and transparent insect-like wings. The leading stray was commendably overzealous, graciously sacrificing itself in advance of the coming onslaught, and there it remained on the callous surface of ground, convulsing dismally as its spirit prepared for departure while leaving its innards and body to lay there to waste, lengthwise split nearly right through by my swift and skillful swing of blade.

A second wave of devils were now fast approaching, dozens, perhaps scores in number, with an innumerable contingency trailing further behind. To the credit of my eager young apprentice, he was eerily quick in getting to his feet and posturing a ready stance, throwing knife positioned in hand. A spirited although futile gesture for no man or wizard could flail blade so quickly so as to dispatch of such a multitudinous onslaught. Even so, if we were to assume that speed of such legendary proportion could be achieved, one would invariably tire as the invasion persisted and as the accumulation of slain creatures swelled to outlandish proportions, smothering the challenger and cluttering and clogging their sword. It is with wisdom of firsthand experience by which I speak of this, and I must say that at that time, I felt great repugnance toward the fact that Noxerus would think so little of my abilities as to imply that I would twice fall fate to the same maneuver.

"Cristofo, follow my lead. Oftentimes flight serves as the most excellent choice of weapon!" With these words I threw down my capable staff and leaped nimbly upon it as it spontaneously flattened into the form of a thin and wide sheet of resilient attribute. The boy quickly followed suit, and at the precise moment that both of our feet touched down upon the uncannily responsive material, it swiftly curled about to form a cylindrical covering, enclosing us both within its protective skin as we continued on, trotting along the interior of the shape as it rolled and made way toward the nearing watercourse.

An intense buzzing sound soon befell as the swarm of creatures enveloped us. The hollow echo of inexhaustible vibrating wings wrought havoc upon our ears, and the congestion and clutter of bodies tampered with the smoothness of our pace, forcing both of us to the limits of our skill as we trotted and balanced ourselves within the safety of our cylindrical shelter. It was a contrivance forced to bounce and sway as it met with flattened and hurtled mounds upon mounds of the devilish obstacles. None too soon, we felt that unmistakable airiness as we took to flight, vaulting a great distance while overrunning a final ramp-shaped heap of the miscreants, a maneuver that sent us both off balance and scattered us about our shell until we came down harshly and awkwardly upon the sanctuary that was the river's rushing flow. The bothersome buzz of onrush finally dwindled for a few moments while we accommodated ourselves within our uncommon transport.

"What the devil was that? What a treacherous incursion of repugnant pests!" contributed the boy as a lull in intensity finally presented itself.

"Treacherous indeed," I retorted distractedly, as my concentration was focused elsewhere for the moment. A wave of my hand signaled instruction to my favorable staff, and once again it fluently transformed; a container still protected us, but this time it assumed a sleeker and more seaworthy form.

"There now—that's better. Well done, Maleabar. I see that your homecoming suits you quite well!"

"Homecoming? Maleabar is from this foul world?" inquired young Cristofo in a startled manner.

"Indeed, this is the place of origin for my fine instrument. One of the precious few treasures that can be found in this dreadful whereabouts is a singular material that only a wizard's charm can enliven. It is of this rare mineral that my trusted accessory is comprised, a mineral that was harvested painstakingly and diligently over ages of time, an arduous task that was commissioned by none other than my resourceful nemesis himself."

"You mean Noxerus? Are you saying that Maleabar is Noxerus's staff?" Once again, the boy's enquiry emitted an aura of surprise.

"Maleabar is my staff!" I exerted with an imposing tone. "And I am its guide! That is the incontestable truth of the matter!" I paused briefly to add emphasis to the blurb. "But that is not to say that this has always been the case," I then offered more tamely to my insatiable young apprentice, together with a presumptuous, revealing wink. Before much more enquiry could be put forth on the matter, that irksome droning sound returned, and Maleabar quivered, reddened and reverberated.

"Those cursed, tenacious scoundrels! All right, Maleabar, let us make evident the hardship of task they face in once again vying to sink fang into this venerable and stiff wizardly skin." And with that, a wave of hand once again solidified the melding of mind with apperceptive material as several minute and circular apertures materialized throughout the upper portion of our sheltering vessel, save for a sizable covering that remained uncompromised overhead. Cristofo remained still, squatting resiliently on the bench-like arrangement of seat, wide and intrigued eyes examining what they could of the fascinating landscape as he peered with an obstructed yet sufficient view, delighting in the novelty of it all as reddish and wrinkled embankments passed by on either side of the rushing water flow.

On one side, the outlook was undeviating, consistent, and unchanging as far as the eye could see. Plains of hardened liquid flow amassing tediously and painstakingly as magma crept forth over ages of time. It was a relatively tame terrain of similar characteristic to our convenient landing pad, which provided a suitable welcome for us as we crashed down upon the unconventional world. The other flank, however, was contradictory. A mountainous range overhung and overshadowed, menacingly presenting itself as though to forewarn. Vivid leakage oozed from the multifaceted peaks and spilled down into vast pools and multitudinous tributaries, wherein the glowing substance accumulated and persisted—a preeminent mixture from deep within the bowels of the world, molten portions of its mineral-like makeup regurgitating and recycling as it saturated and nourished the environ. A hot, hazy emanation guarded the scene and furnished it with a sweltry ambiance that conferred significant unwelcomeness. The flock of aggressive and noisy creatures of determined pursuit obscured the view before long. Biting fangs punched through the spattering of holes, dripping a clear fluidic liquid that spilled onto the deck of our craft, where it gradually accumulated.

"Do not ingest the potent toxin and you'll be fine, Cristofo, and be sure that it stays clear of your pervious wounds," I blurted out audibly in an effort to outdo the ear-splitting droning sound now made more intense by the empowering mesh of holes, and then I stalwartly stood to action. A profound gesture of the hand incited Maleabar's remarkable material as tiny perforations clamped shut, cleaving quantities of fang in turn as the oscillating motion circled our position. Pointed impalers were hewn unrelentingly, guillotined and discarded as they compiled upon the vessel's venom-drenched floor. And the battery continued fluently as the apertures were instructed to reopen and then close in proper sequence. The shrill shrieking chorus of victimized monstrosities prevailed as they withdrew in agony, several of them faltering in flight and tumbling into the incinerating embrace of the river's flow, while countless others caught the discharge of burning lavalike splatter and spray. Still onward they charged, stubbornly attacking as creature upon creature bit down with force, surrendering tusk and jeopardizing continuance—brainwashed drones conditioned for the singular task of capture.

In the meantime, our admirable young Cristofo could do little but conduct himself with caution, adeptly balancing himself atop the accumulating pile of callous fangs.

"Altarius, do something or we'll soon be buried in this ever-growing mishmash of poison and tooth," offered the boy with an increasingly alarmed tone. He was not partial to the uselessness of his contribution to the situation at hand and so dagger once again found place in his reliable hand. "Fashion an opening overhead and I will show these detestable creatures the effectiveness of thrashing steel!"

"The only thing that you will show them is how an impetuous young Earth dweller keels over from snap of fang!" was my brazen reply. "Now sit tight, my boy; our objective nears. Up ahead, a section of the river branches off and leads the way to a cave of sorts. Therein a small opening will chaperone us into a rock shelter, where water flow will carry us forward toward our goal."

"But we're not going to make it, Altarius," cautioned the boy as he clambered atop the amassing pile of discarded tusks. "Please just seal our enclosure and allow us to think for a moment."

I had to concede to the notion, as the boy's request seemed rife with logic; furthermore, I would have soon been buried in the vile medley, which had grown to the point of titillating the caps of my knees. Therefore, the apertures were no more. We accommodated ourselves in the awkward capsule, where a relative quietness once again befell despite the clatter of colliding drones and the muffled shrieks of the unyielding attackers.

"Goodness, a reprieve at last," mustered the boy as he struggled to find a position of comfort within the closed and cluttered quarters.

"Crouch atop the bench, boy," I offered as I did the same, arranging my lanky form accordingly. And although the rudimentary seating was buried in stony fang, a simple adjustment of the marvelous material of my staff heightened it, elevating us up above the muck. A further adjustment overhead was necessitated in order to prevent the compaction of our frames.

The boy looked on in amazement as a honeycomb pattern appeared, progressively solidifying to create a new floor for the vessel just above the cumbersome pile of soaked and severed fragments. Then a jolting force flared up from our underside as a burst of steam was generated, while the previous floor receded, dumping the jumble of debris into the incinerating thrust of rushing water.

"There now—is that a more pleasant arrangement, my agreeable young apprentice?" I offered to the boy, a tad gloatingly, I must confess.

"Much better. Thank you, Altarius. Now to the matter at hand ... Would you consider fashioning a few flaps about the front and sides of our craft? A scattering of square and flat contraptions immersed in the water halfway should do the trick, angled slightly in an effort to inundate us with spray. About yay big should suffice," offered the boy as he demonstrated with a parallel spread of his hands, repeating the illustration as he displayed first lengthwise and then up and down.

"As you command, Master Cristofo," I replied with an approving nod of agreement, rather impressed with the suggestion, I must concede.

Therefore, a mediocre window upon our bow was construed; a dispersion of small openings served this purpose, giving an obscure yet nonetheless necessary view to our course. A predictable reshowing of the pests immediately ensued, once again clogging holes and obstructing the scene. The flaps were then accommodated, as Maleabar was quickly made to perform, first devising the accessories and then slowly adjusting their angle as prescribed. Within moments, shrieks and shrill cries echoed, annoyingly amplified within the hollow walls of our shell. But only for a moment did they endure, as the hissing and fizzing sound of charred creature took center stage, indicating at that instant that the adjustment of angle was ideal. The burdensome pursuers fell from the makeshift window as fangs retreated and bodies cleared way of our view. Steam dominated as the spray of water wreaked havoc upon our enemies, and then it cleared up at the front of our craft, where the luxury of sight was consequently restored.

"There it lies, up ahead," I declared contentedly as a section of the river veered off, deflected to the right by a rugged and pointed land mass of enormous proportion. It was a striking monolith with a primordial feel that lay there as if to serve purpose; a colossal tool of tapered rock was seemingly planted firmly within the river's floor, where it remained, forcing the water off course and subduing it as it flowed more lazily toward our objective. I hurriedly steered toward the direction where the streaming current was tamer and terrain grew steeper and more mountainous as we advanced. In the intermediate distance, our cavernous opening in the rock structure became visible, a modest aperture wherein a mere sliver of our preserving water flow trickled.

"Excellent, Altarius. Now invert the flaps to create a V shape and make them slightly narrower and taller. This will compensate for our slower pace and help to maintain a sufficient spray, although I do believe that our inertia will suffice in getting us to our goal before we become overrun by these dastardly relentless fiends. Incidentally, do you know by what name they are called?" I forgave the boy's commanding tone, as a life of affluence had accustomed him to such manner of expression. Nonetheless, a scowl of warning made my disapproval clear as I responded in proper turn.

"Mutophasms! That is the operative term used to describe the foul breed. Punished spirits of various localities given purpose in this dark and gloomy world. Noxerus commands them all, an army of hollow souls numbingly obedient to his every whim. Therefore, we come to the marrow of this cursed place; it is a world of penalized entities, a prison of sorts wherein all manner of depraved life forces come to reside, sentenced to inhabit foul carcasses of dismal embodiment and form. A great variety of species are spattered about this sphere, teams of warring brutes fighting and battling without rationality and to no end. Our excellent wizard of the nether rules, situated there upon his diabolical throne, where he directs the chaos and revels in its ruthless display. A wasted vocation, in my humble wizardly opinion, but who am I to judge such undertakings? That task appertains to the overseers alone."

"Overseers? Tell me more, Altarius. Are you implying that Noxerus is the devil himself and a wizard no less, appointed by the overseers? Are they the ones who have similarly chosen me as well? And yourself, for that matter …? Are all wizards chosen by the overseers of which you refer? And in this world where we find ourselves, this netherworld of earthly assumption, it is a planet as you imply? Likened to the earth but obviously different? What other manner of creatures reside here in this forsaken place—and are they forever condemned or do they endure with some meager hope of deliverance?" Yes, indeed, our newborn wizard was hungry for answers, and I intended to give nourishment, but only in small digestible morsels, of course.

"Aye, my good Cristofo, all in good time. You must consume these fantastic notions and let them dissolve gradually into your mind. Let us begin with discourse about this world since it is herein that we currently find ourselves at bay. Indeed, it is a sphere like all other places of creature and mass, an imprisoned globe long ago ensnared and held captive by a powerful and omnipotent force of star."

"You mean a star like our sun on earth, Altarius? Is it one of the infinite number we see in the distant darkness of a clear night's array?" the boy interjected excitedly, wide-eyed and enthralled. Truly he presented a most exuberant passion to become versed in all aspects of knowledge and understanding, a most wizard-like peculiarity, I must concede.

"Yes, Cristofo, a star just like the one that holds your precious world in its snug embrace. And it is assuredly one that comes to view upon the curtain of a clear night's display. Magnificent entities, these stars of which we speak, comprised of a phenomenal material that burns brightly and with determined force, powering the cosmos and bringing light to an otherwise shadowed existence. We creatures of spark have them to acknowledge for our inception; all creatures light and all creatures dark owe praise to these divine bodies—enormous reservoirs of fuel energizing the totality and actualizing us all."

"And so when will day break in this foul place, for my eyes grow tired of observing in this gloomy dimness of sky? Although I must say that I do not look forward to the accompanying escalation in temperature; already I feel as though I am roasting within my skin in this sweltering forsaken environ," offered the boy curiously as we glided nonchalantly toward our goal. I opened a window upon our bow once again to assess our course and steer us true. The hot spray of mist provided a surprisingly refreshing interlude, one that was cut short as the indomitable onrush of mutophasm persisted and the ferocity of attack strengthened noticeably in force as it reacted inversely with our currently deteriorating rate of speed. The openings that furnished our view were then clamped shut once again as several dripping fangs tumbled fruitlessly to the vessel's floor, and the relative quietude gave ample opportunity for an explanatory reply.

"Oh, I would say just about a dozen earthly seasons of time or so would bring light to our current position," was my response to the boy's enquiry, a response that garnered a look of much confusion. "You see, this place is a sphere," I continued to explain, "likened to both your home world and mine. However, unlike our places of commencement, it does not have an occupied surface. In fact, the surface of this place persists as a barren and scorching wasteland, one that can only be frequented for short distressing jaunts. It is a more or less molten whereabouts wherein various incrustations of firmness glide nonchalantly along. Any lengthened excursion upon the torturously searing covering would invariably culminate with a most unpleasant end. Truly rare is the privilege to boast witness to the unobstructed and breathtaking view of this planet's brilliant and overpowering bright red sun. It is a mature star of agedness and wisdom that has grown to dominate the sky of this relatively trifle orb. Only a scant shadow persists, cast upon the obverse side of the distinctive world. Once in a remote while does the leisurely spin of the mass bring relief of nightfall to a small portion of terrain that remains otherwise mostly baked in the relentless rush of massive fieriness."

"I do not understand, Altarius. So where are we situated? Do you mean to imply that we are existent somehow within this blistered and encrusted surface of sphere?"

"Yes, precisely, my dear Cristofo, within it indeed—a world within a world as multiple layers of crusty surface endure floating and gyrating haphazardly, islands of crust bringing solidity to a molten and churning swirl. Soundness necessarily augments as the layers step downward toward the planet's indelible and icy core. A most interesting formation, this misunderstood netherworld of human lore, a singular place wherein only spiritless shells are spawned. Herein they dwell aimlessly, patiently awaiting to host the chastised souls of otherworldly existences. We currently find ourselves situated on the third level of inhabitation, the stark outer covering being the first. It is the most sustainable and populous stratum and the one in which our capable Noxerus resides. Here he shepherds the warring broods with help from his three cohorts, other wizards who wander about and manage the chaotic interactions of the vast number of empty yet barbarous creatures. Seven spinning and churning layers in all are defined, distinct subsections of the place autonomously ensconced within its hold. Each layer shifts about its gelatinous foundation, intermingling with its neighboring domain as mountainous formations grind and support their undersides, while down-reaching canyons and rifts open the way below. Lava falls spill down and trickle about the various layers, churning and regurgitating throughout the substructure. Quite unique in its arrangement is this world, I must say, a surprising qualification based on the vastitude of planets that exist as a means to compare."

"I see, Altarius. Quite fascinating, I must admit. So, this meager luminosity that we currently indulge in … What is its origin? The radiance of discharge from the abundance of glowing lava, I suppose?" the boy inquired, reckoning aloud, a characteristic that was reminiscent of his grandfather's exemplary mind.

"Precisely, my boy. Well surmised! And when your eyes get adjusted to the faintness of it all, much detail is surprisingly revealed. In fact, it is the rare exposure to the brilliant sun that ushers in a blinding cover to the overall surround."

"And the water? Obviously, it's derived as it trickles and permeates upward from its source, namely the icy and resilient core succumbing to the relentless allure of the giant red star's inescapable and forceful pull, right?"

"Correct again, my astute apprentice," I interjected, but I was cut short in attempting to add more.

"Well then, Altarius, the lower planes should afford a safer surrounding for creatures more akin to our breed—you know, creatures of meat and bone, so to speak. For certainly the additional water flow would increase the proportion of much needed safe haven?"

"Yes, Cristofo. You comport yourself with a good sense of sound logic," was my reply, "but logic alone will not suffice as a means of your necessary advancement. You must take account of the fact that as water flow augments, so too does the invulnerability of the creatures upon which the wondrous element is imposed. We would find creatures below with much more affinity toward our viscous ally. And besides, the only portal to which I have knowledge resides on our current position, and on our current position we shall remain!"

"I understand, Altarius, and I do not mean to question your course; however, do you not assume that Noxerus is also aware of this circumstance?"

"Assume?" I darted out forcefully. "My dear boy, I unequivocally assure you of it!"

At once, both my young apprentice and I became distracted from the ongoing discussion at hand as an innate wizardly awareness indicated that our target was on fast approach and that the water flow began to quicken as we declined. Sure enough, as a revealing dispersion of openings was immediately contrived, we found that the cave-like aperture within the rock structure was upon us and a hard steer toward port was obliged. We smoothly glided into the cover of our precious shelter within the towering ridge, narrowly avoiding a collision against the passageway's rigid side. At once, the incessant swarm of mutophasms was brought to an end as demonstrated by a chorus of shrill outcries that suddenly erupted, followed by a quietude that abruptly befell as a wall of incinerating mist and water droplets brought the persistent invasion to a long-anticipated end. A delightful dripping patter resonated off the roof of our vessel, providing a welcome sound that ushered us into the next leg of our campaign.

"Ha! So long, you dastardly creatures, but in all candidness, I cannot bid thee farewell!" The hot water condensed under the relatively cooler umbrella of rock as misty vapor rose up and accumulated. Much of it dropped down, slithering along various smooth-surfaced stalactite-like formations that riddled the steeply arched canopy. A great deal of relief ensued as Cristofo and I delighted in the airiness of an open vessel since Maleabar was now accommodated into the form of a simple skiff and therefore we were no longer confined and enclosed. The refreshing down drip of moisture sprinkled us, much to our satisfaction and delight. A smaller apparatus made its way to my tenacious grip as the excess of remarkable material branched off and reconfigured itself as per my command. It was certainly a lesser device, more of an overstated wand than staff, I would say, yet still it felt satisfying to clasp.

"Illumination, Maleabar!" I exerted aloud and quite unnecessarily as I tapped down with my makeshift and more diminutive staff. At once, the inherent radiance of my good implement heightened moderately, as did the remarkable material that comprised our modestly constituted craft. Again, I struck a light blow, escalating the luminance and heightening the clarity of our view. And a third time as well did I thump down with slight force, bringing brightness of an acceptable degree to the surround.

"There now—much better, wouldn't you say, Cristofo?"

The boy hesitated in response. Bright eyes scoured the scene as the boy's sinewy neck swiveled methodically and almost mechanically. It was as though he was observing in sections, analyzing each fragment in turn and emblazoning each detail to memory.

"Wow! I wish Grandfather were here to witness such a sight, Altarius," the boy eventually replied. "It's simply magnificent!" Crystalline structures hung majestically from the topside of the peculiar cave, where a sparkling luminosity enlivened the space, all brought to life by the virtue of Maleabar's shine. The pointed and multitudinous formations were encrusted with gleaming deposits that exuded out from the intricate framework like gemstones of various types and hues.

"I must garner a sample or two to bring back to him for examination," exerted the boy as he stood up from his roost and reached for his throwing knife.

"No, Cristofo!" I shot back, reacquiring his immediate attention. "Sit down, my boy, and enjoy the display, but do not disturb the exquisiteness of it all. Look closely upon the glittering canvas and tell me if there is anything of interest that you see." And with that, I left my bewildered companion to scrutinize of his own accord while I subtly reached into the pocket of my robe.

"Glaring eyeballs! I see them, Altarius! Puny glowing peepers peering at us from behind the cover of their hanging hiding places. Remarkable! What manner of creature resides here within the glittering ambience of our passageway?"

"Why, they are a delightful and inoffensive sort, my dear boy. Micro arcuspods is the name that I have bestowed upon them. And the samples that you so eagerly wanted to gather? Well, they would be the incubation shells of their broods, and I am quite certain that they would be considerably distraught if you were to encroach upon their hatchery with a sharp digging knife. Gentle as though they may well be, do not think them incapable of considerable deterrence."

"No, of course not. I didn't mean to infringe, Altarius. I simply had no idea …," offered the boy in an apologetic manner.

"It is entirely all right, my boy, for you had no way of being aware. But they certainly wouldn't have understood that had you actually attempted to pry loose their progeny. Here now, let us place a better view upon these gentle fellows." With that, I withdrew my hand from the bountiful compartment of my robe. A black and grainy substance was blatantly exposed. It was a mineral-like nourishment that the beings invariably enjoyed, and I tossed up a small quantity of the material as I tootled and chirped in a most unfamiliar manner of expression. Of course, there was no need to vocalize my aim, but I do enjoy hearing the unique sounds of articulation that exist among the various assortments of species, and besides, there was the matter of my eager young apprentice whom I was obliged to impress—or I should use the term *instruct*.

Tiny bodies of faint blue emerged from their hiding spots, charming little creatures about the measure of a man's hand. A number of them leaped dexterously in an effort to snag a quantity of the precious tidbits; only a scant few grains remained uncaught and fell downward to face surrender in the inescapable absorption of the running flow. A chirping and cackling chorus ensued as the enchanting nymph-like creatures deliberated among themselves with regards to our presence, then they quickly came to conclude. They were an enduring lot, and a few of the more elder in the congregation had memories of my previous terriance a dyad of centuries afore. All at once, a thumping pitter-patter ensued, dwarfing the modest reverberation of the ever-present drizzle as arcuspod after arcuspod jumped down agreeably. Within moments, scores of creatures were upon us, some landing about our persons and others littering the deck of our boat.

"Ha ha, welcome aboard, little fellows!" I blurted out contentedly, while Cristofo remained silent and mesmerized. A wide-eyed tiny being settled itself comfortably on top of the boy's motionless thigh, reciprocating his eager gaze.

"Why, hello there, little friend," offered my captivated young apprentice as he nudged his face gradually closer to the unusual curiosity. In turn, spirited eyes returned the scrutiny. In fact, the pocket-size rapscallion was so bold as to reach out slowly and touch hand upon Cristofo's gentle yet firmly chiseled face. I would say that the creature was just about on equal par with the boy as far as level of maturity was concerned; both were late adolescent or early adult in stature for their respective breeds. A good-natured grin appeared, adorning the face of our budding wizard as he wallowed in the otherworldly interaction. Nonetheless, his scientifically oriented mind worked on in the background, analyzing every aspect and retaining each detail.

The creatures' physiques were surprisingly humanlike in detail and form, although donning a more burnished and hardened covering of skin. Two legs and arms of similar assembly hung off them, with relatively larger hands and feet. Fingers and toes of equal number to humankind protruded, while sizable suction cup–shaped protuberances clung to their undersides. Delicate cracks overspread their outer surface, delineating inconsistent fragments that seemed to be all pieced together to form the whole of a complex animated puzzle. Tiny faces beamed jubilantly between a pair of slight and pointed ears, and atop their dainty crowns, a darker, crusty, scaly covering prevailed, sparkling ever so slightly when hit just right by Maleabar's steady glow. Faces were similarly encrusted on a few of the band, bringing a bearded appearance to those that seemed more aged and of higher status. An off-white and almost opaque outcropping of mineralization camouflaged their groin areas, a garment-like covering comparable to calcite or a similar crystalline mineral-based blend.

"Altarius ...," offered the boy succinctly, outreaching his hand in an obvious gesture. I myself was mildly preoccupied with discussion and collaboration among a select few chieftains of the band, while the others chirped about curiously and indulged in the delectable goodies that I had sprinkled conveniently about. Nevertheless, I understood the hint and coolly responded by retrieving more of the alluring foodstuff from my robe and placing some into the boy's outstretched hand. The balance of nutriment remained invitingly in my palm, where the leaders freely helped themselves to the indulgence as they continued to jabber and chirp along. The boy succeeded in acquiring a new friend as the newfound curiosity all but devoured the irresistible treat. What little remained was briskly gobbled up by the other tiny onlookers that were shuffling and bouncing about. All the while, Cristofo reveled in the arrangement of the fantastic creatures as he mingled and played along until my discourse with the counsellors concluded, after which point the lot of them abruptly sprang up into the intricacy of the hanging precipitates, where they instantaneously disappeared from sight.

"Where did they go, Altarius?" inquired the boy excitedly. "Is it possible that there is no sign of them anywhere? No movement or jumping about? It's as though they became invisible—could it be so?"

"Hardly, my good boy, that coveted ability does not form part of the gentle species' repertoire. These dangling formations that we are privy to observe remain as a mere boundary on the outskirt of their domain. They inhabit a significant territory that is hidden away deep within the cover of this unearthly and rocklike material. Indeed, up there in the jumble of pointed pikes of innumerate size and variety, a sophisticated labyrinth of narrow channels and passageways exist, which lead to comfortable compartments and hollows of sorts, wherein they thrive in their secluded habitats, safe from the eyes and ears of Noxerus and his malevolent underlings. Long ago, and I refer to eons of time past, these beings were no different from the abounding variety of mindless drones who wasted away their existences wandering and warring about this maniacal world. Somehow, somewhere along in the line, an impetus of sorts took hold of the band's leader, and through either chance or fate, the entire clan managed to escape the scrutiny of their tenacious overseers. And herein they remained, unbothered and content in their peaceful existence, a spark of benevolence amidst the abundant hostility. Exceptions to the norm will always germinate; always will there be allies among the enemy, and enemies among the allies, my good apprentice."

"They appear to be magnificent creatures indeed, Altarius. That wondrous little fellow captivated me—such a curious and good-natured spirit. I felt a bond with it. An understanding of sorts became evident between us. Is it fair to suggest that a wizardly intuition is developing within me, an ability that facilitates a connection with other animate beings, perhaps? It would certainly explain a lot, as I experienced a similar unification with Cimtar earlier—and also with Brunella this morning, for that matter."

"Developing in point of fact, Cristofo," I responded to the delightful expression of my good apprentice's query. "More so burgeoning, sprouting like the outreaching foliage of a vivacious plant. You must practice the skill, my boy; use your mind to purvey and to extract thoughts. Thoughts exist. They are tangible and concrete. They are possessions of a kind, ideas that can be probed and inspected. Think of it in this manner and the rate of progression will intensify."

"I'll do that, Altarius. I'll make a point of it."

"All right, Cristofo, now to matters of a more pressing importance. We must make ready for conflict, for our sojourn will not be a dull and passive affair. At some point up ahead, our path will intersect with an opening along the edge of this subterrane. It is a channel of sorts—a chute, if you will—that cascades down from within the structure of this mountainous arrangement. Therein lies the most probable avenue upon which our pursuer and/or one of his dutiful miscreant bands will travel with hope of overtaking us. And heed my words well, boy: the sharpest and most resilient of earthly steel will do little more than scratch the surface of the majority of these mineral-made beings. Here on this globe, think more a target of rock when you think of your offensives. Know that only a blade forged of this world will suffice in cleaving away at your adamant adversaries. And to this point, we have had no opportunity to furnish you with such a weapon."

"All right, Altarius, I understand, as do I understand that all creatures of breath can be stifled and all those that bear eyes can have them forever closed. Bring on the confrontation!"

"I will not bring it to realization, my boy, but rest assured that it will come nonetheless of its own accord. Maleabar!" And with such command and a concentrated wave of the hand, a meager weapon materialized, and then a duplicate likewise appeared, exuding out from the hull of our further emaciated boat. Hardly a boat at all remained, transporting us along speedily as the waterway rushed on more vigorously, and the two of us stood at the ready, albeit excessively cramped. I remained sufficiently armed with my diminutive yet effective staff, and the boy held adequacy of two makeshift throwing knives, those of enhanced ingredient, of course. Before long, the perpendicular aperture became visible, still a good way distant but aglow of a curious and brimming shine. Unexpectedly, an effulgent globular mass emerged from the passage, dropping down at once and cascading along the short pitch at the base of the cave wall, where it proceeded to spill headlong into the running water flow. Steam erupted, bursting up into the cave's cylindrical enclosure and diffusing in both directions as the molten creature broke down and hardened amid the lethal fluidity. Then another mass followed, and another one still, as we came to realize that a succession of the beings were advancing, rushing out into the space unrelentingly and spewing forth like a bright and fiery red blood oozing out from an artery within the mountainous configuration. The discharge of vapor blinded us as we stood there idly floating, my staff having been moments before extended as I held it horizontally and embedded it between the rigid cave walls, where it remained a slender yet secure crosspiece upon which we held our position.

Before long, it became apparent that the dynamic rushing flow of the waterway had abated and that a passive backflow now prevailed, calming the motion and stabilizing our stance. I proceeded to extricate my stiff wire like formation of staff from the craggy cave walls, having it retract back to its previous abbreviated form. A hot and heavy condensation enveloped us, generating a smothering blindness that at the same time scalded the water underfoot.

"Disregard the swelter, Cristofo," I instructed in a commanding tone. "It's incapable of causing you any relevant harm; instruct your mind accordingly!" And with those words, we sustained our posture as I proceeded to make our circumstance more clearly understood. A concentrated and forceful surge of breath served this purpose as a calculated exhalation created a tunnel-shaped breach in the fogginess that spewed forth and clarified the scene. A sizable embankment became visible, blocking our course and spreading outward in both directions as it expanded in an effort to establish a workable platform upon which an adequate offensive could be arranged. Gelatinous and molten creatures emerged in a systematic and orderly fashion as they slumped along their sacrificed and solidified comrades, adding themselves to the expanding hardness. Soon enough, a commodious battlefield lay at the ready, and a pause in the assembly line of appearing creatures ensued.

"Prepare yourself, boy," I cautioned as a reddened and reverberating Maleabar fluttered slowly ahead, advancing us to our imminent fray, "and wait for my instruction or follow my lead, as I must first determine what manner of adversary is to be thrust our way." I peered meticulously at the idle mouth of the adverse passageway, sensing several figures that were soon to emerge, when lo and behold, a bulky ogre-like frame barely became visible before slumping inertly to the floor. It was a premature casualty of the boy's impetuousness as a lustrous and capable throwing knife shot through its ash-white hulking mass of a neck. I eyeballed the boy forthwith, summarily conveying both disdain for his impulsiveness as well as impressiveness toward his initiative and skill. The boy perceived my meaning at once, not daring to reciprocate the gaze and instead pressing onward with the offensive as a second weapon of esteem was launched with might. This time, however, the projectile found its ambition to be a dense, round, and resilient shield capably wielded by the second monstrous creature who emerged, stepping over its fallen colleague indifferently and posturing with a readied and prepared stance.

Similar callous battlers followed suit, exiting onto the hardened mass of their lesser colleagues and representing a collection of competent soldiers sporting emerald likened encrustations of shield, armor, and helmet, holding intimidating massively bladed spears and swords. Concurrently, the initial throwing knife blade dislodged itself from the fallen carcass and speedily returned to the boy's capable hand, its duplicate subsequently and similarly complying in turn. And now a dozen plus one of the menacing beasts stood at the ready, systematically dispersed upon the newly devised rigid landing. Icy glares secured themselves upon us—creepy, undeviating stares that remained fixated as though all else was inconsequential, except for the wide-eyed boy and strangely garbed elder that now advanced, floating toward them at a leisurely pace.

Water droplets trickled rampantly down upon the congregation, most of which deflected and dripped off resistant helmet and armor. The occasional bead, however, made its way toward the exposed parts of their husks, mainly the face and neck and joints of their limbs, touching with a fiery clout as the coarse and chalky alien skin sizzled and charred. The clear flowing globules ran down, leaving a striated trail of grayish-black damage along their path; all the while, the fierce creatures remained motionless and silent while maintaining their persistent gaze. They were large and stout beings of sturdy mass, and as we encroached within engaging distance, they rooted themselves securely, shields and spears at the ready. Cristofo persisted with his throwing knife attack, launching blade upon blade futilely as Maleabar's remarkable material repeatedly embedded itself into capable shields. Moments would pass as the blade would wag and shimmy itself free before returning to the boy's qualified hand, only to be relaunched with equal vigor and accuracy. The brutes we faced were surprisingly skilled and agile considering the size of their frames, and they managed to intercept each delivery handily, biding time patiently and waiting for the melee to be brought to their feet.

I too patiently remained, pondering my arsenal of offensive attacks as we drifted within range. And after Cristofo's eighth stubborn hurl of throwing knife, a ninth peculiarly was yet again let fly. It drifted ridiculously over mark, up and above the stalwart formation of adversaries, off target to the point that it was entirely ignored. A thwacking and cracking sound broke through the singular drone sound of dripping waterfall, causing one combatant to break his stare and glance upward toward its source; a grievous error on its part, as a sharp and pointed stalactite formation was dislodged and came crashing down with impetus, making quick work of piercing a fragile target of eyehole. And the projectile continued through the softer inner matter of the being's crown until an abrupt stoppage was imposed by the rigid backing of its skull, in combination with the frontal wedge of a completely embedded socket as the conical shape of the structure immersed itself near full. I must concede that the boy possessed an uncanny ability to find a way to carry out his ambition whenever the situation required. Although the ever-present need to keep him unharmed as we traveled ahead was a most palpable concern that undoubtedly hindered my customary doings and happenings, there was no true sense of burden or hindrance felt on his account. And any such consideration would most definitely dwindle and recede with the passage of time and as each precarious encounter would come to pass.

"Dismount and break through, Cristofo, and do not waste a moment of time," I instructed as we encroached just beyond the outthrust of spear and my outstretched hands came together with a resounding clout as shock waves echoed and inundated our unwavering barricade. Momentary paralysis ensued as the creatures remained rigidly imposed against the powerful emanation. Most creations would have been flung and hurled about with the force of such a profound wizardly conjuration, but not so for these resolute warrior protectors. Indeed, they held position of esteem as personal sentinels to our infamous Noxerus. And there they remained, firmly rooted and unwavering, albeit temporarily immobilized as the surge rushed through. Time became of the essence, for their unresponsiveness was certainly to be short-lived, hence I sharpened my awareness and rocketed to action as I concurrently felt the imminent presence of my veritable adversary. And so, the next moments came to pass with fierce swiftness, happenings that occurred ever so hastily that the slackened pace of words retold could not adequately bring justice to the speed of the circumstance, yet nonetheless I shall do my best to explain what transpired in the subsequent flash of time.

The boy and I nimbly leaped up from our makeshift craft and touched down just at the onset of the stable landing, where I took position of lead and Cristofo followed closely behind. At once, Maleabar fluently transformed, discontinuing its boat like configuration and rejoining the familiar form of my staff. The now—more robust device was spontaneously modified once again, instructed to take on the equally familiar shape of my most excellent sword, which felt good as it lay sturdily clasped in my capable hand, as did it feel good to touch foot on stable ground once again. I wielded my precious Maleabar with a skill that brought forth pride as I darted through the imposing barricade at once, managing to slash away at three dense and menacing bodies as I swept by. Maleabar reverted to previous form as the end of the solidity was at hand, allowing me to once again set foot on a meager yet adequate and seaworthy craft that now lay afloat on the other side of the maliciously concocted barrier. Cristofo was also quite nimble in pace, although he found himself substantially lagging as he came to rest at the outer edge of the newly poured and hardened ground. The boy was absent two proficient throwing knives, which wobbled and danced side to side in an effort to free themselves from their deeply imposed burrows, each just beneath the rims of a pair of his adversaries' resistant helmets, directly at the atlas of their hulking necks. Maleabar and I were too far adrift to board, and Cristofo found himself still at the edge of the newly formed solidity, as the resolute warriors were now swiftly regaining their awareness and form.

Seven stolid combatants remained, shaking off their sluggishness straightaway as weapons were upheld and robust arms shifted to throwing position. Cristofo vaulted aside just as his persistent throwing knives returned to his hand, and he leaped dexterously and with great skill, attaching himself to the craggy cave wall, where he implanted a throwing knife for grip. A swinging motion then ensued as the boy vaulted farther along, employing the same technique for a second surge of advancement. Spears were let fly with vigor, seven deadly and accurate projectiles with a similar and determined aim, yet none could match up to the swiftness of my young apprentice as springing legs bounded off the rugged walls and his agile body somersaulted gracefully before coming to rest with force upon my capable and receptive arms. Frowns of outrage befell our attempted capturers as they stood in failure, in line along the edge of the firm landing pad, with swords drawn to hand but no plan of action to mind.

A gust of wizardly breath set us to sail and distanced us from the menacing hoard just as idle spears were retrieved from the group's fallen companions and desperately launched with might. The boy and I made quick work of dodging the scant barrage, writhing and twisting our bodies nimbly as we watched the massively spiked blades whizz closely by. And we felt ease in mind from the situation at hand as we glided along safely, resuming course toward our ultimate goal. Just then, a rumbling sound and sensation came to pass, immediately amplifying into a fierce, thunderous roar that overcame us entirely and at once as an imposing bestial creature thrust itself down from the guts of the monolithic formation and came crashing upon the hardened firmness of ground, where it assumed a position of lead among the remaining guardsmen. Our momentum was immediately stifled as we stood there idly in our craft. Moreover, in the moderate distance, a towering devilish creation stood there menacingly, grimacing and grunting while watchfully calculating the situation at hand. An enraged and powerfully built figure with a brutish and callous physique tensed itself as its reddened, steaming eyes peering fixedly at our noble young Cristofo with ravenous ferocity. Noxerus had now entered the scene.

CHAPTER 5

Certasus's Crater

"So here we arrive face-to-face with your little pet of Earth, eh my 'old friend', animus Prime, a feeble human no less, who has been bestowed with a rank of essence equal to my own. And equal to yours as well, I might add. Humph ... The wisest of the wise seem to disregard the creature's unremarkableness, and so it seems that I too would be prudent in doing so. Hmm, impressive spark indeed, although blatantly unbefitting in shade. What does your abundant wisdom offer on the subject, my fellow wizard, animus the Prime?" A profound and ominous voice echoed through the expanse in a most brazen and ill-sounding tongue. Walls of rock resonated, and hanging structures rumbled and shivered as though a soft tremor had passed in the wind of the monster's breath.

"Have you uncovered the treasured future leader of your meager band of organic misfits? Ha ha! You will forgive me if I am somewhat less than impressed with your newfound protégé. Perhaps your powers have deteriorated somewhat, eh, old 'chum'? Ha ha ha, succumbing to the boundless weathering of time? And do not declare to me that you had intention of circumventing a stopover at my humble abode during your tarriance on this quaint world upon which I so proudly choose to make my home. I would take great offense to such a blatant disregard toward our unbounded 'friendship', particularly on account of your traveling companion—or should I say your newly appointed cohort? You above all others should be well aware of my insatiable curiosity. So then, would a proper introduction not be in order, my distinguished fellow Prime?"

I stood there listening quietly while remaining alert as Noxerus had his say. His intimidating demeanor had little impact on my seasoned resolve, and as for the boy, not only was he peculiarly unafraid; he was downright irate. He sensed indignity toward his good name as he remained statuesquely positioned while enduring the coarse and boorish foreign-tongued barrage. My mind settled Cristofo's impassioned urge as his hands clenched masterfully upon familiar handles of throwing knife and rash, as though the boy may very well have been, he acknowledged my cautioning thoughts and held his impulsiveness at bay. This was no ordinary belligerent opponent that stood before him after all, and he unquestionably recognized the situation's high demand for caution.

"Well then, my good 'old friend' fusile-favoa the Prime, perhaps you should put your presumption to the test in order to determine just how much the 'weathering of time' has affected my powers." I ended the words with an aggressive intonation and stare, appropriately conforming to the coarse and rustic undertones of my nemesis's native tongue as I tensed my grip on Maleabar and readied my hand.

"And a proper introduction would logically follow a proper invitation," I added in English for the boy's benefit, but with a similar rugged emphasis, "not a crude and unauthorized abduction carried out by your foul and vulgar vescolumen swine!"

"Hmmm." The monster grunted out the sound; a long and resounding rumble noise that permeated the environ as he studied and considered the circumstance. "Unauthorized?" the brutish fiend finally offered in a calm, nonaggressive tone and in an English tongue nonetheless.

"An interesting choice of word you impart from your lips, Prime. Only on the rarest of occasions would such a term be used in regard to me or any of my affairs. Perhaps you should consider your words more carefully, for such blasphemy could be grossly misconstrued were it not for our great and longstanding 'acquaintanceship,' of course. Bah! But 'friends' forgive, do they not, Prime? Come be my guests for a while. Let us acquaint ourselves with the human wizard while enjoying some of my rare spirits that you so invariably enjoy."

"Sir, where I come from, an invitation is only considered when given genuinely and in kind …," Cristofo interjected politely, despite delay, but he was cut short in attempting to carry on.

"Ah … and so an agreeable voice at last presents itself, a fitting accompaniment to a splendid specimen of boy. My ears thank you for reminding them of just how eloquent and seductive the rumble of a human voice can be. Long has it been since last encountering one of your breed, a captivating race, to say the least. Such a soft and delicate framework, it is hardly an ample shell for a warrior or for a fledgling wizard of little seasoning. Of course, it does allow for nimbleness and flexibility in maneuvering, that I cannot deny, but hardly worthwhile in my humble opinion, at the paramount expense of vulnerability and lack of strength. Might I suggest outfitting yourself in proper armor if ever you should find yourself again wandering about the less-than-accommodating territories of my world? Or helmet and shield to consider at least, young human, for many dangers abound. And of course there is the matter of that tantalizing rich red fluid that flows throughout your meager fabric. Mmm … a tepid drink of luxury more satisfying than the most refined of lavas."

The boy did not enjoy the threatening course of words as they spewed forth disturbingly from the mouth of the intimidating beast, yet he allowed the flow to continue uninterrupted, listening reservedly as he examined the creature in search of weakness or opportunity. A large monolithic figure stood there towering above a considerable and steadfast line of guards. A fiery deep red form of consistent hue displayed itself throughout the creature's anatomy, which accentuated an exorbitant musculature as it postured with a tense and nervy demeanor. A glabrous body shimmered, exhibiting a smooth and stony almost metallic sheen with elongated legs and arms of humanlike design. Substantial feet supported the massive figure, with seven rapier clawed toes burrowing into the hardened surface of floor, curling and digging in, hoisting the creature slightly as though setting preparedness for a flying start.

Hands and fingers were similarly equipped. One remained open and available for use, while the other remained occupied, clenched securely about the circumference of a charcoal-black polished and sleek glass-like formation of pole. It was a relatively short apparatus, reaching almost but not quite up to full height of the beast's rugged frame. The top and bottom thirds of the device branched off into three narrower and poignant ends, while the middle section remained in the shape of a standard staff, circular and comfortable to grasp. Eyes were red with pupils completely black, black holes that could swallow your mind and soul, entrapping abysses within which there would be no escape. They highlighted a long and narrow skull embraced by drawn-out form-fitting ears and tightly wrapped with skin. Chin was cleft and pointed, underlying a brutish mouth with thin lips and grayish acicular teeth. A slight nose arranged itself like an isosceles triangle, a directional arrow pointing the way toward a bony and hearty forehead, where four horizontal rugged ridges dominated the space like miniscule mountain ranges. Two stout horns crowned the aggressive beast, dull, chamfered, and ossified—age-old fossils depicting traces of a former geological age.

Silence lingered. The boy looked to me for guidance or encouragement of sorts, but the proper course dictated abeyance. I continued to steady Cristofo with the use of my mind, preferring to grant the luxury of the next move to our anxious foe.

"Well?" Once again, rumbles and shakes took hold of the surround as Noxerus spewed out the word with gust. "Your little pet looks to you for instruction, Prime. No nuggets of wisdom to allot? No instructional counsel to purvey? Your lack of zest makes for a most disappointing turn of events, I must say. Perhaps your feeble tagalong impedes your normal course, eh, 'old friend'? More of a burden than anything else, I might assume?"

With those words, the boy could be held back no more. A throwing knife was let fly with blinding speed and surprising force, and a second immediately followed. The first projectile flew high toward the mark of Noxerus's lofty skull, a well-thought-out decoy which was easily handled by a protecting guardsman's uncomplicated leap with shield. The second, however, was more stealthily unleashed as it flew low and true, an impossible shot for the airborne sentinel to block. It looked to make an impression on the creature with a good and solid strike upon its unsuspecting foot. It wasn't a bad effort on our young wizard's part, finding a glimmer of chance in a more or less impossible offensive, yet he learned his lesson well regarding the formidability of our exalted adversary as a nimble and effortless sidestep brought any vulnerable body part easily out of harm's way. And a flash of staff bit down into the hardened slag of ground, imprisoning the remarkable throwing knife within the hold of its triple pronged bars.

"Ha ha ha! So it seems the boy has some fire after all." The demon laughed ridiculously and then almost immediately reverted to a more serious and threatening tone. The initial throwing knife had shimmied itself free from shield and had returned obediently to Cristofo's hand. The imprisoned one, however, banged and clanged against its prohibiting prison bars of staff, unable to break free despite appearing to have enough space to fit through. Noxerus stooped ever so slightly and cupped his hand upon his chin in a pensive effort to study the enlivened device. Cristofo took note of the gesture and observed a substantial ring on the beast's finger, a peculiar band of the same color and sheen as my unfailing Maleabar.

"Ages of time expended and countless efforts exhausted in order to compile such miraculous material. It pains me to witness its soiling by such an inexperienced and unworthy hand. I would not have granted you such a treasure had I anticipated such frivolous misuse on your part, Prime!"

"Granted? And you dare to maintain that it is I who should choose my words wisely?" I could no longer hold my tongue in check. I had no real qualm about engaging in immediate fray, despite the fact that young Cristofo's requirement for protection afforded my opponent a slight advantage.

"Your trusted sentinels bear witness to the fairness of our famed contest, through the time-honored tales of their forerunners. Do you now disclaim the legitimacy of my triumph and deny my rightful claim of the spoils?" The devilish fiend hesitated in response, and then a characteristic maniacal laugh ensued.

"Ha ha ha, you hold advantage of semantics in English tongue, Prime, for centuries have passed since I have practiced the soft flowing and tedious melody. My honor is indisputable! That is a fact well known to all who roam throughout this world. A fair agreement of contest is law in this land, and so has it been since the beginning, and so shall it remain until the end. Now state your terms."

"I have no desire for contest," I immediately replied, "nor do I have any need for a prize. And Maleabar is now my comfortable companion, and my comfortable companion it shall remain. It is off limits!"

"Ha, it's not your worthier device toward which I am inclined. Time and effort will eventually reunite me with me such weaponry, two variables that I happen to enjoy in abundance." The brute held his hand up and twisted it back and forth as he stared admirably upon the meager amount of miraculous material that encircled the middle finger of his elongated and clawed hand. Then a seemingly harmless flick ensued, unleashing a dozen or so miniscule shrapnel-like fragments that became dynamically airborne, metamorphosing from the creature's treasured finger ring and heading speedily toward the boy.

Haste and smallness afforded the projectiles imperceptibility, yet my quick action managed to block all but one of the tiny bullet-like shreds as Maleabar was thrust forward, employing the configuration of a long and narrow shield. A number of slivers embedded themselves into the protective substance, where they remained lodged for a brief moment until returning themselves upon the finger and shape from which they initiated. A sole scrap of a morsel evaded capture, attaining mark of the boy's tender ear. A biting pain was immediately brushed aside as Cristofo stared wittingly at his aggressor. And the bloodied tidbit returned to its master, who in turn touched it delicately with a dark, devilish, and pointed tongue.

"Mmmmm, a nectar fit for my divine palate ... It is your boy who is my ambition, my fellow Prime, for I would have him as my eager young wizardly apprentice! I too could use a fourth to lend hand in managing the ceaseless chaos of this dynamic world, not to mention the service of a replenishing fountain of such exquisite ambrosia!"

"The boy? He is no chattel upon which one can wager as a prize!" I angrily countered in response to the absurd notion put forth by my rival. "He is of his own free spirit, wizardly spirit no less, and animus by design. With what authority do you propose such a ludicrous challenge? Stick to procuring colleagues of your own hardened kind!"

"Do not speak to me of authority!" the beast angrily reciprocated, harshly and in fervor. "There are no formalities upon which to base your assertion. The boy is of his own free spirit, you say? Then of his own free spirit, he will decide. What say you, boy?"

Cristofo somewhat understood the back-and-forth exchange, but at the same time, he was somewhat confused. He understood that a challenge had been placed at his feet, and that comforted him. Such provocation enlivened him and brought energy to the very marrow of his bones. He knew not why the random spin of destiny had placed him in that current circumstance—in a strange world and in the company of such commanding beings—yet he did know that he belonged there, and he was eager to prove it.

"What have you in mind, fierce creature? Propose it and speak plainly and in clear tongue."

"Battle!" was Noxerus's terse reply. "I have battle in mind, young human, a simple contest for prize."

"You against me?" Cristofo made the enquiry with a moderately serious tone, as though actually considering the prospect.

"Ha, you against me? I do admire your fire to a degree, boy, although I begin to question its luminosity. No, not you against me—you against an opponent of mine and your good mentor's fair choosing."

"I accept!" was our rash fledgling wizard's abrupt reply, a reply that I felt I simply could not oblige.

"No!" I interjected forcibly. "There will be no such contest under my authority." I conclusively brought together hands with force once again. A shock wave followed, affording precious moments of time as sentinels once again found themselves debilitated, and Noxerus was briefly caught off guard as well. A gust of wizardly breath propelled us away from the congregation and hastened us forward in the direction of our goal.

"After them!" Noxerus quickly spewed out after shaking himself free of abstraction. At once, his proficient staff was tossed deliberately and delicately into the restrictive water flow, where it touched down vertically, immediately rooting in an icy foundation as the clear running liquid became crystallized. The device remained there resolutely in a perfectly upright plane as the solidification emanated forth with a relentless pace.

In little time, the iciness passed underneath us, encasing Maleabar in its vessel-like form. Cristofo and I both leaped onto the sleek, hardened surface and scampered along on foot, struggling to make decent ground for lack of grip. And the balance of remarkable material now joined into the shape of a more hearty and agreeable staff, which I utilized in helping to balance myself and in digging down for composure as I made my way along the unstable footing. Cristofo seemed to manage decently of his own accord, adapting quite admirably to the all-but-forgiving surface upon which he had precious little exposure, considering the more favorable climatic whereabouts of his home. The sentinels did well on the sleeted surface as their heavy masses plunged down upon it with solidity, impacting soundly and cracking the thick, frozen veneer underfoot with each surprisingly brisk step.

The intimidating group of sentries bounded forward, narrowing the gap of pursuit as Cristofo and I trudged onward down the icy passageway. Noxerus lingered behind, preferring to remain alongside his staff as he monitored the chase with a scrutinizing eye. In predictable fashion, my young apprentice turned and launched throwing knives intermittently and with skill. Competent shields make quick work of the calculable offensive, yet still he would thrust projectile after projectile immediately and stubbornly just as soon as one would return to his capable hand. The odd launch would find aim of some hanging pointed formations, bringing them down with deadly force. However, the acutely attentive combatants also handled these assaults with relative ease by sidestepping the danger with indifference, and the precipitates would become implanted into the unyielding covering of ice. The distant sound of a raving chuckle echoed along the tunnel-like passage as Noxerus looked on in merriment while his contingency closed in on our position.

"Keep pace, Cristofo," I urged as enormous swords readied themselves and as I sensed the boy's compulsion to turn and take a stand. Whistles then chirped and chimed as they exuded forth from my lips, signaling that the time for support had come to arrive.

A battle cry filled the domain. Shrill tweets and chirrups monopolized the setting as a splattering of blue came into sight, sporadically dispersed among the irregular framework that was the pointed and hanging canopy. Our little friends the arcuspods had come to provide the advantage of surprise. A torrent of armaments came crashing down, catching our pursuers unawares. Stalactites plummeted down with force and in great number, some unattended and some toting miniscule passengers of determined ability. Other tiny creatures also swooped to action, descending directly upon the unsuspecting attackers in aggregate, swarming them while thrashing frenziedly with tinier but equally sharp and rocklike precipitates. Overall, the bombardment was an overwhelming success. By the end of it, seven sizable corpses lay there dilapidated and defeated, strewn about randomly upon the cold and icy battlefield that was turned into a cemetery. A multitudinous variety of ruthless pikes littered the space like so many grave markers, impaling hardened frames and biting into the icy covering resiliently, weakening it as hairline cracks emanated forth about their circumference. With their work completed, as quickly as they presented themselves, the wondrous little creatures receded into the intricate network of passages, shafts, and crawlways that made up the labyrinth-like architecture of their home. Cristofo and I immediately resumed pace just as a loud and fierce roar of anger rumbled past our ears. Noxerus bolted forward with furious intent.

"Move with haste, Cristofo. Our ambition lies in close range," I blurted out eagerly as a cavernous opening came into view. A rushing waterfall could then be heard, dropping down from a pair of cavities within the rounded enclosure and disappearing into the depths of the funnel-like formation of floor. The frozen pathway upon which we traveled led into the basin, overhanging it considerably in a solid mass that was directly representative of the waterway's moderate depth. It was as though the natural pour of it had been halted by Noxerus's wizardry; only a scant dribble remained, where once an outpouring of water cascaded downward with might.

"Launch yourself into the conduct, boy. I'll stave off the brute and reunite with you later," I commanded as Cristofo pressed on, scurrying incautiously toward his aim. I halted pace, pivoting and balancing myself as I harnessed my wizardly energy escalating it to apex as my raging and formidable nemesis advanced with tremendous impetus.

With staff in hand, he bounded forth, crashing down upon the weakened sheet of ice just at the onset of the scattered debris of battle, leaping onward just as the encrusted coating yielded and collapsed under the shear jolt of force. Hairline cracks fractured and jagged; multifaceted pieces of various sizes and shapes tumbled violently into the liquid below. The rummage of battle was cleansed in one fell swoop as corpse and clutter alike were swallowed whole by the current's newly resumed sweep. Noxerus touched down on the farther side, offsetting another less profound dismantling of slab as he vaulted forward still, intending to hurdle over the barricade that I presented in a wholehearted effort to take hold of the boy, who had concurrently propelled himself headfirst along the glistening surface in a desperate and dramatic attempt to slide toward the unfamiliar precipice.

A balled-up flash of power was thrust forth, an impenetrable upsurge which cut off my adversary's attempt to vault over my anchored frame. Hanging formations crumbled effortlessly as the brute torpedoed overhead, and although my efforts succeeded in halting the offensive, an outstretched arm in mid launch somehow managed to break free. A qualified staff shot out vigorously, exiting through the back of the fortification as Noxerus lay wedged overhead, crunched against fragmented stalactites and crushed of wind. The spiraling instrument flew downward and onto the frozen waterway, drilling through the callous coating of ice in a shot, whereupon it disappeared for the briefest of moments before breaching upward from underneath, just at the onset of Cristofo's aim. In a flash, a wall of sleet came into being, cropping up on the tail of the enchanted device and blocking the passageway in its entirety as it expanded violently and unequivocally, thwarting the boy's aspiration as he impacted the barrier headfirst and with clout. Alas, the lad was left denied and utterly senseless. The implement then proceeded downward, once again impacting firmly onto the icy surface as it clamped down onto the boy's inert wrist and secured it amid three sturdy prongs as they entrenched themselves into the rock-hard bed of frozen water.

"Cristofo!" I blurted out worriedly as I lay down my guard and turned attention to the seemingly comatose boy. Noxerus dropped down indifferently, sluggishly reaffirming his bearing as he brushed tiny bits and chunks of debris off his backside. The boy moaned and clamored a bit as he regained consciousness, and my worry abated to a large degree as my broad awareness returned and I realized that he was not much worse for wear after clanging his durable crown onto the inflexible barrier wall of ice. His hand had been merely moored in place, not pierced, severed, or damaged to any meaningful degree.

"Well, Prime? What say you now …? As though there was ever any doubt … Do we have agreement of contest?" the brutish fiend belted out gloatingly as he nonchalantly commanded his staff to increase its pressured hold. In turn, the boy groaned resentfully as pain completed the task of awakening him from his haziness.

"Yes, we have agreement of contest, you relentless, unshakable fiend!" I countered sharply as Maleabar was let fly, impacting the demon's staff with vigor and disengaging it from its tenacious hold. The boy righted himself and remained, angry and astir.

"Ha ha! I see that Maleabar performs well under your guidance, Prime. Surrendering it in contest is certainly not considered among one of my crowning achievements. *Reckless* would be the term best used to characterize the action that heightened the capacity of my foremost of rivals. The time will assuredly come to pass wherein the occasion for my re-gratification will be at hand, and I relish the thought of that, my fellow Prime; patience and willingness to endure will simmer my bitterness until it becomes the most flavorful of dishes … and then I will indulge. Then and only then will I indulge and savor the most delectable of fares. Oh, indeed, the feast will be had, my 'old friend,' of that you can certainly rest assured." The fiendish brute belted out the dialogue with a passion worthy of the greatest of performances, a heartfelt articulation, to be sure. Then he pressed on, conveying a habitual shift of tone.

"Bah! But that is mere fodder for a future tale. Come, let us discuss terms as we make way toward my palace. Come, boy, for the backlog of water flow will soon end, furthering a most unpleasant singe upon my excellent feet … Well? Put yourself in motion, boy!" Cristofo was urged on as he stood there defyingly, still heated and eager to engage.

"Ha, save your enragement for Certasus's Crater, human. You're going to need it!" With that, I reluctantly gestured a nod of acquiescence to our exceptional young fellow. The three of us headed off in the direction from whence we came.

Certasus's crater; a legendary arena of battle and death whereupon countless entities of assorted origin had left their indelible mark upon the enduring and callous surface of the blatant concavity. Originating from a time long-passed as a stray meteorite struck down upon the side of the imposing display that is Mount Immotus, the unwavering peak that somehow remains unchanged in an unstable and turbulent world, complete with root embedded deep and true as it runs endlessly along the planet's lengthy radius near full, until eventually finding home within the planet's perpetual and icy core. Swaying with the limited flex of an iron bar, it churns through the various layers of habitation, wreaking havoc upon the immediate geography until touching the underside of the second netherworld strata, whereupon it scrapes aggressively back and forth against its underbelly. Eons of time have worn, chipped, and frayed away at the tip of the structure, sculpting it into the tapered arrangement that Noxerus pleasantly refers to as home. A vast palace sits comfortably at rest about three-quarters up the mountainside, below which several edifices lay subserviently dispersed.

Stables, armories, warehouses, barracks, huts, and houses of all kinds find themselves littered throughout the lower portion of the mountain's cone-shaped base. And beyond still, the scattering of a mediocre city remains interspersed among the myriad tails and islands of hardened ground, surrounded by flowing rivers of slag and currents of lava that spew forth an abundant mass of volcanic matter that is derived from nearby eruptions. Overall, it was not the most disagreeable of locales, boasting its own unique and beauteous character save for the sporadic assailment of cascading boulders and hot debris that tumbled down from above with violence and moderate frequency. Moreover, in the middle of it all, our hollow crater of interest displayed itself flagrantly and on a modest slant, imposing itself with an unnatural air like an empty socket picked clean of eyeball. Enter Certasus.

The race of goliaths was an above-average band of combatants at best, just one of the numerous lines of empty-souled fiends spawned of this most unnatural world upon which we currently find ourselves embroiled in tale. Despite their considerable size, near impenetrable shells, and abundance of brute strength, the creatures seemed to lack for quickness of hand and alertness of mind, a function of the insufficient room for ample brain inside their dense and tapered crowns—save for Certasus, the supreme specimen of his kind who stood alone. He was a remarkable being of random occurrence abounding of mind and soul, rising above all others as he slashed and clobbered his way through the unending succession of brutal campaigns and senseless battles that would radiate from the heart of this uncommon place. The years wore on, and the relentless stroke of battle hacked away at the enduring clan of cyclopes until a mere handful remained, at which point the scant and worthy few were subjected to the servitude of Noxerus, a common practice that affords the demon no shortage of slave or lack for minion.

Certasus, as anticipated, would be thrust into the circular arena of choice for combat's sake and for entertainment purposes alone. There he would amuse his overlord as he practiced and perfected his craft. Battle upon battle would be waged as time and turmoil eroded away at the oblique depression, tattering the rim and floor as falling particles impacted the lowermost portions. Weaponry would clang and chip away at the various surfaces, and callous bodies and frames of all kinds would chafe and wear away at its veneer as they were hit, smeared, and crushed against the opportune creation of meteor strike until eventually tedium set in. None of the multitudinous and competent array of battlers could succeed in besting the indomitable champion. It was an eventuality that Noxerus tested well and tested heavy, testing repeatedly until finally conceding to the being's unfailing spirit, a spirit indeed worthy of wizardly induction. So, a competent cohort was born and a resilient arena was given the name of its foremost incumbent, who in turn retired his reign and went on to endure and thrive as wizard—Noxerus's chief of command and attendant for all who raged and resided in his favored netherworld vicinity, the upper strata one, two, and three.

I will not disinterest you with the tedious detail of the subsequent transpiration of time as we made our way toward the netherworld's regal dwelling. Suffice it to say that as we trudged along, Noxerus and I carried on back and forth in an effort to designate the boy's forthcoming opponent, terms of battle, and determination of prize. Of course, as far as opponent was concerned, he would propose a candidate with excessive advantage, and I in turn would counter with a much less capable offering. A laborious yet necessary deliberation ensued in which several from the brute's immense stable of warriors were adequately deliberated upon and weighed. The debate concluded at the logical juncture, where reluctance and confidence abrade and both parties are left somewhat unsatisfied.

"Clavus it is, Prime. Always you must wear me down to an arrangement that leaves me disturbingly unfulfilled." The brute offered under pretense that somehow an advantage of sorts had been surrendered. A mere glance was my retort, sufficing to expose his audacity for making such an insinuation.

"Do not play your games with me, Prime, for I think to be well above such triviality. The pairing is fair, with victor undeterminable to either of us, and this you know as well as I do. Now, as for terms of battle, the usual, I suppose, would be adequate, with the boy receiving the choice of two weapons from your arsenal—and Clavus none." I proposed this to the devilish fiend because I was no longer in the mood to have meaningless back-and-forth. And for the sake of my good audience, I will clarify. Usual terms were uncomplicated, were twofold, and were as follows: battle was to the death, and battle gives way to no rules.

Noxerus caught my meaning yet would not concede altogether. "Agreed. However, the choice of weapon must be limited to the training stockpile. The boy should not be granted superior devices to which he would be wholly unaccustomed. And the throwing knives revert back to Maleabar!" To this, I grudgingly agreed. The training depot held a stock of armaments more familiar to the boy: blades of steel, staffs of wood, lariats of chain and such, implements much less effective than those forged of the nether, yet still they could be quite capable in the right hand and under control of the right mind. Herein I had ample confidence in the boy, to whom I relinquished decision of the final circumstance: prize.

"Now, Cristofo, be acutely aware of the venture upon which you presently embark," I cautioned with a serious tone. "Let us be clear that defeat will bring death, or death insomuch as you will struggle to overturn the circumstance as per our prior exchange, and an unseasoned wizard such as yourself could struggle with such a task for quite some period of time. Decades may very well pass—or even centuries, perhaps—before reinvigoration prevails and you return to that familiar life of breath about which you are principally aware. And then, at that point, when at long last you have succeeded in thwarting your foremost of challenges, you will be thrust upon the volatile fancy of Noxerus ... for an indeterminate duration, I might add."

"I see," the boy casually acknowledged. "And do you see me as vanquisher, Altarius, in your infinite wisdom? Do you have faith that I will triumph in contest against this rival of your contributed arrangement?"

"Cristofo my boy," I replied with sincerity, "in all honesty I cannot ascertain the victor in my mind and nor can Noxerus, for that matter; an indeterminable conclusion stands testament to the fairness of contest. My faith in you, however, is as clear and outreaching as a cloudless sky, and that I can offer with utmost certainty. Now to more jubilant considerations. What is it that you yearn for? What is the bounty that fuels your flame of desire? Contemplate well and contemplate purposefully, for the life of an outstanding young wizard such as you is indeed a treasure with little comparison."

The boy took no time at all to deliberate. "A sword! An exceptional sword forged of this world. A choice of sword about which you will have final approval, Altarius. And the ring of remarkable material. The hearty band that our aggressor seems to lust after with such passion, I want it for my own, a miniature Maleabar for me to carry and command as I see fit. What say you, Altarius? Would such a consideration be fitting as a prize?" Red eyes squinted disapprovingly at the question, progressing into a furious gaze with my reply.

"It is reasonable, my young apprentice, for such miraculous material would serve you well. And the sword? If blade is your weakness, then you will find that one forged of this world will forever be unmatched."

"Never!" The word was discharged with an unfaltering firmness, exploding from the beast's mouth with a pent-up strain that had been culminating since the boy made first mention of the treasured ring. "Never will I concede to such a pledge. Millennia of wisdom and struggle serve as the prerequisite for the claim of such a wondrous acquirement. I would never hazard even the slightest of chances that such material would find its way to an inexperienced and still wholly unproven hand." His stance was unquestionably sturdy, and his pain from the loss of Maleabar obviously festered despite the ever-persuasive remedy of time, yet still I attempted to overturn his mind-set.

"Do not allow your sentiment to cloud your honor, Prime. The request is fair and absolute. Do you place so little value on the life of a fledgling wizard of such quality? I think not, for if that were the case, you would not carry on so enthusiastically in an effort to take him as your own." A brief pause gave semblance of hope that the beast may acquiesce after all.

"Ha ha, I had all but forgotten your outstanding aptitude to sway, my fellow Prime. Well done, for you did succeed in sparking some contemplation on my part concerning the matter at hand; however, my resolve is unbreakable and my answer still firm: no remarkable material will be put up as a prize! A choice of sword will more than suffice, for if it is so destined, the boy will be brought together with a blade of unparalleled fulfillment. Of this, I am certain that you have no doubt!"

I looked over to Cristofo, and his meaning was immediately implied. "It seems we come to agree. A choice of blade from your personal cache will suffice in mollifying the boy." Once again, red and angered eyes came to the forefront of an ever-hateful face. A molten fury pressurized to the boiling point before the eruption of a voice brought much-needed release and the fiend imposed himself in a most aggressive manner.

"My personal cache is not to be weighed! Is that understood, Prime?" The last word of the warning had just barely been exuded in full when I stepped in and retaliated with an even more grandiose and ferocious uproar, amplifying my words and augmenting my form until it was I who towered over the taken aback beast.

"The miraculous material or your personal cache! Decide forthwith or you and I will immediately engage! Do not think to take unjust advantage of my capable companion!" And with that, suffice it to say that agreeance was fashioned and a pivotal crater match was brought to bear. Exhilaration began to take hold of the boy as we approached the base of the awesome mountain and he laid eyes on the breathtaking castle from afar, catching a glimpse of the menacing and formidable basin whereupon our novice young wizard intended to leave his mark of distinction.

"Does the boy have need for any preparation?" Noxerus offered with a customary respectful courtesy conferred similarly upon all forthcoming combatants.

"No," Cristofo intervened, preferring to answer on his own behalf. "To the arena at once. Call upon your designate and have him, or her, or it readied for fray, for already I grow tired of this place and my impatience upsurges with each passing moment. I have matters to attend to at home, obligations to satisfy, and unpleasantries to deal with. Unpleasantries of your evil doing, I might add, you callous and impudent creature!"

"Ha ha! How I relish the sensation of excitement that precedes such a purposeful contest. Fight well, boy, and make for a good spectacle, for I do place considerable value on your fellowship. It would be most disappointing if you lacked for skill of any exceptional kind. And do try to go down with the presence and style befitting of a champion; try not to stumble about abashedly as you are bested, bumbling and blundering like an innocent animal lost of its herd, in desperate panic as it attempts to stave off an inevitable dispatching. Ha! Fight well, boy!"

Cristofo all but heard the words; already his great mind began its deliberation as each perceivable variable was weighed. The distant crater exposed its usefulness of form and structure, divulging to the boy just how to manipulate the notable shape to his advantage. The air and ambience would also require consideration, and therefore he accommodated his breathing and mind-set, setting firm his purpose as the density of crowd increased and as indiscernible buzzings and mumblings came into being. Pairs and groupings of strange and unfamiliar creatures gawked and glared at the sight of Cristofo and me in the company of their intimidating king. All was good in the mind of the boy as it hardened and acclimatized for battle. The sentiment was reinforced as we approached the illustrious landmark and skirmishes came into view: training exercises, drills, and spars were autonomously set in motion, rampant and in great number. The boy basked in the delightful flavor of it all, feeling comfortable and almost at home. Noxerus veered off succinctly, barking commands and instruction to nearby attendants who attentively lingered about.

At once, sprightly creatures appeared, purposeful of speed and in quantity. Their forms were slight, displaying a strangely obscure outline that remained sufficiently cloaked behind a shroud of discharging whitish and radiant light. They scurried about frantically and with frenzy, stringently task-oriented minions of the excitable and energized variety. Three of the spirited beings besieged Cristofo, encircling him as they advanced the way toward a ramshackle structure that lay there tiredly amidst a sparsely attended patch of training ground. Our young wizard obliged to the momentum, pleasantly amused by the energetic onrush and by the chipper and animated strange-tongued prattle. Others of the rambunctious breed made way to the foreboding crater of action where swift preparation would be undergone, and others still set course to fetch Clavus, the practiced and proficient challenger of which Cristofo knew naught. In all fairness, the effective battler knew naught of Cristofo as well: a deliberate condition of fair contest and rationalization for separating me from the boy. Still other creatures attended to Noxerus and me as we kept each other in check while making way to our choice arrangement at the forefront of battle view. In the meantime and all the while, our capable adolescent prodigy remained entirely unaltered by the segregation, for his mind was securely set to purpose.

Weaponry lay negligently dispersed about the opening and surround of the shoddy rocklike structure toward which Cristofo was delicately yet deliberately led. Thin panels resembling shale or some similar sedimentary materials of earth-wise comparison endured, placed together in a simple arrangement of wall and covering that presented itself with poise; a proud shelter determinedly serving its function with a dutiful disregard to the wear and tear of neglect and time. Swords of extreme variety caught first consideration of the boy: short swords, long swords, great swords, broad swords, curved swords, warring swords, two-handed swords, and ax-like swords. Swords of all kinds and conditions littered the approach like so many worthless scraps of ineffectual tools of the hazardous trade, arranged along the periphery of the pathway that led to the edifice, forming a disordered soldier course type of pattern for the boy as he approached and then entered the dark and dank interior of the ageless stock house. A soft effervescence provided much-needed illumination as the unrelenting chaperones followed course, bringing light to a bountiful stockpile of diverse range and collection. Monolithic ledges of the same thin rocklike material lined the circumference of the building's interior, two rigid runs of reinforcement that also served as shelves that partitioned the elevation with perfect symmetry and spoke to the lasting integrity of the shelter's otherwise unimpressive exterior display.

Upon the sturdy racks, a multitude of arms lay in crowded repose, lingering through a long-lasting stasis where dreams of bygone battles gave a faint glimmer of rejuvenation: clubs, hammers, daggers and small swords, chain whips, knives and darts, maces, flails, pellets, orbs and balls, devices of all kinds, both familiar and not. On the floor below, another row of dreary implements remained with similar disdain: those with less inclination to balance, those that were obliged to lean. There were shields, for example, a multitude of differing size, shape, and contour. Swords as well resided below, alongside axes, picks, sickles, bars, and bows. At the center point in the space, five segments of support frame came together to resemble a star like formation, and thereupon devices of linearity loitered: poles, staffs, spears, lances, javelins, and the like remained perched and propped and in full view. Cristofo deliberated well as he slowly paced the room. The thought of the empowering grasp of expertly held sword enticed the boy, yet he refrained. The recollection of my cautionary remark stood sharp in his memory and was well weighed: "The sharpest and most resilient of earthly steel will do little more than scratch the surface of the majority of these mineral-like beings. Here on this globe, think more a target of rock when you think of your offensives." Choice of weapon was of instrumental concern under the circumstance, a fact that young Cristofo recognized beyond question and a truth that would give cause for him to deliberate in turn.

And so, eyes turned to instruments that favored the delivery of a more resounding blow; clubs, hammers, maces, and flails were evaluated carefully, with few of the devices left unturned. Single-handed operation was a crucial consideration, as was powerful force of strike. Ergo the dilemma of the moment; which implement embodied the perfect harmony between maneuverability and fierceness of impact? Then it appeared to him, an unremarkably presented hammer that lay there inconspicuously amid several bludgeons of similar strain. It would be his pick to wield, a certainty that came to pass even before his validating grasp and trial stroke of confirmation. It felt true in hand, and thus and so accessory number one was named, a modest hammer no larger than the boy's arm. It was forged of a single mass of rugged steel with handle and head fused together in molten tie. The head was dense and two sided; one face boasted a rugged sledge design, square with slightly cut corners, and the diametric side tapered to an almost flat length of steel with a sharply chiseled termination. Overall, the device represented an ideal configuration that accommodated the transfer of momentous force into an acute and concentrated impact. A course and durable band of braided hide afforded a dependable grip that culminated in a convenient loop for hitching onto one's wrist if so desired.

Attention now shifted to the second choice of armament. Ordinarily, the boy would prefer to battle bereft of shield, for his agility was indeed masterful and his propensity was toward the offensive, but in this particular instance, good sense prevailed. Cristofo knew absolutely nothing of his forthcoming opponent; therefore, sound logic would favor items with a more preventive inclination. Large, cumbersome types of shield were not to be considered because of their awkward and ungraceful comportment. Moreover, those with angles would simply not suffice, for such shapes could hinder a properly sheltered view. A circular-shaped buffer would rule, as far as the boy was concerned, a device of limited size but substantial girth, one that could be used as an effective, aerodynamic, and spiraling projectile while at the same time having value as a striking force when up close in the affray. Thick and dense, split resistant timber constituted one such arrangement of shield, a rare enough material to be found in such a place to be sure. It was of suitable weight and size, resembling the butt end of a moderately sized whisky barrel and the perimeter was reinforced with a generous band of iron; a substantial mass which clamped the panels tight and true before narrowing into form of a not quite sharp but sculpted edge. And so with his selections complete, the finely arranged boy stood there sumptuously for a moment, reveling in the confidence made more potent by wise choosing before exiting battle ready, with shield upon shoulder and hammer in hand.

Crowds of strange and unusual beings had begun to gather about the boy's vicinity, accumulating and progressing as he made way toward the venue of the impending bout. A supporting number of sprightly attendants showed up to provide reinforcement to the situation, shepherding the increasingly boisterous crowd and clearing passage for the invigorated young combatant, who seemed to bask in the enthusiastic display while remaining focused and fixated for fray. Indeed, the entire congregation of the dreary locality seemed to share in the curious disposition that was displayed by their menacing king as the fringe of the monumental crater became overcrowded with an influx of additional observers who adjoined the insubstantial few who had already taken up position in view of the regularly scheduled, ongoing, and less noteworthy campaigns. Discourse of a dynamic and heated nature overspread the masses as terms of consideration were debated and wagers were ratified in good fashion.

Cristofo astutely examined the unfolding arrangement as he was steered to position at the lowermost edge of the facility, where settled rocks and boulders of erstwhile cascades accumulated in a convenient grouping to form makeshift stairs. On the farther side of the rubble, a curious entity was similarly advanced to station. Cristofo's mind enlivened, and his determination was invigorated as he laid first eyes on his challenger; Clavus the mighty had entered and neared.

A blistered and abscess riddled hardened mass of a creature settled rank on the opposite side of the crater's rocky and rugged flight of practicable steps. A cobalt and violet hue painted the entirety of the being's abundant frame, which towered well above the shimmering scurry of his own personal trio of attendants, reaching a height that was loosely twofold that of the boy. The battler's center mass presented a most striking display wherein pointed protuberances abounded. Stalactite-like structures of moderate size covered the entirety of his midsection, protrusions reminiscent of the recently frequented subterrane where a canopy of a similar sort remained. Upon each of the strapping arms of the monster, a single and drawn-out formation sprouted out boastfully amidst a patch of similar offshoots with lesser esteem—a pair of finely pointed and vivid pikes somewhat akin to a unicorn's magnificent display of horn. The crowd roared and grew riotous as the recognized conqueror shrieked and hollered, hoisting arms and clamoring with an exaggerated strain in an effort to convey an intimidating display that all but lost its intended impression on the boy. He had shifted his gaze toward the monolithic seating arrangement that was centered behind the length of bouldered staircase, wherein I calmly positioned myself in the company of Noxerus and others of a more or less elevated status. His glare was a curious one, as best as I could characterize it, and for my part, I returned it with a nod and a reciprocal stare that was replete of a calming and confident air. Cristofo shifted his attention back to his overly enthusiastic adversary, who still excessively provoked and goaded his entourage and the audience on.

A penetrating glare infiltrated the flashy facade, intensely scrutinizing the head and neck of the foe. Every boil and blister was analyzed; each contour and crag was pondered and weighed. And focus maintained its concentrated study even as the crowd's uproar further intensified with the fall of one in the current contest; it was an outburst fueled not of the ongoing battle but of time made ready for the harped-upon battle that was now imminent and in store. Effervescent attendants made quick work of cleanup, and before long Cristofo was nudged and propelled downward. He was suddenly left alone to negotiate the irregular run of steps as he staggered down into the belly of the deep-seated crater. He continued up the steady incline until nearing the further embankment of the depression's face, whereupon he turned preparedly and readied himself as Clavus began to descend, still boisterous and blaring.

At long last, the creature seemed to conclude its drawn-out and clamorous production, growling and grunting and growing more serious as it began to converge upon the boy. At the same time, the enthusiastic crowd followed suit, taking on a noticeably quieter and more concentrated mood. Ten oversized paces or so brought the beast to the midpoint of the space, where it took pause to consider the springiness of the saltating yet otherwise unmoving boy. Then a gasp overcame the masses as the being's body tensed and a fleeting spike was immediately let fly. Cristofo stumbled deliberately as he feigned difficulty in dealing with the capable projectile, clumsily sidestepping at the last moment and watching as the arm's length pike pierced halfway into the callous face of the timeworn crater wall at his hind. From such a distance, the boy could have effortlessly handled such a discharge, but there was no need to demonstrate such skill to his presumptuous opponent. The young champion contentedly gave false credence to the monster's efficacy as three more launches were initiated and then narrowly dodged. If only the indomitable Clavus had known of the boy's training regimen. If only Clavus the overconfident had been aware of the fact that the boy's agility was almost unnatural and wholly unsurpassed. In that moment, the boy's mind brought him back home to the familiar training grounds, where barrages of blunted bolts were regularly unleashed from a less-than-reasonable proximity and where a trio of the king's finest archers were regularly denied of their intended mark.

Cristofo now began to move briskly along the perimeter of the deep-seated enclosure, crouching down slightly as his opposer advanced and let fly with a small cavalcade of in-built missiles. A few were crudely swatted by his shield, while others became firmly embedded in the craggy surface of the crater's wall, where they would remain sticking out like so many nails subjected to a carpenter's insufficient blow. The boy advanced a few paces along the downward slope before stopping to cope with another violent spray, and he would continue in this manner, making headway intermittently as he advanced in small increments. Each time Clavus inched nearer, Cristofo would elevate his poise; with each turn, Clavus would grow more frustrated as Cristofo's true skill came to the surface. In no time at all the boy became satisfied with the ongoing state of the engagement, decidedly sprinting forth from alongside the pike-riddled wall and distancing himself substantially while veering to face his opponent from the center scope of the arena. Clavus was discontented and standing there ungratified, with body fractionally but not entirely spent of spike. The crowd had now become notably enthusiastic, and what's more, they began to turn favor toward the boy. At once, long, uniform, and polished lances extended out from the forearms of the outraged monster as tinier spikes shot out like darts and the creature began to dash toward its enemy while exerting harsh and savage screams of rage.

For his part, Cristofo continued to remain composed and calm, a habitual manner of conduct for the boy when engaged in fray. It served him well while he continued to make good use of his wise choice of shield, swatting tiny spears away with ease, and his legs began to dance with a steady and nimble acceleration. With a calculated and controlled stride, he led the beast on, proceeding toward his previous position along the now–spike-pervaded wall, but not directly so. Instead, he chose an arc-like path that would more slowly approach the circular perimeter of the crater's confining wall. As the boy quickened his pace, Clavus adjusted and followed, unable to establish a firm footing from which to negotiate an accurate launch of poignant extremity. The odd abrupt burst fell well short of its intended moving target of the boy. The brash assailant now chose to close in with a mind-set that attempted to anticipate his vexatious opponent's course, intending to converge upon him at the terminal point of his rat like scurry, whereupon Clavus the almighty would endeavor to conclude the drama in a decisive, flamboyant, wrathful, and audience-pleasing finale. Cristofo, on the other hand, had a different outcome solidified in his exceptional mind, knowing that although he would indeed be regarded as victim in the eyes of both Clavus and the crowd, he would actually be the true predator, operating shrewdly under the guise of prey.

So now the time had arrived for our crafty young newly established wizard to bring his ploy to fruition. With a confidence akin to the most expert of trainers of beasts, the enraged brute was drawn in as it continued along on a path of intercept intended to cut off the course of the scampering boy. Cristofo's course now converged him with the contoured shape of the crater's wall, but with a slightly wider arc that lengthened the distance while accentuating his stride. He approached the sheer face of rock ever so gradually as he advanced forth in flight—a tangential bearing with the precise goal of directing him back toward the location on the crater wall where the interspersed and deep-seated spikes were found. All the while launches of projectile would be swatted and dodged with increasing difficulty, as closeness had now conceded more favorable odds to the shooter, yet still the boy's aptitude would prevail as the fitting shield earned its honor and as its wielder basked in the glory of a perfectly unfolding stratagem.

The boy's objective was now at hand, as was a charging and volatile Clavus on the verge of strike. At that instant, an alert and well-prepared young Cristofo leaped upon the protruding pikes with graceful balance, clambering up the crude formation of rungs to achieve an elevated standpoint. Just as an optimal height was attained, the simple and steadfast shield was tossed with a precise arrangement as Clavus let fly with the entirety of his arsenal. The boy followed suit, soaring off the uppermost foothold while bringing knees to his belly and crouching down in the refuge of his protective flying wooden buffer.

His arms were concurrently set to fluid motion as they heartily grasped the hammer, while his legs shot out firmly, propelling the rounded barricade forth into the face of the dastardly fiend. Spikes then shot off with an inconsequential frenzy, and massive lances swatted futilely as the chamfered edge of the sledge came down from an unstoppable apex with the perfect combination of force and precision. A previously studied indentation on the top of the creature's skull was impacted dead-on, and a consummating crack was instantaneously discharged, shearing off a considerable portion of the being's head, which then listlessly thumped down bluntly onto the compacted thickness of slab that made up the crater's dense and unyielding floor.

Cristofo touched aground gracefully and calmly advanced himself a few paces just as a faint rumble crept up from behind and tickled at his heels, a rumble spawned of the collapsed, dense form of his foe. Silence thrived in the awkward wake of the crowd's bewilderment as the boy shed his hammer with nonchalance, and the fallen carcass at his rear lay there tranquilly stilled amidst an ever-growing puddle of viscous ooze that flowed from the honeycomb like interior of the defeated monster's crown and spilled out onto the callous and coarsely laid ground. And just like that, silence vacated the premises as the crowd erupted with unprecedented intensity. Cristofo continued down toward the peculiar steps of rubble with indifference to the masses and with mind centered fixedly on his well-deserved bounty of sword.

CHAPTER 6

A Well-Earned Prize

A ferocious outcry pierced through the persistent cheer of the exhilarated crowd and jostled young Cristofo from the pleasurable daydream of his forthcoming bounty of a superlative sword. He continued on, unaltered in his victorious yet lackadaisical march down the gradually sloping and slightly bowed crater floor, advancing upon the rugged ramp of boulder and rock that arranged itself as the solitary point of egress from the profound and down-reaching arena. Casually he aimed a glance in the direction of the distinctive noise, where sharp eyes confirmed the reckoning of his dependable ears; massive creatures barked violently amidst the kerfuffle. Colossal hounds, an earthly breed of which the boy was keenly familiar, paled in comparison to these monstrous and vicious mongrels made conscious of the nether. A pair of them surged forth savagely and with a fierce demeanor, even though they were collared and tethered to enormous chains of substantial girth that were held taught by stoic arms as rigid as tree trunks. Gray and sculpted as stone, yet limber and aroused, were these beasts of which I speak, with beady black eyes and darkened teeth of unparalleled sharpness lining powerful, unyielding jaws. They raged on relentlessly with fixation on the boy, dominating the attention at the arena's crowded edge, where the multifarious array of spectators cleared a wide berth for the brutes and their imposing rein holder, Certasus.

With a keen eye, I beheld the spectacle on the crater's craggy fringe while standing tall and cheering in unison with the elated crowd. Noxerus, in the meanwhile, remained settled on his imposing chair of authority, where he weathered the storm of applause with a most disgruntled bearing. An intense suspicion came to being as I weighed the rationale for Ceratusus's sudden appearance, and it heightened further still as I made an effort to uncover the mental goings-on within Noxerus's mind. However, his unfolding thoughts were well barricaded from my attempted raid. Indeed, my shadowy nemesis had surely intended for some form of treachery to come about, conspiring with his sadistic and cyclopean second-in-command. As a result, a warning to young Cristofo was concurrently conveyed, and at the same time, Maleabar was more sturdily grasped. Having acknowledged my cautioning thoughts and digested them with fearless composure, the boy simply continued with his nonchalant stroll, still lacking of shield and hammer yet seeming unaffected by the impending likelihood of peril. Noxerus would certainly not risk face or reputation by stepping in to bedevil the aftermath of a fairly established contest, so his deputy would be called upon to instigate such impropriety, thereby affording his master the luxury of sitting back and enjoying the violation without implication. It was a shrewd maneuver from his dark and devious perspective, yet he would be a fool to assume that I would stand idly by and allow such an unwarranted incursion to take place without reaction.

A heavy chain fell to the compacted ground with a thud and then immediately clanged and clattered while being dragged along speedily behind one of the massive beasts as it plunged heedlessly down from its position atop the crater's flaring brim. The remarkably agile creature easily negotiated the substantial drop and maintained excellent balance upon landing, whereupon it immediately darted along the rugged arena floor and savagely advanced toward the honorable boy. In the meantime, the second raging monstrosity was more than bothered, to say the least, as its tether remained tenaciously grasped while it lunged forth and shrieked in a raging frenzy. It could scarcely be held back, notwithstanding the notably powerful grasp of Certasus, and so it too was liberated in short order as a burly chain was released of its constraining buttress. At once, I positioned myself into throwing position, with Maleabar clenched firmly and with a focused conviction. Then, unexpectedly and all of a sudden, petrification ensued as distraction got the better of me and Noxerus surreptitiously caught me with a spell. The boy would get no help from me. I watched helplessly while the first of the charging anomalies converged.

Cristofo, contrary to the most conventional of logic, turned to face the menacing monster and spontaneously began to sprint forth in an effort to meet with it dead-on. Blackish and knifelike teeth presented themselves as the creature pounced with voracity while unlocking its massive and boxy jaw. I must confess that for the moment I could foresee the boy's entire head being chomped upon and gulped in one fell swoop, forfeited as a snack to the ravenous mongrel of enormous proportion. But lo and behold, the little rapscallion surprised me yet again as he slid underneath the up-surging underbelly while pulling out his own trusted throwing knife, all but forgotten but still readily at hand and cozy in the customized sheath of his ox hide boot, thereupon proceeding to slash away forcefully at the beast's tough and hardened midsection. The exceptionally sharp earthly blade could do little more than scratch the surface of the creature's nonpermissive shell, yet for some reason, as the wild and demonic brute pivoted angrily in a second attempt to dispatch its prey, it dropped down unexpectedly and at once—bereft of breath, lifeless. Do not be confused, for there was no luck or supernatural occurrence involved in the cessation of the ominous beast. Instead, it was the severely potent mutophasm venom that could be credited for abruptly ending the unpleasant ordeal, not to mention the skill and quick thinking of our esteemed young wizard, I might add. A half-dried sticky residue lingered stubbornly, clinging to the steely handle and blade of the boy's reliable half-pounder, which was smothered and drenched, thanks to his sodden woolen lining of boot.

With no time to rejoice in the triumph of conquest, Cristofo righted himself forthwith and readied for the second savagely advancing creature. However, this time he would be alleviated from the requirement for yet another brilliantly orchestrated display, as my temporarily imposed paralysis was successfully overthrown and Noxerus's efforts to stave off my meddling could no longer keep hold. Maleabar was launched with force and aim true, and the device was predictably unfailing as it modified shape while flying toward its surging and bloodthirsty mark. A vacant core manifested itself about the remarkable staff as it transformed into a hollowed-out and cylindrical projectile with an acutely thin, sharp, and resilient perimeter. The formidable implement barely suffered stagnation of speed as it plugged fully through its target, coring out a perfectly rounded portion of dense, grayish, and hardened mass from the chiseled skull of the attacking mongrel. A substantial void now remained where once the top of an all-powerful jaw met with a crown, and what was a ferocious, vigorous, bestial creature an instant before was now slumped down to the ground ineffectually—a ruined bulk of lifeless matter sprawled carelessly about the weathered crater floor. Certasus remained there for an instant, aghast and brimming with rage as he stood atop the craggy ledge that overlooked the all-too-familiar stomping ground, devoid of pet and wanting for retribution.

Cristofo readjusted his posture in an effort to maintain balance as the furious behemoth plunged down into the depth of the industrious cavity, landing harshly and triggering a vigorous rumble that dispersed instantaneously as it passed underfoot of the boy. Wide eyes gushed forth from the sockets of a startled young Cristofo, and a desperate leap ensued, narrowly preserving him from the flattening blow of an immense and forceful club. Once again, the ground shook vigorously from the force of impact. The boy grappled for proper equilibrium as the mighty bludgeon was raised anew. A fresh scar was brought to pass upon the battle-worn surface as a decisive indentation lay there proudly, its periphery shimmering of newly tilled scree. A furious Certasus swatted away with force and vigor, creating gusts of wind that whisked and wafted about our budding wizard of quality as he scampered and swayed deftly until finally managing to distance himself sufficiently from harm's way. Never before had a creature of such enormity shown itself to be so swift and skillful in the eyes of the boy, who now stood in advance of his aggressor and remained confident, in ready stance, with throwing knife securely in hand.

"It is no skill-less hollow battler you face before you now, meager boy of Earth, nor senseless and savage pet. Let us see how well you fare in opposition to the true champion of this land and superintendent of the strata one, two, and three." The words barreled out of the boorish barbarian with a course and amplified loudness and with a foreign discourse still wholly incomprehensible to the boy, yet still he managed to perceive the brunt of the words. However, it mattered not, as no response was forthcoming, for words were not deserving of utterance and action was more befitting the circumstance. A throwing knife responded in lieu of ineffectual speech, set to flight with potency as it zoomed upward en-route to the behemoth's solitary and aberrant eye. An awkward whack of club somehow ended the threat with ease as the surprisingly virile giant batted the projectile away.

Certasus then nimbly leaped forward in a continued and uninterrupted motion while raising his bulky weapon of choice overhead and proceeding to bring it down eagerly with the boy the intended target and with the full strength of a powerful two-handed stroke. The blow may or may not have hit the speedy sidestepping boy; it was too close to estimate. Moreover, it was of no consequence for the moment. The substantial weapon clanged stiffly upon impact of an unperceivable and immoveable dome of protection, conveniently conjured by yours truly. By then, I had begun a fast approach toward the commotion, with the full intention of ending the contemptible and tiresome display.

"Stand down at once, you dastardly and disreputable monster!" I uttered with an aggressive cyclopean slur, and Maleabar concurrently reappeared in my hand. "Lest you face a similar fate as your impulsive and barbaric quadrupeds."

"Your shallow commands have no power or basis in this distinguished realm, prime wizard of the weak and mushy domains." The behemoth retreated a few paces as he voiced the disparaging words, giving semblance to a dissatisfactory withdrawal, "You and the boy present little challenge for the elite of the nether land, as we would quash such soft adversaries with ease. And that is a proclamation for which I will now gladly give a lesson." An unexpected smack of club immediately ensued, not a direct strike aimed at our position but a simple yet forceful swat upon the terrain planted strategically a short distance at our forefront. Stable ground gave way, convulsing and then crumbling underfoot as it swallowed us whole and sent us reeling into the bowels of a voracious and deep-rooted void. A furious reaction was spawned, and Maleabar was competently and at once thrown down. My hands then opened forcefully, inciting the remarkable material to spontaneously expand and latch onto the cavity's durable bounds. A resilient netting arrangement conveniently yielded to our harsh impact before springing up with a snappy elastic force that propelled us out of the sunken hollow and flung us high overhead of an arrogant and overconfident Certasus.

Cristofo touched down cleanly on the adjacent firmness of ground, where he could do little more than make his way downslope in an attempt to retrieve his displaced throwing knife in the distance. On the contrary, I would take charge of the situation at hand, rightly so given my seniority and efficacy in dealing with such foes. Only a wizard can hope to oppose another wizard, with scant exception, and to be frank, I relished the opportunity. Challenge of battle sometimes brings a pleasure of unique value wherein the possibility of defeat can provide for unparalleled exhilaration. And so Maleabar returned to my capable hand as I hovered momentarily overhead of the startled behemoth before letting fly with the device, aimed off target and slightly askew.

Certasus dismissed the substandard hurl and surged forward with ominous intent, but little did he realize that the offensive was not at all insufficient; aim was intended and not at all untrue. Maleabar swung round and circled the stampeding brute, taking form of a stringier ropelike apparatus as it twisted and looped around the creature swiftly and with frequency, entangling appendages and frame as it concluded flight and met up with my anticipatory grasp. Then at once, a swift pull was applied, slackened bonds tightened, and malleable material turned stiff and rigid as steel. The constricted abnormality was then toppled with ease, falling steadily yet unequivocally like a towering superstructure detached of foundation.

A hard thwack brought forth a soft tremble as the mighty giant came crashing down with clout at the edge of the newly conjured aperture.

Certasus tensed his body with a fuming rage with aim of bursting the tenacious binding, and all the while, I concentrated intensely to keep Maleabar steady and unbroken. However, my hard effort would seem to provide little recompense for the moment as the wriggling and writhing barbarian became of lesser concern. Hordes of armed and able sentinels poured into the notorious crater with zeal, while Noxerus stood with poise atop his throne-like arrangement of a chair on the edge of the prominent stadium, where he conducted the flow fervently and with a passionate flair. Cristofo looked on calculatingly while backtracking to my position with throwing knife now retrieved and held in hand.

"Quickly, boy, to my side," I called out with urgency as the onrush swelled and came near.

"Remain calm and motionless," was my command as I settled on the hardness of floor and conjured with an intense fixation. Just in time, a thick, imperceptible, and impervious dome met with a buffet of blows as frames and weaponry alike hit down with malicious intent. Rugged arms pummeled and pounded, while massive swords and spears clanged and clattered and pried and heaved as the chalky skinned defenders endeavored to overturn our refuge with the aim of apprehending both the relatively untrained boy and myself. Shackles of bulky and dense design were toted by several the relentlessly advancing sentries, implying that confinement in lieu of annihilation was the ultimate goal, yet still the undertaking would assuredly include harshness with little qualm toward the infliction of injury and pain.

Certasus burst free of his bindings as Maleabar was absent the benefit of my focused attention. Shrapnel-like bits and fragments discharged with explosive force as the device's rigid configuration reluctantly gave way, hewing down a number of the ardent sentinels who worked away industriously while endeavoring to upheave our impervious shelter. Portions of sheared anatomy and gobs of gluey innards spattered upon our transparent stronghold as Cristofo looked on in bewilderment and as I endeavored to maintain strict focus. A pounding wallop then befell, shaking the understructure of our modest covering as fists like anvils came crashing down with repetition; Certasus was now upon us and was clobbering unrelentingly.

Deeply did I delve into the annals of my mind, where distraction was a distant triviality of negligible concern. A hard and thick husk was solely relevant, an impenetrable fortification with roots planted profoundly as though unified within the uncompromising bedrock. Powerful fingers pried their way between solid ground and conjured dome, lifting with a Herculean effort but failing to achieve the slightest of shift, as my strength of mind proved undeniably sound. Soundly it prevailed as the hulking goliath switched his strategy and gave turn to his monolithic bludgeon of choice, which delivered dynamic blow upon dynamic blow, testing the very limits of my stubborn tenacity and determination to maintain a firm hold.

Time is a whimsical notion; on occasion, the briefest of moments can bear unequivocal value, and now and again, an abundant quantity can bring naught save emptiness and futility. The former truism would now come to relevance in our tale, as the limits of my resolve had begun to draw near and as Noxerus happened toward. Then at once, and without warning, a blinding flash impressed itself into the turmoil of the scene, and then another and another still came to pass as a volley of clamorous blasts struck down with destructive clout and an assorted quantity of sentry men sequentially burst into the air—shattered and damaged products of the prolific discharges.

Attention then turned toward the source of the outbursts, and in the moderate distance, an extraordinary sight came into the range of view, speedily advancing and on approach toward the edge of the illustrious crater of interest. All were baffled as to the identity of the oncoming attacker, except Noxerus, who suddenly took on a most bothered and dispirited mood. It was by way of my beckoning that the commanding creature came to intervene upon the precarious situation at hand. At first hint of Ceratusus's disquieting presence, a wizardly summons was concurrently transmitted, a communiqué that was acknowledged and answered with fierce swiftness.

A dense and ominous cloud hovered overhead of the nearing entity, an utterly dark and dreary mass of modest size that imposed a sense of gloom even in such a place where gloom persists as the mean. Rainfall descended with violence upon a sleek and saturated form that became more discernible by the moment as it converged with haste. Raven-black hair lay flattened by the weight of drench, the sculpted cascade flowing full down the being's striking and curvy backside, where a splendid scabbard of sword buried itself in comfort, an exquisite and capable accessory deemed noteworthy enough to share the beauteous space. A tightly drawn suit of black cradled a delightful anatomy, now distinctly visible and noticeably animus by design.

Before long, the creature slackened pace and proceeded less hurriedly, taking on a calm and dignified poise as it came to settle upon the edge of the busy and brimming crater. Crowds gave a wide berth to the formidable figure as droplets fell with power and fizz, accumulating to form deadly puddles and pools that crept forth toward the huddled masses, who apprehensively retreated to safer spans. Still, the odd blast of lightning would be casually dispelled, with an offshoot of sentry men spewed forth in all directions. Then the discharges stopped altogether. The obliging cloud began to disperse and lighten its hue as it maneuvered overtop the crowded arena. A mild drizzle then descended with a light and delicate air, touching down with potency as coarse and chalky skin sizzled and charred; robust, strapping sentinels cringed and winced as they made a valiant effort to disregard the pain. The point was well made before the murkiness dissipated completely and a sense of relief overtook the besieging horde.

A luminous hunk of crystalline rock dimmed and returned to opaque upon its perch atop a braided staff of unique composition as a majestic figure remained there at the crater's edge with a silent congregation's focus and attention firmly in hand. Then a foreign-tongued assertion echoed with amplitude as it rebounded off the cavernous caldera's fully rounded wall. It was a sound wholly unbefitting the graceful and refined lips of its bewitching orator.

"Oh, how I despise this foul whereabouts of hostility and distress where the native tongue belches unpleasantly from one's mouth with a most crude and rancid spew. Ruthless barbarism remains as the language most readily understood in this forsaken place, and so I profess with a most rambunctious and lightning-based zeal, would you like to give ears to yet another chorus, my esteemed wizard Prime of the nether? A long while has passed since you last had the chance to appreciate the resounding melody of my illustrious and undiscriminating stone."

"Sing away, then, unwelcome wench of meat and bone," Noxerus shot back with a riled sneer, "for that cursed rock of yours may well bring devastation to half my kingdom afore my persuasive grasp takes hold of that sinewy little neck of yours. Aye, it will be worth it then to watch the light fade from your eyes as I send your spirit off on a long and arduous journey. Sing away, Bellatrix the divine of roxus-orbus, sing away!"

"Now now my fellow conjurer, speak not with haste but with the compassion befitting of a worthy king, for the continuance of your subjects depends on you at this moment, you and your consequent actions and words." An icy glare followed, boring its way into the crux of Noxerus's devilish eyes as our proficient wizardess struck down firmly with her staff. Light and life instantaneously returned to the dull fragment that crowned her curious scepter, and elsewhere and all around, a tempestuous dance ensued, wherein every molecule of moisture was drawn together to form an ominous accumulation once again. It was as though each sparse drop was summoned from the seemingly barren and arid surround, set to preparedness, set to unleash a lethal bombardment swiftly upon command.

"Grrrrrar!" Noxerus bellowed with a turbulent roar as he walked off disgruntledly while gesturing to his soldiery. Sentinels promptly cleared away from the impervious dome and made way methodically toward the bouldered exit. Only Certasus remained, stationary and sullen as Cristofo and I dispensed with our barricade and stood fast.

"Time will reunify us once again in battle, paltry little human of Earth; escape is but a temporary reprieve for creatures of lesser worth." The quarrelsome goliath calmly exuded the words from a stifled mouth that struggled to keep its true aggression at bay. I mostly ignored the words, knowing that the danger had dissipated at Noxerus's command. The boy, however, seemed to deem it necessary to respond.

"Time will not bring you favor when once again we meet at arms, you belligerent behemoth. Time will only bestow upon thee a more experienced and capable foe. What's more, a being's worth is an ambiguous variable, calculated differently among those who endeavor to calculate it. Until our next encounter, 'champion' of the land. Enjoy such title full well, for it is a distinction that surely exists for merely a temporary span."

Certasus grimaced with a fuming rage, much to the delight of the boy, as he walked off proudly with a smug smirk upon his face and a sense of satisfaction in spirit. Invigoration was restored, and thoughts of a well-fought victory came back to his mind as the promise of the prize once again nudged its way to the forefront.

"About my sword then?" Cristofo inquired in a tone much louder than required for my adjacent consideration yet much too soft to overtake Noxerus's distant ears, or so one would assume if one were a creature of more modest understanding. Therefore, a simple gesture was conveyed annoyingly and with indifference as our outrivaled netherworld king continued along, not bothering to turn or acknowledge the circumstance. Instead, a trio of sprightly chaperones then appeared and made their way toward our position, traversing fluently against the steady flow of retreating guardsmen. Indistinguishable though the creatures may have been, Cristofo did well to perceive that they were the same escorts as those that previously attended. The radiant threesome hovered alongside tolerantly as our graceful rescuer approached and made words.

"Well, I see that you did not misrepresent the splendidness of our youthful wizard of newborn rank, my venerable Prime. A finely developed form graces our esteemed descendant of Mother Earth, it seems. Yes indeed, Altarius, a soul ablaze with fiery virtue resides within this impeccable framework. Well discovered, my long-standing companion and friend, and cheers to the prospect of a lasting and favorable fellowship to come." A firm yet compassionate arm came down amicably upon the bewildered boy's sturdy shoulder as he stood there speechless and in awe. The figure before him was commanding, to say the least, replete of a fearless and comforting air. Like an infant pleasantly nuzzled in its mother's arms, Cristofo was silent and composed as he basked in the euphoric aura of the magnificent being. Beauty defined itself in the embodiment of our admired wizardess, and she too construed the term, defining it by way of her very presence and manner—a beauty not bound by fleshy interpretation alone but instead an all-encompassing variant that radiates from within and produces a truly rare and unique aftereffect.

"So, it is a sword you seek to secure, eh, my good Cristofo?" She now had both hands cordially placed on the boy's shoulders as she peered forthwith into his alluring eyes. "A nethersword nonetheless? Well played then, my youthful fellow, for mine has served me impeccably for nearly a millennium to date." An unexpectedly swift and fluid motion immediately followed the words, and an impressive blade presented itself to Cristofo for perusal, masterfully grasped and drawn spontaneously from an elegant backside. Glimmering eyes acknowledged the offering, while a succinct nod confirmed the gesture as Cristofo cautiously took hold of the unusual weapon. An ornate and bejeweled hilt burrowed comfortably into his skillful grasp, and a finely fashioned blade emanated forth markedly, moderate in length and black as the darkest night, with an obsidian-like scheme. It was a surprisingly airy device, much to the amusement of our newest compatriot as he rotated and swiveled the implement with expertness and skill.

"It's unbelievable, Altarius, so light and easy to manipulate. It's simply a pleasure to wield." The boy unnecessarily stated what his overall demeanor made obvious. "Is it as impressive when utilized to purpose—you know, hewing, piercing, and such?"

A lightning-fast motion responded in lieu of words as Bellatrix snatched the handle and hurled in one fell swoop. A soft thwack quivered through the air imperceptibly as the outlandish blade penetrated fully through the callous crater wall, a sturdy cross guard halting it with clout and preventing it from disappearing altogether into the solidified slab. Cristofo remained dazzled as he witnessed the event, which included a captivating retrieval.

"Return, Annabel," the intriguing enchantress commanded as she held out her hand in welcome. The magnificent sword extracted itself with ease and obediently reappeared into her grasp before being effortlessly restored to scabbard. The boy's mind was brimming with questions and queries, and just as the overflow began to spurt out of his mouth through words, I interrupted the impulsive tendency, taking full advantage of the perfect opportunity to initiate a more formal introduction.

"Cristofo my boy, I forever ameliorate your soul by introducing to you Bellatrix the divine, keeper of the rock of Tempestas and wizardess of the animus realm, and least but not all, friend and companion of unrivalled quality ..."

My presentation was abruptly cut short with a witty yet respectful snub. "Bellatrix will suffice for short, my gladly received young master. Our admirable Prime tends to overemphasize formality on occasion, whereas I prefer to acquaint in a more casual style. Come. Let us converse as we make our way toward the palace, where we will retrieve your prize among swords of comparable distinction to my treasured Annabel. Lead on, resplendent creatures of servitude and toil, to your master's personal cache as instructed, straightaway and without distraction." So, questions found replies, and queries were fulfilled as the three of us trailed behind our sparkling convoy, chatting and familiarizing, discussing and deliberating. And Bellatrix was not to be outdone, inquiring intrusively about Cristofo in equivalent turn as we made our way toward the towering palace entryway.

It was an opening, to describe it more accurately. No door, gate, or barrier of any sort barred entry into the fluid structure. The extravagant interior space was gouged out from the within of the mountainous arrangement, chiseled and hewn with painstaking and meticulous effort, until only the desired palatial ambience remained. Throughout the peculiar place, a grandiose atmosphere prevailed—not your typical stately and extravagant yet formal monarchial arrangement, but one that was darker, macabre, and foreboding. Nonetheless, a certain undeniable majesty persisted in the vastly arranged corridors, caverns, and coves, notwithstanding the uniformity of color and finish, for a darkened and polished stone like surface composed the entirety of ceiling and wall and floor. Fissures and cracks of older and more recent occurrence pervaded uncaringly and everywhere, mended with skillfulness and soldered with molten slag yet still discernible like a network of telling scars healed and fused to a degree but undeniable and revealing former separations, quakes, and faults. Sensational adornments lay widely scattered about, artifacts and sculptures, portraits and paintings, knickknacks and novelties, and decorative pieces of the most wonderful and unusual of kinds, flagrant and eye-catching as they lined the walls and walkways throughout the unconventional space, where they shared the limelight with the intermittent inclusion of on-guard and attentive sentinels.

Cristofo took note of every detail as we were led unrestrictedly along a number of ramps and passageways and as we moved ahead into the guts of the singular mountain structure, where sentry men became more densely arranged and where miniature streams and trickles of lava slithered and swayed downslope with an almost arrogant nonchalance. And the overall environ became increasingly dreary, until at last a dome-shaped enclosure revealed itself. It was quite sizable in breadth and towering in height as it lay there engagingly. A pair of sturdy guards displaced themselves, acquiescing to allow passage first for our luminous attendants and then for the three of us in turn. A dozen tall and narrow archways lined the circumference of the globular expanse, intriguing passages into subsidiary chambers of wonder and mystery, each lined with a pair of steadfast guardians and each with a teasing display of items invitingly dispersed as hints toward the classification of treasure that lurked within.

A twisted sculpture of some strange and unrecognizable figure lay upon a pedestal adjacent to one such curious door, surrounded by paintings and portraits of various unrecognizable types and forms. Gemstones, crystals, and hunks of precious metal and stone overlaid the surface of a monolithic table of sorts, which graced the entryway to another identical door. Lavas, strange claylike bowls, and urns of the stuff lay dispersed about another approach—glowing, bubbling, and frothy varieties of assorted tinctures, densities, and so on. A diverse collection of inexplicable items wainscoted the room: skulls and bones, body parts and fluids, devices and doohickeys, and all sorts of alien and undefinable items and things.

And weaponry, of course. A pair of lustrous swords flanked the opening toward which we were being relentlessly led, along with a spattering of spears and hammers and a sprinkling of pikestaff and shields. Cristofo eyed the aggregate with meticulousness as we were escorted through the exhilarative passageway and into the cache of our ambition, where a brief stretch of empty corridor ushered us into yet another alcove, a round and vaulted compartment of equal form to its precursive anteroom. Sprightly attendants desisted and remained in wait, emitting a most helpful and radiant offshoot of light, while Cristofo perused and inspected with intensity. At once, a spectacular sword caught the boy's eye, hanging there strikingly upon the rocklike wall, where it was precisely arranged on top of elaborate hooks with scabbard directly below and situated exactly counter to the entryway's arched opening. It was an apparatus of considerable size, much too large to be seriously considered in the mind of our young prizewinner, yet still he was drawn to it and remained overcome with a strange sense of affinity.

"What do you think, Altarius? 'Tis much too broad and lengthy, yet still it is quite superb, is it not?"

"All items that occupy this distinctive vault could be classified as superb, to say the least, but the choice of prize must be yours and yours alone, my young apprentice. I wish not to impact your decision in any way, but rest assured that I will give a final evaluation and opinion only after the determination is freely made. Evaluate full well and let your intuition be your ultimate guide."

Cristofo made an effort to heed my words as he glanced around and took notice of the various items that arranged themselves about the room, randomly dispersed yet somehow orderly and meticulously displayed. Bellatrix seemed preoccupied as she too perused, taking note of a pair of blades with similar composition to her precious Annabel. I, on the other hand, took a more subtle approach in my scrutiny, being careful not to show interest or favor to any specific blade or weapon of any type, thus minimizing the possibility to sway the boy in any way or manner. However, my effort was seemingly futile in any event, for he could not maintain focus or attention on any device save for the beguiling sword of excessive stature. Cristofo wasted little time considering the supplementary items that lined the hollowed-out and vault-like room as he proceeded toward the impractical yet strangely engaging broadsword.

An almost magnetic allure invoked the boy's right hand as it converged, cautiously at first as it neared and then abruptly grasping the silvery handle, which seemed adequate, notwithstanding its apparent mediocrity and general lack of impressiveness or visual appeal. The blade was then hoisted up rather effortlessly from its roost on a pair of sturdy and ornamental hooks, and then it was immediately brought down, its blade skillfully placed on its side and supported upon an anxious and vibrant palm. Cristofo gazed at the unusual blade, swiveling his head to and fro as he took in the entirety of its oversized length. It was a curious color of gray that was light and wispy but with an underlying and undefinable darkness that manifested itself subtly, like a budding yet burgeoning thundercloud.

"It's unbelievably airy for its size, Altarius, and it emits an almost innate sense of sharpness and potency. 'Tis chiseled and slightly serrated upon edge like Annabel, yet it's somehow different, obviously different in composition but different in essence as well. It is as though honed by the divine Altarius, a supreme blade of unmatched design right here in my presence, forged long ago and persisting through ages of loneliness, enduring the company of mismatched possessors, unworthy wielders who could do naught but dishonor her with their unworthy touch. But the wrongdoing ends now. Finally, mystical blade will conjoin with its intended companion, and never again will it lack for adventure. Never again will it endure inactivity, arranged complacently upon a callous wall within a dark and dreary vault inside a colorless dredged-out and hollowed palace, situated on a drab and dismal world. Never again!"

The boy heightened the intensity of his words as they progressed. Then his eyes pierced forcefully into a sprightly attendant, and the sprightly attendant inferred in turn, immediately snatching an invaluable helmet of sorts that happened to be situated on a nearby pedestal of stone. The seemingly ordinary handle softened as the boy intensified his grip, molding to conform to every nuance of finger and knuckle, wrinkle and hair, transmogrifying and coating the hand with a form-fitting and protective covering complete with cross guard and pommel. It stiffened, and then remained; the epitome of comfort fusing with hardness as Cristofo swung fluently and as a soft thwack was made salient while the enormous blade sliced through both helmet and the rectangular pedestal with ease. And a satisfying grin declared the boy's contentment as an angular cross section of the monolith lazily dropped to the floor.

"Well then, Altarius?" Cristofo requested with a childlike inflection that was both imploring and optimistic, as though an infant seeking approval to procure a newly encountered pet. A casual nod affirmed my acceptance of the choice. The weapon's uncommonly large size may have dissuaded me under normal circumstances, but the boy's powerful inclination toward the device could simply not be ignored. Furthermore, its lightness would more than offset the awkwardness of its size, and what more could one ask of a blade but to perform and cleave flawlessly apropos any and all object without dulling or requiring sharpening of any form or kind?

Therefore, with subdued glee, Cristofo threw down his newly attained prize, affixing it rigidly into the hardened bedrock with little exertion. He then looked to the scabbard, which appeared desolate and abandoned absent its counterpart but still seemed valiant as it hung on the callous wall. It was necessarily massive by design, plain and stone like in color, as though intending to mask the true remarkableness of its precious consignment. It flew off the hooks with the lightness of a feather as the boy held it up for a more comprehensive study.

Although rather dull and ordinary in appearance, the sheath was found to have a most distinctive characteristic; it was completely open along the entire length of its side. Cristofo found this peculiarity fascinating, knowing that it would exist by design since such a treasured commodity would simply not identify with any type of flaw. Two looped straps with a decorative chain-like appearance flung themselves about wildly while their newfound proprietor swung the scabbard into position and watched them flail through the air and lash about with a power equal to that of a fluffy strand of yarn. With his right arm, he yanked at the implanted sword and withdrew it with ease from the rigid and unyielding bedrock upon which it was secured. And as the two separate yet corresponding components were drawn close with the intention of sheathing, they snapped together with magnetic force, unexpectedly, violently, and passionately, like a pair of forlorn lovers reunited at last after a long and unsought segregation.

"Well then, my good companions, I do believe that our business here is done." Cristofo took a moment to fasten his newly acquired prize, ensuring that both straps were tightened firmly and securely. One was fixed snuggly under his armpits and tied soundly above the top of his chest, while the other was anchored similarly but in the more common location of the waist. As he finished his task, he remained quite simply in a state of delight as he stood there sporting an invaluable new weapon, a device appearing to be most awkward and cumbersome as it ran along the boy's backside, near three-quarters the length of his unmitigated and tallish span, yet it nestled against his spine almost weightlessly, as though a paltry load of insignificant burden.

"I do believe that I have had my fill of this foul place for the time being. Let us return to my homeland at once and without delay, for my worthy loved ones are in need of comfort, all on account of that vile beast who blemishes the essence of the common characteristics for all those who hold claim to the rank of king. Indeed, matters remain quite unsettled between my attempted enslaver and me, but the time for restitution will inevitably come to pass. Maybe even sooner as opposed to later should we happen to cross paths in short order now that a glorious sword serves to bolster both my efficacy and confidence—a sword whose first deed under my charge may very well be to strike down its former proprietor!"

With that, Cristofo boldly took the lead as he scuttled onward through the vacant corridor, paying no mind to the sprightly attendants and employing a decidedly quickened pace. Bellatrix and I exchanged a terse and unsettled glance before following in haste, darting out preparedly into the more sizable and sentinel-laden anteroom, where guardians sprang to ready positions. Startled by the sudden advancement, they anxiously arranged themselves into a hold position while remaining primed with sword and spear. A smug look revealed our novice young wizard's enthusiasm as he reached back and uncoupled his newly acquired and yearning-to-be-utilized sword. Resilient defenders of the monumental palace stood fast and remained unruffled despite the fact that Annabel was also unbridled; Maleabar was also readily arranged. That particular moment, however, would not afford the boy familiarity with his newfound sword in battle as the three shimmering custodians diligently intervened, appeasing the loyal wardens of the treasure chamber and prompting them to unconditionally stand down. Noxerus had made his instruction clear, and his triad of sprightly attendants would ensure strict adherence in that regard.

A sense of relief came over the boy, perhaps in conjunction with a touch of dismay as he reached back to re-sheathe his magnificent weapon, whose handle readily receded from its protective encrustation of hand and returned to a more modest display. Its blade snapped harshly into place of its mated scabbard at the very instant that the two compatible items approached and drew near. At once, the boy resumed his quickness of pace, rushing down and around the various ramps and passageways with ease as he navigated back through the murky palace interior until exiting out into the equally drab yet considerably more expansive outdoors, with Bellatrix and I utterly and unequivocally right upon his heels.

"Where to now? Lead on to the nearest gateway, Altarius. Or, Bellatrix, perhaps you can discern a more convenient portal."

"Indeed I can, my good Cristofo," my splendid and more alluring counterpart interjected with certainty as she glanced in my direction and dispensed with a gesture of acknowledgment. A subtle nod revealed the fact that I concurred, and none too soon, I might add, as Noxerus, Certasus, and a bevy of other assorted and belligerent followers began their approach from a not-too-distant standpoint.

"Haste would be favored, Bellatrix. I sense that something is amiss," I compelled our extraordinary wizardess, who wasted no time in slamming down her proficient staff with impetus. At once, the miraculous stone on its apex turned aglow, awakened with vigor from its dull and somber repose as the crystal-like fragment hurriedly gathered up and harnessed vast amounts of air from all around the arid and mostly constricted surround. With a furious swirl, the atmospheric gases began to advance and whirl in an effort to create an excessive and volatile span of wind. Noxerus and crew were taken aback by the forceful gusts as they passed through and advanced to the forefront of the angrily advancing congregation at the behest of their omnipotent rallier, creating an effective distraction and affording precious moments of time, moments well utilized as Maleabar was transfigured into a convenient disc-shaped vessel.

"Hop on board, Cristofo," I declared resoundingly as the gale-force gyrations of wind pressed firmly against our hair, clothing, and skin. An instant afterward, we were airborne. Upward we soared with remarkable speed and equilibrium, riding on the cusp of the torrential air currents yet remaining curiously balanced and settled with Bellatrix at the helm and her mighty Tempestas energized and generating vast quantities of unadulterated power.

A desperate volley of arrows and spears were aggressively hurled with destructive intent, but they readily became deadened and disenabled, thrown off course and tossed around haphazardly like so many leaflets scattered adrift by a healthy and cleansing burst of autumn wind. Noxerus, however, would not be so easily deterred as he and Certasus promptly gave chase mounted on a pair of robust vespertillions. These vigorous bat-like creatures were commonly used as carriers in the nether strata number three, complacent critters of extraordinary composure and velocity, with stiffened, glassy, and angular wings jutting out in a perfectly triangular symmetry. They suffered no stagnation in speed as they vaulted along at an exorbitant pace, although the unluckiest of the pair did seem to lag to a minor degree as it was saddled with our colossal club-wielding and raging cyclopean opposer.

In seemingly no time at all, our pursuers were within striking range. Bellatrix readily unleashed blasts of pounding wind, but to no avail, for the balanced and well-laden vespertillions resiliently maintained their course. Noxerus veered onward in an attempt to situate himself at our forefront, while Certasus cast his mighty club with full strain and from a lower position, swinging his enormous arm around full circle until letting the device fly with impetus and bolstered speed.

Aimed straight and true, the enormous truncheon barreled forthwith as it headed directly toward us. With no time to spare, I skipped back onto the edge of our makeshift aeronautical apparatus and took hold of young Cristofo while impelling Maleabar to transform immediately. At once, a considerable hole manifested itself into the device, expanding outward from the center of our soaring disk as it mimicked a centrifugal impulse, absent the generally required spin.

Ceratusus's malevolently launched missile-like projectile shot through the newly conceived hole in our craft and continued on up into the limited span of sky, where it soon after collided into the gyrating understructure of the surprisingly near-at-hand yet more altitudinous nether strata number two, impacting and embedding itself into the doughy semi-molten material as we looked on anxiously in our unwavering and now–halo-shaped vessel. The stubbornly pursuing cyclops maintained his upward course as Bellatrix continued to navigate us higher and higher, riding forth on the cusp of a powerful and uninterrupted tailwind and thrusting toward the outlandish bounds that separated and bordered the adjacent layers two and three. A narrow yet obvious opening was her aim as she veered to the horizontal for a moment until continuing to ascend through the permissive rift and into the considerably more sweltering and phosphorescent strata number two. A brief deviation to retrieve his implanted club cost Certasus little distance as he followed through the aperture with swift ferocity.

At once and seemingly out of nowhere, Noxerus soared into view at the head of our position, and a sinister stare shot down at us with potency as it was delivered with no less effectiveness than if a spear hurled with vigor and striking dead on to the eyes of our fair flier. Bellatrix handily absorbed the blustering gaze and returned one of equal weight as she decelerated and made good use of her magnificently adorned staff, discharging violent bursts of lightning that flew straightaway and struck directly on target. Our malevolent opponent and his exorbitantly winged yet competent ride became instantly engulfed in the electrifying bursts of powerful current, both seeming to be temporarily immobilized yet at the same time strangely bolstered as though absorbing the impacts with eagerness and appearing almost invigorated while harnessing the energy's tremendous potency.

At our capable wizardess's behest, the almighty Tempestas reassembled our forceful tailwinds, and in a flash upward, we fled, following alongside the flank of a rugged and precipitous yet oddly smooth flowing mountain structure. Herein lay our goal, a scarcely visible opening nestled within a sizable indentation on the steepness of a slope—a wormhole brought to light by way of a divine swipe of pickax upon the mountainside, to describe the anomaly in terms that would better depict it and make it more evident and clear. And as we flew along taking full advantage of Noxerus's temporarily imposed paralysis, Certasus happened dangerously near.

Swiftly I prepared myself for action as pulsating waves of energy were channeled toward my steadied extremities for immediate discharge. However, I was suddenly forced to desist, and my forthcoming burst of energized matter was discontinued altogether as the well-formed figure of our presumptuous young wizard passed precisely in front of my aim, leaping off our stable foothold and lunging heedlessly down toward our advancing cyclopean foe. Stone-gray scabbard unlocked the full way down its length as the boy's steadfast hand took hold of the silvery handle of his newfound sword. A firm yet snug encrustation overspread his grasp synchronously as the impressive nethersword was unsheathed and a far-reaching weapon of severe potency took form: an intrinsic and unified extension of his capable and battle-ready arm thirsting for its first taste of conquest. Now although it would certainly not be my preference for our relatively unseasoned apprentice to grapple with such a qualified adversary, I found myself unwilling to interfere in the overzealous attack. Perhaps my curiosity took hold given that the boy had consistently surprised me—or perhaps my exceptional tutelage shone through as I determined that the circumstance should unconditionally play itself through. Nonetheless, I remained uninvolved and impartial for the most part, limiting my influence to a slight modification by way of Maleabar as a tensile strand was concurrently brought forth and lassoed around the boy's drifting and airborne ankle.

A welcoming grimace met Cristofo dead-on as the boy bounded down with breakneck speed and deadly aim, aligned and unswerving like a bolt of arrow on a collision course with its intended target as a perfectly executed swing came down upon the unyielding goliath, struck skillfully and wisely from the advantage of a higher and more balanced position. However, Certasus presented no ordinary objective; the accomplished battler and second-in-command would hardly fall prey to such a transparent offensive, nor would he be found bereft of experience in dealing with the efficacy of an exceptionally well fashioned nethersword. And so the massive club was brought to bear with uncanny swiftness and scheme, striking precisely upon the edgeless face of the momentous swipe of blade, knocking it aside and impelling the boy off his course. A quick twist and flip granted our brazen protégé time enough to reestablish equilibrium even as he continued along on the abrupt descent. And with the benefit of remarkable dexterity and with the service of a truly exceptional sword, he managed to slash fluently and effectually upon the frontward flank of the behemoth's superlative ride.

An ear-piercing shriek overspread the surround as the severely wounded vespertillion swerved and pivoted in desperation, but the damage had theretofore been done. A jagged segment of dissevered wing coasted unassumingly down as the sizable beast fluttered and cawed in a last and frantic effort to retain awareness. Gobs of glutinous fluid exuded from the deep laceration on the creature's side as it surrendered breath and body, leaving the latter to plummet precipitously down while necessarily bringing its appalled and maddened rider along with it. Cristofo's free fall was handily arrested as his ensnared ankle succumbed to the springy clutch and abrupt recoil of magnificent material. The fantastic vessel upon which he was secured wrenched him forward with speed as Bellatrix heightened pace toward our goal. Just then, he laid eyes on Certasus who had elected to relinquish his ruined transport in favor of a harsh and substantial vault down on the steep and unyielding mountainside. The unruly giant swiftly shook off the coarse impact and began to scramble up toward the wormhole with urgent fervor. As the boy shifted his glance in favor of our forthcoming objective, he noticed that we were virtually upon it and that our momentum had slowed as we approached the strangely symmetrical aperture. His pliable snare had all but flung him back on board.

"Cristofo, to the wormhole straightaway!" I bellowed at the boy just as he began to reestablish footing onto our provisional craft. It was a desperate effort to incite the boy toward the portal and his freedom, for once again Noxerus had plans to the contrary, and once again I would be charged to provide a much-needed blockade. Unexpectedly, the unrelenting beast converged to within striking position, enlivened and energized as he approached bestriding his equally invigorated and noticeably maligned and aggressive vespertillion. Somehow, the crafty devil had managed to absorb and store the abundant potency of Bellatrix's vigorous discharges, and with sadistic joy, he let fly with a sweeping blast that was designed to encapsulate our entire position. With excessive strain, I planted firm and braced myself for the onrushing burst, raising arms and positioning hands to bolster the transmittal of an intense force field, one that struggled to repel the tremendous forcefulness of Noxerus's billowing thrust.

Bellatrix swiveled as she impelled our vessel to slow on approach along the mountainside in an attempt to prepare us for dismount. "Make a break for it, Cristofo, right now!" she blared as she turned to face our threat and to provide an infusion of much-needed aid. Cristofo adhered to the command, taking a few lengthy strides as he arranged to leap off the transport's firm deck and onto the oblate ridge at the foot of the wormhole.

Unanticipatedly, the three of us were all caught unawares as Certasus vaulted onto the opening's foothold and a savage blow of club struck forthwith upon the bow of our makeshift craft, abruptly halting our forward momentum and throwing both Bellatrix and me altogether off balance. In the meantime, Cristofo had been propelled more vigorously toward his goal, as he had already begun his vault at the exact moment of impact. A sudden wave of debilitating current then took hold of us and our airborne vessel as the distraction threw us off our focus, and as a result, Noxerus's offensive managed to break through. Numbness permeated throughout the core of my being, an immobilizing radiation that rendered me all but frozen. Bellatrix was caught in the irradiant web as well, suffering a similar inability to break free. I worked hard to overcome the unrelenting surge of electricity, but alas, I came to realize that the task was too formidable and that freedom, for the moment, was wholly unattainable.

Through the haze of excruciating discomfort, my eyes beheld that at once a sharp jolt took hold of the boy, who had just become airborne yet remained linked to the gripping current through the remarkable material still bound about his ankle. However, one with such a resolute spirit would not so easily succumb, despite the tenacious grip of the crippling surge, so the previously drawn sword was difficulty swayed and the strand of remarkable material was cleanly dissevered. Cristofo was liberated from the electricity's tenacious clutch as he continued with his prior upsurge and overleaped the ample and agile frame of Certasus. The belligerent behemoth took hold of his club in a frantic effort to halt the unwanted exodus, but his swing was decidedly hampered by an impeding obstruction of Maleabar's design as I was able to intervene, barely mustering a final exertion of power. A graceful landing upon the portal's sculpted approach then ensued, immediately followed by a fluent and sword-first leap into and through the circular opening. All at once, our young apprentice had disappeared. I felt a reassuring contentment on account of his liberation—a sensation replete of comfort and one that ushered me to dimness just as my senses faded and unequivocally submitted to the dark.

CHAPTER 7

An Overwhelming Aerial Surge

An abrupt landing ushered our newly declared wizard back into his native domain. His earthly- based senses awkwardly reactivated with an intermittent zeal as though resetting themselves to acclimatize to the formerly familiar surround. Gasps of breath fought hard to fuel conforming lungs as stagnant and foreign air was slowly replaced with a more agreeable mixture, helping Cristofo along as he struggled to regain his bearing. The faint scent of smoke was first to creep its way into his perception as consciousness inevitably was restored. Eyes opened to a blurry haze of murkiness and soreness took hold as the boy made an attempt to right himself from the noticeably stiff and rocklike substructure while coughing and wheezing almost mechanically. His firmly clenched fist still held an eager grasp on the magnificent nethersword, which jutted out awkwardly and at length, with its handle still encrusted and forcibly overlaid. Cristofo loosened his grip, and the tenacious covering receded forthwith, releasing the blade and freeing his hand to facilitate a much-needed straightening.

In the near-at-hand distance, muffled bursts and blasts became audible as obvious and frequent explosions of significant magnitude somehow weakened and waned before reaching the boy's acute and now rejuvenated earshot. Heavy billows of smoke drifted while darkness was fully actualized and not just a function of his debilitated sight, as our novice young realm jumper attempted to stand but was impeded forthwith by a moderate slope underfoot, the apperception of a cramped whereabouts, and by an awkward stumble on account of a tenacious obstruction, the likes of which was immediately inferred.

"Maleabar, illumination!" was the command coarsely blurted from a recovered but still gasping voice box. At once, clarity was shed upon the uncertain situation at hand as the modestly sized segment of remarkable material obediently exuded a healthy glimmer, and a factory borehole was unmistakably deciphered as the boy's current circumstance.

Many a time would he find himself romping about within the variously positioned and symmetrical tunnels, cavorting and exploring as a carefree child with a curious mind and an insatiable spirit. In this particular instance, an early evening's bearing on the great timepiece of inexplicable origin was inferred based on intuition, orientation of footing, and more specifically, degree of incline. Cristofo reestablished his balance while maintaining a slightly crouched-over position as he carefully sheathed his nethersword and decisively prompted Maleabar to unbind itself from his ankle, reconfigure, and relocate to a more convenient station around his sinewy wrist. Then he anxiously made way toward the outward facing mouth of the proportional borehole, grappling through the blurring obscurity of lingering smoke and the worrisome intensification of detonating blasts.

The boy quickly emerged from his cylindrical locality, stepping down from the broadened and fractured mouth of the imposing passageway and onto a heap of fragmented rubble, a startling indication that he had just narrowly missed a forceful strike upon his secluded landing place. Desperately he drew in much-needed air, gasping emphatically and with importunity as though surfacing from an inexplicably lengthy submergence in a vast and unfamiliar sea. A long and restorative breath consummated the effort, taking precedence over the shower of blazing cannonry that descended relentlessly and widely upon the far-reaching range in advance of the factory's expansive entryway. In the meantime, a barrage of fiery and explosive arrows and a bombardment of catapulted ordnance shot up in reply, a countercharge of immense proportion that completed the task of irradiating the cover of a shadowy dusk sky. Cristofo looked on in amazement as his coloration spontaneously returned to its familiar and healthy beige hue; his vitality was necessarily restored to its usual remarkableness. He took a moment to study and contemplate the startling situation at hand, and in that moment, an unimaginable measure of information was surprisingly revealed, inciting a sharp and biting sense of vexation as the boy came to realize that a completely foreign and dominant aerial attack had devastated the man-made infrastructure leading toward the all-important factory, not to mention the presumable loss of countless men and soldiery.

And what of his beloved Myrina? How he yearned to clamp her tightly in his inflexible clutch and feel the rousing press of her shapely frame and the reassuring pulsation of her precious heartbeat as it resonated against his firmly pressed chest. The assistance of his newly befriended wizardly compatriots would certainly be of great benefit, but he feared and felt that this too was unrealizable for the moment, as they had disastrously fallen prey to the unrelenting imposition of capture. All at once, the boy dispensed with his dispiriting thoughts and sprang into motion, expertly negotiating the various drops and declivities that delineated the trajectory down the mountainous ridge and unto the crowd of bustling Nephashan battalions and infantries.

A considerable degree of dodging and weaving was required as Cristofo snaked his way around the multitude of foot soldiers and archers while progressing through the dense arrangement of squadrons and brigades that were strategically scattered about the assorted blockhouses and fortifications that secured and safeguarded the approach to the celebrated factory. Indeed, much had changed from the early days of the monumental discovery when our old friend the alchemist happened upon the strangely housed stockpile of explosive powder. Long since, the industrious manufactory had evolved into a mammoth operation of enormous proportion, harvesting and refining vast quantities of the desirable material and processing it into salable products of various categories and kinds. Fire sticks, of course, is where it began. A perfected formulation ultimately took hold, and then cases and crates, and eventually cartloads and wagons full doled out the commodity with brisk frequency, thusly inciting a partnership with the king, which in turn bolstered growth to an unfathomable degree. Commerce and governance naturally became of regal concern, leaving the magister free to focus and formulate, design and devise. For once the relatively simplistic fire stick was perfected, both passions and pocketbooks looked to more fulfilling concerns.

Within a matter of seasons, a diversity of explosive weaponry was being churned out with regularity—coveted devices with no shortage of buyers, all of whom were agreeable to the hefty price tag, a small premium to pay for the peace of mind that came with such effective deterrence against all potential aggressors. A full array of products with differing potency and size ensured satisfaction without exception. The basic design was brilliantly simplistic: launchable shells encasing a quantity of explosive powder, the ignition of which was regulated by a slow-burning and inextinguishable fuse. The fuse itself was the most critical component, requiring the lion's share of the magister's effort to develop and perfect, the final version of which consisted of a thin paper-encased tube filled with powder and wrapped with a waxy chemical mixture to prevent external exposure of the burning core. Length of fuse and/or density of powder were modified to adjust for the duration of burn. The resulting product was a powerful projectile that could be launched without restriction, without worry of smother, and with a perfectly timed detonation, all initiated, of course, with the utilization of the indispensable fire stick.

Slings, catapults, bows, ballistae, spears, and simple hurls or tosses were all implemented to set the disparate assortment of detonative contrivances in motion. Stationary designs were also sold with volume, catering to those with a more industrious mind-set, their pursuits much facilitated by use of controlled blasts and explosions. Substantial purchases were frequently made by cities and towns, boroughs and hamlets, and colonies and communities who held a penchant for mining, tunneling, demolishing, burrowing, and the like. In any event, a sizable number of institutions from far and wide would needfully expend a good percentage of their financial resources on the invaluable products. Both industry and perseverance were in mind, thus vaulting the bustling town of Nephesh into the forefront of richness and power, with the magister and his family naturally following in the path of the meteoric rise.

"Ho there, brigadier!" Cristofo blurted forth upon making approach toward one of the king's battalion commanders, who staunchly oversaw the sizable assortment of factory workers and king's guardsmen that banded together in defense of the staggering onslaught. The engrossed veteran turned indignantly, disturbed from his toiling as he dispensed with orders from a makeshift command station at the edge of the expansive factory's approach. "Status report?" Cristofo continued in a necessarily loud tone as he leaned into the ear of the weathered serviceman in an effort to overpower the deafly loud resonance of bursting ordnance. The strikingly capable officer dispensed with his irritated tone straightaway as he turned and recognized the source of the interruption.

"Master Cristofo! From where did you emerge?" he uttered in surprise but with a pleased undertone; the young aristocrat was well known and respected among the court of officers and governors who knew of the boy's remarkableness and of the eventuality of his future reign. "The status is grim, young master. Our defensive efforts are futile. We haven't the range to impact the outlandish vessels of strange design. Our sentries first spotted a pair of the contrivances just as the shade of dusk had begun. Scouts, I imagine, who aimed to inform themselves of our geography and of our defensive capabilities as a number of their explosive projectiles were let fly. Within a brief period of time, a swarm of them was upon us, dropping devastation and death the likes of which you now see the latter portion of."

"Cease fire!" the resilient commander exclaimed as he passed Cristofo a pair of field glasses and veered off while instructing his lieutenant to spread the command. The invading fleet had seemed to reach the end of its bombing run, and the defensive countermeasures served little purpose anyway, except for lighting up a portion of the rapidly darkening sky. Cristofo peered through the convenient oculars and at once confirmed what he had previously inferred while watching the unfamiliar airships from his perch on the mountainside, where he observed a good measure of detail, thanks to the bombardment's offshoot of radiant light. Mechanically altered beasts of flight; thusly did the boy presume to characterize the individual components of the unorthodox armada, and thusly would he portray the strange vessels to his father and/or grandfather, hoping he would find them without delay, conveniently sheltered within the factory's impervious lookout, a hollowed expanse carved from an outcropping of stone some dozen paces or so above the towering entryway.

Each peculiar member of the menacing flock imparted a most ominous and sinister display, with a bulging saucer-shaped form and darkened scabrous coverings akin to that of a tortoise shell, the top and bottom portions of which affixed to each other with an obvious fissure-like seam. Two sets of cylindrical protuberances poked their way through the noticeable seam and dangled below the exotic craft like awkwardly fitted appendages, where they revealed a mechanical peculiarity as steely components outthrust back and forth in a dynamic effort to send off bursts of artillery. Jagged and sizable teeth were viewable, giving semblance to a gaping cavity of mouth upon an otherwise thick protrusion that jutted out from their foreparts like husky consolidated masses of head and neck that swiveled clumsily and randomly with an organic mien. Wingless, they sailed across the targeted position as a soft blue effervescent discharge emanated from their tails, a means of propulsion wholly unfamiliar to Cristofo at that time, yet still he held astuteness enough to conclude that the contrivances were indeed unearthly and from a more advanced progression of design. The outlandish airships were most certainly piloted, for atop the resilient husk-like framework, a transpicuous bubble-shaped nodule appeared, modestly sized and camouflaged to a slight degree yet still plainly revealing of an obscured operator.

Meanwhile, at the location of Cristofo's forthcoming objective within the spacious factory antechamber, an assortment of hirelings and wage earners scampered about, some still diligently manning their posts and tending to their affairs and others more apprehensive and jittery as they jostled around confusedly. They didn't seem to know whether to loiter about the chamber's opening in an attempt to view the precarious situation outside in the open air or to withdraw into the potential safety of the numerous compartments, nooks, and niches within the fantastic enterprise. The majority of the assemblage consisted of women and those of inappropriate age and healthfulness and of those who lacked in the characteristics generally required to take up arms and engage in a defensive effort. In any event, all unquestionably shared in the commotion and confusion of the moment, observing and taking note as Cristofo dashed through the space hurriedly with the wholly conspicuous and seemingly cumbersome nethersword bumping and bobbing against his backside. When he reached the end of the stretch, he bolted up the considerable staircase that led to the guarded watchtower.

"Father!" Cristofo exclaimed as he spotted his esteemed guardian in the near distance. He hurriedly weaved his way through a handful of guardsmen stationed in the lookout's relatively spacious anteroom. Deep thought and deliberation had monopolized the factory's troubled overseer, who paced back and forth as he contemplated the current circumstance, a peculiarity passed down from his own father, the magister. Others of elevated status bustled around, advocating and elucidating as they intermittently took turn peering out of the watchtower's mediocrely sized rectangular porthole, a thickly framed aperture carved through the mountain's impermeable crust where visuality was imposed upon the exterior surround while maintaining a reasonably sheltered vantage point. On each flank of the distinctive opening, well-made viewing devices with state-of-the-art lenses poked through small holes in the precipice, where they swiveled fluently to afford an intensified and more detailed view. Officers, administrators, and the like were all tactfully ignored by their respected director as they interjected, advised, and opined. All the while, he maintained an undistracted and introverted focus, until his deep concentration was welcomingly broken by the resonating cry of his treasured firstborn.

"Cristofo! Thank the sun and stars you're all right, son!" A measureless sense of relief befell the boy's father as he locked his arm in salute and then enthusiastically pulled his son in for a vigorous and much-needed embrace. All the turmoil of the present circumstance dwindled away like the breezy afterthought of a frivolous dream as the proud father took a step back and inspected his esteemed offspring.

"Well now, you look slightly worse for wear, son, but still in good shape, vibrant and healthful, to say the least. It befits you well and brings warmth to my core. Now what of this endangerment about which your grandfather refers? An abduction no less? Strange and hellish creatures appearing from thin air? If not for the blemished and broken state of your dragons, the account would not be so easily believed, or so your grandfather disclosed after attending the whereabouts and speaking with your admired female companion."

"Myrina? How is she, Father? Grandfather frequented the scene of the spectacle? Thank goodness for that! Well then, how is she, Father, and where is she? And what of Cimtar and Somnia? Have they been tended to? And Iggy as well? The poor creature fell adrift for lack of powder and touched down far afield of the circumstance, marooned somewhere in the sea of untamed grassy meadow."

"She's fine boy, just fine. You needn't trouble yourself about her constitution. She's back at the palace being tended to, where the worst of her suffering can be ascribed to you and her apprehension regarding your well-being and whereabouts. As for your dragons, they too find themselves back at home being cared for in the comfort of their man-made habitat. They were more grievously injured, but not beyond amelioration, at the capable hands of their qualified caretakers, or so the magister informs me. As far as Iggy is concerned, there was no indication of the creature's whereabouts. It had been assumed that he remained in your company or that he would be sought out eventually when time was more plentiful and the circumstance less critical."

"I need Iggy, Father, sooner as opposed to later. And where is Grandfather? I need to speak with him straightaway."

"He's down in the testing room with the fabricators. They have in mind to make operational our prototype tubular launching devices with hope that they can be actuated without delay and utilized against these foreign foes."

"That's a well-deliberated plan, Father. I shall go to him forthwith. And Mother and the twins? I assume they're still safe and out of harm's way in Sienoro with the sales contingency?"

"Aye, my boy, or so we hope. Little do we know of the extent of this strange invasion. I say it is fair to assume that they remain oblivious and unharmed, but still, messengers have heretofore been sent by steed. And what of this babble about wizardry and wayfaring and such? Where is our esteemed Altarius, anyway? Had he not taken charge to come to your aid? His involvement brought much solace to both your grandfather and me."

"Father, we have much to discuss. Meet us in the testing room when the occasion allows for your leave … Sentry!" the boy bellowed to the most decorated guardsman in the vicinity. "Have word sent to the princess. Tell her that I have surfaced and am of good health and mind. Tell her that I will call on her as soon as an opportune moment arrives."

"Yes, master Cristofo, straightaway," the obliging officer acknowledged, but he was halted in his effort to break off and carry on.

"And as far as Iggy is concerned, take a score of men with four wagons full of powder and no shortfall of torch. Ensure that the contingency constitutes at least two men from the magister's convoy from earlier on in the day and have them lead the way to the bank of the rivulet where the princess and our dragons were previously found. From that standpoint, navigate exactly eleven and a half stades in the direction west-northwest. Be precise in your calculations and note that you will find yourself in the middle of an open meadow. Begin here with your dispersion of powder and progress outward until Iggy is found. Have each wagon attend to a quadrant and have a rider ready to call for more powder if need be. Make haste, for I want to be reunited with my fiery companion this night."

Off the loyal sentry man went, beckoning to a pair of fellow journeymen, who in turn followed behind as he vigorously marched through the anteroom and proceeded down the adjacent staircase and out into the expansive factory lobby area in an earnest effort to carry out his charge. Cristofo, in the meantime, took leave of his father and proceeded toward the innovative though secluded and restricted testing room.

"Oh, and by the way, son," the director added before his boy could get very far, "what's with that monstrosity of a sword? Did you pillage and loot a giant's lair somewhere along in your travels? Please dispatch with that bulky encumbrance and fetch yourself a proper brand from the armory."

"Father, as I've said, we have much to discuss!" was the boy's reply as he smirked and turned to recommence the brisk pace toward the whereabouts of his respected grandfather.

"Yes, much to discuss indeed," the director whispered to himself as his boy had formerly run off and he had slipped back into the somber mood of the lookout tower and its rambling occupiers, who had gravitated toward their venerated leader like a swarm of bees clustered about their queen. He re-immersed himself into the turmoil of the moment as the undesired load of obligation and responsibility bore down on him with the weight of shackles and chains.

Divert to the factory's testing room, a massive whereabouts stealthily tucked away a short stretch below grade and a good distance from the busyness and bustle of the dynamic goings-on that persisted day to day in the industrious manufactory. Digging, dredging, boring and burrowing, sifting, sorting, carting and carrying, filtering, refining, mixing and measuring, and so on and so forth, ground away the limitless moneymaker that was the jewel in the crown of the marvelous city of old that was Nephesh. It was a cold and indifferent mass of strange and foreign stone brought to life by the flowing swarm of bodies and beasts teeming through every orifice and vein as they worked systematically and to no end in an effort to perpetuate the enterprise; lifeblood without which only lifelessness and indifference would remain. And at the core of it all, an aged but far from withered heart beat with fervor as brilliance was brought forth once again, and a wrinkled face tautened under the stress of an insuppressible smile.

"Gentlemen, come quickly!" The excited voice echoed through the vast chamber-like the hull of the factory's renowned epicenter. "I believe it should work toward its purpose. Call for the casters and mold makers to begin straightaway with prototypes." Technicians and testers broke away from their concentrated workings in turn and made way toward the monolithic wooden worktable in the farthest corner of the expanse. It was a resolute fixture that had endured many a year's toiling and trials, notwithstanding innumerable spills and burns, let alone countless poundings and bumps, scrapes and scratches, and smacks and dents as trial upon trial came to pass and as invention, model, and prototype alike traversed the unbending worktable to be subjected to the critical and scrutinizing eye of the city's most famous and revered alchemist.

Down the hall, a half dozen more or less unremarkable instruments passed across Cristofo's path as they were being ushered along hurriedly by a convoy of attendants and marksmen while he concurrently made his way down the tedious incline that led to the guarded laboratory. Unremarkable, I say, in that you would expect more girth and complexity from a device that was touted as the most advanced innovation of its time as far as weaponry and items of warfare were concerned. With hopes of making obsolete the bulky, cumbersome, and tedious to make ready catapult, these tubular launching devices were being mobilized to their inaugural utilization against the unusual attackers who rained down destruction and devastation from the refuge of distance, high up in the sky. Hopes were high, as was desperation, for the assaulters would certainly return in droves, and nothing in the city's working arsenal could furnish proper deterrence. To imply that the contrivances were wholly untested would simply serve as fallacy. The rockbound northern wall of the expansive testing room could attest to that, along with its pitted facade and rubbly base of loosened debris. Not even a fortnight had passed since one of the devices was brought out into the open air, where umpteen launches were undertaken under the watchful analysis of the factory's foremost of scientific minds, the magister himself included.

Overall, the weapon was found to operate satisfactorily and a general sense of contentment pervaded the assemblage. At last the typical, rounded and explosive projectiles could be fired competently and with frequency, propelled by the combustion of a quantity of powder and discharged through the shaft of a heavy steel tube. Now, granted that the contrivance was indeed quite simplistic in concept, one could still rest assured that the intricacy of detail was exhaustingly weighed. The optimal length of the barrel in proportion to the diameter of shell—the exact quantity and composition of powder to be used for the propulsion of the shot, taking into account that the convention powder required much tweaking before the possibility of detonation upon firing could be confidently discounted; the ingenious addition of small jagged chunks of lead mixed into the powder which would be released en masse upon ignition to create a formidable spray of lethal particles when considered in conjunction with the fragmented portions of the burst casing of steel; these variables and more were heavily tested and deliberated before the ingenious invention could be extolled. Yet two things remained unsettlingly in the mind of the magister. Firstly, the timing of the fuse left much to calculation with regards to controlling the detonation. Secondly, distance was still felt to be suboptimal. The relatively cumbersome catapult was indeed to be successfully replaced; however, the range of impact was not substantially improved.

"As you are all well aware, the typical spherical design of our launched projectile can be quite effective, albeit lacking in its relentless pursuit toward escalated distance in flight. This new design, however, will combat the unrelenting hindrance of gust and breeze." The boy's ingenious grandfather rambled on with ease as the crowd of eager listeners swelled and as Cristofo advanced upon the setting more or less unnoticed. "Three distinct parts will comprise the device. At its front, as you can see, a conical shell leads the way, cutting through the air with a much-reduced stagnation of speed. And within the thinly walled casing of steel, our explosive and destructive admixture is enclosed, lingering calmly in anticipation of its eventual and tumultuous release. But that isn't all, gentlemen. Note the inconspicuous nodule at the very tip of the nose. This mechanism depresses upon impact, triggering an abrasion of flint and steel and thus igniting our charge. No longer is the lighting of a fuse required prior to the launch, and in addition, the delicate complexity of timing the blast becomes a burden no more!"

Cristofo gleamed with pride as he listened to his admired forbearer, knowing that a marvelous creation was spawned from his excellent mind yet again. Still, he realized that the invention, although sound and constructively practicable, would be insufficient in and of itself to ward off another concentrated aerial attack. He listened on nonetheless with a contented smile and a bolstered heart.

"The middle portion of the device serves a most rudimentary purpose; a cylindrical housing accommodates a quantity of propellant that in turn combusts consistently to provide a steady and forceful thrust. And what ignites the propellant? you might ask. Well, that brings us to the third component of our invention, where the same contrivance found at the front of the shell is duplicated to serve purpose at its aft; immediately upon impact, the encasement will drop down and percuss onto the bottom of the cylindrical conduit, initiating the depression of the starter nodule, creating spark and consequently igniting the propellant, which will in turn incite the launching of our fleeting projectile. What's more, these three fin-shaped attachments will serve to stabilize flight and maintain the trajectory straight and true." Chatter and buzz initiated and was interchanged as the cluster of invigorated colleagues weighed in, every one of them excited about the product and each with their own idea on how to optimize the particulars and technicalities of design. "Very well then, my good collaborators, work out the details at once, for I require an assortment of working prototypes put forth without delay."

"Cloud Cutter, eh, Grandfather? A fitting name for yet another impressive invention!" Cristofo infused the compliment from his subtle perch at the magister's rear as he looked over the intellectual's slightly hunched shoulder and considered the familiar precision of his meticulous schematic, the heading of which was scrawled below.

"Cristofo, my precious boy!" the magister exerted with force, barely managing to contain his euphoria at the sight of his treasured grandson as he bounded off his chair and administered a vigorous embrace. "Ha ha, what a relief to hear your voice; it's only a working title, my boy, but never mind about that for the moment. Are you all right, son? Here, let me get a good look at you!" The overjoyed ancestor retreated a pace or two and scrutinized his grandson's commanding frame. "What a sight for exhausted old eyes! Come, boy. Let's sit and share drink while you tell me all about it. Are you hungry? Bascomb, send for some cheese and bread forthwith," he abruptly instructed one of his nearby colleagues. "The rest of you go to your work stations chop-chop." The ecstatic patriarch incited young Cristofo along the room and in the direction of his lounging area, where comfortable chairs flanked a small serving table and a crowded bookshelf and brimming storage chest brought up the rear. "And what of Altarius? Did he not meet up with you and assist at the scene?"

"Come sit, Grandfather," Cristofo urged invitingly as he took to his seat rather awkwardly while adjusting the obstruent nethersword.

The magister rummaged through his storage chest for goblets and a decanter of wine. "My goodness, boy, that's quite the sword you've come across. Would something more conveniently sized not be more to your style?"

Cristofo held off on replying, instead choosing to unfasten his treasured new device while his grandfather set up the glasses and poured. "Here. Take it, Grandfather, and try it out for size." The boy handed over the substantial broadsword, still resting in its scabbard and with no hint toward its legitimate bearing.

"Oh my, 'tis much too weighty for my aged and rickety old bones," the magister offered semi-jokingly before taking the instrument in hand. "Let's have a look-see then." He took hold of the weapon forcibly, in anticipation of a more resistant load. At once, he sidestepped in an attempt to recapture his balance, as he had postured for a hoisting of a different kind, and then a pleasant astonishment immediately took hold.

"My word! 'Tis indeed miraculous. It's enchanted, wizardry no less. I'd wager that Altarius played a hand in this magnificent bounty."

"No, Grandfather. Well, kind of, in a way, but not really," Cristofo began to explain, but then he remained silent as he watched his grandfather unsheathe the magnificent sword enthrallingly. He continued to observe as his grandfather's eyes swelled, his grasp inciting a protective encrustation of hand.

"What an outstanding metamorphosis. It feels so natural and inspiriting." The magister then proceeded to support the blade on his free palm as he evaluated the extraordinary weapon with care. He slackened his grip and reveled at the fluidity with which the durable coating appeared to recede back into the substance of the broadsword, and then he reestablished his grip and watched attentively as his hand became wrapped in the wondrous material once again.

"Outstanding! I may have to confiscate this weapon for a while, my boy—you know, in order to fully evaluate its capabilities and so forth." The seemingly unformidable old-ish frame of the magister danced around incongruously as he emitted the words, spinning, lunging, and thrusting away with the skill of a seasoned swordsman half his age. Slashes, strikes, and parries abound as the enraptured scientist lost himself in the majesty of the remarkable sword, bolstered by its incredibly liberating airiness.

"Ha, careful now, Grandfather. You wouldn't want to strain yourself or dislocate any of those rickety old bones of yours."

"Oh, hush now, boy. Your grandfather was quite the capable swordsman in his day, as I'm sure you are already aware."

"Yes, Grandfather, and so I've heard on more than a few occasions," Cristofo quipped jokingly.

"Oh, really? Did Altarius share any anecdotes on the subject, pray tell?" the magister inquired curiously, wanting to know.

"No, not a word was said about the subject, but much of interest was thoroughly discussed. Please relinquish my blade and sit; we have some important business to discuss."

"All right, son, all right." A more serious tone established itself in the comportment of the wise patriarch, who immediately braced himself for potential concern. "Let's have it, then," he requested as he handed back the nethersword and took to his chair attentively.

"It's nothing terrible, Grandfather. Bring an end to your serious tone," Cristofo retorted reassuringly, easily perceiving the unfavorable aura in his grandfather's mood and smiling in an effort to restore some cheer. He took back his blade agreeably and lobbed it with the greatest of ease, paying no mind to its course as he knew of its aim. The magister's eyes bulged with disbelief as he watched the incredulous blade land just next to the serving table, impaling itself a good distance within the inflexible bedrock.

"My word," the astonished elder managed to utter. "Such incisiveness has no explanation in this world. It is indeed an enchanted blade."

"It certainly is, Grandfather, wrought with an enchantment of an unfamiliar kind and with fabric and skill native to a wholly extraneous place. It was afforded to me as prize—the purse, in a manner of speaking—for a contest of battle." Cristofo began to explain about his preposterous adventure during the most recently transpired measure of time. "You see, it was another world from which I effected escape, a strangely dissimilar place with strangely dissimilar creatures and a strangely dissimilar quality. To be sure, it was a totally different realm of existence that was the terminus of my unsolicited abduction."

"Go on, boy, go on," the magister incited as Cristofo took pause in his dialogue to partake in a quick swig of wine. The velvety attribute of the drink enlivened the boy's palate and jolted him into a stark revelation; he had experienced no appetite for food or drink, nor had he desire for rest or recuperation of any kind since his early morning rise and moderate breakfast. Even still, after an assiduous day of exploits and undertakings, he lacked for thirst, hunger, or repose of any type or kind. This realization struck the boy as curious since he would usually indulge in the significant consumption that would be typical for a growing boy of his stature and age. Little did he imagine that trivialities such as sustenance and slumber were no longer to be of concern, for in the capacity of wizard, one is nourished and revitalized sheerly by will of the overseers. From that day forth, only when time and circumstance conveniently obliged would the boy gratify his penchant toward the most basic of earthly compulsions. And to that end, he quickly caught on as Bascomb approached the vicinity and laid down a hefty and inviting platter of cheeses, meats, and bread. And although the display was utterly inviting, no craving or wanting desire established itself within the boy.

"Why, thank you, Bascomb, this is much appreciated," Cristofo offered to the hospitable company deviser.

"You are quite welcome, Master Cristofo," the loyal staff member returned, along with a respectful nod.

"Yes, yes, many thanks, Bascomb. Now back to your drafting table on the double; much work is to be done, and time is of the essence. Hop to it now." The magister all but shooed away the loyal researcher as his grandson nibbled a small portion of cheese and bread while donning an uncertain look on his face. The mouthful was indeed enjoyable, yet still there lingered perplexedness with regard to his lack for appetite.

"All right, then, my boy, you were saying? A different realm of existence? Go on, please, son—don't leave me hanging with anticipation. I'm nervous enough already, as you are very aware."

Cristofo began to make clear the transpirations of earlier in the day, opening with an account of the vascolumen demons hatched of a thunderous blast from an incongruous cloud.

His grandfather looked on with intensity as the boy went on to describe the creatures' unworldly abilities, the ensuing confrontation, and all of the commotion that led to his eventual capture and conveyance back through the maleficent cloud and unto a dissimilar world.

"It was such an unusual sensation, Grandfather. I felt an all-encompassing, suffocating heat—not the typical radiant swelter as you would expect but more of a firm and consolidated kind. It was as though I was frozen numb within a continuous mass of the stuff, if you will excuse my use of the contradictory term."

The boy's enraptured grandfather urged him on from the edge of his seat. "My goodness, child, go on. What happened next?"

"I was lost within myself. There was only darkness and fieriness and nothing else. My senses were inoperative for the most part. Lungs brought not breath, and my heart scarcely fluttered, yet still I knew that death, although predominantly represented, was not fully upon me."

"Unfathomable! Please continue. I only interrupt from anxiety. How did you overcome such horror?" The magister struggled to absorb the recounted hardship of his treasured kin.

"There was a flicker of light! A flash of sentience in an otherwise hopeless transfixion. And from thereon in, awareness painstakingly was restored."

"Altarius," the astute elder said in a whisper, "but how could you persist in such a foreign environ? It flies in the face of logic that one could breathe of unearthly air or that their very core could subsist in a place of disparate physicality—the gravity, pressure, electromagnetism, and so forth—all of which can wreak havoc on the body in such deviated and disproportionate forms ... but of course!" the magister reckoned as he said the words out loud. "Wizardry and witchcraft, no doubt, Altarius must have taken you under his wing and protected you from injury."

"Well, not exactly Grandfather." The boy wrestled with the correct terminology. "Yes, Altarius was indeed invaluable in effecting my rescue and safekeeping but ... you see ... I was able to subsist in light of the fact that—"

"Naturally!" the magister decidedly interrupted. "You are in truth a genuine wizard!"

"Why, yes, Grandfather, that is correct, but how ...?" Cristofo was caught off guard, for he did not expect that deduction to be forthcoming, not even from the likes of such a formidable intellect.

"Now now, boy, don't be so taken aback. Altarius confided the fact to me last night after you had gone up to bed."

"I had no idea that you knew; I was struggling to find the words to explain, while ...all along you knew? And what's more, you became aware well in advance of my being informed? Is Father aware as well?"

"Aware of what, exactly?" The resounding voice cut into the conversation as the connecting member of the outstanding line of succession promptly encroached himself onto the scene, where he proceeded to corral himself a goblet and pull up a closely placed chair. "Never mind. You can tell me later. First, we must discuss this unexplainable onslaught," the earnest director pronounced matter-of-factly as he thirstily maneuvered the half-full decanter of wine.

"We have not been singled out in this unwarranted offensive. Noise and blasts of cannonade have been observed in the direction of the palace, and so it seems that our aggressors have a more ambitious design that encompasses more than just our simple factory."

"Or perhaps they are well aware that it would be impossible to overthrow the factory without defeating the royal soldiery, along with the entire city, for that matter," Cristofo returned with a heightened state of vexation. He worried not about his fair Myrina, for he knew full well that she would be safely harbored within the comfort of one of the many strongholds strategically dispersed within the belly of the monumental castle, but still the incursion brought him much consternation—a feeling that would generally give cause for the boy to take immediate and appropriate action. And he would have done so forthwith were it not for the damaged and downtrodden state of his dragon. For the moment, the boy would have had to patiently hold firm. That is not to say that he did not already have another game plan in mind. Indeed, it would be no easy task to accomplish what his dauntless judgement had outlined, and he was anxious to get started with the undertaking. But for this, he would first have to wait for the reappearance of his cherished companion, Iggy.

"Well, in any event, there are a few certainties with which we will have to contend, two at any rate, upon which the cabinet and I summarily agree," the boy's father continued with a grim and somber tone. "First off, the invaders will most certainly deliver another air raid of equal if not more intensified weight. And this time a ground advancement will necessarily follow, for surely they realize that bombardment from above will only go so far against the impenetrable mark of mountainside. If our humble little factory is the prize to which they aspire, then they will have to enter within and fight on equal footing with all who stand firm to defend her. The palace, on the other hand, and more so the entire city, would be much more susceptible to an airborne offensive, where falling explosives would have a most devastating impact and where the consequent sweep of a ground invasion would most logically follow in the advantage of the aftermath."

The magister broke free of his silent contemplation." "And the second certainty, son? What might that be?"

"Well, that brings us to the all-important question, Father. How do we fare regarding our tubular launching devices? For the other certainty upon which we can all agree is that there is currently no measure or method available for us to deter the aerial onslaught. At the moment, all we can do to prepare is dig in and wait. And this is certainly not reassuring by any means."

"Yes, not reassuring indeed, son," the magister replied almost under his breath, as though biding time while preoccupied with his inner thoughts, which were being instantaneously churned and contemplated in turn until his more coherent sentiments could be properly formulated and disclosed. "The outside of the factory is to be completely abandoned. I see no need for our men to be sacrificed needlessly like sitting ducks. Clear out whatever items are of value in the exterior structures and let these confounded wretches bomb to their hearts' content. Let them bring the fight to us in here, where we will be waiting with a multitude of eager men and with no scant share of explosive surprises."

"But, Grandfather, we know nothing of these alien foes ...," Cristofo began to interject, but he was untypically cut off with a harsh and abrupt reply.

"And they know naught of us as well!" the magister vociferated fiercely, with a most startling pounding of fist. Then he immediately calmed down. "Sorry to display such a sharp reaction, Cristofo. Believe me when I tell you that my anger is intended toward them, not you, my boy." The magister then continued with his usual excited yet more levelheaded tone. "Have all six tubular launching devices sent to the palace, where they can be positioned as the commanders see fit. A dozen wagons full of powder shot to accompany should suffice in enlightening our eager attackers as to the fact that Nepheshan resolve is not to be so lightly weighed! And to answer your question, my boy, the launching devices most certainly will fare quite adequately, and depending on how much time we have until the next offensive, our unnatural invaders may just learn to dread the foul taste of Cloud Cutter as well!"

Both Cristofo and his father listened appreciatively and with respect as the magister spoke with command. The wise elder was highly regarded by both of his exemplary descendants, an indication of high honor that was well earned through years of hard yet courteous upbringing and by virtue of his measureless examples of genuine foresight and guidance.

A terse silence afforded Cristofo the opportunity to opine. "I believe it would be of benefit to set up small bases around the mountainside as well. Not randomly dispersed, of course, but strategically placed about the handful of boreholes that share orientation with the factory's approach. From each of these six standpoints, a trio of marksmen with slings and bows can instill substantial hindrance to any form of ground invasion by launching our most lethal and destructive shots and then retreating to the cover of the borehole in proper sequence."

"Yes, yes, that would indeed be advantageous," the magister agreeably concurred. "They could store a good amount of munitions in safety, a number of paces back into the crawlways, where there would be no danger of detonation from incoming fire. Make sure they anchor themselves with enough security rope to make possible a successful retreat to within—should the need arise. But I don't have to tell you this, son: my intention is not to micromanage. Go on and send forth instruction and let's be done with this matter, for Cristofo has a story and news of a most fantastical nature to relate."

To that end, the director summarily called forth his ardent associate, who had been tolerantly lingering at attention just inside the testing room's outspread and otherwise unguarded archway.

"Buonapart," he beckoned rather succinctly and with only a moderate heightening of tone. At once, a strapping and able-bodied whip of a man trotted forth with enthusiasm, employing an adequately brisk pace as though he had been biding time and listening attentively.

"Yes, Director?" was the man's simple and singular reply as he stood there fastidiously with a studious and concentrated focus, absorbing the bevy of instructions that the director barreled forth flowingly in an articulate and precisely clarified mode.

"Oh, and one more thing, Buonapart." The fleet-footed attendant was barely halted in time, caught just at the onset of his accelerating spring. "Be sure to have a convoy dispatched to the palace, via the undisclosed byway, of course, bringing details of our intentions and plans. The royal carriers are certain to be encountered en route, as reciprocal messages will be pressingly forthcoming in return. Call for me at once as the king's messengers approach and have them escorted to the watchtower, where they will report directly to the cabinet and me straightaway."

"Aye, Director, I shall make it so at once." And just like that, the loyal Buonapart was gone like a flash.

The boy's father turned his focus to the platter of foodstuff and to his eager-to-be-emptied goblet of wine. He rejuvenated his previously imposed interruption while munching with a distracted demeanor. "Now then, boy, to what end do you inquire about my awareness, exactly?" And then he abruptly put an end to his mastication, propping his chin upon bolstering arms and attentively laying focused and fixated eyes upon his treasured firstborn.

Cristofo took center stage as he barreled out a most eloquent recounting of his adventures and exploits on that which was a most unusual and unimaginable of days. His adroit adherence to detail did well to alleviate the impulse for either of his forbearers to find cause to interrupt with either aim of question or request for clarification. Instead, they remained enchanted and enthralled for the most part, with the magister scarcely managing to suppress his excitement as he maintained a tense and jittery posture accentuated by the shameless stare of wide and childlike eyes. The boy's father similarly affected a focused silence, one that contrarily gave way to a calmer and more motionless demeanor, with unblinking eyes voraciously absorbing the discourse. Overall, it was a most enrapturing recounting, one that was able to carry on uninterrupted for its entire rather lengthy duration, due mostly on account of the fascinating turn of events but with no small betterment owed to the boy's natural ability to narrate and to hold his audience firmly at bay. A most wizardly quality in its own right, I most certainly must concede! A healthy silence accompanied the verbal account, affording the eager listeners a much-needed interlude with which to digest the unfathomable recapitulation and make it palatable to their unreadied minds. The magister was first to come around and break the silence.

"Well then, Cristofo, I have so much subject matter upon which to inquire but let us begin with the most important point in question. Are we safe to assume that Altarius and this female wizard of which you speak—Bellatrix the divine—have both been taken captive or, worse yet, been done away with at the hands of these foul creatures?" The boy's grandfather had a myriad of inquiries in mind, but none so pressing as would be his concern for such a highly regarded acquaintance—one that had saved his skin on more than one occasion, I might add. Not to mention one who had just risked pitfall and peril to extricate his most valued kinsperson from a most precarious circumstance. Nonetheless, it was quite heartening to know that the thoughts of one with a truly radiant soul were with me and my unforeseeable well-being.

"Not done away with, Grandfather, of this I am most certainly aware. Don't ask me exactly how I know, suffice it to say that I can feel it inherently as it rings forth from the very marrow of my bones. But captured yes, without question. They are being held forcefully and within only a wisp of being aware, of this you can be sure."

"I see," the magister acknowledged with a pensive nod of the head, which in turn progressed into an empathic glance toward his son. "In that event, we must dispatch a special convoy forthwith. Son, make ready a small squadron of our best warriors while I accommodate myself with a proper coat of mail and an appropriate accessory of steel. Cristofo, I don't suppose we can keep you out of this pursual? Make whatever arrangements you deem fit and prepare to lead the way toward our decisive recapturing! You do know how to get us back to this forsaken place, do you not, boy?"

Cristofo paused briefly in advance of his fitting reply, a necessary discontinuation that served to appease his enthusiastic grandfather and give fair warning to the forthcoming denial.

"I think I do, Grandfather, as do I think that you know that your accompaniment is altogether infeasible. The portal will simply not accommodate whatever form of man, woman, or beast that you would have in mind to chaperone me on this substantial quest, a burden which I gladly welcome with the full weight of obligation."

"But, Cristofo, you mustn't go alone! I forbid it. Your wizardly companions will manage sufficiently on their own. Need I remind you of your recent overpowering and abduction at the hand of those otherworldly fiends since it is yet so fresh in your memory? We'd not be having this conversation were it not for Altarius and his matronly counterpart. You'd be, well, let's just say … in a most unthinkable situation."

"Now that's not necessarily true, Grandfather, although I do not make light of your concern. And I won't be alone. I'll have Iggy with me, as well as my sensational sword, not to mention a notably dynamic fragment that I carry along enthusiastically while safekeeping it for a friend. What more could a boy ask but for such high-ranking company on such an intrepid and worthwhile quest? And besides, the argument is entirely in vain, for only I can achieve passage through the gateway, so either I go alone or our highly regarded captives are left to fend for themselves."

The magister desperately sought to find cause to deter his obstinate grandson. "Are you absolutely certain that Iggy is adaptable to the opening as well?"

"I am certain beyond question," was the boy's immediate reply. "In fact, my intuition screams to the fact that my loyal companion is altogether befitting to this distinctive domain."

"Well, don't just sit there in silence, Tiberius. Talk some sense into your son!" The wise elder knew that the effort was futile, yet still he carried on with a last-ditch effort of words intended to bolster support from his son.

"Father, much time has passed, and much has my son sprouted and matured since his eleventh season, whereupon I learned without fail that it would be of no use to attempt to dissuade him. Do you not recall that abnormally bitter winter's eve when our stable hand was found slain and our outbuilding lay absent our tetrad of rare and inestimable gorallions? What purpose came of my forbiddance then? And what end was served by my persistence and by my eventual confinement to his room for that teary-eyed and unbending moppet who howled and screamed insistently in an effort to run off and initiate a search forthwith?"

"Yes, yes, I do recall it all too well," the magister reminisced with inspiriting pridefulness. "The king's detail of a dozen men had combed the surround at full length during the whole of that bitter and biting night while you and I were up till the wee hours, troubled and tormented by the unsettling ordeal. And we were all none the wiser to those happenings in the dark until dawn broke and Timalty came to rouse us in a fervor, ushering us to our iron-willed boy's room, where a gaping door exposed the unforgettable image of a cozy and peacefully sleeping Cristofo nuzzled up against an equally tranquil and snug Brunella. The little cub's parents and sib were reposing well in the comfort of their agreeable stable, while their murderous abductors lay bound to nearby softwood, fractured and broken to no small degree and frozen to within a wisp of breath. To this day, the mystery remains as to the transpirations of that unnerving and chilling night, a turn of events perpetuated and safeguarded exclusively within the tenacious mind of our unparalleled descendant."

The magister laid eyes upon his reticent grandson as he finished speaking, initiating a not-so- subtle effort to draw out the episode. It was the most recent of umpteen prior attempts, yet again his endeavor had failed to evoke naught of his target, save for an evasive and inward smile. Cristofo carried on with his guarded silence, displaying a casual and apathetic air, but all the while, the genuine occurrence replayed itself in his mind with the all-too-realistic detail of an unforgettably riveting theatrical performance. The savage, biting wind was like fire upon his unguarded visage as he raced through the proximate and vast woodland with the burn of anger and the vigorous surge of blood coursing through his veins and sufficing to keep warm his less than adequately clothed frame. His keen eye made quick work of discerning the villains' path of escapement, for it was a trail none too easy to conceal in light of such a bulky and cumbersome haul, especially when under scrutiny of one with such a gifted and innate ability to perceive. Neither the wispy blow of cloaking snow nor the random, scattered arrangement of fallen branch or broken twig could serve to sway the boy from a proper chase. He saw the reckless footpath that lay in hiding under the shadow of that grim and tempestuous night, and he followed unrelentingly with a pace more befitting that of a beast in its fierce and hungry pursuit of sustenance, as opposed to that of a simple boy who held aspiration to personate a man, with proper heart but insufficient physicality. Suitable footwear and ample mitt accompanied the young lad as he slipped out of his bedroom window while still sporting his insubstantial nightwear and armed solely with steely determination, a moderate length of plaited rope, and his weighted and best-liked baton.

Time wore on into the dead of night, steadfast in its relentless and unwavering course as Tiburon danced along its prearranged path in the trail of twilight and as Tamar entered the scene with its quarter moon shine and ample light. All the while, the boy ran and ran with an equivalent pace and a decisive plight, knowing the forbearance of the gorallions in hurried flight. Soon enough, he apperceived the chase's end as tracks came to be less covered and prints arranged themselves decidedly less spread out. And so, he primed his mind for the approaching clash, quickening pace as he accommodated his reliable baton; the sturdy press of the rigid leather-wrapped shaft of consolidated leadwood brought a comforting assurance as it ran the full length of the boy's muscled forearm, continuing along to jut just beyond his bony elbow. Course wind ground away at young Cristofo's unblinking eyeballs as his mark became evident and his focus approached formidability. Two men came to be discernible, gracelessly mounted upon their sizable rides with unsettled cubs carelessly tethered in tow. One was quite massively arranged, while the other was more moderately disposed, but each could soon be heard shouting vile insults to the gentle beasts as they urged them on ruthlessly and with no lack of heel or shortage of flog.

A deep-seated wail burst forth from within of the exhilarated boy, an impulsive outcry brought forward by cause of the uncommon emotional blend of both joy and rage that bore comparison to the bellow of a savage brute as it cut through the air violently, overpowering and all but stamping out the fiercely imposed howl of shrieking wind. Both of the villainous two turned to face the alarming sound, and the weightier of the pair found immediate clarification to his curious perusal, an elucidation by way of a swiftly rotating cylinder impacting with heavy force upon his unsuspecting skull. Training and intuition coincided to create accomplishment in all exceptional combatants, a certainty that young Cristofo embraced as he prudently let fly his initial attack with aim of the more threatening of the duo. An unpleasant crack was transmitted with a deadening tone. It signified to the boy that the whole of his efforts could now be put forth toward his remaining opponent, a taken-aback wretch who had already fallen to the strangling squeeze of limbs upon his throat, as Cristofo had concurrently leaped legs first in an effort to expertly apply the debilitating maneuver.

Both man and boy wriggled and twisted in a desperate manner as they were thrown down from atop the shoulders of the magnificent mammal before proceeding to writhe and roll on the icebound and snow-covered landscape. One was frantically trying to free himself from the suffocating hold, while the other remained firm and forceful in his unbreakable clench as hearty muscles of thigh bided time patiently until the inevitable collapse of the outmatched prey. Forevermore would the memory of that unforgettable journey back to the warmth of his luxurious manor remain emblazoned in the cognizance of the boy, as neither fatigue nor biting cold could succeed in washing away the prideful elation in his bosom as he pranced and trotted his way back, playfully and in the company of the frolicsome cubs. Their parents trudged behind steadily and stoically with their beat-up and blemished cargo trailing behind, bumping and bobbing in the rugged and rough terrain as they were mercilessly dragged along in tow.

Our bestirred young prodigy brought forth a successful effort to reset the subject matter at hand after an overly lengthy and borderline uncomfortable pause. "Altarius made mention of a conduit deep within the bowels of the factory, a locality that someway maintains the capacity for water. I shall set out to hit upon this place, and once there, I will recognize the standpoint from which to traverse back into the diabolical domain."

"It sounds to me as if you … don't exactly have a proper plan in place, son," the boy's father remarked with a seemingly cynical tone, yet in truth the comment was more of an affirmation to the fact that Cristofo was never the type to establish a drawn-out and specific procedure or strategy. Instead, he favored a reliance on intuition and instinct to guide him along as he set forth with a general scenario in mind.

The magister proceeded to interject in turn. "There is indeed a location where water is found, rooted far into the depths of the factory's underside, well below our nethermost station at the millenary step. I know this by way of firsthand observation. Long ago, I delved that far into the belly of our mountainous arrangement, where Cedric, my bygone companion of old, joined me in spelunking the caverns and cavities that lay sporadically dispersed among the substratum under the last run of the carved and sculpted staircase. Therein I saw the trickle of meandering water and stream flowing unhurriedly yet persistently. I had initially set off to confirm what I had long since reckoned, that eventually water flow would become unhindered in running its inevitable course once our inexplicably constructed boreholes' prearranged drainage channels were done diverting the commodity from going awash onto the factory floor, that is. From that point on, I cannot say what is to be expected for lightness of air, and the thought of the fatiguing trek back upslope had unquestionably halted the desire for further exploration. I can say, however, that by way of logic and collaborative agreement, it follows that the course of running water will likely lead to a greater and more abundant accumulation."

"And so it is settled, Grandfather. Father, I shall retire to my personal quarters for a brief period of preparation, after which point I will take leave on my subterranean campaign to carry out the objective at hand: to free Altarius and Bellatrix from their improper confinement and to bring them back to us healthful and in the here and now where they can provide advantage in our difficult and demanding defensive. Both of you please take heed, let soldiering be done by soldiers and stay back of the conflict where you will be safer in the refuge of command. Stand firm and hold at any cost while awaiting my fleet footed return." Cristofo proceeded to embrace both of his esteemed forebearers as good wishes and good hopes were alternatingly exchanged. Then he made way to the refuge of his private chambers, reluctantly satisfied with the fact that he had prudently restrained from divulging to them a crucial circumstance, namely that he saw practically no chance of them bringing about any measure of success in defense of the oncoming onslaught without the forceful and integral impetus that could only eventualize in the capacity of a combined wizardly effort.

The boy's private quarters represented a modest enough place, modest at least with respect to the larger than average spans to which he would be more routinely accustomed. Still, the space was quite grand

and accommodating by your more typical standards, with chiseled and rough-hewn walls, ceiling and floor defining the character of the hollowed-out and boxlike abode. Fancy furnishings and fixtures could do little to mask the drab and stark reality of the circumstance. It was a nook in the ground, a burrowed-out little compartment hidden away along a softly traveled edge of the vast and far-reaching mountainous arrangement that was the Nepheshan fire powder factory of old. Much credit was due to the warming sprawl of a magnificent rug of pelt that bore down on the drabness of floor and quelled the area's monolithic ambiance as it covered near its entirety, save for the scant border that remained viable and evenly apportioned along the rectangular periphery. A fashionable bedstead arranged itself imposingly with broad and richly carved headboard and posts of wood abutting the fringe of clean and tightened linens. A sturdy armoire and matching writing desk stood well-arranged and organized among the rather rampant sprawl of table, ledges, and shelves lined with books, articles, and accoutrements of diverse varieties and kinds—a vast assortment of items all grouped, sorted, and systematically arranged.

"Maleabar, illumination!" the boy declared as he concurrently removed the remarkable fragment from his wrist and tossed it lightly upon the leather inlaid panel of his sturdy and well-proportioned desktop. At once, an agreeable luster permeated throughout the space, bringing a new and refreshing aspect to the domain that had previously only ever been subjected to the tedious and lackluster sheen of sparsely dispersed candlelight. Cristofo then proceeded to unbind himself of sword as he threw himself upon the comfort of the taut and resilient bedding, where he cradled hands behind his head in an effort to repose and reflect upon the forthcoming crusade. However, confusion befell in lieu of solace as discomforting thoughts raced about in the mind of the exceptional young aristocrat, unsteadily vaulting from subject to subject as his newly enlivened awareness struggled to rationalize the fantastical transpirations of the preceding day. Noxerus, Certasus, Clavus, Altarius, and Bellatrix, the attacking monstrous hound-like creatures, the sprightly minions of unknown designation, steadfast sentinels, delightful yet slashing arcuspods, swarming mutophasms, and vile vasculomen swine, Iggy abandoned, pierced and seared Cimtar and Somnia ... It was a collage of spinning and swirling memories rampantly awash in the subconscious of the newly declared wizardly boy, who felt no desire for the convenience of slumber but instead seemed to suffer from an entrancing delusion of the wakeful kind.

Then solace at last reared its comforting head. The shrill yet beguiling cry of Myrina in need of rescue burst to the forefront of Cristofo's visions and served to snap him free from reverie. All else faded from focus as the indelible thoughts of his true love brought much-needed soothing. But recollection then shifted to the panicked realization that he would be unable to forestall her forceful abduction—and then to the overwhelming relief brought to bear by her unanticipated rescue at the hand of a heroic wizard of age and his magnificent dragon. It was a dichotomy of unrestricted emotions swaying back and forth like a cleansing scour, washing away all but the most basic of desires, more specifically to be enraptured by a compatible body and soul and to feel the gratifying warmth of the reciprocated sentiment. The exhilarating sensation of adoration delighted young Cristofo and provided grounding for the rampantly racing thoughts that had atypically taken hold of his mind.

Indeed, the peaceful rejuvenation of sleep would not come to the boy's aid on that inaugural wizardly night, and nor was it needed for that matter, not then and not for any other day or night moving forward. Of course, that is not to say that the welcome commodity would be vanquished forever; instead, it would happen on the odd occasion and when convenient, like the infrequent yet gladly anticipated visit from a favored and far-off friend. And so up he stirred, and to his soundly fashioned desk he bounded, where a sheaf of stationery and a thirsty quill would do well to harvest the eloquently composed bounty brought forth by way of a bit of free time, his unparalleled penchant toward the art of exposition, and the indelible thoughts of his precious Myrina which were fresh and foremost in his mind.

Meanwhile, a good distance beyond, in a comparable yet blatantly more lush and sizable station, a fair princess found herself comfortably settled upon an absurdly oversized bed top, where a deep and billowy mattress yielded obediently to every curve and corner, bend and bow. The well-proportioned gentlewoman lay sufficiently sprawled with a thickset book of learning at her forefront, giving semblance to a studious fixation, while in actuality her firm glare was unfocused and her attention was thoroughly entrenched on her beloved companion of interest. Worry permeated throughout her being, infiltrating her mind with the clout of a stark and incalculable wound as the agony of Cristofo's unknown circumstance etched itself upon her mind-set in pulsating waves of realization.

Thankfully, thoughts and memories of their numerous adventures, undertakings, and tender moments during the whole of their many seasons together ran abound in the princess's fair memory, bringing alternatingly pleasant periods of mend that did well to aid her along as she suffered the ordeal. From the gentle touch of innocent lips upon a young girl's abraded knee to the fierce and fiery throw of comradeship in battle, her unhindered reflections churned out memories with unbridled frequency, and all the while, she fought to quell the bitter undercurrent of uncertainty. She knew deep down in the crux of her soul that her champion was adequately existent and that he too was nurturing himself with thoughts of their drawn-out and unrelenting relationship. And with that, a purposeful knock at the door disengaged the lovely Myrina from her contemplation. The muffled sound of an earnest voice prompted a surge of relief and invoked an uncontainable smile.

"Greetings, Your Royal Highness. I bring word at the behest of Master Cristofo …"

Next, we revert back to our waiting and composing youthful protagonist, where the doleful strain of longed-for togetherness lingered about with an almost visible substantiality as the boy poured out his emotionalism in the form of masterfully crafted phrases and terms. Then, all at once, the resounding thwack of fist on wooden door served to break him free of his undertaking just as it drew to a close.

"Yes?" An excited undertone exposed itself through the boy's word as he quickly signed off on his letter— "Your counterpart forever in spirit …"—and hurriedly executed a crisp and capable fold and seal.

Elation once again presented itself, a much-sought companion whose emergence altogether vanquished the persistent hover of the melancholy mood as Cristofo sprang up from his seated position and headed toward the entryway with premonition of a welcome surprise. Well, lo and behold, if that fiery little sidekick of his didn't slink under the heavyset slab and burst into the room before his bearer could dispense with the opening of the heavyset and cumbersome door.

"Iggy, there you are, you little rapscallion." Cristofo delighted in the presence of his flickering and flaring attendant, who had altered to a more jubilant hue while whisking and whirling around his faithful companion in a frenzy. "Ha ha, settle down, Iggy. You're going to squander away your powder." The boy luxuriated in the much-needed laughter given cause by virtue of the creature's exaggerated contentedness. "You missed me all the while as you lay stranded amidst the overgrown blades of sod, didn't you? Ha ha, I missed you too, my diminutive dynamo. Never again will we dragon ride absent of satchel! You fought well, little friend. Do not bemoan your outstanding performance, for you were gaining the upper hand on those diabolical creatures."

Despite delay, the incredible pint-sized creation eventually nuzzled into its golden sanctuary, where comfort and coziness were brought about by way of the metal's soft and spellbinding tactility and by the soothing rhythm of his master's pulsating chest.

"It's good to have you back as well, my whimsical wonder, and worry not, for although you were absent in the course of my most recent adventure, circumstance dictates that you will indulge in the subsequent foray … Well done, sentry man. I thank you for your good work in retrieving my invaluable companion." Cristofo's attention turned to the allegiant man who stood at attention just inside the chamber's threshold.

"Not at all, young master. The little fellow was precisely where you had indicated."

"Nonetheless, it is no easy task to diligently follow instruction; splendidly done. Now take leave and report at once to my father. Inform him that I have rewarded you with promotion to a rank and posting entirely of his choosing. Furthermore, see to it that this letter finds the fair hand of princess Myrina without deviation." With an obedient nod, the sentry was off with a vigorous stride and an insuppressible smile.

"Well, no need for delay, Iggy," the boy enunciated aloud, although he knew that there was really no need, for Iggy was certainly able to appreciate the boy's thoughts. Moreover, he found himself much more in tune with the creature's reasoning as well, much more so than usual, thanks to his newly acquired and steadily developing wizardly abilities, I might add.

"Off we go to undertaking and adventure! Altarius and Bellatrix are assuredly in need of our best efforts, little wonder, and our best efforts are always at the ready for those who are decent and deserving."

Cristofo scuttled about the room as he fastened his newly acquired sword and conferred with his unique and diminutive chum, being sure to grab one of many satchels of powder that lay at the ready upon a shelf among a number of duplicates all in a row and arranged like soldiers at attention.

"Today begins a new chapter with regard to our exploits, little one, places and predicaments like never before, creatures and creations like never imagined. Off we go into the bowels of this phenomenal factory. Altarius had warned of strange and unusual things and of freakish phenomenon that dwell deep down in its mysterious underbelly, the very location of our aim. And from there, stranger things still once we transverse into the dreary domain of my usurpation; I'll tell you all about it along the way, Iggy, and who knows, we may even get another chance at engagement with those dastardly vasculomen demons! Maleabar …"

And with that they took their leave of the lonely antechamber as the miraculous and lustrous material flung itself around the wrist of the exceptional young boy as he made his way along the drab and dreary factory corridor, a magnificent and imposing sword bobbing about his back and the radiant hue of a contented fiery creature exuding spiritedly from his bosom.

CHAPTER 8

A Planet Left in Ruin

The Defluous Highlands was a unique mountainous arrangement remotely situated amid a vast expanse of lightly forested timberland some distance beyond all persons or populace. It lay isolated and nearly a clear horizon's distance away from the nearest population, which just so happened to manifest itself in an extensive sprawl of creatures and characters that had over time coalesced and clustered in a comfortable corner of actuality that centered around what has since become known as the Nepheshan city of old. The curious formation resembled a bubbling encrustation, fashioned of the hardened spew brought forth of the molten undercrust that churned away with fiery vitality under the skin of our magnificent hostess, the incomparable Mother Earth. Nestled about the craggy and undulating far-reaching framework, the odd aperture established itself sporadically and with infrequency; hollowed and hardened conduits hidden away within the plethora of bumps and berms, brought to bear long ago by the pressurized flow of molten undertow and by its irrepressible urge to burst forth and settle anew.

For a multitude of time, the otherwise insignificant structure lay passive and dormant as though a neglected protuberance scantily overlaid by shrubbery and underbrush and scarcely visited by the occasional bucking goat or bristle-bird—or by some similar sustenance-seeking stray. But not so in the course of the current interval of our story, wherein the desolate locality would display barrenness no more. Alternatively, it would be all of a sudden alive and teeming with extraneous beings, exotic creations, extrinsic materials, apparatuses, and other things. Like an indignant swarm of industrious ants, a slew of completely foreign and seemingly ambitious beasts materialized, gushing forth through the mouth of one of the aforementioned long-established apertures with a persistent flow that displayed similar steadiness and strain to the tunnelway's inaugural and molten payload. The continuous stream served to feed an already extensively accumulated gathering. All the while, a solitary member of the association lay crouched unassumingly upon a high-reaching and optimally situated vantage point from where the outrushing progression was intensely observed and quietly studied. Indeed, the reticent onlooker was the conductor of the momentous undertaking, a formidable individual whose name I knew not then but know well now.

Aleregeni the unwavering, a creature of more determined spirit had yet to be uncovered within the whole of the recognizable cosmos. No task was beyond the grasp of her tenacious mind and no chore too thorough so as to free itself from her unfailing hands. Indeed, she was a unique entity, this Aleregeni of which I speak—a wizard for certain, and what's more, conceivably the first of our kind. She was a being of uttermost age and of uttermost essence that was spawned of the foremost of her species' evolutionary base. Yes, I will reiterate, a being of tremendous age and henceforth of tremendous wisdom, and more curious still was the nature of her spark. You see, although free from rule, regulation, or restriction of any kind, guidelines and axioms necessarily come into being in order to reconcile the general course of wizardly behavior. In the animus realm, for instance, a great respect for life and creation is substantially regarded among all her wizardly custodians. Other realms also share a similar sentiment—others, not so much. Whereas some would go so far as to not harm any form of existence in any way or under any circumstance, others still would conduct themselves in the opposite modus, executing and eradicating without discrimination. Once again, our paradigm of a spectrum comes into play where extremities subsist and a plethora of differing positions endures in between.

Corbomite was the name of Aleregeni's home world, an ill-fated sphere with an unbalanced rhythm spinning away desperately and erratically somewhere beyond and in a distant galaxy along a far corner of the universe. And the race of Corbominians were unique in their aspect, which in and of itself does not impart much significance since the same could be said for any and all of the vastitude of disparate races that infest the countless wandering specks and shreds of solidity that persist throughout the far reaches of endlessness. What was particularly notable about the Corbominian strain was their neutrality of spark—neither good nor evil, not of light or dark, but rather situated in the absolute centrism of the all-important array, the benchmark upon which all of existence reconciles their most fundamental condition. Consequentially, they comported themselves with complete neutrality as far as their interactions are concerned, carrying on with preassigned functions and duties in a wholly methodical manner while progressing unwaveringly in their course. Not a thought would be given to mobs, masses, observers, or onlookers who kept their distance with no penchant for interference, nor would a trace of hesitation be found should the need arise to thwart any form of obstruction. Ruthlessly they would engage, if that were the case, and ceaseless they would be in their efforts to carry on.

And so, the quandary comes to pass upon the consideration of another wise and rational wizard of age who would be placed in the position to decide upon and act with consequence regarding the situation that theretofore presented itself at hand. To thwart the onrush and actualize the extinction of an entire species or to stand idly by and watch the callous and unsympathetic overthrowing of but another ...? Such are the determinations that fall at the feet of wizardly responsibility from time to time. Could the mother of a race be faulted for attempting to conserve and keep safe her flock at any cost? Should the mother of one race not recognize that preservation should not be seated on the destruction of yet some other? These are questions upon which we may all contemplate and come to conclude. For my part, I will divulge my biased inclination; I side with the realm about which I have been destined to superintend. And no deliverer of destruction or notion of neutrality would serve to diminish my resolve in any significant way.

In any event, I fear that I may have digressed yet again and consequently may have foreshown substance that belongs further along in our tale. Therefore, to Corbomite we return, to a time long past, where the carelessly spinning orb was whirling around and whizzing about its own system of scraps and segments that merged and mingled as so many others of similar strain that subsist throughout the vastitude. The Corbominians proceeded harmoniously about their various pursuits, tending to duties and deeds and whatever other carryings-on they ordinarily undertook, until an indiscriminate stroke of fate came down upon the populace with an unsympathetic smash of ruination. Darkness all of a sudden befell, giving light to a massive and fiery object cascading down with ferocity and gleaming of its own conflagrant blaze; a tired and travel-weary asteroid had finally come to berth upon the random fragment of hardness upon which Aleregeni and her ill-fated race just happened to be found.

Indeed, the indomitable asteroid reared its mighty head; these are shattered shards and displaced remnants of planets, planetoids, and planetesimals alike wandering about unwaveringly and without any perceivable goal. Unfailingly, they fly for a time and distance of varying degrees, but in all cases with an absolute finality, for the ceaseless capacity of lastingness would eventually bring each and every one to bear. Many become fodder for famished and fiery stars, while others entrap themselves in a spinning and stabilized equilibrium. Others still collide and conjoin to create their own segments, or offspring, or merely continue their course with an enduring albeit altered trajectory and form. However, the one thing that can be said for certain is that many inhabitants upon many a sphere have fallen prey to their all-powerful and undiscriminating wrath.

Therefore, the brimful planet of Corbomite was dealt a mortal blow. A devastating impact shook the ground throughout the entirety of the robustly proportioned sphere as a sizable and velocious mass of consolidated rock struck down with the force of a thousand thunder strikes and lodged itself firmly inside the sediment-based bedrock.

Shattered portions of outer crust and mammoth sections of mountain ridge burst off into the heavens like so many seeds of the indigenous land, a new wave of celestial spores set to sail on an uncharted journey with the aim of eventual convergence and conjointment and with aspirations of carrying forward in their own alternative yet ultimately conclusive way. A resounding shock wave radiated throughout the entirety of the planet, bringing instantaneous death to a good half of her unsuspecting inhabitants as the unfortunate souls were swallowed down and consumed by the seismic stress brought forth by the abruptly afflicted trauma. A colossal crack of vast proportion was discharged, and an ensuing fissure propagated, shearing off a significant segment of the valiant sphere, which in turn exerted all its available energies in a desperate effort to keep the valuable arc-shaped appendage secure. And believe it or not, it succeeded in doing so by some indiscernible act of intervention or by some generally occurring activity of natural law— either way and in any event, she was somehow able to survive the ordeal while managing to remain barely whole but not quite intact.

Not quite intact indeed, for the fragmented segment hung off her with disproportionality as though it were haphazardly mended yet still in a state of disrepair. The planet's grievous injury extended a full half diameter length of chord, leaving the valiant celestial body significantly disfigured, a spherical teapot with a damaged and dangling lid. At once, a dense and heavy upspring of dust and debris wreaked havoc upon the planet's populace as immense and consolidated clouds of the stuff propagated and persisted in an orbital gathering, where it hypnotically conducted and steadily flowed as it was drawn into the irresistible lure of gravitational equilibrium. Precious and nurturing lifeblood from her ever-giving star would be substantially blocked and obstructed save for pockets and pinpoints where it seeped through here and there. As a result, another good portion of her prodigious parasites fell victim to the ensuing frigidity and lack of breathable air. As if that were not enough, her stability was additionally injured beyond any foreseeable repair; an unbalanced core gave cause to an erratic rotation about her axis, which incited her orbit to gradually deteriorate and decompose.

Yes, the unfortunate adolescent planet of Corbomite, along with its burgeoning band of luckless inhabitants, had indeed been dealt a mortifying blow. Little hope remained for the handful of surviving dwellers that managed to subsist sporadically about their lifeboat of a sphere, howbeit little hope is not no hope, and so the story goes on. Generations came and went as though subsisting with the constancy of the alternating seasons, and the race of Corbominians regained their vigor and vitality of old as their atmospheric blockade became increasingly cleansed by the tireless scrub of time. A populace that once boasted a densely abundant congregation one hundred billion in number now proudly endured with an enhanced and heartier lot one fraction of one hundredth its former size. Still, it was strong. Moreover, Aleregeni was there to shepherd her precious flock all the while, safeguarding and preserving them with desperate determination. The veritable mother of her race and a being of extraordinary abilities was nurturing and protecting with singular intent.

But while the next number of centuries served the population relatively well, enabling the surviving multitudes to stabilize, regroup, and eventually replenish and thrive, not so for their irreplaceable host. One of the planet's three modestly sized moons had been previously struck and realigned by some shrapnel from the aforementioned catastrophic planetary event and had since strayed farther and farther away from her captivating ballast, increasing orbital span in an effort to create distance and eventually break free. And outward she veered, gaining freedom and momentum with each and every revolution, until time and fate brought forth her consequent crossroads and she converged upon her lesser and more far-off sister moon, percussing it with momentous force and fragmenting it to no small degree. Thusly, an assortment of additional projectiles were sent off into space, where they would progress of their own accord and wreak their own brand of havoc or whatnot, and the struggling sphere more cordially known as Corbomite was forced to carry on absent two of its beloved moons, propelling it into a state of even more hectic disrepair. Her elliptical solar rotation could no longer maintain its much-needed though erratic equilibrium and had instead become nudged toward a course that was significantly foreshortened, or flattened, or more stretched out. However you care to describe it, the end result remained the same; it was a planetwide death sentence.

Life persisted for the resilient and assiduous race with focus on day-to-day survival and lesser concern toward the eventual imperilment that was imminent according to the planetary interpretation of time, but millennia then forward with respect to the relatively accelerated Corbomite chronology. The coldest seasons grew more unbearable still while the hottest scorched and scalded with unprecedented ferocity, limits that were amplified to heavier extremes as the planet's course about her sun progressively flattened. Aleregeni, for the most part, had focused relentlessly on the restoration and rejuvenation of her embattled species, foregoing the usual outward divergence that would typically overtake a wizardly heart and force it to explore and survey its limitless bounds. Well, eventually and inevitably, the persistent flame of inquisitiveness, coupled with the undeniable need to arrive at a solution for her doomed progeniture, had forced the hand of change, prompting Aleregeni to take leave of her developing people and delve outward into the unrestricted immensity. With the spirit of a bewildered child, she bounded and capered about the far-reaching network of wizardly wormholes, cogitating and considering as the doors to the universe unfolded before her exceptional mind, which in turn became more cultivated and matured to an unprecedented degree. And at long last, after century upon century of consideration, her glorious stratagem had been birthed.

Ergo we arrived at our humble little planet and principle setting to our story, the valued and venerated earth, a relatively modest sphere with a somewhat uncomplicated inhabitancy that just happened to exhibit a decent measure of congruence with its far-off and comparable counterpart, Corbomite. Even more noteworthy was the fact that she just happened to be the unsuspecting landing place for a rather exorbitant hunk of intergalactic shrapnel brought forth by the momentous Corbominian asteroid strike, an occurrence far too coincidental to allow Aleregeni to overlook the opportune orb's suitability for the broken and battle-fatigued planet's ambitious mass migration. All that had remained to be reckoned was the method with which she would avail in transporting her colony to its new and suitable resting place. Now this, of course, was to be no easy task. Indeed, the undertaking took all of an age and more. The unwavering one considered and contemplated with diligent determination and indefatigable resolve until at last her ambition had been foreseen. She had accomplished the unrealizable task of successfully transporting temporal beings through the specifically prohibitive wizardly wormholes. To no small degree, two principal contributing factors had been credited with facilitating her success, the first being the wayfarers' neutrality of spark and the subsequent ascribable to the relative congruence of atmosphere betwixt the planet of their outset and that of their ultimate destination.

To that end, our wise and iron-willed Aleregeni had begun her migratory campaign, moderately at first, as would be expected from a wise old wizardess of age, for the circumstance was not yet grievously desperate and the suitability of the chosen locality was prudently postulated yet still wholly unproven and untested. Accordingly, dozens of denizens were transported at any given time and implanted upon the logical encampment for a displaced and dedicated band of colonizers. It was a mountainous hunk of their previously pulverized home world that would eventually and inevitably develop into that bountiful locality of which we are all too familiar with at this point in our tale, the noteworthy Nepeshan powder factory. Herein they were placed to the task of accommodating and habituating their newfound home, and industriously they would do so, getting the process underway with steadfast and painstaking effort and with the unfailing resolve that would epitomize the true nature of the assiduous race.

As time passed, more and more inhabitants would be sent to join their ever-increasing band of colonizers, with the eventual aim of transplanting the entirety of the race well in advance of the inevitable demise of their distressed home world. With every passing season, their Earth-based faction would swell and they would delve deeper and deeper into their terrestrial mountainous abode. And within a matter of a few solar revolutions, thousands of the resolute beings accommodated themselves about the massive morsel that had once been attached to their former home, digging and dredging and consuming of the mineral rubble, as was the Corbominian way. Although they seemed to be progressing and prospering in their transformative endeavor, Aleregeni became increasingly unsure about the lasting viability of her evolutionary crusade, knowing full well that any measure of success would be contingent on her people's capability to branch out into the outskirts beyond the mountainous arrangement, where they could subsist of the foreign land and breathe free.

Well, be it by the subtle differences in the newfound atmosphere and air, or by the slight discrepancy in the diffusion of their new and similarly proportioned yet undeniably disparate star, or be it by some indiscernible influence that was recognizable solely on a planetary scale, for some reason the determined colonizers struggled to proliferate and propagate in their recently inhabited and unaccustomed surround. It was not for lack of effort that they failed in their quest to spread out and broaden scope. It was simply due to a lack of capacity to acclimatize to the newfound earthly environ. Breath was achievable yet feebly so, and it was not nearly as invigorating as when taken in inside the confines of their underground and mineralized abode. Sunlight bathed and shone brightly yet seemed to provide little by way of nourishment and vitality. In fact, any more than a modest exposure looked to be more harmful than healthful and brought on infirmity and fragility, resulting in eventual demise.

Overall, things seemed to worsen progressively as time barreled on and as more and more efforts were made to sprawl and proliferate the struggling species. Aleregeni, for her part, responded with a heartless and methodical discipline, delivering more and more bodies to the earthen colony and sending substantial numbers out into the surrounding stomping grounds in an attempt to set up some manner of sustainability, but to no avail. All that came to pass was death and downfall to all who were cast away, and sickliness prevailed for the fortunate numbers who endured within the comfort of the mountainous arrangement, although "fortunate" would be a most arguable adjective used to describe them as they struggled to accomplish any viable measure of propagation. The majority withered away suffering and in discomfort as they retreated deeper and deeper into the belly of their desperate sanctuary and delved deeper and deeper into the depths of despair.

Alas, the unwavering one had seemed to waver from the relentless affair, at least for a limited period, for although she accepted and embraced the essentiality of her strict and heartless command, she did indeed have heart as well as spirit of the particularly admirable kind. No longer could she suffer the torment of sending her kinsfolk out to dissolution and eventual demise, so the portal was shut down immediately and the determined wizardess retreated to the domain of her home world. There she would immerse herself in the profundity of contemplation in an effort to unravel the complexities of her most imperative predicament, with the preservation of her beloved species at stake and all the while under burden of the scant and insufficient deadline celestially imposed a millennium then forward, give or take a fractional time span or two. And the remaining Corbominian Earth dwellers? Well, their intergalactic entry point accommodated a one-way journey alone, leaving them to fend for themselves on the remote and unsuitable outpost, with little by way of hope for survival and even lesser by way of option.

Now let us return a thousand years henceforth, back to the principal setting of our story and back to our reticent onlooker from a number of passages prior in our portrayal. And let us give more attention to the contemplative figure who studiously overlooked her subsequent migratory campaign; hence and so she perched herself with a concentrated and statue-like air and a more or less humanlike proportion, although noticeably slenderer and considerably taller. Ample and shadowy eyes flashed of the lucent moonlight like two orbicular mirrors tinted black, stark beacons of contrast against an otherwise dull and charcoal-like visage and frame, both of which remained predominantly concealed within the brim of a sand-colored heavily protruding hood and its corresponding covering loosely akin to a robe. It was a thickset and meshy garment resembling a potato sack that left little by way of exposure except for extremities and a frontispiece with a silhouetted trace of a display. Lackluster streaks of chalky red meandered about indifferently along the whole of the surface of the otherwise carbon-correlated being, as though robustly nurturing veins were coursing through the entirety of the non-animal and mineral-like anatomy and, if for no other reason at all, serving to provide a colorful distinction to the drab and desolate shell. This effected a perception that would be considered much more intriguing to the unacquainted eye.

An appropriately proportioned staff overhung the creature's crouched limbs, resting there with the palpable obedience of a devoted and well-disciplined pet. It was quite the majestic device, an intricately carved and remarkably ornate rod of polished and sparkling material blatantly exquisite and awash of the bewitching characteristics more commonly associated with precious stones and rare gems. A brownish tinge emanated from the implement, analogous to a hunk of smoky quartz that reflected light brilliantly and habitually by nature of its myriad facets and faces of every angle and kind. Bony and blackened fingers tightened grasp on the accessory as the formidable figure leaned upon it and righted herself. A prismatic spray of reflected luster burst forth as the staff was manipulated and as a dutiful subordinate approached a fully heightened Aleregeni, who stood there statuesquely in wait amidst a momentous gust of wind that spontaneously wore away at the granular crust of her exposed and outer coating. It blew away bits and specks in a grainy breeze as the eroded layer of outer skin regenerated almost instantaneously.

A coarse and gritty voice in a foreign tongue addressed the stoic wizardess with a resonance quite unpleasant toward animus ears. "The bombing squadrons return from their mission, my mistress."

"And what word of the migration?" An equally disagreeable yet softer and more womanish tone countered the obvious phrase, as the returning fleet could be quite easily observed in the not-too-distant beyond.

"We have yet a way to go, matriarch. At current reckoning, one-tenth of our populace has been supplanted upon the replacement terrain, along with a good stockpile of provisioning and stores. Accountings from the home world allude to a rapidly unsettling state of affairs; tremors and quakes intensify like never before, and unyielding disturbances escalate. Our beloved Corbomite is being pulled apart, my matriarch, and it is unbeknownst how long she will be able to hang on." A brief pause served to solidify the seriousness of her reply as Aleregeni perused the rumbling convergence of her returning armada and complacently deduced that their extraneous opponents were unequivocally outmatched.

Then she glanced over toward the swelling egress point of her latest and most desperate colonization attempt, and a confident determination was transmitted through her words, although deep within a worrisome uncertainty stewed and bubbled as it grew more and more difficult to subdue.

"Have the facilitators continue to arrange things as planned and see to it that the flight commanders submit their reports forthwith. At the next eventide, we proceed with a full invasion; quadruplicate the attacking flock of flying turtibrida and prepare the infiltrators for a subsequent ground assault. Our treasured remnant of home world must be reoccupied in haste and at any and all cost." With that, our dynamic wizardess of age withdrew in a flash, jetting away atop her sparkling and spellbinding staff as she traversed the industrious scene of the mass migration and shot directly into the mouth of an obscure aperture that lay nestled farther along the bubbling Defluous topography. She then disappeared into her own brand of portal, which led somewhere among the endless unknown, leaving no trace or track save for the flickering afterglow of her lustrous device, which was scarcely visible and dissipated almost immediately thereafter.

Now we divert and change course once again in our tale and back to our fond young protagonist we proceed wherein the monotonous and purposely produced run of stairs decline unto the cavity of the monumental mountainous formation until coming to conclusion at the foot of the so-called millenary step.

"Yes! There we have it, Iggy!" our excellent and eager adolescent cried out in a voice that was exuberant if not moderately winded by cause of the rather tedious yet exceptionally fleet-footed descent. "Just as Grandfather described." Cristofo paused and took a breath as he leaned over and studied the course of a meandering trickle that was evident at the base of a modest opening. The mouth of it encroached upon a cramped and irregular landing of bedrock that seemed to represent the endpoint of the exhaustive effort of chiseled and carved steps as well as the starting point of a supplementary passageway with a different and considerably more arduous way. In a fluid motion, the boy took hold of his wrist, and a simple fling ensued.

"Brighter, Maleabar," our young wizard proclaimed, and a moderate luster then grew, bringing clarity to the wholly uncharted formation at hand. A curious yet cautious head then proceeded to poke its way into the aperture, where it was able to peruse with more precision. The adjoining body followed suit, snaking its way into the subterranean area while making a deliberate effort to steer the oversized nethersword through.

At first glance, the tunnel appeared to be similar to many that Cristofo had negotiated before. Size-wise, it had breadth enough to just barely allow for a decently spacious and upright traversing, and with regard to composition, a crusty and irregular surface wrapped the entirety of the walls, ceiling, and floor as though a chunky coat of mire had been haphazardly smeared by some crude and undiscriminating applicator. The ground underfoot was particularly craggy and uneven, with the trickling stream rippling carelessly along its own eroded channel at the relative midpoint of the span. Broken-off chunks of the adjacent embankments dispersed themselves randomly along the waterway's substratum, where they littered the liquid's pathway with debris of various contour and size. The channel way stretched in both directions from Cristofo's prevailing vantage point, so the boy concluded his scrutinizing surveillance of the surround and carried on in the same direction as the meandering flow.

"Return, Maleabar!" the boy commanded as he outstretched his wrist in gesture to the morsel of miraculous material. A luminous wristband reappeared at once. Thoughts of former expeditions with his admired grandfather brought tidings of fond memories as he advanced swiftly along, straddling the narrow watercourse while delving deeper downgrade and farther into the depths of the unexplored.

Cristofo trudged along throughout the while, observing and analyzing as he conversed one-sidedly with his loyal little flaming companion, Iggy, as he so often did on his plenitude of prior arbitrary

outings and excursions. And although the diminutive dynamo returned
not a word, plenty was communicated and cognitively inferred, especially
at this point, as the boy's wizardly perception had steadily matured.

"And just like that, a consolidated mass of ice came shooting up
from the ground just as I was about to delve headfirst into the cauldron-
shaped pit of water. I was flattened for an instant, momentarily knocked
out cold … just like the time we were fleeing from that gang of hoodlums
way out in Aspera, remember, Iggy, where we accompanied Father on
that sales concursion? I should have been able to avoid that pelting of
rocks. To this day, I rue the fact that I let one of those bouldered rockets
get the better of me …

"I know, Iggy. Yes, there were a lot of them. Why do you think
I chose to flee from the encounter? You know that such a course of
action goes against my better judgement and conflicts with my overall
inclination to meet with endangerment dead-on … At any rate, that
memory prompts me to express gratitude to you yet again, my fiery
friend, for your circle of raging flame did well to keep those barbarians
at bay. Thank goodness the senselessness faded in short order and
likewise that we had a sufficient stockpile of powder and a significant
enough allotment of steel to liberate ourselves from that precarious
predicament—and in the process leave a good number of our asinine
assailants with intensely regrettable recollections of the entire ordeal!

"In any event, back to the here and now, my friend, and back to
the objective at hand. We need to come upon a connotative display of
waterfall, a cascading flow of sorts or a plunging down rush, wherein we
can be flushed away and into the territory of our outlandish aim. I will
recognize the locality when I see it, Iggy. I know I will." A noticeably
more excited tone accompanied the boy's words as he progressed farther
along the subterranean passageway and as the watercourse swelled and
strengthened. His saturated footwear succumbed to the unavoidable
submergence, no longer capable of straddling to keep dry. The cavern
itself had opened up considerably as its traveler had journeyed along,
and a much more expansive span threefold its previous breadth now
resonated and echoed Cristofo's recounting words as they mingled

and merged with and lost themselves altogether amidst the repetitious reverberation of water flow.

"Look there ahead, Iggy!" the boy exclaimed in reference to a noticeable change in the tunnel way's underlying composition. At once, he halted stride and recoiled his arm. Synchronously, a luminous throwing knife of miraculous material appeared and was hurled with a smooth and seemingly effortless zeal. A soft thwack then ensued but went unheard as the mentally manufactured throwing knife became lodged in a faraway section of the cavern wall, where a more intense brightness was now shining as intended and on cue.

A fork in the channel now lay evident in the relatively distant range, an obvious divide brought to light by the embedded segment of Maleabar, which remained obediently aglow in the precise midpoint of the divergent passageways. Water was now seen to trickle and seep from various locations along the cavern's craggy and rough-hewn facade; moreover, small and scattered cavities became evident, randomly sized and flagrantly more numerous as the foreground progressed. Our intuitive young wizard immediately surmised indentations, or breaches, or burrows, perhaps. At once, Cristofo took hold of a pinch of powder and sprinkled it precisely upon his golden talisman. It was gobbled up thoroughly by a surging blast of flame brought forth courtesy of a ravenously responding Iggy, who then felt compelled to withdraw from his agreeable hideaway to take a more vigilant position upon his master's broad and well-sculpted shoulder. At that point, a more intense flicker actualized and brought a more luminous viewpoint to the entire scene. The boy then drew tight the waterproof lining of his powder bag and adjusted his satchel to lay more snug and secure. Next off, the lengthy nethersword was fluently drawn and held in ready position as he advanced cautiously along the progressively deepening watercourse, wherein the saturation upsurged steadily along his tailor-made leggings until tapering off as it approached the height of his tightly wrapped midsection.

Caution followed as the young wizard continued along to the definitive and well-lit branch-off point, where a lustrous gleam reflected upon a multitude of tiny beady eyes that were quite easily discerned but hidden away within the plethora of holes and crawlways that riddled the cavern's bumpy and scraggy sides.

"Yes, I see them Iggy. Enliven and remain alert," the boy commanded with a more or less ordinary intensity of tone, and his fiery companion obediently responded by augmenting and enlivening his naturally occurring flame. Even though Iggy's irradiation effected a noticeable retraction and withdrawal of the vast majority of the proximate and miniscule eyeballs—those more toward the forefront as well as those more abaft—they seemed to be more or less unstirred by the aggressive gesture. In fact, they began to take leave of their shadowy hiding spots, drawing their corresponding crowns and bodies along into the exposing ambience of the artificially brightened subterrane.

And that which was then revealed... well suffice it to say that a vast majority of the immeasurable sum of all sentient beings would be genuinely repulsed by the features and forms of these unsightly beasts. Indeed, classifying these deep-seated cavern-dwelling creatures would be no easy task. *Grotesquitons*, I call them, for lack of any better term. They were not insects, rodents, or bore worms yet somehow an abnormal assimilation of the mismatched and unrelated crew. Most likely, they represented some cross-mated subcategorization of a species derived from both earthly and netherworld-originated lines. In any manner, the creatures conveyed a most unpalatable presence, to say the least, with each specimen donning a variant number of the aforementioned beady and minuscule eyes, all of which seemed to outline a bulging and prominent frontage wherein drawn-out, triangular, and curvilinear teeth combined to form a compacted and skull-like resilient crown. And routinely they operated, these predominant incisors of which I speak, opening and snapping with an almost mechanical regularity as though dredging or biting or directing all manner of material into its stout and tubular body, which in turn processed the procurement that moved through a modest succession of segmented passages that flexed and thrust as they carried it along.

As if that were not revolting enough, their blubbery and blemished whitish chassis were overspread with a slimy, translucent, and mucous-like ooze that dragged and distended and latched onto the immediate surround as the creatures wandered along. Short, dark, and rigid whisker-like hairs bespeckled the lardaceous bodies in a random and completely inconsistent manner, creating a striking contrast that only added to the overall hideousness of the bothersome beings. And trailing behind, a stout and conical-shaped tail-type of apparatus brought up the rear, secreting its own brand of gelatinous and slimy goo. All the same, they were quite quick on their feet for such sludgy and awkwardly appearing beasts, with credit due to the sextet of clawed and rodent-like feet that helped them to cling onto all aspects of the craggy cavern's surface as they speedily scuttled and scurried along.

"Back off, foul creatures!" Cristofo offered aloud, not expecting any form of compliance or understanding in return. "Lest my nimble nethersword make quick feast of your plumpish and full-bodied forms." The words rang out with amplitude in the confining surround and were intended more for the benefit of the boy himself, who took solace in the familiar resonance of his voice in a place that was otherwise wholly unfamiliar and unknown. He continued to advance carefully and alertly while still managing to assess and survey the surround. The portside branch-off stream appeared to carry on with a more or less consistent bearing to his prevailing vantage point, whereas the alternative route seemed to quicken and cascade with spirited haste. A more turbulent disposition overswept this right-side watercourse, eliciting the stark impression of a much more profound and vigorous downrush of water situated farther along. Therefore, it was decided; toward this blatantly more treacherous standpoint, he occasioned to veer.

All at once and from all directions, several the assertive creatures swept into action in an attempt to fall upon our daring young wizard. And with respect to this foreseeable eventuality, he was well prepared. A fervently whisking wrist manipulated the airy nethersword in a seemingly effortless manner as would be wielded the implement of a master portrait painter who makes quick work of a customary and frequently practiced background scene. Chunks and globs of disseered grotesquiton flew off the magnificent blade in plenty, and nary a sound was transmitted as a dozen or so of the dastardly things were cut clean through with incomprehensible swiftness and ease. Splashing sounds, however, were flagrantly heard as the blubbery segments spattered about the watercourse directly at the forefront of Cristofo's way. And a contemporaneously crackling and flickering flame contributed to the melodious symphony, as did the searing and bubbling of glutinous flesh while Iggy blockaded the boy's backside with an airtight wall of impenetrable flame, thus causing the contentious creatures to sizzle and burn and drop down in droves. However, the onslaught persisted as the boy endeavored to mosey along, and the number of aggressors grew as monstrosity upon vulgar monstrosity materialized, seeping forth from the cavern walls like relentless and coagulating ooze.

Soon enough, the creatures began to submerge into the watercourse, where they made way toward their mark from a safer and more sheltered vantage point. Cristofo felt more underfoot than the usual squishy and doughy settlement of fragmentary corpses and carcasses as he advanced onward. Indeed, wriggling and writhing was then quite obviously discerned, progressing without delay toward nipping and snapping as the boy bounded and hurdled in a futile effort to stay on top of the ever-growing buildup of attacking beasts. They steadily advanced from behind as well since Iggy's blockade became easily circumvented through the buffering obscurity of the subaquatic bypath. An irksome and unpleasant impact then descended upon the shoulder of our daring young adventurer, immediately followed by another gluey and clinging thud that stuck more firmly and in close vicinity to his disapproving face.

"Maleabar!" the boy screamed intensely, stretching his free arm, and at once a most effective throwing knife shimmied itself free from the cave's craggy wall and flew with velocity and accuracy directly into his waiting hand. The nethersword was then meticulously flung in the direction of Cristofo's backside, where it cleaved straight through a latched-on beast before being vigorously snapped upon by its complemental scabbard, and in one fluid motion, the boy's hand then snatched hold of his half-pounder, which neared as he lifted his leg to facilitate the retrieval of the well-planted blade.

With the use of the two masterfully manipulated weapons of close range, the fastened monstrosities were severed and slashed efficiently and without hesitation just as their anxious chompers were preparing to strike. And their tacky tenacious corpses eventually fell off the boy as he continued to swing and slice furiously upon a number of the creatures as they flung themselves in his direction tirelessly and in multitude. Iggy, for his part, engulfed the boy's body in flames, yet still the foul creatures were able to break through by sheer will of their abundance, which was extensive enough to create a smothering effect to some degree. Quick thinking was certainly required in order to extricate the young wizard from the troubling situation at hand, and fortunately enough for his sake, such an attribute was one of many with which Cristofo was luxuriantly endowed. Like a flash, his half-pounder was re-holstered and a sturdy grip on the effective nethersword was reestablished with ease. In one fell swoop, the substantial blade was let fly sidelong, where it came to quick impact and embedded itself firmly upon the scabrous cavern wall. Well-wielded throwing knives then continued to slash and flail as the boy laboriously strived to make forward progress toward his aim, and before long, he was within reach of his netherblade's silvery handgrip.

By this point, a pyramid-shaped accumulation of disgusting ingredients had all but immobilized the boy; a writhing and snapping pile of unwavering and vulgar creatures intermixed among the dead, detached, and divided portions of their counterparts, which had now amassed to the extent of Cristofo's waist. Sizzling, searing, and bubbling flesh furthermore contributed to the outrageousness of the situation as Iggy pressed on with his propagation of sheltering flame, producing a most unpleasant aromatic offshoot of burnt body and tissue that was powerful enough to be overbearing even in the bustling turmoil of the preposterous scene.

"Ready yourself, Iggy!" the boy declared as an outstretched hand took hold of the nethersword handle, which served to provide leverage for an agile hoisting and subsequent setting down upon the commodious face of the implanted blade. Iggy receded at once, dispensing with his radiant offshoot of flame and withdrawing back into the solace of his golden refuge, where he firmly arranged himself before proceeding to take in a healthful quantity of powder. A springy lunge forward then ensued as the boy dove headlong toward the choppy flow of the quickening stream, overshooting the congestion of aggressing grotesquitons and piercing through the waterline with the impetus of a cleanly launched harpoon.

Quietude then befell, or at least was drawn near insomuch as the boy wallowed in the harbor of the underwater sanctuary, which seemed altogether a different world from that upon which he had just escaped. Long fluent strokes carried Cristofo deeper and deeper away and farther along into the evolvement of his underwater fantasy. Gone was the desire to surface and take breath, for the boy was quite comfortable and content with his current mode of advancement He was also quite capable in the art of underwater maneuverability, thanks in large part to the plenitude of lessons rigorously prescribed by the strong-willed and resolute Lady Valencia. His pace began to quicken rapidly, more from the water's downward momentum than by way of the boy's impeccable technique. A broader cognizance then necessarily returned as Cristofo's mind reentered the necessity of the moment, and he began to strive for the surface in anticipation of a soon to be required breach and breath. Additionally, a telepathic command was contemporaneously transmitted and a dagger-shaped segment of miraculous material then flew. Rearward and with velocity it zinged, back into the locality of the previous scene, where it transmogrified and sprouted a ropelike tail that twisted around and took hold of the still-reverberating nethersword hilt. A liberating jolt thereupon ensued, loosening the invaluable blade and freeing it from its craggy hold, thus facilitating a towed-along transport that would soon see it returned to its proper station at its master's backside, snugly at rest in the embrace of its tenacious scabbard.

The boy broke through the waterline with throwing knife in hand and a vigorous thrust, not knowing what to expect upon reentering the breathable aspect of the surround. Turbulence greeted him with a whisking swirl as mist and drizzle and resounding splash swept over the transitional fringe betwixt the two inconsonant elements. The rapid flow accelerating in accordance with the declivity of the underlying groundwork, as well as the forceful slam of rushing wave upon the jagged and rockbound edges of the cavern walls, which happened to be acting as the waterway's embankment as well at this point in the stream, both combined to wreak havoc upon the intermediate stretch of erratic and inconsistent borderline. And Cristofo was swept away in the torrent for lack of any better portrayal, a powerless scrap of rubble washed along in the tide of an increasingly vigorous flow. He knew better than to fight the inevitable, choosing instead to succumb and acquiesce to the whirlwind drag-along, taking breath when able to and focusing on composure and calmness in an effort to battle the overall dizziness of the unavoidable ordeal.

Accordingly, the boy continued along until complete free fall was unmistakably discerned. He came to perceive the associated disequilibrium of center mass and lightness of ear that would be typical to such an occurrence—a circumstance the likes of which he had oftentimes experienced before. The plunge seemed to drag on for a while, lingering to the extent that the boy had all but acclimatized to the vertigo of the situation, until eventually, when a more solid and substantial aqueousness was blatantly endured and our young wizard became profoundly immersed at the completion of his mesmerizing ride. After this point, he proceeded to surface with carefulness as he poked his head out of the water unhurriedly and began to survey the surround, knowing where he had landed but not being able to distinguish precisely how he had gotten there.

The noisy rush of descending waterfall and the modest sprinkle of mist and spray did little to distract Cristofo from the otherwise strange sense of complacency that was felt as he found himself in the near middle of a peculiar cauldron-shaped and extensive cavity that seemed to accommodate a number of inpourings and outflows, all of which blatantly differed in configuration, quantity, and kind. It was an intricately fed hourglass with substance of water in lieu of sand, craggy stone walls in place of glass, and with basis apparently rooted upon an endless and indeterminable setting of time. Within its cavernous and semi-filled upper bulb, the boy assumed to be situated, or so Cristofo correlated as he gasped and fought for breath with moderate difficulty while treading water and devising his procedure to extricate himself from the relatively profound and onerous formation at hand. His coloration transformed to once again take on a recently familiar pinkish-red hue.

CHAPTER 9

A World of Battles and Brouhahas

Cristofo's tender and aching fingers gladly took advantage of the repose that was afforded by way of an opportune outcropping of stone or, more fittingly, an adequate foothold that came to be stumbled upon as he climbed near the peak of the jagged and rockbound wall just adjacent to the rim of the uppermost waterway whereupon the cauldron's heaviest inpouring cascaded down with momentous force and fed a considerable current into the outlandish and incomprehensible mechanism that was a transcendental hub of some mystical type and kind. He elected to take a brief pause in order to rejuvenate overworked muscles as well as to contemplate his next maneuver at hand, so the freshly apprized nethersword was put to good use once again. In quick order, the unique blade was drawn and thrust into the dense and impervious surface of the cavernous wall, just up and over from the boy's prevailing standpoint and just far enough along to make feasible a moderately strenuous reach and climb.

Up and onto the flat edge of the implanted blade he accommodated himself with mild difficulty before proceeding to sit in comfort and survey the foreign and strangely multifaceted surround. From this vantage point, the previously traveled upon rivulet was not only clearly visible but also reasonably attainable as well. His soaked and sodden frame brought no discomfort, and in fact it refreshed him to a degree while keeping him inclined toward continuing along the wet and waterlogged course that lay ahead. A much different appearance presented itself upon the locality that now gushed and surged with potency; it was in stark contrast to the deathly still and frozen setting that he had encountered not long before.

"How are you making out in there, Iggy?" His extraordinary little companion doubtlessly heard the boy's words, yet they went unanswered and were unequivocally ignored. Although impregnable with regard to the water's quelling attribute, it was still an interaction with which the fiery morsel was wholeheartedly willing to oppose.

"Hang in there, little comrade. You will have to maintain your hibernation for yet another spell." Cristofo had thoroughly analyzed his forthcoming course as he sat there briefly and enunciated the words. Without hesitation, he propped himself upright onto the netherblade and proceeded to spring into action with yet another flawlessly executed bound and dive. He plunged down into the river's midst, cutting straight through the hastened flow until reaching the more manageable pace of opposing current that mixed and whirled about the rugged and craggy undersurface of the subterranean riverbed. A telepathic message was then once again transmitted as our young wizard reentered the pleasantness of his underwater fantasyland, wherein he would swim along unconcernedly while the miniaturized portion of Maleabar obediently reassumed the task of retrieving the magnificent yet unmoving netherblade once again. Onward the boy progressed, taking full advantage of the considerable momentum brought to pass by way of his impeccable freestyle technique and notwithstanding the substantial drag of the resistant flow.

Soon enough, his pace had slackened to a degree and he had come to realize that forward progress could be just as steadily yet more easily achieved through the clutching and yanking of the various pointed and spiked components that made up the majority of the riverbed's subaquatic skeleton. Thusly he advanced with fervent strain and focused determination until such time as the snapping thrust of his affixed scabbard signaled the return of his priceless sword. Maleabar reattached itself upon his wrist, jolting Cristofo from his dreamlike and deeply focused state, prompting the young adventurer to take pause for a restorative breath as he subsequently surfaced just atop of the moderately turbulent gush of the streaming water surface and rapidly gulped down the netherworld equivalent to his oxygenated fuel.

At once, he resubmerged and continued down to the coarse and jagged river floor, where forward progress was reestablished by way of wrenching ahead with pulling arms bolstered by kicking legs, until such time as his anchored handholds became noticeably taller and altogether irregular. Shortly thereafter, the boy became frantically more aware as he came to hit upon the previous battleground, whereupon pointed and deadly projectiles flew aplenty, piercing and putting an end to the onrush of persistent sentinels before becoming lodged and littered along the riverbed. This was thanks to the service of our befriended and frenzied band of teeny blue collaborators, the arcuspods.

Sizzled and charred yet for the most part intact faces with a deathly feel now greeted the boy as he glided through the underwater and carcass-laden scene of the sentinels' last foray. Fully exposed and still seemingly aware eyes stared with icy resolve and conveyed an aggressive air as though the will to lash out at their proximate passerby was altogether alive, although lacking the much-needed revivification of thrashing frame. What once was a band of prolific and high-ranking warriors now lay scattered about the coarse and brambly river bottom like snagged and skewered refuse that the cleansing current was unable to whisk and wash away. And so churns the oftentimes ironic course that imposes itself upon pretty much the collectivity of sentient beings, for one knows not when the humbling smash of fate may come crashing down with inescapable wrath. The thrill and rush of adventurous and dangersome entanglements presents to all a double-edged circumstance in that they attempt to accentuate and heighten the exhilarative aspect of creatural life, while at the same time drawing it closer and closer to the brink of an unsolicited yet inevitable end.

"All right now, Iggy, we're done with our watercourse for the time being," Cristofo exclaimed with satisfaction as he hoisted himself up onto the hardened platform that lay stoically positioned at the foot of the ample shaftway whereupon Noxerus had previously made his diabolical debut. It was comprised of the solidified slag-like remains of his globular sacrificers. A shallow flow had overlaid the smooth and level surface, which could no longer manage to hold back the waterway's relentless surge. Instead, the current pressed on and persevered, indifferently running its course over the boy's saturated footwear before gaining rapidity and intermixing into its more turbulent and further along blend. A pulsating glimmer had then ensued, emanating from the boy's chest, where his golden pendant flickered with an increasingly powerful and intermittent zeal. The flaring discharges continued until Iggy deemed it time to exit altogether from his agreeable abode.

"Welcome to the netherworld, little one. Well, what say you? How does the extrinsic environment feel?" Cristofo offered with a most curious mien. A gyrating and spinning gesture was undertaken in response to the enquiring words as the fiery morsel wobbled and unsteadily swayed while flying about his taken-aback master, who had never before seen such an erratic maneuvering unfold.

"What's the problem, Iggy? Please, make an effort to gather your bearings," the boy urged his companion along with a tone that was both slightly puzzled as well as noticeably concerned.

"You're whirling about like an inebriated buffoon!" At that point, our disquieted young wizard had decided to attempt to intervene favorably. Diligent fingers made quick work of the powder bag's unstringing and subsequent exposing of the dry contents within. At once, a modest handful was taken ahold of and thrown, and straight into the pathway of the erratic creature, it sprayed with precise calculation. Much to the boy's surprise, the powder passed through his fiery companion with negligible consequence before spattering ineffectually along the rapidly streaming flow. A rare lack for words then befell as our heroic young protagonist stared with increasingly widened eyes as his predictable companion of many years began to metamorphose abruptly and straightaway.

The creature augmented in a most noticeable way, growing twentyfold or so in size until reaching the approximate proportion of a newborn of humanoid strain. Coloration as well was quite conspicuously remade, deepening and solidifying synchronously with each throbbing burst of enlargement. Within moments, a striking mass of flaring flame hovered in the forefront of Cristofo's view, a strangely displayed creation brandishing the configuration of fire—but with a most incongruous facade. A deep and ominous shade of pink overlaid the complete surface of the combusting being, a solid coating of completely uniform tincture and of a consistent, lustrous glaze.

"Iggy, my word! That is quite the transformation that you have incurred. Are you still as cognizant and familiarized as before?" The boy thoroughly scrutinized the glowing and glossy form, taking a moment to circle around and eyeball the entirety of its surface. "Yes, there you are, little fellow. Now I can perceive your essence yet again, although I don't feel obliged to call you 'little fellow' any longer."

A cautious palm then reached out with curious intent and pressed itself into the creature's newly formed protoplasm. The duo's mental interconnection was still indeed existent, albeit shaky, unsteady, and scarcely intact.

"Well, you don't feel any different, and you don't seem to have any penchant toward the scorching of my relatively susceptible hand. So onward we continue, my little—I mean, my rather substantial— companion, up and through this passageway we advance until reaching the parching and peculiar surface of this hellish land, whereupon more quickly and much closer to our objective we will land!" Cristofo proceeded to lead the way with Iggy trailing closely yet not quite so affectionately behind. Something had indeed altered the basis of the exceptional being, who now conveyed a darker and more diabolical flavor that was blatantly perceived by our resolute and relentless young rescuer, and an increasingly heightened measure of power was obviously exhibited and unquestionably inferred.

After performing the rather strenuous ascension, Cristofo emerged from the smooth and scalable channelway to find himself on the edge of a moderate hillside that overlooked the unmistakable panorama of the unique and extraordinary Mount Immotus. Amidst a band of turbulent, trembling lava-rich crusts, the imposing land mass stoically remained, a stubborn and unwavering ballast stuck in the middle of a violent and ever-changing fiery sea. Thereupon lay Ceratusus's Crater, round and obvious in the distance as though sculpted intentionally upon the terrain to serve purpose of decoration, adornment, or ornamentation of some significant kind; it was a striking accessory to the spectacular focal point of the mountain, the shimmering and shining eye-catching palace of Noxerus. Like a massive and crystalline outcropping of stone, the unique manor imposed itself, resolutely displayed on the flank and more than midway up the mountainside, where long and slender columns of jagged and juxtaposed rock brilliantly reflected the meager offshoot of illumination that came to derive from the lava, fire flashes, and dullish overall fluorescence of the netherworld air. It was a blemish, a growth, a beautiful protuberance on the face of the sphere's most noteworthy landmark, which crowned the cavernous abode of its diabolical wizardly overseer.

What's more, crowds, factions, and all manner of beings and brutes bespeckled the vista, serving to further enliven it and to provide a more animated feel to the already active, vibrant, and combustible scene. Battles raged on with wild and unquenchable flare as savage cries circulated throughout the dark-hued sky, where they intermixed with the echoed crack of seismic ruptures; the spouting bursts of volcanic spew; and the general crackling, sparking, burning, boiling, and bubbling tones that comprised the unmistakable and melodious flavor that formed part of the already distressing and boisterous netherworld feel.

And for some particular reason, and by some random or perhaps contrived progression of fate, Cristofo relished the overall quality of the surround, taking in a foreign breath with invigorating boldness until his insides burned yet felt replete of power and life. So too did his fiery companion seem to be bolstered by the unique and unfamiliar air, taking on an almost humanlike enthusiastic pose as the two vastly different yet intimately interlinked beings stood there almost mesmerized. They were soaking up the excitement of the multitudinous forays and preparing themselves to trek onward unto their meaningful crusade with a most fearless disposition and the most aggressive of intentions. Thusly they advanced, with Cristofo scurrying down the mildly rugged hillside employing his typical hastened pace, and with Iggy trailing obediently yet somewhat unorthodoxly and disconnectedly behind.

In short order, the confident and courageous pair happened upon a seemingly weathered and well-traveled perpendicular pathway whereupon a rather aggressive and raucous band of battle-ready travelers proceeded riotously along on a coincidental path of intercept.

"Well, well, what have we stumbled upon here now, my most dutiful and battle-thirsty warriors? It seems a swig of gratification has made itself available by some arbitrary and fortuitous chance!" A sizable and hulking creature spewed out the words in some strange and foreign tongue, yet Cristofo did quite well in deciphering the implicit meaning. Many a time afore had the exceptional young adventurer encountered brutes, blowhards, bullies, and gang leaders of similar persuasion, yet admittedly none with such a towering physique and threatening disposition.

"Hmm, let's see … Who among us shall be rewarded with the amusement of slaughtering these unusual and repulsive wanderers who seem to have come across the most unfortunate of circumstances?" The being's voice was deep and sinister, resonating out into the surround like an amplified warning cry. Four muscled and oversized arms dominated the towering frame, hanging off a torso with a comparable and fleshier type of grain. A hardened and scaly shell overlaid the backside of the strange entity's enormous anatomy, extending rearward along an elongated hind toward a hearty and menacingly swaying tail. It was a centaur-shaped creation so as to bring your mind to compare, but with a scorpion-type component in lieu of the more typically imagined element of a mare.

"Come now. Such inadequate displays of enthusiasm will surely not garner claim to this wonderful and unexpectedly furnished prize!" The overpowering words echoed with fortitude, all but drowning out the uproarious bellows of the dozen or so enthusiastic band members, who called out in response as they ruffled about the proximate portion of the modestly wide and decently planate pathway. "And so it seems that I myself must take on the exemplifying role yet again. Watch well and take lesson while your master demonstrates the proper way to sumptuously feast!" Two sturdy blades then hastily appeared as the towering creature pulled them from his backside holders with eye-opening speed. "Greetings, strange and privileged ones, and welcome to the company of the infamous Educortex tribe! Now you may ready yourselves to meet with your makers, whereupon you may boast of being theretofore conveyed at the skillful hands of Corpelius the Great!"

Dullish gleams sparkled and displayed a most unusual aspect as they shot off the face of each of the encroaching creature's highly held netherblades, and all four of its muscle-bound limbs became tense and taut as they prepared to strike amidst the incitement of a fiercely disgorged battle cry. Cristofo scarcely wavered in the intervening time and only slightly decelerated from his moderately hastened pace. He felt neither desire nor need to defer to the loud and rambunctious beast, particularly not when focused on a meaningful objective, and generally not when in a position of higher ground, and especially not when in possession of the most unique and effective of swords. And so, the most graceful of downwardly directed leaps then ensued, performed in conjunction with a seamless and fluid unsheathing of blade, which in turn progressed and brought to fruition the smoothest and most eloquently executed of strokes. The clanging and acute sound of dropped metal reverberated into the suddenly quieted surround as the aggressing beast's netherblades noisily came to rest upon the flat and rocky footpath. This was followed promptly by the more subdued thud of fleshy meat and knock of hardened shell as the blowhard's blade-wielding limbs surrendered to the consequence of being instantaneously and unequivocally severed clean.

Then the two formidable companions simply continued to mosey along, all but ignoring the flabbergasted band of quieted onlookers as they cut across the congregation with indifference and as Cristofo nonchalantly tossed his blade to his backside, where its corresponding scabbard aggressively snapped it up. Iggy followed close behind with similar posture but with a bias toward a more disappointed and dissatisfied air as the leaderless Educortexians let them pass with no obstruction, therefore creating no motive for further engagement. What seemed like a ridiculously lengthy transpiration of time then ensued while the twosome became well distanced from the assembly and as they ignored the delayed reaction that had occurred before a portion of the defeated creature's upper body slithered lazily along the angled demarcation point of its flawlessly dissected torso. It finally flopped down with a thud and came to rest upon the callous ground of the flattened and well-trodden pathway.

Onward did the determined duo advance as a diverse assortment of battles and brouhahas continued to present themselves throughout the foreground as they continued their march toward the prominent eye-catching palace. Nary would a moment transpire before they would find themselves intruding upon and interfering in a distinct and unfamiliar melee of some unusual sort and kind. All the while, Cristofo forged ahead with his usual boldness, not hesitating to take part in the odd engagement, which would come to present itself to his more than capable hand while taking the opportunity to familiarize himself further with his newly taken in blade, thusly enhancing and improving upon his already outstanding swordsmanship. Many a fallen creature from either or any side of the various forays littered the rearward trail of the boy's beeline course toward his blatant objective. All the while, Iggy continued to tag closely and attentively along, being sure to keep a protective eye on his long-standing companion by acting as would a fierce yet loyal and disciplined guard dog; granting Cristofo the freedom to actively engage and take on opponents at his sole and unimpeded discretion while taking a back seat to the bountiful action but still remaining aggressive, alert, and at the ready should the need arise.

Somewhere at or about the midway point of the boy's raucous and ... well, let us just say 'unsubtle' and obvious approach, he and his companion came upon a most startling and most pleasantly unexpected display. Humans! Or persons! Or creatures of Earth nonetheless, all abuzz and frenetic while engaged in a most tempestuous foray with rocklike and thickset creatures of substantial girth and a stumpy bouldered design. It was a most abnormal and outlandish breed, with origination seemingly not birthed but instead torn away from the verge of some rock-ribbed mountainside whereupon some simple kneading and molding would polish the creations off prior to their being dispersed and scattered upon the adjacent countryside. A pair of shortened and concrete-like legs moved the creatures along at a gradual yet surprisingly progressive pace as they came down upon the ground with resounding and tremor-generating thuds, while at the same time serving to make quick work of the pulverization of any and all parcels, portions or things that found themselves in the unfortunate trappings of their underside.

A consolidated midsection seemed to endure upon the beasts with the simple purpose of anchoring its tetrad of limbs, which also included a pair of matching but longer arms that hung down idly and stagnantly alongside of them as they maneuvered clumsily along. Built-in sledgehammers that were at the ready to undertake any requirement for pounding or hammering or clobbering that may come to transpire. A relatively undersized crown topped off the massive and mountain-materialized beasts. It was a boulder-shaped finial with no discontinuity save for a pint-sized and perforated pair of dark beady eyes and a fissure-like aperture situated some ways below. It mimicked a mouth as it opened and oscillated to dissipate loud and obnoxious outcries that echoed out with fortitude and created ear-piercing shrills that traveled through the airwaves with the vibrating modulation of a heavily advancing rockslide.

"Strike them down with your blunted scimitars!" The resounding voice barely cut through the overpowering chorus of the bellowing band of bouldered battlers who made up the members of the Eo-saxum tribe. Cristofo was somewhat relieved yet not so much surprised to hear the words that were shouted out in his own familiar tongue. And as a consequence, he began to focus more attention upon a tall and statuesque man who stood out as he maneuvered and swayed about the foot of one of the swinging and stomping brutes, swatting away with his sword while continuing to call out commands.

"Entangle their legs with your chains to bring them down and then rain havoc upon their fallen frames!" Shards and fragments of rock flew off the creature as the obvious leader of men made contact with the odd stroke of blade while continuing to dodge and dart about the circumference of the powerful and determined yet relatively sluggish and dense attacker. Cristofo came to rest for the first time during his downwardly directed crusade and took a moment to observe the unusual battle involving a quantity of his kinsmen—so to speak—with which he felt an understandable affinity given his current interfusion into such a strange setting and among such a strange agglomeration of unfamiliar creatures and things.

As he stood there in a somewhat fascinated state of observance, a number of ongoing skirmishes presented themselves in the proximate range wherein a dozen or so of the rocky constituted beasts fervently exchanged blows with ten times the number of the merely muscled and boned battlers. Chains wisped through the air in plenitude and wrapped themselves about the forelegs of one of the mammoth and consolidated beings. Shrill cries roared through the vicinity as a half dozen men heaved and pulled with might until firm and grounded legs of stone were forced to come together, allowing gravity to gain favor over an unbalanced load. Once felled, a number of scimitar-wielding attackers were directed to get astride of the capsized mark, whereupon their weapons came down with repetitive and resounding blows. Thus did defeat happen upon the hulking and seemingly undefeatable creature with which the well-bodied warriors were rigorously engaged, and in no time at all the capable behemoth came to remain smattered, scattered, and permanently stilled.

Indeed, the battle-worn humans reaped the benefit of their wise choice of arms: the blunted scimitar. It was a uniquely fashioned bludgeon with an appearance similar to its bladed namesake but with a thick and tapered striking edge in lieu of the typical sharpened kind. A broad and lengthy mass of metal with thickness measuring two fingers wide could certainly make for a wallop that proved to be quite effective as it came down upon opponents of the more rocklike and breakable variety. It was akin to striking with the backside of an ax, but with much more potency delivered because of a much more easily maneuvered stroke. A slight curvature on the overall length would serve to intensify the force of impact and to allow for a more fluid percussion, thereby facilitating a more rapidly pronounced flurry of recoil and chop and thus allowing one to make quick work of the required chiseling and hacking away. This would lead to the shearing off of chunks, the breaking apart of blocks, and the eventual converting to rubble of the unfortunate Eo-saxum prey.

Elsewhere around the relatively widespread battleground, similar skirmishes and encounters were concurrently well underway. Blares, bellows, and all sorts of clamorous commotions and cries rang through the stuffy and sweltering netherworld air with an almost reassuring usualness. Gravel-like pieces and shards flew off the rocky giants in abundance, while squashed and swatted away morsels of meat and fleshy fabric were simultaneously strewn. At once, the nearby engaged-upon creature barreled toward the site of its fallen comrade, seemingly oblivious to the relentless pursuit of its persistent attacker, who continued to chase and swat away at the heels of the outraged and infuriated brute. Pounding fists came down like sledgehammers upon the humans, who were caught off guard and who had scarcely begun to revel in their latterly gained triumph. One such unfortunate soul was knocked clean away by a deadly accurate and pendulum-like stroke that was let fly as though shooing upon a bothersome and insignificant insect. Another such combatant found himself unable to evade a dynamic and well-placed stomp that came down upon his legs with the force of a hundred slabs. Hardly a shriek or a cry was transmitted from the dazed and deadened soul in the split second that transpired in advance of his upper portion being swatted upon and tidily disjoined from his already flattened and inert lower frame.

At this point, Cristofo felt an overwhelming urge to interpose himself into the foray. The brutally delivered fatalities gave rise to a sentimentality of sorts that swayed him toward the favor of the tribesmen of relatively equal strain. Suddenly and straightaway, the spirited young wizard bolted down upon the setting of the immediate melee. With nimble speed and skillful execution, he bounded up and onto the substantial midsection of the fallen Eo-saxum's rocklike remains, continuing his upward surge until it brought him to a more or less equal plane with his raging and rampaging, stomping and swatting prey. The comparatively heavy and sluggish behemoth stood little chance against the fast-moving and formidable adventurer. In fact, it had just been quick enough to turn its head around in time to perceive the flash of nethersteel, which would serve to represent the final image upon which it would bear witness, at least insofar as that particular manner of existence was concerned. A nearly perfect medial blow split straight into the crown of the almost pitiable creature and continued down well into the pith of its broad and rockbound upper trunk.

The symmetrical segments of cleaved upper frame proceeded to bend and curl at an increasingly widening rate until the V-shaped void down the center of the partially slivered beast broke down completely as a consequence to its crumbled and fully collapsed sides. The lower half of the being remained upright as Cristofo steadily came to rest at the foot of the rubble-laden foreground and as a relative quietude befell. A simple moment seemed to pass as both men and boulder-like beasts surveyed the scene of the decisive defeat in an effort to make sense of what had presently transpired. Then a resounding bellow rang out from elsewhere in the surround; a far-reaching outcry emitted from the mouth of another member of the stonelike tribe, which signaled immediate retreat for all the remaining Eo-saxum colossi. Concurrently, in the approximate distance, on a conveniently arranged balcony carved into the side of the majestic mountainside, a nervy and devilish head jolted around in reaction to the peculiar yet somewhat familiar sound. Indeed, it was our old friend Noxerus, who had caught wind of the circumstance and at once and implicitly inferred the gist of the boy's escapade. A diabolical smile crept its way into form along a set of thin and wispy lips as sharpened and shady teeth necessarily became exposed and as muscle-bound forearms settled atop a monolithic banister, whereupon they helped to facilitate a comfortable and unrestricted ongoing view.

"Three cheers for the mysterious and incomprehensible boy!" a random band member suddenly cried, only to be immediately followed by a jubilant and all-encompassing celebratory uproar. The victorious humans then began to converge as the surviving rock giants collectively foregathered and fled.

"What say you, my remarkable and inspirational brethren?" The strong voice greeted Cristofo with a most pleasant and appreciative tone. "Are you lost or adrift from your tribe? Have you perhaps transmigrated from one of the lower sectors of our notorious sphere? I hear that there are many such hominoid hordes situated in the lower and more aqueous and less scorching tiers. Undoubtedly, it is a much more compatible environment for creatures of muscle and flesh and bone—simple creatures of servitude such as ourselves." The gregarious band leader offered up the words while exhibiting a unifying gesture with his arms, an associative motion that served to foster a sense of welcome and familiarity.

"Am I correct to assume that you lead this band of barbarous and able-bodied men?" Cristofo's retort was somewhat authoritative if not more than slightly snobbish.

"You would indeed be correct to assume so, young man; Thaddeus the intrepid of the third-tier Terra-pario tribe at your service." The battle-worn veteran presented himself strikingly and with agreeable charm, a much preferable type of response as far as our wizardly protagonist was concerned, although he had been entirely prepared to take the appropriate action should the response have been one of the more offensive or assertive in variety.

"Cristofo, wizard of Earth," was exuded with obvious confidence as the boy sturdily grasped the arm of the well-postured man. "And in the company of Ignatius, the unequivocally inflamed. We venture with haste toward the palace on a quest to liberate some companions of ours who have been involuntarily enslaved."

"And so have we all been involuntarily enslaved. Each and every one of us creatures who find ourselves struggling and scraping away at a meager existence on this godforsaken plane. Indeed, we are here not by choice but in consequence to the conduct and actions of our previously held existences, slaves to the anger and wrath that festers and is forcibly infused into every encounter with dissimilar factions or crews. Here we remain, scratching and clawing beast-like beings desperate to persevere despite our torturous continuance and notwithstanding our underlying appetite for the sweet release of death and the consequent shift to a better-suited domain. Imprisoned wretches who are free from visible shackles or chains yet remain confined nonetheless, savage and salivating barbarians brought to pass with each and every encounter. Ferocious and fearless brutes putting on performance after ruthless performance while under scrutiny and to the amusement of our devilish and diabolical overseer."

"I hear your plight and feel for your circumstance, although I know naught of your previous and formerly lived ways," Cristofo began with a resounding tone and with an all-encompassing posture that drew in the entirety of the hominid clan. He continued with his professing speech-like dialogue, which at once drew the full attention of the unduly receptive audience.

"Furthermore, it seems to be quite apparent that your current situations are likely, and dare I say undeniably, very well deserved! Yet let us not harp upon the irrelevant rationalization of how you have come to arrive here or for what reason you have come to be arraigned, but instead let us quite simply accept the fact that we have all been brought together by some random happenstance or perhaps by some calculated turn of destiny. Nonetheless and whatever the case, here we stand: a robust and capable well-built band of fighting men, a small yet powerful army of iron-willed warriors at the ready and unequivocally unafraid. So, I propose to you that you join me in my endeavor, taking the fight to the heart of the matter, so to speak, in lieu of lingering and leaving your encounters to the discretion of unassociated parties or to the arbitrary spin of some devilishly inspired fate."

"Am I to understand that you intend for us to join you in a bold and brazen charge toward the palace, young man of mysterious mainspring and manner?" the reddened and respectable leader of men inquired in a rhetorical way as a buzz and overall chitchat overspread the remainder of the manageable and overly agreeable crowd.

"Why not?" was emitted sporadically, in random and affirmatory ways.

"What have we got to lose?" was set abuzz among the multitudes, with little worry and no opposers with anything otherwise to say. Eagerness and enthusiasm began to quickly steep and stew as cheers of encouragement sprouted and excitement spread through and through.

"We all know that our ends will come in due course anyway."

"We wouldn't be the first who have tried, but maybe we can be the first to succeed."

"I, for one, grow weary of lingering and lagging along in this domain."

"I also tire and no longer desire to subsist as a creature who suffers while others are entertained."

On and on the encouraging banter whistled and flew like the spirited and snappy sparks of a softwood fire, until Thaddeus the well-spoken warrior settled the masses and vocally and unequivocally intervened.

"Well then, my loyal and experienced band of brethren, it seems that we are all on the same wavelength and that we all overwhelmingly agree. We shall proceed to grasp vigorously upon the throat of circumstance and to take cause upon those who impose restriction against our precious and much-longed-for free will. To the nearest weapons depository at once, whereupon the devices of a more poignant variety shall unmistakably be our aim. And shields in accompaniment; buffers and bulwarks to suit your particular comforts and needs! Onward, my fellow champions, and make haste as you set forth upon our objective. Lead on toward the sweet song of victory, for it shall certainly overwhelm us with its mesmerizing serenade, albeit through the skillful sway of our well-worn and sharpened instruments or through the merry foray that will see us depart this forsaken continuance and usher us unto a better and more tolerable plane!"

Shrieks, howls, and battle cries consummated the rendering of the befitting leader's well-placed words as the crowd of rambunctious humanoids collectively set foot upon their goal. Maces, bludgeons, and blunted scimitars alike were released and discarded like so many scraps of valueless debris, and straightaway to the nearest weapons depot the lot of them summarily convened. In little time and with little deviation, in stride they arrived at one of a multitude of customarily arranged depositories that littered the surround, a modestly arranged structure similar in composition to that which Cristofo perused in advance of his latterly fought contest. In contrast, however, this one had a much more polished presence, with vitrified and well-reconciled walls loftily at ease amidst a spotless and well-cared-for perimeter. Cristofo lagged and lingered to a degree, preferring to observe from the perspective of a limited distance, while his otherworldly kinsmen cluttered and congested the building's solitary entryway in an effort to arm themselves to a T.

For a brief period, the tumultuous scurry obscured the differentiation between enterer and evacuee until distance could be achieved by the armed and readied departers, bringing to clear view a variety of blatantly exhibited shields intertwined among a myriad of dullish and dancing flashes of nethersteel. A spirited charge began, a raw and unhesitating onslaught fueled with the fire of an irrefutable gain. Steadily and in a constant gush, the battle-ready warriors marched upon the palace's sizable entryway with the unwavering drive of a stream of attacking army ants. Determinedly they did flow on a beeline course toward the structure's cave-like opening, which lay flagrantly visible but still remained a considerable distance away.

Rearward, in the meanwhile, a resplendent offshoot of radiance caught the corner of the boy's eye and drew his attention away from the otherwise inspiriting scene. A quartet of familiar and sprightly creatures had suddenly come into view, custodians of the battleground, or so they appeared. The zippy and spirited operatives made quick work of the gathering and organizing of the abandoned implements and of the tidying and taking away of corpses, carcasses, and the various other segments and sections associated with the ravaging foray. A regiment of muscled and mule-like beasts accompanied the prolific processors, each of which displayed a similar sheen and equivalent vigor to their meticulous and methodical masters as they dragged along barrow-shaped wagons, which were speedily laden and instantaneously taken away. These so-called facilitators of the nethersphere brought a certain agreeability and cordiality to the otherwise harsh and uninviting air, and the boy felt a genuine affinity toward them and a spark of goodness that was definitely sensed and unequivocally gleaned.

"I feel beyond alive, Iggy," the remarkable boy who was blossoming into a man declared unanticipatedly as he breathed in the distinctive air with the force of an exaggeratedly powerful set of lungs. "I feel the blood coursing through my veins like the cascading rush of a downward stream. My heart reverberates like the pounding beat of a battle drum, wherein each and every stroke heightens my awareness and bolsters my every muscle and pore. My eyes see more than mere refracted rays, Iggy; instead, they scour the surround and perceive detail that would ordinarily hide among the shadow of the obverse side. My ears draw in every nuance, forceful magnets that attract not metal but rather modulation and tone. And it doesn't end there, Iggy. Nostrils draw in the essence of all that presents itself in their range, with lips that can taste the surround and decipher the truly whimsical nature of its raging and rampaging way. Toes grasp upon the ground with an explorative air, bypassing the wall of footwear as though it were not even there, while fingers stretch out with an eager yearning, itching to take hold and anxious to maneuver and mold. I feel beyond alive, Iggy. I feel ready to thrive!"

Ah yes, to feel the blissful onrush of a germinal wizardly enlivenment. Millennia have flown by and washed away a vastitude of memories with the whisking swirl of a temporal whirlwind, yet still, that moment so, so long ago sits fresh in my mind as though it occurred only yesterday. The unequivocal feel of powerfulness and the stark bite of realization that ensues when a wizardly invocation spontaneously begins and when that first infusion of overwhelming dynamism all of a sudden, and without any question, thoroughly takes hold. It would be untruthful to deny my envy toward the boy at that particular juncture in time, as would it be improper to assume that a genuine lean toward peacefulness and a contented feel were not also a part of the emotional fray. Indeed, the two conflicting emotions can and do certainly coexist with each other, as do a number of other sentiments from time to time in comprising the insuppressible mélange of an animus being's psychological disposition.

"It is difficult to explain, Iggy, but I can see that you feel it too, and in fact I sense a similar mind-set within you as well. My senses are heightened beyond constraint, and I would go so far as to say that they burst forth with the drive of a wild, untamable stallion! Onward, my fierce and fiery companion; it is now our time to join in the parade!"

With those words, our flourishing young Cristofo began his belated charge, racing toward the already engaged clash that had instantaneously generated an overly abundant measure of carnage and bloodshed. Humans and sentry men alike did battle and swayed in great numbers as the imposing palace entryway's immediate foreground became painted with bodily spew and came to be littered with miscellaneous chunks and fragments that were ruthlessly severed and wantonly hewn. Many brave tribesmen succeeded in freeing themselves from their torturous existences, as did a fair share of rugged and robustious guardians who were forcibly ushered unto their consequent and wholly uncharted campaigns. And the battle raged on for a good period of time as more and more of the resilient sentinels poured forth from within the meandering and mazelike interior of the staggering structure in an effort to ward off the attacking tribesmen with a consolidated attempt to join in and bolster their brethren's defensive barricade.

A fleeting and unswayable force then arrived as Cristofo delved headlong into the husk of the merciless foray. All opponents in his path were voraciously engaged upon and dealt with by way of the conclusive stroke of skillfully wielded nethersteel. The boy's extravagant blade served him well against the sizable and well-armed band of battlers, as did his newly invigorated spirit and supercharged zeal. Slashed away segments of sword and severed sections of spear rained down upon the terrain in the forefront of the boy's rampaging sortie. Heads were lopped off with unsettling ease, and they crashed down upon the ground with resounding still-helmeted thuds as coarse and chalky white flesh intermixed with slimy, sludgy fluids as well as steely plate and shield, all of which served to cover the ground below while accumulating in muddled heaps and piles. Nimble footwork automatically came into play as Cristofo balanced himself atop the jumbled masses while continuing his aggressive charge. Leaps and bounds advanced the boy forth as he maintained his savage onslaught from the comfort of a more elevated standpoint, while shields, helmets, and bodies alike were utilized as stepping-stones to bring him ever nearer toward his imminent goal.

In short time, our daring and newly invigorated wizard had succeeded in advancing beyond the primary guardian blockade, and a minor reprieve now presented itself as he crossed over the accessible threshold and into the palace's expansive reception hall. All the while, Iggy had remained closely at the rear of his venerated master, following intently but quietly along while delivering only the occasional burning and brandishing with what seemed like only a meager and moderately emitted discharge. Once inside, a triad of deadpan and determined sentinels stood at strict guard in the forefront of every available passageway that lined the massive antechamber's perimeter walls with muddled symmetry, thusly blocking any attempt to gain further entry into any other part of the elaborate mazelike domain. Ridiculously large and heavily barbed spears cast aim upon the boy, with points aligned like so many sets of impassioned and fixated eyes. Waves of rushing sentry men continued to gush forth sporadically, all the while exuding out through the various passages and passing between their statue-like comrades' bodily blockades. Most of them continued toward the palace's more actively boisterous exterior, while a mere foursome methodically chose to remain, placing themselves evenly spaced and at the halfway point between Cristofo and the perimeter wall's protected access ways.

At once, an eager spear was launched with considerable force and accuracy, but it was easily steered clear by way of a swift and skillful swat of nethersteel. A simple flick of the boy's wrist then quickly and deliberately ensued, unleashing the meager amount of miraculous material with deadly precision and with a strictly focused mental rule. The scarcely visible fragment jetted straight through the unsuspecting guardsman's focused eyehole until it pierced the back of his helmet with the implicit ease of a comparably shaped needle passing through a simple tract of wool. The three remaining approachers drew swords and barreled concurrently toward the boy just as their compatriot's slumped body gravitated inertly toward the smooth and rigid ground below. Before the resounding thud of impact was distinctly heard, the portion of Maleabar returned to its interim master and was yet again successfully and similarly hurled. A second successive attacker then lay similarly stagnant on the polished and hardened floor.

Two remaining riled and raging guardians were now fully upon the readied and qualified boy, who proceeded to engage them in some disciplined swordplay with the intent of evaluating their general skill level and speed, a beneficial nugget of information that would prove useful in deciphering the overall abilities of the persistent yet little-known sentinel breed. Mere moments passed, and Cristofo had garnered the required insight while employing a quantity of casual blocks, thrusts, sways, parries, and turns. With no further need to prolong the uncomplicated charade, he abruptly supercharged his execution and pace, serving to dispatch the remaining two ogre-like beings simultaneously and straightaway.

"Maleabar, conjoin with your bulkier proportion!" the boy declared with a bold and vigorous tone. At once, the metallic wonder veered off hard and to the portside with an obedient ambition and moderate velocity, shooting squarely through the midsection of the selected pathway's centermost and bodily fashioned barricade while en route to its larger and more significant staff- shaped guise.

Cristofo wasted no time in chasing after the morsel of Maleabar, trusting full well that the primary portion of miraculous material would at least be situated in the vicinity of his ultimate goal. It was a speculative notion bolstered by a mental interconnection that began to take hold as the young apprentice apperceived the presence of one and the other of his impounded wizardly compeers. Broad blades of spear swerved and veered as the remaining two determined guardians attempted to fend off the boy's undaunted forward advancement into the mouth of their assigned passageway. The lengthy weapons were indeed skillfully wielded, yet the capacity of our singularly talented adolescent was simply beyond compare. There was no laxness of speed as Cristofo holstered his magnificent blade and continued headlong into the wall of slashing and oscillating weaponry, wherein a headfirst dive then purposefully ensued, bringing his body safely below the range of the flailing display and advancing it smoothly into a forearm-assisted skip and surge. This maneuver served to jostle him up and onto the body of the sentinels' medial and most recently fallen peer. Blades then whacked down as though swung with the brutish stroke of seasoned lumbermen, intending to cut short the boy's unrelenting crusade, and indeed both sharpened steely implements bit down into flesh with a satiating plunge. However, the flavorless and cadaverous tissue was what the serrated edges felt as they chomped profoundly into the pith of the previously dispatched sentinel's lifeless carcass.

Yes, indeed, a considerable measure of space will necessarily ensue in the midst of a triangular arrangement wherein there is meaningful length to all sides. A longish guardian frame coupled with an even more prolonged arm's length outreach of spear leaves more than enough leeway for a simply executed and perfectly timed shift and veer. Thus did our young champion serve to avoid the intended lethal strokes, rolling sidelong onto the brink of one of the attacker's monstrous feet. Likewise did he succeed in negotiating a fluid drawing of his throwing knife and a subsequent upsurge and plunge that drew the blade deeply into the pith of the hapless warrior's unsuspecting throat. A mightily executed outward thrust then savagely ensued, rupturing and detaching a considerable portion of jawbone and jowl alike as his forward motion continued to follow through until the blade exited its initial objective before being released momentously, straightforward and true. The compacted half-pound mass of flawlessly forged and sharpened earthly steel then proceeded to cement itself profoundly into the skull of its proximate and crosswise foe, putting an end to the combative situation as both osseous matter and spew from the firstly assailed victim splattered upon the face of the more recently defeated opposer, just as the two of them crumpled and dropped lifelessly down to the ground in unison.

Once again, Cristofo made haste as he continued with the pursuit of the fleeting fragment of Maleabar, barreling down the tunnel-like channel with countervailing speed as several auxiliary sentinels from the reception antechamber changed course and proceeded to chase and relentlessly pursue. However, their efforts were soon to be proven futile as each of the onrushing guardians came to hit upon a vivid consolidated and impassable barrier. Indeed, it was Iggy who had remained behind to keep all of the aggressive pursuers at bay. One by one, they would brashly charge; one by one, they would instantaneously fall upon impact with the burning and blazing solidified wall. The fiery creature had indeed metamorphosed into a more powerful and substantial being, brandishing an equivalent measure of loyalty but with an inclination toward a more callous and unsympathetic mien. A glassy and globular barricade now sealed the entirety of the passage's bounds, as Iggy had swollen to a tight-fitting size and bolstered intensity to an almost unfathomable rise. A deeply shaded mass now lay ominously at guard while exhibiting a fluorescent and darkish magenta hue as it remained stoically in place with a simple and solitary charge, preventing all advancing assailants from giving chase to his highly regarded master.

Many a loyal guardsman made an effort to breach the impenetrable blockade, rushing headlong into the nearly solid form of absolute blaze, in the process conveying themselves to instantaneous dissolution with an incinerating flicker. One can only imagine the degree of dynamism required to generate a sufficiently hot combustion so as to immediately consume creatures that made feast of slag and took drink of lava, yet in some such way, such power did indeed put on a display, sizzling tips of spear and spontaneously combusting blades forged of resistant nethersteel. Many devoted and determined sentinels suffered instant disintegration of their extremities and limbs alike as they stubbornly, and might I add stupidly, continued to test the veracity of the formidable palisade.

In the meantime, Cristofo maintained his relentless pursuit as the fleeting fragment of wizardly wonder raced through the various curves and corridors while negotiating several twists and turns with a seamless and implicit ease. Each of the intermittent oncoming guardians who would be so unlucky as to cross squarely into their path would either be met with an inescapable and lethal piercing straight through courtesy of the scarcely visible metallic material, or they would otherwise come to terms with a similarly swift and sudden slaying at the hand of the skillful boy and his extraordinarily compatible new blade. In short order, the aspect of the chase veered noticeably downward, and although the network of twists and turns maintained their sporadic consistency, at one point, an obvious and precipitous downgrade deviation became blatantly apparent and clear, until the portion of Maleabar eventually and finally proceeded to burst into a large and cavernous, cluttered laboratory-like room.

Cristofo slackened his pace and surveyed the surround as he passed through the threshold and into the peculiar chamber. At once, a vivid assortment of contraptions and creations of differing measures and kinds took strong hold of his attention and served to pique his sense of curiosity while concurrently heightening his alertness and overall verve. A sudden and boisterous smash then ensued as the fragment of miraculous material concluded its most recently mandated charge, crashing through an irrelevant and glassy canister atop a crowded tabletop and conjoining with its more massively proportioned and staff-shaped side. This consequently succeeded in interrupting the inharmonious yet strangely soothing dripping and bubbling, squeaking and creaking, pecking and knocking tones that defined the essence of the unusual workshop, or testing room, or research lab of some unconventional nature and style.

"Maleabar, return!" the boy commanded, but surprisingly he found the utterance to be ignored and disregarded and altogether without comply.

"Welcome, Master Cristofo, hatchling of the most nurturing and fructiferous Mother Earth!" A modest and crackling voice brought these words into the otherwise clattery and rackety space, clearly and concisely spoken in proper English tongue, nonetheless although somewhat devalued due to an inherently coarse undertone such as that which would be associated with a creature of excessive and obvious age. At once, a diminutive being leaped up and onto a nearby worktable with surprising dexterity and unexpected speed, only to be met dead on with an expertly wielded and instantaneously drawn-upon length of nethersteel.

"What manner of foul creature be you?" the boy exerted authoritatively, with the endorsement of a pointed blade abutting and betwixt a pair of grayish-blue unflinching eyes.

"Ah, my old friend Azrael! A befitting prize for the prospective successor to the illustrious animus clan—and one well-chosen indeed, I might add, Master Cristofo."

"You know this blade?" the fledgling wizard spontaneously let fly, knowing perfectly well that an affirmative response would almost certainly comprise the strange being's imminent and oncoming reply.

"Know it? Indeed, I do, yet 'know' is not the proper term to be used in such an intimate context. Does a mother simply 'know' her child?

Would a lover simply claim to 'know' their kindred soul? I think not, Master Cristofo, and likewise do I disagree with the use of the word as a frame of reference to define my unfathomable knowledge toward this exquisite blade! Its conception began eons ago, brought forth by a spark of thought enkindled by my own ever-contriving mind and nurtured to fruition over the course of several lifetimes, inasmuch as the intervals would pertain to those whom you would refer to as peers. No words can properly describe the manner in which I made sharp the unmatchable blade, and no mind can grasp the degree to which I toiled and slaved, whetting and honing with numberless hours and strokes, crafting and conjuring with unmatchable diligence and scope. Ah, if only you could fathom the intimacy in which we both share, my fair Azrael and me. Much that is me is embodied in her, and much that is her exists within me ..."

A brief pause then fittingly ensued as the wrinkly earth-toned and infant-sized creation seemed to abruptly emerge from a pleasantly mesmerizing fantasy. "And so is the case for many and most of my comparable creations, Master Cristofo, which brings us back to the gist of your first, and might I say discourteously placed question. Fingo would be my name, and the title you may use to refer to me. Yet, 'The Imperial Alchemist,' 'Supreme Forger of the Nether,' or 'Magisterial Mastermind of Weaponry', would be some of my more formally declared and ceremonially bestowed titles. At your service!"

The diminutive creature concluded his long-winded diatribe with a humble bow, a forward shifting veer facilitated by way of a latterly laxed blade. Cristofo had long since recognized the agreeable nature of the undersized individual as well as his obviously animus-classed kind. A brief interval of quietude followed as Cristofo further analyzed the talkative being while also taking in a more detailed view of the surround. Mutophasms! An arrangement of those strange and tenacious nuisances were first to enrapture the boy's mind, as were they the first and foremost of entities brought forth to welcome our valiant campaigner into the parching and peculiar land on his inaugural drop-in not long afore. A dozen or so lined up comatose on a linearly aligned contraption connected to a tabletop that stood near at hand.

Tenuous and transparent tubes reeled into and around their unmoving frames until reaching an end just above the cusp of a rather large and columnar openmouthed beaker wherein small droplets of venom dripped down and reverberated with what seemed a thunderous echo as the boy intensified his focus and stare.

Elsewhere, other abundant devices and contraptions were also analyzed with similar concentration. The staff of Bellatrix, for example ... There it inconspicuously lay absent its crown and haphazardly placed upon a dim little crook in the room. Cristofo chose to repress the fact that it had been utterly gleaned and continued on while presuming that the crafty little rascal had dug full into the deciphering of the wizardess's enigmatic and mystical stone. Here and there and intermittently scattered everywhere throughout the space, simple and stunted worktables planted themselves resolutely in the manner of prevalent and unshakable fixtures whereupon well-used and unfamiliar yet obvious tools of the incredible trade contentedly lay among the various objects and articles and inconceivable items and things—reluctant victims subjected to all varieties of experimentation, dissection, and whims. Although a large quantity of information had been diligently and deliberately ingested, only a brief moment had in fact passed until Cristofo's eyes returned to their principal target, who yet remained anchored in place by the tip of an authoritative and still steadily upheld blade.

"You speak heartily and with unexpected eloquence, little Fingo, the fabricator of contraptions and blades. My words will ring much more simply and will be more clearly presented and concisely unskewed; bring me to my wizardly companions at once, lest your precious Azrael gets thrust straightforwardly into your throat!" The humble little curiosity remained calm, motionless, and seemingly unstirred by the earnestly placed threat. And what's more, a soft and inspiriting smile crept its way onto his rumpled and wrinkly undersized face."

"Ah, it would be nothing short of a pleasure, young master, to face an end at the hand of such grace. One of age in the same manner as I would not be brought to their knees by the means of such blatantly placed duress. Indeed, joyance would ensue in its stead, ushered by way of the freeing and fanciful notion that you present, wherein a different and more desirable continuance of mind would result from the culmination of your decisively threatening deed. Nonetheless, your eagerness is certainly to be expected, and furthermore, it is thoroughly understood. Yet I propose to you for your consideration and contemplation, of course, young Master Cristofo, that patience is a power that has served my creations quite well, and moreover it is a factor of value that you would be wise to consider for the moment and make dwell."

With that, as well as with a casually launched hop off the tabletop, Fingo gestured for our adventurer to follow as he proceeded casually along and further into the expansive chamber. Cristofo, of course, stayed close on his trail and thereupon took note of the fact that the curious creature actually sported a tail. It was a modestly sized appendage from the looks of the bulge on the backside of his well-fitted and lab coat–like garb, revealing a substantial stub that tapered down to a slender and curled point that protruded out and up from under the garment's well-tailored hem. Indeed, it was a rodent-like feature of the otherwise rumpled and stout two-legged being who sauntered merrily along by the virtue of his clawed and somewhat curvilinear and relatively oversized feet.

"And do not entertain any deceptive maneuvers, master fidgeter of gadgets and things—" The boy was abruptly cut short in his partially uttered forewarning.

"Yes, yes, I know full well, Master Cristofo. You will run me straight through with my own invaluable creation. Worry not, for my master keeps me not for my ability to deceive."

"And if either of them is damaged or harmed in any meaningful way—" Once again, he was interrupted.

"You will indeed find them fully intact, young master. You must still learn plenty with regard to the implicit nature of wizardly interrelationships. There exists an underlying sense of respect that unmistakably comes into play, inspired by the overseers nonetheless, a necessary dose of cordiality without which an undesirable imbalance would necessarily emerge and make way."

A considerable measure of patience was required in order for Cristofo to composedly proceed, for he was not accustomed to being so wantonly interrupted, nor was he comfortable being so indiscriminately led.

"Surely you feel it as well, Master Cristofo, the inherent inter-wizardly courtesy of which I speak. Verily, it is there without question, despite the fact that in the present course of time, you may not feel so graciously inclined toward the likes of your nether-categorized compeers. That is not to say that exceptions do not exist with regard to this intrinsic and fundamental way. In fact, oftentimes clashes and quarrels can rage and stew until reaching culmination, as would a bubbling and boiling brew. And so, although it is somewhat rare for one or the other of the transcendental fraternity to deliver their equal-ranked associate into the realm of the unequivocally unclear, it is certainly not unheard of!"

At this point in our young adventurer's single-minded campaign, he opted to continue quietly while his talkative hostage prattled habitually along. Cristofo could not help but feel a conflicting affinity toward the seemingly enlightened and peculiar being who brought forth warming thoughts of his grandfather and, as a consequence, a more comforting air. Fingo, the foremost of fabricators, carried on with his incessant recommendations, opinions, and so forth as he traversed a number of openings and passed through various compartments, tunnels, and rooms. All the while, Cristofo discreetly absorbed the vast array of unusual and unfamiliar detail, emblazoning it all to his mind for further analysis while haphazardly lending an ear to the ramblings of his seemingly more than willing captive, until all at once, when the disconsonant pair set upon an expansive and cavernous factory-like area of operation.

"More, you fruitless and incompetent beasts!" The tiny creature roared out the rudely exerted directive in a graceless and coarse tongue that brought out a manner and method most incongruous with his modestly constituted frame. "Much more platinous matter is required in order to soften the wrath of the master!" A dozen or so monotonous and ogre-like beings in the immediate foreground turned sluggishly toward Fingo in response to the vociferously placed words, barely breaking pace from their labors and almost uncaringly ignoring the words. What a sight it was that presented itself before Cristofo at that particular moment in time—a heavily industrialized factory floor that brought forth a memory of the most familiar kind. It was an expansive space teeming with strange, steady, and slow-moving beasts of burden, primarily those of the giant two-legged and muscle-bound variety, all of whom rummaged about systematically, consistently, and with an eerily synchronous rhythm.

"Flagello, send word into the shaftways that these ores are not sufficient in quality or kind!" Fingo commanded as he scrutinized the contents of one in a line of primitive yet adequate and brimming carts that were being conveyed into a farther along section of the factory, wherein blocks and hunks of the broken-off fragments from within the bowels of the magnificent Immotus were being additionally evaluated, processed, and categorized. An even larger but equally sluggish, slag-composed, and vitrified brute nodded clumsily in reply as he stumbled forward toward one of the multiple dark and desolate passageways while concurrently unravelling a relatively short, segmented and metallically disposed flog.

"You will excuse my abrupt burst of barbarity, Master Cristofo, as it is absolutely required in order to effectively communicate with these dense and single-minded beasts." Our young protagonist had already surmised the rationale behind the laborious and intense propensity to mine, as well as its eventual and most rare and valuable of consequences. Of course, it was none other than the miraculous wizardly material toward which he was by this time conclusively inclined.

"Teams and numbers of the inexhaustible breed pervade all along the multitude of tunnels and veins that course throughout the ever-reaching root of our unwavering, monolithic, and mountainous host. Developed and derived over countless generations of species and seed with no alternative purpose but to burrow, extract, and breed. 'Tis doleful indeed to consider the menial and subservient existences of the perpetually burdened classification and kind, yet still we must remind ourselves that all forms of continuance have a relative diversity of emotions, experiences, spirit, and drive. And all for what? you might pry. Oftentimes, I am forced but to reflect and to ponder; such an exhaustive and all-important undertaking in order to produce a mere droplet per every odd century of the nowhere near necessary or required but indisputably miraculous wonder ..."

Once again, a brief pause was habitually construed—a requisite reset that seemed to preclude our forcibly begotten chaperone from falling adrift at the hand of his inherently concocted reveries.

"Nevertheless, Master Cristofo, I fear that you admit neither the time nor the frame of mind to continue farther along on a tour of the metallic marvel's incredibly laborious and toilsome extraction. Moreover, we have reached the juncture that sets you upon the target of your ambitiously initiated crusade."

"Lead on, then, you aberrant and long-winded creature. Make haste so as to facilitate the upper hand with regard to the looming approach of your master."

"Ha, my young fellow. No manner of haste would assist in preventing his and your eventual encounter." A fabricated chuckle initiated the remark, a mocking-type discharge that lacked the more customary whimsical flair in favor of a cruder and almost maniacal air. "Do you really think that it is merely your aptitude and skillfulness that has gotten you this far? Come now, my good boy. Surely you realize that my master maintains a sturdier grasp on the goings-on of his treasured stomping grounds? And with that thought, I declare to you that we have succeeded in achieving your goal." A slight bow was then construed as a set of miniscule and outreached arms pointed Cristofo toward the immediate foreground and gestured for him to assume the position of lead. "Intact and unharmed, as promised, Master Cristofo."

A series of conventional and simply laid out prison cells drew command of the boy's eyes as he walked along and scanned the length of a broad and drawn-out hall. Tapered, honed, and narrowly spaced vertical lengths of sword-like pillars stood at guard in lieu of the more traditionally rounded and more widely dispersed bars. The relatively wide shafts served to partially obstruct an angular view, but not so much as to prevent Cristofo from inferring the presence of an assorted number of alien entities and beings—a ragtag collection of curious and peculiar creatures representing those of the more questionable and unrecognizable kind. Nor did the knife-edged and parallel run of balustrades preclude him from distinguishing the occupant of a proximate cell wherein a longish frame lay upon a simple cot while wrapped in an earth-tone robe. Crosswise from that location, a similarly disposed form was arranged with a more modest breadth and garbs of a more blackened kind. At once, the boy leaped forth to facilitate a clearly placed and perpendicular view, wherein a side-to-side glance immediately confirmed that his ambitions were indeed recognized and their identities true.

"Fingo!" the boy exclaimed in a blaring and frustrated manner as he came to realize that his moment of distraction had granted the accommodating hostage an opportunity to break free. However, it mattered not, for although the boy wished that Iggy, his luminous companion, were nearby, his senses were sharpened and his wizardly intuition brought strict order to the precarious situation that presented itself with a view to immediate action.

"Altarius!" the boy clamorously declared with a resounding wail that discouragingly seemed to fall upon oblivious ears. His sharp and scrutinizing eyes squinted ever so slightly in an attempt to compensate for the overly dark and shadowy surround—a sufficient effort, which, together with his other heightened wizardly senses, served to overcome the existent veil of obscurity. A pair of sizable pouches were the conspicuous items that stood at odds in the otherwise bare and uncomplicated cell. They hung there ominously above and overtop the simple cot whereupon the formidable figure of none other than yours truly lifelessly lay. A narrow and flexible tube streamed down from the bladder-like and liquid-filled containers, running a slightly twisted and turned course until transfixing into the arm of the temporarily helpless yet otherwise impressive and singular being of the highest repute: a steady stream of mind-numbing mutophasm venom that was being continuously transmitted!

"Fret not, my good mentor, for your alertness will unhesitatingly return." The harmonious ring of lengthy sword frictioning against the grip of scabbard then echoed robustly throughout the space, a resounding modulation that paralleled a lover's reluctant and undeniable plea intended to dissuade their better half from being compelled to dutifully part for battle. The clangorous wail struck a chord deep within my memory, wherein it will forever represent the embodiment of undying loyalty, as it also at that point served as the initial indication that my liberation was indeed imminent, advancing, and near.

A swiftly executed swoosh of blade made quick work of the cleaving of sharpened and knifelike bars as the severed lengths of metallic cuttings clanged melodiously upon impact with the dense and rock-ribbed floor. A subsequent slash was initiated in conjunction with a carefully placed vault into the dispiriting room, whereupon the motion forwardly progressed into the execution of a liberating detachment of host from poison-delivering cord.

"Altarius, Altarius, awaken at once. Arise!" The boy shook and jostled the inert and lengthy figure that lay helplessly upon the harsh and ill-fitting cot as he vehemently removed the tubular attachment that was latched into its arm. "Time is of the essence my friend; enliven without delay, for Noxerus will undoubtedly soon appear!" A faint grumble and ever so slight sway gave indication that the discontinuance of the debilitating liquid immediately triggered some form of recuperation from the poisonous malaise. Without a moment's hesitation, Cristofo returned to the hallway and proceeded to enter the crosswise cell in a likewise manner, liberating Bellatrix in the equivalent way.

"Bellatrix! Come now, snap out of it!" A series of firm yet carefully dispensed swats to the face gave indication to the urgency of the situation at hand. "I know where they're holding your precious Tempestas. Recover at once and let us get on with things!"

A similar and equally subtle stir marked the beginning of recovery for our distinguished wizardess as Cristofo turned his attention to the cavernous and expansive factory floor whereupon a simple rock-transporting cart represented his present and prevailing aim. In no time at all the boy had returned to the prison cell servicing hall, this time with a conveniently modified and fluently functioning four wheeled wagon in tow. A quick bit of carving courtesy of his superlative sword served to lop off a substantial portion of the otherwise overly heavy and deep-seated cariole.

"Come on, Altarius, up we go." A bit of a struggle necessarily ensued as the boy pretty much single-handedly righted my overly lanky and admittedly heavy-ish frame—an impressive display of strength that I found quite surprising even when considering his recently bolstered wizardly zing and notwithstanding my almost negligible contribution to the required upheaval at hand. A firm jolt then served to boost my awareness as I was slung into the dense and unyielding pushcart with none too gentle of a situating throw. My cognizance was indeed restoring, but not quickly enough for my liking—a stark realization that abruptly came to pass as I was unable to properly maneuver and make way for the additional body that was soon carelessly flung upon my framework, where it stagnantly lay.

"Come now, both of you snap out of it! Your assistance would be greatly appreciated. In fact, it will almost imminently be obliged." The boy raced down the factory floor, backtracking along the direction from whence he had entered just a short while before, employing a decent pace considering the fact that he was propelling us forward in a rather bulky and burdensome pushcart. Little did he realize at the time that his wizardly intuition was indeed thriving and that it was leading him toward a loosely deciphered and soon-to-be exposed portal way. What's more, his overall aura of bolstered dynamism served to stimulate both mine and my fair accomplice's recuperative air. Therefore, the situation became more and more discernible with every moment that whispered along and with every bump, rattle, and shake that befell our rugged and more slowly inclined transport before proceeding to disseminate throughout the entirety of my recovering yet still very much unresponsive frame.

"Maleabar, return!" was what I so desperately wanted to say as the passing scenery revealed a mass quantity of lumbering and lackadaisical and sizable brutes, yet the thought found no means to advance itself into spoken words of any recognizable clarity.

"Altarius, can you hear me? Are you beginning to become more favorably restored?" the boy inquired with a somewhat desperate tone as he recognized the attempted verbalization and noticed that I had regained some form of mobility insomuch as I was able to maneuver out from under the motionless form and fair figure of Lady Bellatrix. Moreover, a wave of enthusiasm took firm hold as he passed beyond the opening that led back into the extensive workshop where he had originally stumbled across Fingo the forger of instruments and devices and innumerable other gizmos and things. Still, no answer came his way as he careened forward through the crowded facility that was teeming with materials and appurtenances, not to mention the gross abundance of monstrous yet still wholly disinterested and seemingly uncaring beasts. The boy eased pace and heaved the cart rearward on approach to the mouth of a seemingly random tunnelway. In fact, his selection was not random at all but rather a viable egress point to which he was somehow supernally inclined.

"Proceed forward through this mining shaftway at once; both of you make your best effort to arise and push on. I shall momentarily be following along." Cristofo anxiously took hold of my lumbering frame and hoisted me up and out of my seated arrangement while making sure to provide the necessary support as I labored to maintain some semblance of an erect posture. Then, lo and behold, I outstretched my freshly maneuverable arm and took firm grasp of the reassurance that could only derive from the touch of fingers upon my steely staff of miraculous wonder.

"Maleabar! It's about time that you decided to come join us," our newly ordained compatriot exclaimed while being somewhat perplexed about the metallically inclined phenomenon's inconsistent conformity and timing. Little did he realize that the superlative substance would singularly adhere to only the command of its master and that at its master's behest alone could such obedience be unilaterally transposed. When the boy unknowingly authorized the morsel's return to its bulkier majority, he relinquished command over the exceptional material and restored it to its previously held standpoint. Perchance it may have been wise to pass on that relevant tidbit of information during the course of our erstwhile wizardly discourse, yet vast is the amount of knowledge that I could have wholeheartedly purveyed, and only a trifle of time had thus far been allotted toward the perpetual task of guiding my apprentice along in his way. In any event, it was favorable indeed that the wondrous device could tune into my reactivated consciousness, taking on the most useful of shapes inasmuch as what was required at that particular moment in time, a simple staff upon which I could lean, an ample prop upon which a meager progression could be respectably mustered.

"Morsel, transmute!" was the command that I intended to verbally relay, but once again the words were unripened and a faint rumble nudged forth in its way. Nevertheless, the sentiment alone was enough to ensure that the miniscule portion of Maleabar would be successfully reconveyed, and so back onto the wrist of my impassioned young protégé did the fragment of material immediately reinstate, joining him on his errand of the moment. It would be at his service as required while he scuttled back into Fingo's workshop on a mission to retrieve the precious property that could only come to be legitimized in the hand of our charming concomitant. Yes, indeed, the precious jewel of Tempestas would most certainly warrant an attempt at retrieval, no matter how grievous the cost as measured by both the likelihood of encountering peril and by the squandering of invaluable time.

The boy was fleeting in his pursual of the extraordinary stone of incomparable wonder, for as has already been hinted toward, he had previously caught wind of its unhidden whereabouts. And sure enough, there it conspicuously lay, only partially camouflaged atop a random worktable amidst an array of utensils, apparatuses, hand lenses, and trays. A quick snatch concluded the ambition without incident, and onward he precariously made way, farther along into the extensive laboratory to the site of the crystal-like gemstone's corresponding yet not altogether irreplaceable stave. Once in hand, a simple effort saw the two married components latch together with a tenacious fuse, and in consequence, Cristofo incipiently perceived the heartening invigoration that only a firm clasping of staff could endeavor to make real. It was a most vitalizing sensation and one that only those of wizardly inclination would be privileged enough to veritably feel. A brief moment's hesitation allowed our daring adventurer time enough to ensure that the device's suitability was sufficiently weighed, and in that terse progression of time frame, my general endorsement of the invaluable implement was fully accepted and undeniably understood. Still, the fantastical sentiment of swaying, slashing, and steely swing of flashy sword could not be dethroned in the meticulous and methodical mindset of the boy. Off he raced back to his dropped-off companions with staff in hand but with unreplaceable longsword fluttering across his backside, still his favorite choice and eagerly at the ready and primed for any impending forays.

"If only Fingo had been kept captive and was forced to remain close at hand," Cristofo pondered as he sprinted across the cluttered object-filled room. He passed a number of vials, potions, concoctions, and brews, wishing that he had been more vigilant in that regard, for not only would that eventuality have facilitated the acquisition of a suitable antidote, but in addition a hostage of such priority would certainly come in handy in the likely event that Noxerus would decide to join the ordeal. At once, a flicker was scantily discerned, a faint glow in the stone of Tempestas that served to indicate that Bellatrix's consciousness was beginning to more firmly take hold. Then a moderate twang reverberated and pulsated through the air; it was the hearkened cry of Annabel, singing and inviting and cooing as it persuaded him near. Cristofo made no mistake in deciphering the sword's tuning fork–like vibratory squeal, and his heightened wizardly senses made quick work of uncovering the splendidly fashioned instrument of nether land–originated steel.

"Come now, Annabel, for your mistress enthusiastically awaits your return." The boy's excitement intensified as he rescued the splendid device and its scabbard from a chest filled with numerous others of lesser quality but similar strain and hurriedly exited the unconventional testing room in favor of the far more expansive yet much less unoccupied factory floor.

An awry sensation hit upon the boy as he shot himself into the bustle of the crowded yet altogether functional factory chamber. Stalwart yet slow-moving beasts continued with their slogging, slaving, and single-minded pursuits, but their overall arrangement had altered somehow and their symmetry still seemed intact although modified with regard to orientation, direction, and line. In fact, a substantial and centrally located stretch of the expanse had become entirely avoided, wholly untraveled, and thoroughly cleared. It was as though a noxious discharge had been haphazardly overlaid, an extremely poisonous splattering that would necessitate a circumvention that was equally directed both ways. Cristofo thought it unusual as he proceeded to traverse the conveniently situated and completely disregarded stretch of terrain, until reaching very near its midpoint, whereupon an overt interruption caught his attention and incited his wizardly senses to instantaneously raise.

"Master Cristofo, hold!" a recognized voice bellowed out with a familiar inflection but an unnatural loudness that resonated with much more potency than its regular tone. The boy halted and turned in an effort to actualize what his auditory perception had already inferred, and thus he once again came to gaze upon Fingo, the mastermind of weaponry, devices, and limitless words. Unto the creature's pint-sized and puckered lips, a strange horn-shaped item was enduringly placed; it was an amplifying instrument of sorts that gave cause to the thundering nature of his otherwise modest and crinkling voice. Yet at that instant, words were not the only appurtenances that the miniaturized minion intended to hurl vociferously. Alternatively, it was a simple, circular, and shield-like object that was let fly with a robust and unforeseeable verve. An acute trumpeting sound was then distinctly heard—a calculated discharge launched from the mouthpiece of the diminutive fellow and aimed altogether above the position of our adventurous rescuer, who had concurrently snatched hold of the rounded and revolving projectile with his free and fastidious hand. A quick glance upward served to solidify Cristofo's consequent and compulsory action as the newly caught and now obviously perceptible shield was rigidly grasped and steadfastly positioned overhead.

Sharpened and piercing shards rained down upon the boy, pressuring his fastened and fixated hold on the instrument that had afforded him a narrow safeguard from the overwhelming shower that was most unpredictable and wholly absurd. Indeed, the scant lifeline that Fingo had conveniently conveyed was but a fraction larger in stature than was the boy's diameter and broadness of frame. In one fell swoop, imprisonment had forcibly imposed itself upon the valiant and intrepid soul—a thickset and dense circular wall of transfixed, translucent, and impervious crystal-like poles had soundly embedded themselves about his circumference. What's more, a towering heap of them had accumulated on top of his recently provided resistant and circular hold.

Powerfully built legs intensified as they planted themselves firmly into the ground while the balance of Cristofo's impeccable musculature system simultaneously followed suit. Backside, shoulders, blades, and arms were all tense and taut and working in unison to countervail the pressure and stress that weighed down with a staggering strain as an impenetrable overhead blockade bore down on him. It had an equivalent measure of force and resistance as that provided by the crystalline wall that surrounded him and now fronted the boy's angered and penetrating eyes. A focused gaze then decisively arose as his wizardly enhanced vision brought forth clarity to the hazy and semi translucent view, unblurring the standpoint to a sufficient degree so as to clearly expose the refracted form of Fingo the forger alongside the unmistakable and overbearing figure of his domineering master. Yes, indeed, Noxerus had finally decided to implant himself into the scheme. And Cristofo's fortitude enlivened and grew as the image of Iggy all of a sudden was made clear, entering in through the laboratory doorway in company with a number of tenacious guardians who had been closely trailing the fiery defender and irreplaceable compeer. And on the boy's face, a devilish smile then necessarily ensued while Annabell reverberated softly, the portion of Maleabar pulsated and teetered, and the stone of Tempestas flickered and flashed as it enlivened in response to its mistress, whom had concurrently begun to come to.

CHAPTER 10

Summon Pumiceus

"Master, behold—the jewel flickers! Our fearsome foe awakens, and her power begins to restore!"

"Caution your tongue, my indispensable little fabricator." Noxerus stood calm and cool as he collectively observed the situation at hand and responded to his subservient's moderately distressful enunciation of words. "Your master fears no foe, whether spirit, creature, wizard, entity, being, or beast. None shall succeed in evoking fear into the heart of your exalted wizard Prime." A subtle nod was then laterally dispensed by the devilishly powerful fiend, an implicit acknowledgment lauding their allegiant tenacity and directed toward the near score or so of his most loyal guardians who had persistently followed and trailed in the path of Iggy, who from their perspective represented a fiery creature of mysterious origin and unsurpassable blaze. It was also a succinct command directing them to stand down and remain in the ready position during the impending unfolding of the situation that was certainly to be determined yet still wholly unclear.

"And besides, precious moments will be obliged to transpire before the effects of the mutophasm venom are to be completely overthrown."

Elongated and clawed fingers then proceeded to relinquish their grasp on the netherworld leader's all-powerful glassy and sleek pole, and upright it remained in an obedient mode, waiting at attention until such time as its wielder would decide to resume his previous hold. A simple yet robust clap would then have vigorously ensued, unleashing a thunderous and shock wave–like blast which hit upon our cylindrical tunnelway's generous opening. Substantial hunks of rock as well as fractured and fragmented portions of stone came cascading down with considerable impetus to create an instant and immoveable bouldered barrier wall that served to decisively separate myself and the fair Bellatrix from our resourceful yet unpracticed and endangered young champion.

The effect of the mutophasm toxin, although adequately dissipating, was for the moment sufficient to ensure that Cristofo would be absent any help from the two of his wizardly associates as the thickset wall of compacted rubble and ore solidified the equation and unequivocally sealed the deal. In consequence, the scene on and about the expansive factory floor was overshadowed by the exceedingly pleased mood of our smug and self-satisfied principal rival and coveter of our recently designated and animus-classed wizardly inductee as the maniacal overseer watched intently and bore witness to the diminishment of the stone of Tempestas's flickering gleam.

"And now let us see the true worth of our meagerly constituted human of fleshy and squishy makeup and feel. I perceive that his peculiar and blazing companion here presents a much more dangerous and powerful threat, although strangely enough I struggle to take firm grasp of the strange being's reasoning, thought process, and will." An intense and contemplative gaze was then set upon Iggy as the devilish wizard probed and analyzed while the unique creation simply yet blazingly remained. And then all of a sudden, a subtle hand-generated gesture initiated the launch of a barrage of sizable and sentinel-wielded spears, all of which came to hit upon the center point of the globular and glossy mass of fiery protoplasm. Instant incineration then became the fate of the strenuously flung lances with tips of nether-forged steel, peaking the attention of Noxerus, who seemed quite content in his observation of the ultra-resistant creature's unbelievably resilient veneer.

"What say you then, my little fountain of knowledge and expertise? About the ability and origin of this unusual entity which seems to be fiery beyond the limits of rationality, at least insofar as our netherworld-rooted physics would make us believe."

"A most unusual spirit to be sure, my exalted Prime. A creature of immense age and capability, and one that would most certainly be of value for you to apprehend and force to remain resident with us on this sphere. Tales of my forbearers spoke ambiguously about such an entity, as this that presents itself before us, accounts from so long ago that the details have since faded and dissipated over the course of their tenuous voyages throughout a number of antiquated and fossilized ears. But I do faintly recollect a residual nugget of an abstraction that likely contains a fraction of that which may indeed prove to be indubitably true; the being's origin is akin to that of your elder wizardly compatriot, the matron of all matrons with whom you have made arrangements and proffered a deal."

"Hmm." A pensive grumble was the diabolical master's solitary reply as he then redirected his focus toward the crystalline stockade that served host to his precious captive and which for some reason had begun to resonate, rumble, and stir.

Well within the rocklike, glassy, and semi opaque yet thickly covered and fortified hold, a more or less buried Cristofo had spent the last number of moments contemplating the onerous circumstance at hand. He found peace in the face of despair, as his training had taught him, and analyzed his potential next moves with strict focus and unwavering logic, as was the true manner of his nature as well as the force by which he was intuitively moved to perform. At once, the young champion solidified his framework and fixated his mind. No longer did he represent mere flesh, muscle, and marrow and bone, for such restrictive depictions need not apply in the presence of one who stands with the endowment of being wizardly infused. Blood no longer furnished his body's necessary fodder and fuel. Lava coursed through veins in its stead with a boiling and bubbling configuration and mood, teeming all about the intricate network of hardened vessels and far-ranging ducts with ambition of a mitigating discharge and an irrepressible drive to burst through. An ever so slight bend represented the whole of the physical readjustment required, and an ear-splitting

roar served to give warning of his imminent and unstoppable demand
to surge forth and break free …

Bits, shards, and broken portions of the crystalline bars then exploded
outward with the force of a wizardly powered volcanic discharge,
blasting high, wide, and barraging upon the locality's intermediate
perimeter. Several of the innocently slogging and slaving, and otherwise
oblivious and unconcerned beasts, fell prey to the abrupt and unforeseen
salvo of lethal shrapnel, while others of the kind lay innocently wounded
and strewn about the rectified factory floor, wriggling and writhing
collateral victims of an otherwise incomprehensible and unexpected
foray. A handful of sentinels were also hit upon with a similar fate,
a quarter or so of the dependable warriors whose shield-wielding
skills were too sluggish to proffer any form of protection as well as
a few with adroitness but no luckiness, who were haphazardly struck
nonetheless. And Fingo the forger did indeed remain unscathed as a
quick bit of maneuvering detached him from the dangers presented by
the formidable and shrapnel-laced spray. To the rear of his master did
the diminutive creature nimbly surge, behind the hulking and broad
framework to safety, and just in time, as Noxerus unflinchingly cast
his will upon the indiscriminately flying fragments, compelling them
to abruptly drop down and just lay.

"Aaaaargh!" The long-winded and vociferous exhalation atypically
burst forth from the crux of the newly invigorated boy, who would more
routinely find himself less exasperated and more mentally composed
when faced with a similarly perilous situation such as the one that had
just left him more or less compromised and forcibly imposed. And a
mad rush toward his enemy was in consequence and thereupon invoked
as the determined young warrior committed his best effort toward the
dismantling of his immediate adversary, malevolent incarcerator, and
netherworld-strained compeer. In furtherance of the boy's impulsive
attack, the staff of Tempestas was used spear-like and was vigorously
hurled with only the slightest alteration of his forward progress and with
a precision that left nothing to chance as Noxerus calmly stood at the
ready and once again signaled for his sentinels to stand down and remain.
A fluently executed clutch and swirl gave rise to an incomprehensible

maneuver wherein the bulky and overly muscular beast did indeed portray a graceful elegance as though in the performance of a battle-worthy ballet, and with an implicit ease, the fleeting pole was steered in the opposite direction, where it now found itself barreling toward Cristofo in a breakneck stream.

In response, a quick deployment and deflection by way of the boy's Fingo-provided shield made quick work of the threat's avoidance, veering the speeding implement up and over his current position and in consequence serving to slow his determinedly exorbitant pace.

"Steady yourself, boy! One must not rush into the figurative flame without first weighing the appropriate manner and way." The denigrating remark elicited nothing but silence from our hyped-up and infuriated young protégé, who in turn let fly with a shrapnel-like dispersion of his proportion of Maleabar, hurled forth his circular bulwark, and skillfully drew upon sword as he continued rushing unrestrainedly straight forward. In a flash, the hulking monstrosity took hold of his patiently waiting staff and spun it with a calculated rhythm and steer, exhibiting a much more agile disposition than one would surmise based merely upon the manner in which his hulking comportment was shown to appear.

"It seems that our ever so wise overseers have infused you with a most generous quantity of zeal ..." The behemoth enjoyably put forth the words while simultaneously conducting his staff in a seemingly effortless manner. It absorbed the fragment-sized morsels of Maleabar and deflected the round and revolving projectile before proceeding to twirl and sway as it sideswiped and turned away the boy's relentless and nethersword-led onrush.

"Nonetheless, it seems that they have faltered in that you would have much more competently remained had the invigoration consisted of an apportionment more intellectually tailored and weighed." An imperceptible swing of inconceivable speed struck with sound impact against the sidelong edge of the frantically thrashing and swaying configuration that represented the masterfully conducting young swordsman's all-out display. Flying sideward up through the air did our daring young Cristofo find himself, inexorably launched out of the way with no hint of fear but an abundant supply of disdain. A moment's pause lingered and drifted, giving rise to what seemed like an exaggeratedly long interval until the fended-off young wizard completed his airborne catapult and came to rest hard upon the callous factory floor some half dozen paces away. His impassioned eyes, however, did manage to remain gazing fixedly upon his enemy the whole while as his body was thrusted and thrown with what seemed like an uncomplicated attempt to keep him becalmed and at bay.

"Enough, my fierce and impetuous young comrade! I may indeed be impressed with your skills, but your carelessness speaks ill of your master. There are infinite concepts that yet remain to be learned, and you have all the time in the world to be taught them. For truth, it pains me to stand quietly by while surmising the course of your forthcoming advancement at the hand of such insufficient and harmful methods as those routinely implemented by the more weakened and delicate practitioners of our timeless handicraft. By what logic do you assert such rigid loyalty toward your animus-kindred Prime? You know naught of his thousands of years and even less about what he intends and requires. Is it by way of the fact that he was first to uncover your unique and particular charms? I assure you that my observance of our ever-so powerful star grants me no claim to her unbridled potency and breathtaking fire. She yet remains to burn free, to shine brilliantly and unrestrainedly as she spreads her esprit. As do you, with your irrepressible zing and impetuous drive, your intuitive boldness and undisciplined ire. Yes, indeed, my pliable and fleshy young champion, let the truth be told as both of us seem to realize it. Your spirit is much more akin to this world, the inferno, the fury, the fire … the rage, the passion, the desire …

Tell me, why do you think that you feel so alive here? And why would our all-knowing overseers choose this locality as the one in which to enliven you? Ha ha. And your resplendent companion here, a creature of likewise predisposition to be sure. Can you claim that it beams with such blatant brilliance and style on your meager little birthplace of a world? A kindred soul put together with yours through a predetermined course evoked ages ago with pathways intricately woven through the fabric of time? Pathways that deliberately led you both unto me; pointers, indicators, and harbingers all pushing you in this direction and all trying to instill upon you the essence of who you truly shall be. And so, young Cristofo, champion and newborn wizard spawned of the fertile and fructiferous earth, I compel you to take your seat as my student and consent to the uttermost advancement of your power, your privilege, and your gain! Look toward Fingo here, for instance. Harken his words and grant him the courtesy of elucidation, for he is a creature of animus pedigree such as yourself, I might add, and an exceptionality in like manner. Please do tell, my indispensable little fabricator. Spell it out for the boy; make it clear and unscrambled. Expound upon it with significance, leaving no room for question; bring to reason the inevitability of it all in the style that only you and your engrossing words could do justice."

"Indeed I shall, master …"

The long-winded and subservient minion was cut short at the outset of his undoubtedly wordy inducement and predictable rallying cry as an unforeseen explosion burst forth alongside him with a dissipating and mist-like discharge. All the while, as Noxerus progressed onward with his attempted persuasion and contemplative tirade, Cristofo had feigned listening and instead had been focusing and intensifying, and in such a manner was his diversion contrived. Flattering words of enticement would do poorly in swaying one of such an exceptional mind, and furthermore, such drawn-out and baseless proposals were no match for the boy's abundant instinctual awareness and good measure of sense and self-pride. Thus and so, the implanted fragments of Maleabar were directed to disperse and unwind, splintering apart Noxerus's sleek and lustrous pole within which they had been previously confined. The fine-grained particles served little by way of fatality but proved to be quite effective as a means of distraction as they spattered upon nearby faces prior to accumulating and reconvening upon the wrist of our power-infused young warrior, who took the opportunity to gain footing and to reequip himself with his steely length of bravura. His netherworld forged countercharge.

"Never shall I be swayed by such miserably fiendish beings such as the ones that present themselves before me and at hand. A garrulous gabber who goes on sans respite and an intuitively deceptive beast who is chock-full of false pretense and by no means contrite. Bring forth your best assault, you foul creature and self-proclaimed devilish Prime, for many of similar strain and significant stature have been shrunk down by mine all-seeing eyes." No, the boy's head did not suffer with haze as though reeling from a substantially hard impact. Indeed, his wizardly infusion brought boldness along with a courageous and spirited drive. Composure took hold in the wake of his recently failed and overly impetuous offensive, and this time his focus was true and his objective uncompromised as the faint silhouette of a flame set itself upon his gaze and as his body steadied and remained loaded with supercharged and ready to erupt nerves as he planted himself firmly upon the terrain and waited intently with a patient yet trigger-happy strain.

"In fact, I struggle not to lose sight of you and your meager form that is all but hidden in the shadow of your proportionally challenged collaborator, who for the moment seems to stand tall by your side. Let us see how you make do absent your precious staff. Let us test your true imperviousness as your hard shell comes to smack against the business end of meticulously forged and netherworld sharpened steel."

"Hrrrrummmm ..." The grumbling exhalation echoed with fortitude in an otherwise soundless proximity. The devilishly jovial chuckle that would more typically exude from the monstrous brute seemed altogether forgotten and ever so far and away. "Well then, you arrogant windbag and pestiferous puny pup ..." The tone intensified, and loudness was amplified exponentially with the utterance of every word. "It seems you leave me no choice but to ferry you away unto a most torturous and faraway domain wherein you will have nothing but the densely imposed obscurity of time within which to contemplate, consider, and come to self-analyze." A sideward outstretched arm rose up from the sizable brute's rigidly chiseled and towering pose, a seemingly mutinous-minded appendage flying adrift of the imposing creature's ominous stature and acting independently of his menacing and unflinching gaze. An opened palm thereupon proceeded to lure, coax, and handily wrench free a sentinel-held broadsword, sucking it into its grasp in a flash with staggering momentum and a superpowered magnetic-like zeal.

A ferocious and never-before-heard roar emanated from the crux of the now–sufficiently armed and infuriated boor as cinder-like spew and semiliquid goo disgorged itself in a rampant and unbridled surge, up and out of a then-transforming frontispiece wherein the brute's already unseemly features took on an even more disturbing and hideously devilish mold. Previously sharpened and knifelike teeth sprouted forth and flourished into a much more assertive and voluminous form, capturing the lion's share of attention from the otherwise and equally distressing transmutation of neck size, cheeks, jawbone, and overall facial structure and guise. A twisting and slithering arm-sized tongue then lashed onward and out of the creature's shrieking, blustering, and fang-lined orifice, a seeking and probing outrider looking to clutch at and capture any in the vicinity that would bear the distinction of appropriate and imminent prey.

Cristofo braced rigidly for impact, as readied as one thusly predisposed could by any means purvey. In a swiftly invoked and battle-readied maneuver, his steady forearm rose up and in defense of him, while its sword-wielding counterpart obediently upheld his spectacular blade. All at once, Maleabar was drawn up from his wrist like a switchblade, whereupon it fanned out and into the form of a serrated and semicircular edge. There it then lay, still anchored firmly upon him, a thinly sharpened and half-moon shaped blade that ran the length of his forearm, inviting any and all incoming appendages to be dissevered or least of all shaved. At that precise instant, the venomously seething, spewing, and smoldering beast shot forward with a speed-induced blur just as our anticipatory young champion let fly with a fastidious and backhanded spurn. A substantial sliver of the monstrosity's fossilized yet mucous-like and muscle-like tongue shot off into the immediate vicinity, a disjoined segment having conclusively succumbed to the boy's not-to-be underestimated ability and sway.

A shrill squeal could then be distinctly discerned, interposing itself into the creature's already blusterous and overblown battle cry. Yet still the superficial blow did little to alter the behemoth's forthcoming and unswayable aggression as the firm and momentous swing of sentinel-grade broadsword came down with the uttermost impetus, straight on top of Cristofo's resilient but otherwise unshielded form. The boy impulsively lashed forth with his unparalleled weapon, bracing himself for impact, for he knew full well that the advancing stroke would result in some form of gratification for the incoming blade. Yet even so, there remained a glimmer of exoneration in that he realized that his bloodthirsty Azrael would revel in some measure of meaningful indulgence just the same.

Then, lo and behold, another imperceptibly rapid flash came swooping upon the precise whereabouts of the imminently conclusive affray. Indeed, it was the boy's most vigilant watchdog Ignatius who superimposed himself onto the scene. A sizzling hiss was instantaneously heard and came to be made clear as incinerated nethersteel broadsword met with dissolution and was made to unequivocally disappear. With the same motion, the fiery wonder came to jolt back the infringing form of Noxerus, returning it back to its former and slightly more palatable monstrousness while at the same time engulfing the entirety of the aggressing and sword-swinging boy. It congealed him into a protective hideaway wherein he remained in relative comfort, unscathed and snugly tucked in and out of harm's way.

Though the combustible wonder's inner protoplasm was made to shelter instead of to sear, its outer casing remained infinitely fiery, resistant, and calamitous to any objects that would come to percuss against it, as well as to most that would choose to come near.

"Back away, vigorous creature of fire and blaze! My battle is not against you, but by no means will I allow your impetuous meat sack of a master to be saved." Angry fists pounded down upon the deeply shaded coating of lustrous and conflagrant glaze, and despite the fact that the powerful wizardly appendages failed to penetrate Iggy's impervious envelope, neither did they incinerate, sizzle, or burn up and wither away. "Impressive, my fulminant fellow. I shall indeed secure your presence here at my palace wherein you must lie in wait until beckoned or until I call upon you at my every whim or behest. Now stand aside and desist at once, for Noxerus is the one who now commands your will. Indeed, it is I..., your new master..., the one to whom from this point forth you must unconditionally yield and obey." A sanguine glow emanated from the demon's beady pitch-dark eyes as his elongated palms and pointed fingers danced and swayed in a seductive wave that saw a hypnotically charged energy make its way along the proximate surface of Iggy's resplendent veneer. 'Twas a powerful and age-old bewitchment with which Noxerus was masterfully adept—a time-tested and captivating maneuver that boasted a remarkably high rate of success.

Initially, the singular specimen's brilliant and burnished facade remained unfaltering and its comportment seemed altogether constant and unfazed. However, as the seasoned and satanic sorcerer immersed himself more deeply with spell, Iggy's super-resilient outer surface began to alternately sink and swell.

"Recede, my fiery wonder. Withdraw and slither away ... Only in this manner... will your undeserving and former master be unequivocally salvaged and ultimately saved." In response, the incomparable mass of gleaming protoplasm continued to pulsate as it throbbed and quivered in whichever way. Then, all at once, it shot off in a stream, barreling straight toward the blocked-off egress way wherein my wizardly compatriot and I were being effectively held at bay. All the while, Cristofo remained snugly inside the fine creation, fastened into the center of its anatomy, wherein he stayed more or less cognizant, albeit thoroughly cemented in place.

Within an instant, Iggy had arrived at the bouldered threshold that fronted and blocked our portal-accommodating passageway, at which point the exceptional being enlarged itself to the exact breadth of the maliciously placed barricade and lightly slithered its way into the space. The thickset and consolidated mass of densely rooted boulders and rigidly disposed rubble and rock was instantaneously set to a glow and spontaneously made to combust, and in no time at all the impassible accumulation was completely incinerated and altogether reduced to ashes and dust. A completely smooth and near perfectly round cavity was created in the wake of the creature's forward advancement, a bored-out hole with clean lines and perfect symmetry wherein Iggy would take position and once again remain as an impenetrable barrier resolutely ingrained. Our recently vitalized wizardly concomitant and unwillingly conveyed passenger was then sternly off-loaded into the interior side of our much-needed escape way. Therein he was quickly reunited with his recuperating counterparts, who were found to be in the process of prying away fragments and digging their way through rubble and scree. They were just about halfway recovered from their venomous contagion and were working with an ever-increasing energy as they clawed and scraped away in an attempt to reunite with their ever-so-brave rescuer and grossly outmatched young protégé.

"Well done, my surprisingly capable and versatile Ignatius! Come now, Cristofo. This is no time for hesitation. Take hold of the fair Bellatrix and hurry along down the straightforward pathway that leads to our exoneration."

The boy was still reeling to a certain degree, feeling the effects of being pretty much swallowed by his unfailing companion, while at the same time wrestling with the conflicting emotions of disappointment and relief in that he had basically been rescued as Iggy extricated him from the unfolding battle at hand. He quickly shook off the quandary while taking firm hold of the stalwart wizardess's outreaching forearm and proceeding to make way down the sweltry and irregularly meandering passageway that ripped through the consolidated mass of netherworld rock and ages old stone like a blood-coursing vein that dipped and declined as it ran along unto the very heart of the mighty Immotus.

And all the while, dozens upon dozens of slogging and slaving beasts continued their single-minded pursuits as an intermittently spaced trail of loaded wagons advanced toward the blocked-off exit, whereupon a few of them had stalled and accumulated along with their operators as they hit upon the stoppage point in a dazed and disoriented stupefaction. I had decided to remain briefly behind with a purpose in mind, as my fortitude was showing signs of regeneration and my mental aptitude had returned to full range. Iggy unequivocally inferred my intention as the creature's coloration tended toward a more semi opaque hue and as its membrane was made to let Maleabar fly through.

Thus, my remarkable instrument was launched with vigor and smoothly whizzed out and into the cavernous manufactory, where both Noxerus and his delusive minion looked on with chagrin as they caught sight of the fleeting staff-shaped projectile.

"Master, the unmerciful Tempestas!" Panic set in as Fingo desperately blew upon his enchanted instrument and as his fuming overlord raced toward the magnificently crowned staff with frantic vexation. But it was all for naught, for the miraculous wonder made quick work of the clutch and snag of the wizardess's incomparable implement, after which point the fantastical formation seamlessly turned and swayed to fly back like a shot toward the direction from whence it had previously come.

The efforts of our nether-foes fell shy of their aim to ensure that the omnipotent Tempestas would stay and remain in their inherent domain, as Fingo's enchantment went cold and Noxerus's exertion came short of reaching the retreating metallic tool that was whisking away the mystical jewel. The creature's devilish frame crashed hard upon Iggy's resilient glaze as both wondrous contrivances passed clean through the blazing phenomenon just as its outer coating returned to its impervious hue. A steady-going singe and char continued to deter and force back the onrush of my determined yet alternately inclined fellow Prime, who had carried on with an effort to wrestle and sway as he tried to uncover a way past the seemingly impenetrable barricade. A decent number of intermittent thrusts and lunges were undertaken, each of which was followed by a countervailing sizzle and neutralizing fry, until finally evoking the abatement of the vigorous beast's relentless and stubborn charge.

Meanwhile, on the obverse side of Noxerus's heavy-handed aggression, a triumphant smile assumed control over the weathered visage of a newly restored and self-satisfied wizard of age who had been quite in need of a victory of sorts, no matter how marginal or slight that victory may or may not have ultimately come to be perceived.

"Slacken intensity, Ignatius!" I felt the need to convey my merciful thoughts unto the sweltering barrier, but only regarding its portal-facing facade and in an effort to mitigate the disintegration of the obtusely advancing and cluelessly continuing beasts of burden. By that point, a number of them had walked straight into dissolution, while others of the more rational strain succeeded in limiting their damage to the odd extremity or obtruded appendage. Nonetheless, the poor brutes were undeserving of such collateral fate, a sentiment about which they obliviously benefited in due thanks to my newfound invigoration and notably improved mood. And with that, a revelation took hold and seriousness returned with intensity as I raced to join up with my far to the fore companions, who were making decent headway in their trek down and along the meandering passageway that led into the bowels of Immotus and unto the depths of the altogether unknown.

"Ahoy there, my vigilant adventurers!" It did not take long for my refreshed and rejuvenated form to converge upon the previously departed journeyers, for my pace was exceedingly vigorous and true and notwithstanding the distinct fork in the channelway, whereupon Cristofo and Bellatrix had elected to take pause and await their fellow evacuee. Contented smiles greeted me as I concluded my approach, with a most brilliantly satisfied variety adorning the elegant visage of our formidable yet beauteous wizardess as her eyes lay focus on my freshly retrieved prize.

"I could not find it within myself to depart this forsaken domain while leaving behind such a noble and magnificent instrument with crown that lies lifeless and cold at the hand of all except for her warmhearted mistress. Take hold of your mighty Tempestas, fair lady, re-acquaint yourself with its infamous manner and mold!"

"Much obliged, my esteemed Prime. A lady reunited with her favored jewel makes for a most gracious and invaluable companion! Now let us not while away the time. Into which prong of this threefold-apportioned divide do we thrust ourselves with newly invigorated stamina and drive?" Our female complement stood radiantly and in good form with all her venomous contamination having been pretty much overthrown now that she held firm grasp upon her splendidly crested staff and by virtue of her previous bolstering by way of being reunited with Annabel, which, thanks to Cristofo, now lay cozily at home in her back-slung scabbard.

"Well, my lady, that choice falls upon our youthful liberator. Lead on, Cristofo, for it was your newfound intuitiveness that brought us unto our current vein, and thusly shall it carry us to the distinctive portal that calls to you and beckons your spirit as well as your physical frame." A prideful grin took hold of the boy's enchantingly pleased face as he nodded in acceptance of the relegated directive. A mere moment transpired before he started upon his chosen trajectory, for he had since analyzed the triumvirate of options while waiting upon my impending return. The main branch of the fork ran headlong into the well-traveled and bustling passageway whereupon the beasts were busy laboring and where a series of deeply grooved track marks ingrained themselves stoically as they served to steer the heavily laden pushcarts back and through. This bearing clearly offered no inkling of significance or sway. The midmost prong was considerably narrower yet seemed to be relatively linear and of a more or less level plane. Its seemingly unused and somewhat abandoned aura appealed to the boy despite its confining and restrictive tone. Perhaps a hint of allure presented itself here, but a hint alone was not enough to draw the boy into its hold.

The third branch-off point immediately dropped down into an abrupt and unforeseeable decline. A modest and mound-shaped formation bedecked the footpath's inductive entryway, laying itself upon the base of the hole-shaped portal like a swallowed tongue that cascaded along before looping around into an otherwise dark and dismal advance down through the throat of the formation and into the gist of whatever was to be found down below.

"Come on then, my fellow wayfarers; bring up the rear as I endeavor to lead the charge." And with that, Cristofo swept up and over the hill-shaped threshold and immediately thereafter dipped and disappeared into the uninvestigated and unconventional trail. A noticeable surge in illumination was then seen as it rebounded off the cavity's downward-flowing canopy, drawing in both the fair Bellatrix and me with its mesmerizing and Maleabar-produced charm.

Elseways, beyond the channel's obstructed gate and unto the cavernous manufactory floor, a more or less turbulent Noxerus pondered and weighed as he tried to overcome the surprisingly impermeable barricade. An ambiguous rage struggled to come to the forefront, managing only to flicker and fade in view of the hellish superintendent's undeniable bias toward being altogether impressed with the resplendently glowing anomaly's remarkable fortification. A number of varying assailments had proven to be ineffectual while being implemented amidst the counsel of Fingo, and to the dissatisfaction of the obediently subdued crowd of conveniently arranged guardians.

"Master, perhaps a solidifying freeze would serve to weaken the creature sufficiently enough to allow you to hastily slip through?" A lingering pause was the demonic being's singular reply, a blatant rejection of the idea that was deemed to have such a high degree of ill appeal to not even warrant a vocal response. In preference, the contemplative overlord continued along in his quiet and studious trance until finally withdrawing, stepping a half dozen paces or so back, and arranging himself for the forthcoming and subsequently initiated attack.

"I would bring the mighty Immotus itself to its knees before succumbing to the whim of an obstinate and uncomplicated entity such as thee!" At once, a deep-rooted roar was extruded from the pith of the intensely concentrating beast. Arms were held out, with hands seeming to emit some strange assortment of vaguely perceptible rays. In due course, up and down and all around the perimeter of the refulgent blockade, fissures began to take form upon the rock as a multitude of fractures and rifts were essentially willed into being. At first, hairline cracks materialized sporadically and in great numbers, only to sprout and grow with a vigorous flow as they matured and spread all around the resistant creature's circumference. In no time at all strips, wedges, and boulders would fall on and about Iggy's highly combustible frame, creating a billowing and dust-filled cloud of soot and smoke and residual scree. This was due in principal to the instant disintegration that befell the vast majority of the tumbling pieces as they happened to touch down upon the obstacle's impermeable and incinerating shell.

At the end of the potently conjured and precipitously cascading rockfall, all around the fringe of the fire-laden orb, random chunks of rubble and sprinkled portions of debris lingered about like a scattering of fortunate soldiers that had somehow survived an annihilating detonation, only to find themselves laid out about the battlefield in a disoriented clutter. A fleeting Noxerus wasted no time in flinging himself through the air with a missile-like charge that was skillfully aimed overtop of the resilient obstacle and straight into the newly created breach in the tunnelway's entry wall. However, little could be foretold as to the degree with which our irrepressible Ignatius would be so bold and tenacious. Like a flash, the refulgent glob of protoplasm expanded, swelling up in size with an unmitigated effort to close the newly established void around its perimeter. The creature broadened with a tremendous speed that proved to be no match for the otherwise unparalleled quickness of our persistent and pigheaded netherworld Prime, who found himself altogether wedged betwixt the forepart of Iggy's incinerating shell and the craggy, uneven, and newly reshaped rock-bound wall. And there he remained like a critter in a trap, writhing and wriggling as he tried to break free, with legs dangling strenuously and an overall disposition that was scrunched and squeezed and scorched and seethed.

More than a few embarrassment-laden moments passed before the egotistical and overbearing wizard managed to drop himself down before his awestruck devotees, who were at a loss and knew not how to react or proceed. Oh, how I wish to have been present firsthand to bear witness to the humbling failure of my inversely inclined cohort, the mighty Noxerus Prime. A sad and dejected figure he would have certainly been, marching away from his ambition with a blackened and besmirched spirit as well as a framework that was left significantly tattered and charred.

"Fingo ..." The dispirited yet determined and unrelenting ruler made no eye contact as he called to his awaiting attendant with a calm but deathly serious tone, "Summon Pumiceus!"

"Yes, master, at once." The eager-to-please minion turned toward the crowd of onlooking guardians and waved his arms about in a furious manner. The borderline frantic gesture was executed with a twofold purpose—first, as an acknowledgment that his obedience was notably evident and for the most part austere; second, as an indication for the lot of them to withdraw and stand considerably clear. For his part, Noxerus continued to trudge wearily along, being sure to give a wide berth to the circumstance as Fingo reflected upon the correct positioning, primed the appropriate locality, stepped back several paces, placed his mysteriously remarkable horn upon his lips, and then blew vigorously and vibrantly with a drawn-out, persistent, and oscillatory blare.

An awkward silence followed the conclusion of the miniaturized minion's blast, but only for as long as a moment's passing, whereupon a faint rumble was suddenly heard and an abrupt crack distinctively appeared. Indeed, a germinating and expanding rupture in the substrate spontaneously came into being—a rift, a fault line, a fissure that broke apart the foreground and opened up as though the crust of the mountain could no longer keep its innards within. A thick and viscous lava-like brew then bled forth from the newly formed chasm, filling it to its brim and satiating the ever-expanding split as it traveled underneath and into the barricaded channel's entryway like an insuppressible and uprising river contrived of the guts of the mountain and teeming with its blood and its boiling, bubbling stew. Up from the frothing slag and magma-like upsurge, a creature gushed forth and materialized into view. It was a fiery and ominous creation that found itself breaching the surface of the molten locality, rising up with an unmerciful roar like a mighty sea demon and rearing its head in an unbridled gesture of dominance, power, and undisputable rule.

No words were obliged to be spoken; no actions were depicted or told. Suffice it to say that the being's summoning in and of itself spoke volumes with regard to its purpose, its objective, and its ultimate goal. Call it a wizardly exaction or word it in any way that you will—in any case, the gist of it all is that the leviathan hungered intently for the three of our fleeing and friable frames. The fluently flowing molten monstrosity waded through its liquefied and lava-rich slush with the uttermost ease as it made its way toward our glowing stopper, who had thus far managed to successfully cork the entrance into our liberating tunnelway and had succeeded in keeping all potential followers at bay. Our ears suffered the consequence as a ferocious roaring sound echoed and reverberated throughout the cavernous domain, rolling and reduplicating in a seemingly perpetual howl as the vigorous creature re-instigated the cacophony before allowing the resounding reproduction to complete its preceding score. Soon enough, and to the contentment of all within earshot, a reprieve from the tumultuous uproar ensued and a relative silence befell at the precise moment when the indomitable Pumiceus stopped in front of Iggy, the refulgent, resistant, insurmountable wall.

A fiery dragon-like scowl gleamed up and down and all around the surface of the lustrous and energy-laden ball as a deep and unhurried rumble spewed forth from the throat of the called-upon monstrosity. It was a profound and intermittent growl that was given rise, a strangely construed mixture of simple breathing with an exploratory and contemplative guise. The sonority resonated for a decently lengthy period of time as the devilish creation sought to make contact with the unfamiliar entity's unperceivable eyes. It surveyed and studied Iggy's resplendent facade with the aid of a continuously progressing broad and stumpy neck that supported the enormous and oscillating head of the beast as it extended up from the surface of the lava flow and correspondingly slunk down as it plunged back below.

Without much delay, the enormity's thickset and snakelike chassis reared and raised up in a sinuous and serpentine manner, opening its prolonged fiery and fang-laden mouth before letting fly with a lava-rich discharge that shot out in a concentrated beam and hit upon the precise center of the obstruction with the semblance and similitude of a solar tongue. Seconds passed as though minutes. The intensive blast smacked upon the surface of Iggy's already flaring and radiating skin, dispersing a thick and gooey offshoot of molten spew that splattered about the vicinity, sticking, bespattering, and splashing about. For the most part, it rejoined with the gushing ooze that poured into the tunnelway and with which the ominous sea serpent seemed to be so intimately interfused. After a brief pause, a second effort immediately ensued, for the creature was required to breathe in out of necessity to reinstate its liquefied and lava-laced deluge.

A second interval of rest then followed after the accompanying percussion of the potently discharged beam, and in its wake, it was sure to be found that even the impenetrable Ignatius had been somewhat compromised—or so it was suggested, or at least so it seemed. A sizable and circular mark tainted the sleek and glossy dark pink coloration of the resilient being, leaving a blemish-like imprint that lessened as it extended outward from the center, where it stood blackened, then blackish, then progressively lighter and lighter shades of blue. However, much to the dismay of the nether-rooted onlookers, the discoloration did not prove to be stagnant, nor did it manage to prevail or keep speed. Instead, it diminished rather hastily as the supernatural wonder's true pigment reestablished itself by reconstituting, overtaking, and eventually swallowing even the darkest and blackest of hues.

Strained eyes spectated amidst the brilliant and scintillating display, for although the netherworld native creatures were quite familiar with the magma-produced offshoot of light in an otherwise dusky and shadowy terrain, the intensive shine of the newly conjured creature, together with Iggy's resplendently glimmering sheen, was rather torturous for their unaccustomed eyeballs to look at. It was almost impossible for them to stare at it fixedly. The fulgent and abundantly flaring creature then rose up from its molten hideaway after briefly submerging and giving way, at which point a near-complete breach of its lava duct saw the mighty creation unveil the full magnitude of its elusive yet magnificently shimmering frame. Shards of blistering crystal covered the entire surface of its massive snakelike anatomy, glittering and gleaming insomuch as was possible considering the faintish and desolate overtone of the underground domain. A behemoth mass of shimmering flare was revealed, wrapped in a coating of resilient scales that hung off the magnificent chassis like whitish-gold flakes, accentuating its majesty like a grandiose mansion's crowning with diamond-encrusted shakes.

Then, in a flash, the wondrous creature dove down and re-submerged, leaving its rare and precious appearance to live on in the wells of its beholders' memories, where it would remain more or less unforgotten since such a privileged exhibition would most likely not be realizable for most of them ever again. Down below in the deep-seated undercurrent of the velocious and choppy lava flow, the mighty Pumiceus glided and slithered and easily circumvented the impermeable barrier that did not fully extend into the depths of the molten river that ran its course through the mountain's preeminent and, at that moment, most sought-after tunnelway. Indeed, it seemed that for whatever reason, the omnipotent beast chose to break off its engagement with our remarkable Ignatius, deciding instead to circumvent the barricade in an effort to avoid the altercation from progressing along in order to facilitate its more pressing objective without any further delay.

Diametrically and beyond the blockaded mouth of the noteworthy shaftway, a section of the rapidly flowing and magma-comprised rivulet burst outward with a significant discharge of its lava-laced load as the resurfacing sea demon breached the obverse surface of the rushing flow and once again came into view. A thunderous roar emerged afresh, reverberating with fortitude but this time with a more purposeful strain as the creature made its display into the mildly crowded passage, where it wasted no time in opening wide its blazing jaws and then snapping them down with a voracious hunger and clout upon a number of wading beasts of burden. A collection of the calm and simpleminded brutes were scattered in, around, and all about the newly generated lava flow and its adjacent banks. They were easy marks and unavoidable fodder for the ravenous and insatiable leviathan as it ebbed and flowed, chomped down, and swallowed with a fluid savagery that carried forward as the incited pursuer glided hurriedly and farther along. Meanwhile, a triad of adventurers pressed along with their precipitous effort to extricate themselves from the tiresome world, which was found to be quite filled with savagery and significantly replete of duress.

"Cristofo, my dear boy, I'm afraid that I must inform you of a rather upsetting turn of events ..."

After a brief period of navigation along the chosen branch-off route, where a relatively constrictive breadth and an unusually rough and craggy footing eventually dissipated and slackened to make more manageable our latterly set-upon road, I felt that the timing was appropriate. I needed to disclose what I had recently inferred at the mouth of the substantial tunnelway when Iggy let down his guard to allow Maleabar and the staff of Tempestas to fly through safely. At that precise moment, a diabolical collusion was uncovered as I caught wind of a lingering thought process betwixt Fingo and my diabolical nemesis, the accursed Noxerus Prime.

"Your breed is in danger, my young apprentice, and it is a happenstance that I deeply regret to advise you of. A great threat bears down upon the whole of your species, with the initial onslaught aimed directly toward your homestead, your people, and your grounds." A unique stare was the response to the initial utterance of the shuddersome words as Cristofo stopped dead in his tracks and turned to face the conveyor of the obviously unsettling news. It was a steely and concerned gaze rife of curiosity, to some extent confounded, and to a certain degree dazed.

Cristofo pounced back with an immediate reply. "You know of the alien aggression? I was just now working on the words to expound upon the circumstance for the benefit of the two of you, my most loyal and battle-worthy peers. For although I aim not to discount the sincerity with which I initiated this liberating quest, truth be told, it furthered with a purpose in mind—namely that the two of you would return with me to the crux of the battle to help ward off the extraordinary and overly powerful extraterrestrial campaign …"

"Well, let us move forward with haste, then, while the two of you give details and carry on explaining," the fair Lady Bellatrix masterfully interjected in advance of the tenuous silence's ability to lengthen and thereby mature to a more awkward and uncomfortable strain. She felt an urgency to step forth and intertwine, an impulse that spoke volumes about her fearlessness and sense of adventure while also demonstrating her willingness to take on the most dangerous and momentous of campaigns. She certainly realized that the fate of an entire race was at stake, inferring from the non-too-specific banter that a considerably significant enterprise was indeed forthcoming and assuredly in store. However, at the same time and more pressingly, she also perceived the onrush of an imminent and quickly approaching threat.

Therefore, at her urging we continued along at a breakneck pace while Cristofo recounted what he knew of the earthly assailment and I in turn elucidated upon the circumstance with whatever shreds of clarification I could proffer and whichever nuggets of information I could manage to incite and sustain.

"But for what reason?" our young protégé befittingly inquired. "What could Noxerus possibly gain from the potential deposition or even the destruction of a good number from my inconsequential and unimpeachable race?"

"Why, it all boils down to his ultimate amusement and pleasure, of course, my dear boy. I fear that you underestimate the true value of your species from the perspective of a battle-driven, unsympathetic, and torture-riddled realm. The hominid clans are highly distinguished and well acclaimed throughout their dispersion among the nether sphere's variegated strata and uniquely dispersed tiers. And although each layer boasts its own distinct brand of misery and diversified versions of ill appeal, all share in their conclusive appreciation of the invariably resilient, spirited, tenacious and determinedly subsisting humanoids—attributes that seems to overlie the whole of your enduringly barbaric yet highly regarded and overly obstinate race."

"And you have yet to mention the apparent fondness that seems to prevail with regard to the propensity toward the taste of our runny and red body fluid!"

"Indeed, my boy. I have yet to mention it, but by no means does that negate the truth of the matter, nor does it imply an unimportant rationale toward the ultimate goal, which is namely to augment the human populace as it exists on the netherworld plane. And to that end, Noxerus would certainly go to great lengths in order to aid or facilitate the effort of any coinciding and likewise campaign." And with that, for the most part, the subject seemed to be exhausted and closed, a conclusion wrought from the ensuing quietude that thereafter seemed to unfold while we continued along. We followed the lead of young Cristofo, who was left quite satisfied with the overall explanations that were proffered, remaining confident about the bearing of our course and its conveyance toward a wizardly portal and its corresponding and imminently forthcoming earthly approach.

"Hold!" I blurted forth more loudly than necessary and with an inflection that was misguided in its jumpy and worry-promoting tone. A soft yet clattery noise was discerned in the rearward distance, an ever-so-slight rumbling movement that echoed forward to expose a speedy follower by way of an untypically careless displacement of rubble and stone. Such a stealthy, sneaky, and catlike pursuit could only derive from one source with which I was familiar. "Cristofo, no!" I exclaimed as our rather impetuous young champion eagerly and prematurely let fly with a Maleabar-contrived throwing blade.

At that moment, an effectively concealed form jumped out from its camouflaging press along the broken and ridged wall of the portal bearing tunnelway, where it proceeded to sidestep the expertly placed and robustly hurtled throwing knife with a startling dexterity and speed. 'Twas a rather large and cumbersome figure to behave in such a spry and agile manner—one that utterly revealed itself as it continued headlong toward our prevailing standpoint.

"Look, Altarius, 'tis none other than a lumbering beast of burden absent the sluggish and burdensome aspects toward which they had seemed to be almost fundamentally inclined!"

"No, Cristofo, stand down at once." I called on our impulsive young apprentice to re-sheathe his hastily drawn sword and take ease. "Malthazar! Slacken pace, my wizardly comrade, before you completely unhinge our excitable, battle-ready, and newly invigorated young boy."

"But there is no time to dawdle, Altarius, my well-received collaborator and unsurpassable Prime. To the portal at once with the lot of you, and we shall save the pleasantries for yet another place and some other time."

"Speak forthwith and with haste, my imposturous old friend." Lady Bellatrix held no inkling toward being left in the dark regarding the forthcoming threat that was ever so near and unmistakably perceived. "And revert back to your more conventional form so that I may reacquaint myself with that long unseen and all but forgotten mold. And also for the sake of our newest associate here so that a more formal introduction can be properly purveyed, no matter how short-lived or quaint it may or may not remain."

"Yes, yes, my lady, of course. At once." Immediately and without forgoing a succinct yet courteous bow, the accommodating cohort began to violently contort, transmogrify, and altogether unwind. And in no time at all that grizzly and feeble old figure about which we were much more accustomed immediately stood at the great wizardess's forefront as well as at Cristofo's and mine.

In the meantime, Cristofo, stared in amazement throughout the entire enthralling and reconfiguring ordeal with wide and captivated eyes that did not alter as his newly beheld wizardly concomitant fully came together and then proceeded to expound vigorously.

"Pumiceus! The savage beast has been summoned and in this direction barrels its boiling and nurturing flow!" A calmer and more settled version of the perpetually excitable and scruffily comported old dynamo suddenly and distinctively emerged. "It is indeed a great pleasure to meet with your acquaintance, young Cristofo ..." And then almost instantaneously, an overly anxious hyperactivity returned as the tranquil composure was summarily re-submerged. "Now in haste and onward to the egress point you go! Take lead and demonstrate the required maneuver so as to allow your fellow evacuees a smoother and more fluid plunge and decline in through the portal mouth and on to the otherworld locality you seek!"

"But ... but I do not yet know the precise manner in which to guide them." A mild uncertainty pervaded as the boy confusedly remained for an instant until he reconciled, recalculated, and began to peruse the existing situation properly. "And by no means will we leave you alone here to face whatever threat is imminent and at hand!" The becalmed and more serious strain of Malthazar once again came to the forefront and stood firm. A sturdy grasp fastened itself upon the shoulders of our distinguished apprentice, and a pair of darkish and debonair eyes beamed fixedly amidst an otherwise scruffy, untidy, and bewhiskered visage.

"Yes, you do, son ... and yes, you will." With that, the withered and wrinkled figure turned and began to glide calmly away.

An atypical hesitation followed as Cristofo was released from the somewhat mesmerizing clamp. All at once, a roaring and thunderous hiss-construed bellow echoed forth from the foreground well in advance of the tunnelway's liberating road. And rearward, in the distance, was a glimmer, an onrush, an ever-nearing and tumultuous liquefied flow. A curt glance my way provided the boy with confirmation that Malthazar was to be left of his own accord and that it was now or never for the three of us to move onward, unto the crux of our extricating sortie.

"Malthazar, are you mad? Come with us at once and save yourself from the oncoming turmoil while at the same time helping us to negotiate further along." Our determined champion still felt the need to implore his newly encountered yet strangely familiar companion, who appeared to be much too feeble and creaky for combat and was seemingly much more valuable in helping to lead him along on his way.

"But you already know the way, Cristofo. Now carry on to safety while I stay behind to deal with our molten and monstrous threat." The bent and broken-down form turned to face the target of his assertion. "And worry not, for we shall reconnect soon, my boy, much sooner that you can hope to imagine or perceive."

An irregular smile then significantly altered the contour and outline of the scraggly and crumpled old visage, exposing a most unsightly arrangement of dentition, a considerably discontinuous, yellowed, and fragmented array. Then the frumpish old wizard turned and once again began to saunter away. An obvious and crooked hobble waned and abated with every step that advanced him forward, and a torn and tattered rag of a shirt did little to conceal a contorted and knobby spine that ran the full length of his backside like the twisted carcass of a long-since burrowed in and semi-decomposed snake.

"Grrrawrawrr! Come now, you foul and fiery creature!" An irrational battle cry served to rile up the deceptively competent and battle-weathered warrior. "Grrrawrawrr! Let me impose upon you the quelling attribute of my enchanted and slaughter-ready blade as it kisses upon your fulgent and fire-laden frame! Grrrawrawrr!" he repeated with an ever-growing vein as his pace decidedly quickened. His posture effectively straightened, and as he jumped down upon his heels soundly, his hand reached back to the topmost part of his cervical tier.

There and then, Malthazar's long and thin yet sinewy and toughened fingers took firm grasp upon what could best be described as a significantly protruding bone. A sharp jolt and fluent swivel completed the disentangling motion as every corresponding bump, or vertebrae, or node detached itself from the rickety and slightly bowed backside to conjoin and meld in a perfectly straight and unfaltering line. A sharp whip quickly concluded the unravelling motion, and a wickedly clean and rectified edge delineated the character of the sword that the transfiguring wizard proudly brandished while prompting the rapidly approaching beast to harken and summarily behold. A seemingly virile and much less misshapen form then pressed forward with a howling and battle-readied frenzy. Within moments, the bold and brazen aggressor shrieked forth consecutive screams that echoed throughout the cavernous domain—profound cries filled of pain admixed with rage and maniacal fervor as the undaunted Malthazar delved headlong into the onrushing molten fluid that ferried along the mighty Pumiceus with its vitalizing and liquid combination of melted and mountainous rock and stone.

Once again, and from the opposing range, a thunderous bellow came down upon our ears with a chilling and spine-tingling hiss-conceived modulation. The roar pulsated forth from far in the foreground, emanating toward us in turbulent waves that actually stirred the air and conveyed a foul-smelling breeze unto our standpoint. A hugely round and cavernous silhouette became increasingly discernible in the distance, soon enough evolving to reveal a mucous-filled and wormlike enormity whose breadth spanned across more or less the full diameter of the passage. A circular array of jagged teeth lined the inward circumference of the foully derived and tunnel-dwelling beast whose gaping mouth opened with significant magnitude as it continued to roar and offensively expel and spew. Indeed, 'twas a creature that bore similitude to the repugnant species with which Cristofo was all too familiar, the giant queenlike version of the ingurgitating devils that hounded him not so long ago, well underneath and to the earth-side depths of the Nepheshan factory's portal-fringed undertow.

"No!" Cristofo exclaimed as Lady Bellatrix and I readied our blades and looked toward the repugnantly large and glutinous larva-resembling foe. "I will take lead in this matter, and the both of you are to follow closely behind while replicating precisely my every action and movement as you see them unfold!"

Then a deeper and much more clamorous roar seized our attention as it smashed upon us yet again and from the opposite pole. At once, we all turned to catch glimpse of Malthazar in the heat of a most inconceivable melee, swimming and bobbing about the guts of the indomitable lava creature while swinging and swatting away with his unconventional but highly effective blade. The dragon-headed and snake-bodied beast's devouring and fire-laden fangs came down upon the meager assaulter in a number of differing yet fierce and merciless ways, and each and every turn was met with swift response from the uncannily agile old wizard and by his netherworld forged and sharpened retaliatory foray. The magma-comprised head of the mighty Pumiceus was repeatedly lopped off, slashed at, and hewn, only to regrow at once and with fluidity after first collapsing down upon its molten marrow, its nurturing and runny lava- composed lagoon. The behemoth's more solid and hardened foreparts were construed from some strain of igneous or more simply cooled-off portions of its nectar and solidified brew, coming to fruition upon its facial features, which consisted of a jawbone, choppers, and lengthy fangs that would blatantly obtrude. The sum of the compacted and callous members would in any event instantaneously soften, turn to mush, and run down into its own liquefied lifeblood with each competent sword strike that our diligent Malthazar administered and with each smiting that he delivered and would unfailingly come to achieve.

Cristofo's enraptured glance was ever so briefly reciprocated by the far to the fore wizard, whose blistered and magma-spattered face turned to convey reassurance by means of a quick beam from a pair of sprightly and spellbinding eyes. With that, the spirited young initiate discerned that it was indeed appropriate timing for us to abandon our wizardly defender, as the earthly realm was beckoning and the portal was primed and ready for us to take leave. And so onward and straightforwardly did our remarkable boy rush toward the advancing slithering and slobbering beast, with blade held high and battle cry unreservedly unleashed. He immediately found himself face front of the giant tooth-interlined gaping-mouthed monstrosity. An odious breeze served to straighten the young wizard's longish dark-shaded hair as he approached his ambition as though trudging forward through a mildly violent gale. The tongueless and drool-laden orifice glared alluringly while inveigling entry unto the blubbery and lardaceous passage within. All at once, our forward companion altered his tactic and unexpectedly sheathed his exceedingly qualified sword.

An agile, flying, headfirst lunge carried the boy straight into the guts of the clueless and otherwise soggy and corpulent beast, and farther along into the bowels of the creature was he directed by way of throbbing and pulsating tissue and sinewy, swallowing thew. Every movement was felt with a stark and clear awareness as our bold protagonist was squeezed ahead unto foul stenching cannula and pushed forward through gross fleshy tubes, where he intermixed with lumpish swill and indescribable materials while traveling along the glutinous monster's entrails until finally, and thankfully, passing right through. A firm and unyielding landing pad greeted the boy as he smacked down upon some good old-fashioned earth and stone, serving to jostle him back to his senses. He got up with some measure of soreness and difficulty before cleaning off what he could of the sporadically adhered residue and posturing with a decent degree of dignity so as to remain more formally in wait for his peers.

In the meantime, back unto the netherworld and in the locality of the mighty Immotus's subterranean manufactory, Noxerus, Fingo, and company had been suddenly smacked with the realization that their ominous conjuring had failed to achieve the function upon which it was wickedly construed. Like a bolt of lightning, our superpowered Ignatius abandoned his stalwart hold by scaling down and retracting before shooting into the liberating tunnelway with nearly unobservable outset and speed. Yet again the shameful cloak of failure somehow came to enrobe the supremely powerful and netherworld-revered wizard Prime, a sentiment that the omnipotent being had not felt (nor longed for) since at least a handful of centuries afore.

"Fingo, call upon Certasus at once and make ready our most noteworthy squadron of vescolumen." A serious, more or less dejected and monotone directive was uttered almost distractedly, spoken softly and with a preoccupied and introverted tone. "Make the necessary arrangements to govern accordingly in our absence and for the indeterminate time being."

"But, master, you vowed never to return to the earthly domain!" A fiery glare responded in turn and served to silence the discussion, ending it conclusively and at the same time communicating the fact that Fingo's counterstatement was one that held substance with which the devilish overlord was not only familiar but also most certainly aware. And in the not too distant Earth-based otherworldly locality, a hard landing wreaked havoc upon my backside as I touched down at the feet of our well-composed young rescuer and alongside of a similarly discomforted Bellatrix. Our trio of conveyed journeyers then stared on in relative amazement while catching a glimpse of Ignatius's grand entrance as the fiery wonder shot into our underground terminus to join us with a lightning-fast, blazing, and comet-resembling sizzle and burn.

CHAPTER 11

Battleground, Earth

The adventure pushed on with the three of us continuing along while sporting a refreshed disposition and a more earthly inspired flavor and feel. Cristofo led the charge with a noticeably more contented and homier aura that overshadowed an underlying and increasing sense of urgency that was progressing almost toward apprehension with a hint of despair. Meanwhile, Iggy maintained position atop and about his master's shoulder before deciding to retreat into the comfort of that cozy little refuge of gold that rocked easefully with every uniform footstep and soothed with every rhythmical pulsation of a dynamically beating heart. It did not take long for the fiery creature to scale back down to a more familiar stature and to a more subtle overall comportment and flare. The same held true about the rest of us, for that matter, as we quickly reverted to our more familiar methods and manners and our oxygen-inspired breathing and shade.

"The battle rages on as we speak! I sense it, Altarius, and I can feel it in my marrow and in my meat. What's more, these subterranes reek of it. It's as though something is brewing here in the factory's deep and uninvestigated undersurface." Worrisome thoughts of his father and grandfather seeped and soaked within Cristofo's mind like indelible ooze, furthering into a sensation of outright fear for his beloved Myrina as well as for the whole of his fellow compatriots, his family and friends, and his peers.

"Then let us quicken pace, my young apprentice, for the warfare will certainly not sit idly by and tarry until such time as the three of us decide to attend. Let it never be said that Altarius the Prime and company should dawdle and dally along while en route to the awaiting enticement of a hostile and slaughterous campaign. What say you of this, my fair and much favored Lady Bellatrix?"

"I say onward with haste, my fellow champions, for Annabell is well overdue for a feast. And what of my precious Tempestas? you might ask. Well, she is bloated and burdened with pressure and is therefore much in need of release!"

The dense and compacted substrate brought a strange comfort to Cristofo as he trudged along rapidly, leading us through the twisting and winding passages and caverns that varied considerably in a number of differing manners and ways. Narrow and nearly impassable bottlenecks that would more commonly unnerve and intimidate would instead be negotiated with the uttermost confidence and ease, usually opening up into voluminous expanses with widespread arteries and tunnelways and with an endless variety of cavities and caves. Bridge-like overpasses would link and combine a large number of intricately woven footpaths, walkways, and trails, as did interlacing catwalks and connectors with diversified breadths, thicknesses, and range. In and out, across and through, over and under we ventured with a progress that remained at all times virtuous and true. In addition, the one consistent factor in the whole of the variegated and irregular subterrane was that the boy led us along with an overall upward momentum in an effort to get us to the factory's principal level—or at least to a proximate and near surface grade.

Vast and disorienting indeed was this deep and bewildering underbelly upon which the boy's chosen portal way had obliged us to drop in at, or more so compelled us to attend. Never afore had I seen the likes of such a naturally occurring arrangement that smacked of the magnificently sporadic proportionality of a galactic supercluster, the fascinating framework of the inconsistently intertwined canals and chambers of the honeycomb sea sponge, or of the meshy maze of fossilized marrow that instills itself within the confines of a petrified bone. In any event, our undaunted pacesetter plugged ahead with a steady if not vigorous resolve and pace, for he knew that somewhere beyond his current circumstance, the battle raged on with a cold indifference and that his allies, associates, kinsfolk, and friends were much in need of a bolstering hand.

"Hoo-hoo." The soft yet focused owl-like cry descended upon our standpoint with an attention-grabbing resonance. All at once, we scoured the multifaceted foreground in an attempt to uncover the origin of the unexpected yet strangely intelligible catcall. But its source was most elusive indeed considering the intense darkness of the underground bearing, which was not fully broken by Maleabar's moderate, if practical sheen.

"Hoo-hoo." Once again, the outburst resoundingly flew by, but this time with more volume and clarity and with our attention level set considerably more high.

"Look to the fore." I directed with an outstretched arm and finger more clearly pointing the way and with a directed beam from Maleabar illuminating the target and putting it on a clearly visible display. "There he be, the beguiling little rascal!" My eyes confirmed what my perception had pretty much already foreseen.

"Well, my word! It's Malthazar!" Cristofo gave voice to the recognition that Bellatrix and I had conclusively unearthed by that time. "But how …? I mean, when could he have …? We left him … 'Tis confounding, to say the least."

Our young companion was surely contented with the turn-up of our recently left behind associate, albeit he remained at somewhat of a loss with regard to reconciling the exact methodology used in his uncanny ability to summarily reappear.

"Ha ha! To be somewhat confounded is simply to know our rascally and most capable fellow wizard. It is in his true nature to amaze and astonish, in his manner to confuse and confound. But if there is one thing upon which we can all be certain, it is that he is a most effective and resourceful ally and one that can be counted upon with the same regularity as the inevitable dawn at the end of each day. Carry on toward his whereabouts at once, my good Cristofo. He signals and urges us his way. We must move fast to catch up with him, for already he has moved on with his typically impatient and relentless pace."

To that end, the three of us made quick work of the convergence toward our considerably competent old comrade and friend, who led us up through a rather random array of pathways, channels, underpasses, and overpasses before maneuvering along a narrow and lengthy tunnelway. He finally halted at one of its various window-like openings, where he stooped down, peered out toward the foreground, and waited for us to draw up and attend. A subtle yet concise signal conveyed the need to extinguish our Maleabar-produced luminance as we hit upon and took position beside our well-prepared collaborator, who then silently gestured for us to peruse without commotion by use of our noiseless and studious eyes. What we saw at that precise moment was indeed a scene without parallel—a truly significant circumstance of great consequence in the overall unfolding of our spectacular tale.

A numberless array of marching bodies filed along methodically throughout a good portion of the expansive vastitude that was the objective of our scrutiny and that ran widespread and for some considerable distance and range. A regimented almost robotic pace advanced the masses forward in precisely delineated rectangular segments of equal dimension and with each grouping also being uniformly interspaced. Slender and tall beings of more or less human proportion were made plainly visible by way of sparkling and sporadically scattered phosphorescent and crystal-like fragments firmly embedded into the underground earth and stone. A light-emitting material and natural component of the admixed minerals, bedrock, subsoil, and clay made up part of the structure of the outstretching cavity's groundwork, far-reaching canopy, boundaries, and facade.

In the distant backdrop, waterfalls, rivulets, and ponds bedecked the otherwise stony and rustic landscape and added some decoration with no small measure of flair. And intermixed into the uniquely arranged subterranean equation, lava flow prevailed in and among its own blend of basins and pools and other runny and rushing stream like formations, accumulations, offshoots, and tears. Overall, it was a wholly incongruous and mismatched habitation with its own blend of steamy hot blasts and refreshingly shivery breezes, its own batches of off-colored spots and randomly dispersed surface encrustations, as well as an assortment of patches and plots that were rife and replete of various types and kinds of seemingly mineralized shrubbery and vegetation. Indeed, it was a genuine and unique ecosystem full of life and activity and engulfed with gust, breath, spirit, and vim. Yes, of course, as by this time you have surely supposed, it was a subterrestrial populace brought forth by the original numbers of Corbominian settlers who had sought shelter in the factory's homey confines, only to recede farther down unto the more favorable depths, where they would eventually find a more revitalizing homestead and a much more restorative admixture of air.

Hence and so, there they then remained at our fore, an army of cloaked and charcoal-surfaced sedimentary beasts marching forth with a firm objective in mind and with a purpose securely set in place. Bony and blackened fingers held consistent grasps upon stone-like and minerally comprised weapons that were tall and staff shaped, with a pickax resembling the top part, which was unmistakably sharpened and incontestably hewn. Nary a step was misguided, nor were the formations out of line on any occasion. Instead, the robotically mobilized and sufficiently armed soldiery was marching forth with unemotional vigor and fortitude, forming a most threatening and apparently proficient force that progressed forward in great volume until branching off and into all manner of channels and junctions and passageways with an even dispersion and a precisely calculated bearing and climb.

"So it seems that our battle begins much sooner than we had supposed or foreseen." I spoke softly and in the direction of Malthazar, who in turn nodded reassuringly and in short order since our thoughts were unilaterally garnered and gleaned. Vigor then throbbed and burst forward as concealment and stealth gave way, and upward I rose with strict posture as Maleabar was at the same time solidly hit down upon the rocklike terrain. At once, a great bow was transacted, and from its limb set a pair of impressively sculpted arrows were drawn out with a most graceful and fluid motion and with no small measure of swagger and flair. The two sharp-tipped projectiles were thereupon set together against drawstring and unleashed with a ruthless precision and with impetus to spare.

A cold thwacking sound shot back to us in quick order and with a reiterative succession that rippled its way through the air, an octet of puncturing and penetrating noises that chimed with a heartwarming resonance as though dragging our ears through a symphonic parade. Crisp yet subdued piercing sounds gave rise to the melody as granular and crusty anatomies were cut clean through by way of the virtuoso's chosen instruments before proceeding to burst outward with a gritty crescendo that sprayed forth a sandy cloud of residue. The chorus continued along as the unparalleled arrows found their subsequent victims in the arrangement, thereby serving to somewhat extend the echoing, evocative, and inspiriting tune. Four chords per arrow, or eight when counted fully in twos, and a corresponding number of the marching soldiery were struck down from their perfect formation, never again to resume.

Several beady and black largely extruded and pupiled eyes stared back toward the direction of the unexpected salvo, which disrupted the uniformity of the company's mechanical march by forever ending the stride for the struck-down members who were effectively reduced to a heaping pile of motionless rubble and grain. In response, four sets of fixed and focused wizardly eyeballs returned the gazes with vehemence until the Maleabar-slung apportionments returned to an outstretched and anxiously awaiting grab.

"Lead on then, my good fellow, for it seems that we have succeeded in precipitating the charge!" Again my words were aimed toward Malthazar but were primarily for the benefit of my other two concomitants since at that time our other senior male accomplice's thought process and mine were summarily interfused. Furthermore, as a result of my preceding action, the squadrons of marching marauders quickened pace and became much more energized as they veered off into newly established directions and pushed on at a more intense and vigorous rate.

"Follow along quickly," Malthazar proclaimed with an authoritative strain, "for it is time to take leave of this decamping subterrane and

to cut off a good number of this attacking and surface-bound race."
At once, the squirrely old figure scampered off at an unpredictably
outrageous pace with the three of us following closely behind, easily
managing to keep up by way of our own proportionally accelerated
gait. "Yee-haw! Yip Yip Yee-haw!" Our forward positioned colleague
shrieked in a most enthusiastic and preposterous manner as he led us
through the maze-like geography with Bellatrix at his heels, followed
by Cristofo, and winding up with yours truly at the back of the charge.
And by "charge," I do speak with a most literal meaning, for a constant
and steady stream of bursts and detonations erupted in a cacophonous
flurry. Far and wide and near and nigh the explosions rang out intensely,
with a few of the discharges near enough to my heels that they spurred
me forward with a more urgent and necessitated haste. In and around,
away and afar, heaps of earth and stone came crashing to the ground,
and bridges, links, and overpasses came tumbling down. Many a
below-surface Corbominian dweller was crushed, ground, smashed,
and thrown around, only to forever remain as spiritless carcasses or
remnants of senseless and fragmented wholes that were thenceforth
merely one of many ingredients of the mineralized surroundings and
soil.

Indeed, it was our exceedingly talented Malthazar who was the
orchestrator of the multitudinous and wide-ranging yet strategically
pinpointed attack. Although only a fractional amount of the surface-
bound intruders was permanently stilled, there was also a good portion
who were altogether obstructed and trapped in passages and corridors—
and more numbers still who were effectively smashed and sealed and
more or less blocked off. Before long, our winding trajectory brought
us into another geologic vein with multiple openings that overspread
the walls in a framework of sporadic and substantial window-like voids.
A ruined and rotted-away pipe-like conduit which connected along as
merely an outreaching tentacle among the myriad of extensions and
branchlets, which were widespread in number and direction and shot
off as though aimlessly strewn. 'Twas Bellatrix who then all at once
halted and obliged our company to draw up and respectfully attend
as she peered out onto the now much farther down massive and vast

subterranean hollow that was the expansive underground homestead of the callous and unemotional Corbominians, who had by then somewhat evolved into a colony of indigenous subterrestrial beings.

"Take a breath for a moment, my fellow wanderers, and observe as your womanly inclined counterpart makes good use of the acid-like tinge that comprises a miniscule portion of this semi-stagnant and sluggish underground air."

The formidable raven-haired figure held upright and projected her marvelously interwoven staff as a focused glare brought life upon the opaquely perched jewel of Tempestas, which glistened and enlivened, then kindled and flashed. A non-brilliant white glow then assumed command of the unparalleled and infinitely precious stone, a dull yet powerfully enlightening diode that radiated with softness while asserting clarity one thousand times fold. Beads of viscous and gooey liquid were all of a sudden drawn out from the walls and ceiling, and generally from all over and also upon the existent surface rind that overspread the hugely cavernous hall wherein an astringent, nervous, and worrisome sweat-like brew was drawn out from the consolidated bedrock by way of the powerfully equipped jewel's magical and mysterious allure. Drips and drops and dribbles of an increasingly showery and acid-based dew fell down upon the masses of marching and mineralized beings as they struggled to maintain strict order while advancing forward upon their momentous and ambitiously embarked upon campaign.

A resounding surge of subtle yet biting and sizzling hisses were then heard as the acidic precipitate hit upon the advancing targets and diluted their outer casings of hardened and sedimentary skin. This incited a gritty and sand-like residue to run down and off the crusty Corbominian veneer as though by way of miniaturized tributaries whisking away their fair share of alluvium and sediments and brim. Soon enough, seepage materialized and came to unfold as the gnawing and consuming liquid pooled and accumulated underfoot, serving to scatter and break apart the squadrons of soldiery that could no longer sustain the aggressively corrosive and devouring foray. Off they scampered with an orderly if not frantic configuration, making a rush toward the proximate holes and tunnelways that spread rampantly along the entire surface of the extensive and outreaching periphery walls of the cavernous and all-encompassing space—a colony of retreating invaders rushing to the exits with an ant-like demeanor and an analogous hurried pace.

Many a tall and charcoal-skinned raider lost breath on that day on account of the mighty Tempestas and by way of Bellatrix's gentle persuasion as robust and indurated bodies and limbs succumbed to the infallible scientific conclusion that the conjured-up chemical reaction would necessarily transfer and bring. Slimy, muddy, and murky goo remained in place upon a large portion of the cavern's undersurface, where fluidified husk, melted body parts, and residues admixed with the acrid pools and shared space with the creatures' burlap-like garments and fallen broken-down tools. The latter were fashioned to be used in the cutting and carving of human flesh with the intention of eradicating and overtaking the dominion of the soft-ish and less worthily viewed species of surface-dwelling and sun- and air-hogging human hordes.

By and by, the unrestrainedly ferocious beast that lies deeply buried within the heart of the much sought-after gemstone was then tamed by the fair Bellatrix's inimitable manner of signal and speak. In addition, the dullish white glow of Tempestas receded back into the pith of the opaque and unirradiated stone, wherein it would hole up and seek harbor until such time as her wizardly conductress would so charmingly serenade her to perform yet again. Onward and upward did Cristofo then lead the four of us hastily on our way, en route to the open air-bestrewn surface with ambition of joining our animus-based brethren in their unsolicited defensive campaign as they yearned for the liberating spaciousness brought forth on the heels of a vivid, clear, unbounded, and Earth-encircling sky on a sun-brightened day.

Meanwhile, in the no-longer-so-distant and far-removed standpoint, a mother of her race and an age-old all-powerful wizardess felt the distress that had touched down upon her long since uprooted, underground relegated, and now–called upon brood. A frown-like scowl barely altered the configuration of her stony and largely unsympathetic face as she was unhappily distracted from her aerial and observational perch atop a lustrous and brilliantly glittering staff wherein she maintained a clear and studious view of her ongoing and well-orchestrated offensive. Fleets of turtibrida riddled the skyline, and bombastic eruptions peppered the ground in and around the heart of the well-established Nepheshan metropolis, with lesser but similar attacks progressing against the venerated palace grounds as well as the factory's mountainous facade and front-facing perimeter. Various squadrons of the mechanized and turtle-like hybrids progressed in symmetrical and well-fashioned lines, dropping their explosive and volatile munitions upon the more or less undefendable targets before veering back to reload at their base of operations in the Defluous Highlands' flatter surrounds.

Farther from the aerial bombing spray, vast quantities of Corbominian foot soldiers advanced upon the masses of Nepheshan infantry and denizens, who were also joined by numerous surrounding villagers, inhabitants, and men. They fought with intensity and with all their heart, managing to do decently but by no means prevailing or conquering or swaying the outcome to turn out well for the conglomeration of them. The densely compacted Corbominian anatomies proved to be quite challenging for ax and sword, arrow and spear, and all other variances of weaponry fashioned of human-forged manner of steel. Buffets and blows from hammers and bars, clubs, maces, pellets, wads, and similar percussional utensils would likewise not carry the fighting humanoids' relentless efforts very far, as coarse and sandy skin would absorb the brunt of the wallop and disperse the physical impact before restorative granules would merely push forth and reassemble from within.

Yes, indeed twas a troublesome circumstance that faced the lot of the bound and determined Nepheshan populace as well as the adjacent and approximal townspeople, including all of their women and children and of course the sum of all men. Peculiarly sharp, rocklike, and metallically fusible tools wrought havoc upon the defending multitudes by slashing, ensnaring, and breaching tough coverings of plate and mail, ripping apart flesh and tearing off skin, severing sections and fragments of bodies and chopping off limbs. Longish and slightly arched blades crowned the top part of staff-like shafts that the Corbominian assailants wielded with intensity and with a practiced and qualified whim. A fine-cornered point tipped the pinnacle of the barbaric devices that resembled sickles, or scythes, or some similarly treacherous things.

Many a ruthless chop would come down with considerable influence, gaining great momentum from its tallish starting point as well as from the impetus of lengthy arms that were held high overhead and came down stretched full out. Into and upon a variety of helmeted or not-so-safeguarded heads would they fall, whereupon the razor-sharp beak of the implement would bury itself deeply through skullcap and embed itself fixedly before finally coming to stall. Outward they would then be pulled with vigorous force, expelling portions of scalp and gray matter while spewing forth morsels of torn-apart tissue and splashings of generously liberated blood.

Truth be told, the human defenders boasted their fair share of small victories, however scattered and scant in number they may or may not have been, taking advantage of their attacker's somewhat robotic advancements, which grew to be almost predictable and were generally proven slower and less agilely placed. Victory came quite easily in aggregate as several frequent blows from all angles succeeded in bringing down their tall-statured objectives before they were able to deliver any meaningful and reciprocal damage and sting. Also, the factory's longtime successfulness with its explosive product lines proved to be more than to some extent useful as vast quantities of throwable armaments descended upon their targets with a blasting fruition that greeted them with a fracturing, shattering, rupturing, and bursting-apart embrace.

To that end, the battles raged on with a vigorous stride and an unrelenting drive and with myriad contests spontaneously unfolding, whereupon the numbers of finished-off factions equaled exactly to the victories won. The overall impetus strongly favored the more advanced and desperate forces who were no longer with homeland and more or less vacant of option or claim—the Corbominian-based swarm that had the intention of first ravaging the nearby populations before expanding outward unto the sweeping countryside, the far-reaching horizon, and eventually unto the whole of the precious and utterly sought-after orb. Indeed, the situation seemed hopeless for the Earth-dwelling species of humanoids or possibly futile at best since the entire Nephashan central infrastructure remained largely demolished by way of the airborne armada of mechanized organisms dropping abundant munitions that exploded with what was at that time unbeknownst fervor and weight. The precious palace, its grounds, and its glorious hall were sporadically pelted and fractured and lay there in shambles, a ruined landmark reduced to wreckage with a broken-down structure and a now-shattered and pretty much ineffectual mainstay, namely the monumental and storied centuries-old barrier wall.

The great factory's frontage was also subjected to rigorous attack as it was bombarded with exploding payload dropped down from above before being stormed upon by ground troops in astronomical numbers and with inexorable clout. Into the rubble-laden principal entryway did the waves of Corbominians ceaselessly flow, whereupon the bloodshed would continue along into the confines of hollowed-out rock and age-old stone. As if that weren't enough of a challenge for the factory's defending masses to face, they were also soon to be pressed upon from the underside by way of the advancing underground forces, the likes of which I have just recently explained. They were namely the offshoots of Aleregeni's initiatory settlers of old, who had since grown to a massive assortment and collection. It was a conglomeration of the otherworldly civilization's called-upon brethren and underground Earth-stationed race.

"The surface is in close proximity, Altarius. I can sense the sweet smell of its breeze. But I see no clear path to its realization, only endless tunnels and arteries with no upward proclivity and openings with no other shortcuts or pathways of any other means."

"Stop relying on your meager little human senses, boy!" It was Malthazar this time, his retort meant to make it clear. "Look beyond the obvious signals of an inexperienced body and a predominantly untrained eye. You have the wizardly endowment coursing through your veins from hereon in. Use it to its fullest, use it to your advantage, and do not doubt its direction but instead submit to its suggestion— follow along and dive right in!" The proximate and scraggly face of the seasoned old wizard was strictly serious while conveying the words, and the bluish- gray eyes of the bedazzling devil were sternly focused, intensified, and altogether glazed. Within an instant, Cristofo's disposition became much more confident, enthusiastic, and self-assured. Excitement overwhelmed him as he came to realize that the crucial encounter was now near to fruition and that his strategically initiated and executed wizardly countercharge was considerably stronger than he had originally anticipated and represented a true ambush upon the alien attackers, which was now undoubtedly imminent, evident and at hand.

"Onward with vigor! Prepare yourselves for conflict and to meet head-on with whatever it is that may come!" A quick sprint toward a not-so-far overhang was instigated and then replicated in triplicate, without any delay. A full-bore unhesitating dive then ensued as the boy leaped off a nearby cliff-like protrusion, a maneuver that was once again repeated threefold and with similar audacity, an equally adventuresome verve, and an evenly matched follow-through. A windless and utterly stagnant air gave no resistance as we progressed unto the depths of our bold and brazen dive. A pitch-black envelope surrounded us and swallowed us whole as though it were a globule of obscurity wrapping us into a bubble and disconnecting us from the awaiting impact of firm ground and stiff, densely compacted soil. It felt as though we were inert and motionless amidst a tranquil and starless universe, not perceiving any inkling of movement or decline or acknowledging any apprehensiveness or turmoil in the metaphorical well that saturates the mind. Indeed, it was by far the most serene of portal ridings that I had ever embarked upon at that point and since; it came to parallel death's journey to a somewhat moderate degree in that the spirit was at total comfort and ease but the body's connection, in contrast, was still intact and stress-free.

Then a brash wind smacked with fortitude and brought life to the inertness of my face. My eyes opened wide to square off against the stinging sensation of the blasting air's unwavering and far-from-delicate embrace. Clouds of puffy white bliss amidst a sun-filled vastitude of blue brought great pleasure and invigoration as I basked in the unrestricted delightfulness of free fall in the midst of open air and brilliantly vivid daylight. In addition, three of my accomplices then came into eyeshot, whereupon I quickly inferred a similarly lightened spirit and flair. Sadly, the euphoric sensation was short-lived, I must say, as eyeballs swiftly began to gain focus and in consequence a grievous and most harrowing display was unveiled. It was a widespread and diversified smorgasbord of destruction—an utterly intricate and multifarious battle scene that I have just alluded to and will now attempt to further describe and portray.

Down upon the distant surface of land, a massive and forceful invasion was well underway. Scores upon scores of airborne raiders dropped their munitions upon the Nepheshan infrastructures. There was an exploding consequence and a shattering conclusion for numerous houses, buildings, and architecture, as well as for crowds, congregations, troops, squadrons, other conglomerations, clusters, and arrays. Swarms of lanky and imposing marauders moved in on the masses like a plague of locusts that would devour plants and vegetation and fields of ripe and ready to consume grain. With their cloth-like robes, they descended relentlessly like the clouds of a cosmic dust storm advancing unremittingly and without any discernible end to the advancing foray. Indeed the long-standing city was under siege, to say the least, as were the historic royal grounds and palace as well as the widely renowned factory frontage and lead. And although the advancing attackers were successfully conquering at a ratio of at least one hundred to three, small and glorious victories kept hopes and confidence alive within certain human pockets of richly exhibited elation and glee.

Cloud Cutters functioned with more success than had been anticipated or even fathomed, bringing down the odd turtibrida with their strategically obscured placements and their far-reaching ordnance that served to reciprocate the high-flying foreigners' otherwise unmitigated bombing spree. Indeed, a few dozen more of the miraculous devices would have certainly served the defending populace well, but at least as an alternative, a multitudinous amount of the more traditional explosive devices were generously and triumphantly hurled—an abundant and diverse assortment of the factory's more typical stockpile and store. Several well-hidden launching pads enjoyed great success in and around the proximate nooks, alcoves, crevices, and quoins that overspread the factory's mountainous periphery and front-facing façade, wherein small groupings of skillful throwers were situated and actively engaged.

Therefore, a considerable number of gritty-skinned attackers were blown apart, disseminated, and altogether pulverized into an outshooting and granular spray.

Elsewhere in the more northeasterly and distant range, dragons roared and erupted in a furious and frenzied fire-expending display that was clearly made visible from our elevated standpoint and sky-high overview of the vast and foreseeable terrain. 'Twas none other than Cimtar and Somnia, still chained up in their habitat but putting immense pressure on their tense and tautened shackles as they aggressively made an effort to free themselves and take off unto the unbounded air while breathing fire upward and in the direction of the airborne alien attackers. The latter were paying no mind to them but instead were strictly focused on delivering ruination upon the surrounding environment and bringing destruction unto the dragons' human cohabitants. Furthermore, a particularly stinging franticness overcame the majestic creatures, a feverish frenzy brought about on account of concern toward their most favorably looked upon and treasured princess. Elation was then all at once thrust upon the glorious and mystical beasts as they caught wind of their precious Myrina on approach, fighting and skirmishing with various bands and bunches of the alien intruders as she maneuvered closer toward the man-made habitat of her most infamous and most beloved of pets.

Yes indeed the two magnificent creations were a fierce, frantic, and fulminant pair, but do not be confused about their vigorous fervor and bustling flair. Although you may be well aware of their recent and grievous injuries and their recently allotted state of disrepair, your obvious perplexity is wholly unfounded, albeit understandable, seeing as how a dragon's unique and incomparable healing powers would represent a fact upon which the vast majority of audiences would not be privy to but instead would be mostly ignorant toward and utterly unaware. Furthermore, their overall resilience and stamina is quite often underestimated as most would not be able to fully reconcile the fact that they are indeed magical and mystical creatures about which there is far too little study, examination, scrutiny, and read. In any event, let us now return to our bird's-eye view description of the wide-ranging alien invasion, for I fear that I have yet again managed to meander off course and to veer, and so back to our illustrious future queen as she made way toward the man-made dragon's den, where her forthcoming course and intention will be expounded upon with hope of making it more clear.

A dozen or so of the more qualified king's guardsmen accompanied her along on the way, as did her magnificently crafted battle sword, not to mention their abundant supply of launchable munitions to ensure fully that her safety would command the utmost importance and would represent all of their principal concern.

"Stay back and secure this position." The commanding tone suited the well-skilled and capable heiress to the king's priceless and illustrious throne. She was splendidly clad in her stately battle gear as she took hold of her cumbersome riding saddle and gave leave to her chaperoning entourage.

"I cross the moat alone. Good warring to the lot of you; hold fast until you see me soaring skyward upon the back of my beloved Somnia, at which point I release you from your obligation toward me and recommission your swords and sway unto the protection of my father and mother. Make your way back to the palace and stand steadfast with them and with the rest of their called upon band."

"But, Your Majesty ..." A weathered but noticeably skillful and qualified officer of the guard looked fixedly upon the fair Myrina with his battle-worn visage and soulful brown eyes. 'Twas none other than the stalwart paladin who'd greeted young Cristofo at the palace check-in point; he was a loyal guardsman and champion of many battles about whom King Reuel spoke consistently and with sentiment of the highest regard.

"I promised your father to never leave your side!"

"Well, good luck with that, my good Giacomar, for unless you have aim to seat yourself upon that agreeable beast over there ..." A glaring pointer was then dispensed immediately subsequent to the obviously sarcastic remark by way of gesturing head and eyes aimed in the direction of a rampant and raging Cimtar. "Or unless you have all of a sudden somehow acquired the ability to spontaneously sprout wings, I am inclined to inform you that your pledge will unfortunately remain for the most part unpaid! Now come and help me harness Somnia before relegating yourself to a much more useful purpose in this most strenuous of campaigns."

A few moments passed as the valiant Giacomar gave a signal for his men to hold and defend their current soon-to-be-seized-upon position and then proceeded to grab away the bulky harness and follow the strong-willed princess's lead across the narrowly arranged access bridge. Somnia immediately took to the ground and steadied herself as she caught wind of the shimmering set of keys and its clanging wail. As for Cimtar, not so much. His chains continued to be tested with stubborn fervor and a determined might until the harnessing process was about halfway complete on his becalmed sibling. Then he reluctantly made the determination to cede. A dissatisfied stance bore little comfort as the magnificent creature bided his time and puffed and wheezed in an unmitigated effort to tolerantly wait to be released. His patience was justly rewarded, as Myrina's saddling was complete in short order. She gave Giacomar instructions for the long-anticipated unlocking to proceed. Cimtar was the first to be unleashed, taking off at the exact moment the key turn clicked its locking pins free, and then up into the air he shot like a bolt of lightning, with a bound and determined beeline and a speed that has yet to be entirely conceived.

A scorched and charred carcass of turtibrida plummeted earthward with a smoke-trailing lead, and yet another was grievously chomped on and torn apart by the time it was Somnia's turn to be summarily un-keyed. Indeed, a good foursome of the aerial alien bombers had been arbitrarily dispatched by the time Somnia reached her brother's battle level elevation. At that point, the pair of remarkable creatures continued with their vigorous assault by way of battering with their skulls and clobbering with their tails. They pierced and gashed with tooth-lined snapping maws used in conjunction with crushing jaws. Of course, there were spewing blazes and fire sprays that were particularly effective against the strangely intermixed hybrid anatomies that would almost immediately begin to lose altitude for a short while until the flame thrower–like assault incited their munition-laden hulls to flare up and discharge in a bursting, fiery, and volatile climax. The extraneous flying structures were not designed as effective defenders. Instead, they were developed with the principle goal of dropping and delivering dangerous and unstable payloads from highly placed spans and unattainable stands. With the courageous princess guiding their course and flow, the remarkable dragons more or less had their way with the relatively sluggish and slow to maneuver turtibrida.

Back on the ground, the undaunted Giacomar was invigorated and renewed in spirit as he stood witness to the princess and her dragons' triumphant aerial blitzkrieg. His men had seemed to be managing quite well in their nearby skirmishes, so he chose to commit himself toward the sporadically smashed, shattered, and largely overridden barrier wall. In no time at all he reached its inner rim, whereupon collapsed blocks of igneous and fallen brickwork, timbers, and bars served as rudimentary stepping-stones that facilitated his ascent to the top of the semi-dilapidated stronghold. Just prior to the apex of his clamber, the fearless champion pulled out a pair of explosive shells from his shouldered handbag and lit them with a steady and smoothly executed abrading grind. A delicate toss onto the wall's damaged and fractured rooftop, landing adjacent to a modest band of the pitchy-skinned marauders consummated the strategic encroachment as the fearless paladin crouched low in an effort to undermine the out bursting Corbominian-shattering spray.

At the tail end of the eruption, a bold advancement quickly ensued wherein a few of the wounded but still cognizant attackers were slashed at and hacked upon with a sharp-edged and hardened steel battle sword, yielded with skillfulness and with an intensified dose of vigor and zeal. It was with no small effort that the remaining bandits were forced to relinquish their continuance as a semi-exasperated Giacomar reveled atop their smoted carcasses and indulged, if for a moment, of the uniquely flavored euphoria of victory, survival, and the ultimate of egotism and self-appeal. From the relatively elevated standpoint, he further paused in order to work out his next course of action as he scanned and scrutinized the unimaginable unfoldings that were transpiring in and about the foreseeable surround.

Dragon fire still ripped through the smoke-filled atmosphere with sporadic intensity as would lightning flicker amidst an abundantly overcast and beclouded sky. The odd object would be seen to plummet listlessly groundward, even though numerous would still press on to drop their payload and continue with their objective while posturing from up high. A preponderance of eruptions would contrarily throw flames and wreckage upward into the aerial medley, adding substance into the explosive mishmash and contributing greatly to the overall combustion and wildfire that exemplified the general state of havoc in the area as well as the flagrant disrepair. Battles raged rampantly and with severity both inside and outside of the intermittently broken-down yet still somewhat delineating barrier wall. Outward and away from the rounded perimeter the human defenders were grossly conquered and overthrown by the swarming bands of raiders, who were noticeably slowed by the imposing stone obstacle although still pouring in through the enclosure's largely breached portions and newly created openings and crannies and crawls. Inward of the largely damaged wall, they continued in the face of more evenly matched challenges, wherein they met head-on with hard blasts from much more heavily armed soldiers and heedful attacks from the more skillfully bent of both warriors and guardsmen as well as a few handfuls of the more generously invigorated lays.

Farther along toward the fortification's nucleus, the valiant paladin set eyes upon a never-before-seen display that was thriving as it unfolded— never before seen by any of the present generation of onlookers as the boundary-lined row of carnivoran trees plucked and crushed the gritty-skinned attackers with outreaching branches of unforeseeable effectiveness and speed. One by one, the methodical advancers would be snatched up and mauled by the formerly stiff and grayish wood branches that were dancing and swaying as though fervently enlivened and altogether enthralled, with limbs reaching widely and snapping and clamping in all directions. A bloodless outcome would seem to frustrate the stout and leafless timbers as they would immediately abandon their spontaneously snatched, scrunched, and dissected prey in favor of the next approaching victim. They had the hope of finding one with a more fulfilling store of entrails that would enable them to ingest their nourishment by way of the spilled rich red fluid's much-longed-for seepage and much-savored spray.

Indeed, it was quite the scene that our brave Giacomar had taken a moment to survey. However, observation alone would neither wage nor win his forthcoming battles. Thence he advanced onward along the fractured peak of the shattered wall, whereupon the turmoil and travel intensified as it led away from the bounds of the dragon's moat in favor of the busier and more blusterous palatial encroachment. Sturdy chests of potent and powerful explosives were still intermittently situated along the defensible perimeter's topside. The odd cache had been crushed or cast away, but they were nowhere near destroyed or depleted. A handy small-scaled enkindling torch was summarily procured and lit from the first nearby semi-smashed and largely emptied-out crate. The fearless paladin grabbed hold of a few shells and made quick work of the lighting and launching of the explosive devices that were aimed downward along the grossly breached channels and farther ahead along the no longer congested but still sporadically occupied rooftop deck. The human defenders had long since been vanquished from their fortified standpoint, so the alien advancers were more strictly focused on hastening through and past the broken-down barrier as they proceeded forward toward their ultimate aim. Unto the increasingly perilous trajectory did the good Giacomar fearlessly sway, sequentially throwing bombs and delivering hard strokes of fine steel at each and every challenger that remained standing or defiantly stood in his way.

Battles and bloodshed of similar sort and equivalent strain were rampant and recognizable throughout the observable distance, which was now considerably shrinking in conjunction with our invariably hastening descent. Therefore, the time to make land had at last presented itself and the shift toward battle was in consequence and accordingly manifest. Bellatrix took firm hold of Cristofo at the precise moment that she had blanketed herself in a waft of robust yet accommodating wind. Malthazar had transmogrified in mid-flight, taking the form of a majestic and broad-winged creature that soared through the air with unmitigated gracefulness and ease. For my part, Maleabar was utilized for a steady downward decline, with unfolded and fanned-out appendages that spread out to accommodate a more controllable and responsive drift and glide. However, the miraculous material was only to be temporarily employed until my more functional ride rematerialized. Indeed, Candilux was most urgently summoned using the more conventional of telepathic behests. As we all came closer to the aggressive and strenuous circumstance, a flurry of activity would ultimately initiate, transpire, and unfold, thereby giving rise to a barrage of riveting and simultaneously occurring encounters about which I will now give my best effort to expound upon and make told.

My magnificent white beast was indeed a wondrous sight, beginning from the moment that she was spotted in the distance and increasingly even more so as she furiously zoomed in on our locality, slowing and swerving on her oncoming approach. Maleabar was summarily sheathed and was shouldered just as my remarkable dragon came to the fold and positioned herself to be mounted. Just as I managed to touch myself down upon the smoothly worn scales of her collar, a sharp and high-pitched shriek of concern was exuded forth. It was a well-intentioned but far too delayed cautionary forewarning. Out of nowhere, a vastly hard and imperceptibly fleeting impact smacked down upon the pith of my staggered and thunderstruck person. 'Twas none other than Aleregeni herself who had come to meet me head-on with the full force of her staff, knocking me well clear of my imminent ride and rendering me senseless and near submission.

In response to the offensive, Candilux instinctively and furiously roared as she moved to pivot her surprisingly agile yet gargantuan form. Malthazar hurriedly fluttered and soared from his not-so-distant standpoint, making diligent use of his magnificent eagle-like wings in an effort to take firm hold of me well before there was any chance of my taking on a splattering disposition. His secure grasp revived me to a moderate degree and worked in conjunction with a restorative spell that helped bring me back to full control of my senses.

A torrent of fire then torpedoed across the near-at-hand sky, delivering a concerted burst of both scorching and blistering heat and a clamoring, crackling sound, as Candilux had concluded her aggressive turn with a dynamic cannonade of dragon fire. However, little did the devoted and well-intentioned creature realize that the primordial of all our species would make quick work of evading even the fiercest and most belligerent of such blasts. A simple motion of her hand sent the magnificent dragon drifting and reeling back away from whence it had previously come, and at the same time, the casual gesture gave Aleregeni command of the oncoming and fiery salvo. This allowed her to turn it swiftly away will a fluent steer and sway, diverting and redirecting it to smack directly upon my ferrying concomitant and myself. As a result, down to the ground did we both crash and come to be found in a flaming and violent display. The two of us were slow indeed to recover as we desperately attempted to come to our feet, knowing that a further attack would be imminent and would carry with it a charge of at least equal if not heightened potency.

Down came the subsequent strike with heavy weight and breakneck flight just as I managed to wrap Maleabar about the two of our figures with a steely semicircular protective dome. A huge craterlike indentation was ingrained upon the shell-like covering, which served its purpose for the moment but undeniably yielded to a significant extent as it was forced to bend and give way. The attacking wizardess's ridged and bejeweled staff struck down upon it with the full momentum of her mineral-like and heavyset frame, which crashed to the ground with a resounding and rumble-provoking thud. A quick pry then ensued wherein the device broke light betwixt the metallic bubble and the topography's proliferant and densely laid lawn. Almost at once, the resolute and tenacious barrier made of remarkable material was effortlessly upheaved and then flung. It did not travel very far, however, before managing to reconfigure into its more combative form, which quickly reestablished itself at my fore. A firm grasp upon the familiar and steely surface of my practical and prototypical pole gave me assurance and fortitude as I held it up in short order to block another aggressively administered, largely drawn out, and heavy-handed blow.

Malthazar was then quick into action, taking advantage of the blocked and thwarted offensive by fluently drawing out his sword and administering a well-placed stroke upon the near-at-hand limb of the wizardess's stately and imposing physique. A clean slice right through decidedly caught the attention of the relentlessly advancing warrior, who instantaneously returned the thrust by way of an energy-discharging wave of the hand that sent my colleague reeling and tumbling a fair distance away. The thoroughly lacerated appendage then spontaneously fused, interblended, and proceeded to mend itself completely within the short time that it took for Malthazar's bowled along body to stop itself from rolling and trundling away. In the meantime, my staff had been furiously spun and swayed in an intensified effort to strike down upon my opponent's statuesque frame, but my barrages in turn were skillfully spurned by my equally capable adversary's efforts to keep them at bay.

The odd blow made contact on both sides of the aggressive foray, wherein my delivered jolts seemed to be more effortlessly absorbed as though impacted against a loosely filled sack of sand. Whacks that I received, however, assuredly were felt and stung as they percussed and impinged against good old-fashioned animus meat and bone. The emotionless and machinelike challenger was indeed frustrating to a considerable degree, and I had quickly come to recognize that a prolonged contest would most certainly favor her more stoic and unrelenting manner. Therefore, vigor intensified and soared. Maleabar was lengthened while being simultaneously thrust and turned into sword, puncturing smack into the middle of my tenacious opponent and piercing well into her dense and mineral-based mold. She was momentarily thrown off guard, and I took advantage by directing my miraculous material to flare up and burst forth with an explosive and heavy discharge of variegated parts and pieces of fragments and shards, causing her to fall back and initiate a pause while evaluating the newly formed void that came to be arranged on her broad coarse-grained midsection.

"Begone, foul mistress! Return at once with the lot of your dark and misguided race! Send them back unto the bowels of the earth's untapped substructure and back through your portal so as to reenter the confines of whenever the time or wherever the place! There shall be no unsolicited incursion brought forth unto this or any other of the multitudinous flocks that fall under the watchful umbrella of animus the Prime!" The momentarily unresponsive matriarch raised her head up and away from focus, as she had been almost confusedly fondling the scraggy fringe of her gaping injury. A grim yet governed stare then shot back at me as though tangibly materialized and launched directly upon my fixated and firmly reconciled face. Malthazar had returned to my side but seemed to be wholly ignored as a rumbling and vibrating voice emitted a never before listened to pitch and tone.

"I too am charged with the overseeing of my precious and irreplaceable flock, Altarius, who is Prime of a mere and meager branchlet that wavers leisurely and lost amidst an infinite forest of endless trees. A capable enough spirit churns and drives your chosen embodiment, yet it is one that knows not its place when it comes to be faced by the Prime of all who are given the name Prime!" Bony and pronged fingers then scraped and scooped the slurry sediment-based sludge that lined the edge of her newly formed and blotchy wound.

"The gateway about which you refer is unconditionally and unilaterally imposed. My most worthy progeny are here to remain and will presume incumbency over this compatible and most suitable sphere, both its nurturing underground as well as its lush and luminous outer veneer." At once and unexpectedly, the gooey muck was calculatedly hurled upon both of our attentive and unsuspecting forms. "Let the fittest and most worthy species persevere and thrive in and among this wondrous heavenly body upon which all manner of beings can be given the chance to flourish and shine and to toil and fight to survive. There exists no mandate that must be maintained, nor is there any birthright or claim that sets aside the freedom of any race or breed to strive for continuance and for the right to prosper and bear seed. And it is not for you or your ragtag animus crew to declare otherwise. That includes your newly prescribed boy, or should I say your much touted and highly acclaimed initiate, who is brash and brave but still soft and naïve. He would scrape and fight with all his might in a futile effort to save the people of his home world."

The gooey muck had dispersed itself over and about the two of our squared-off and readied forms, wherein it proceeded to spontaneously spread, swell, thicken, and gel until covering the whole of our bodies, effectively rendering us motionless. We were fastened and glued by the material's lead-like attribute, and what's more, it continued to pervade as it ran down to soak and overlay the immediate stretch of terrain at our feet. Downward we began to slink as the groundwork became saturated and then was instantaneously amalgamated with the dense and inexplicably initiated paste. Ordinarily and under similar circumstances, either of our minds would be more than sufficient to free us from any analogous trap or ruse. Nevertheless, in this particular instance, Aleregeni managed to block our mental attempts with her own brand of powerful and imposing mind control, which certainly was drawn from higher ranks, leaving us more or less helpless as we slumped unhurriedly down into the pith of the quicksand-like substance. A quick swipe of her staff cleared away a swatch of the uncontainable goop from my mouth with the intention of granting me one last dialogue with which to rebuke.

"Nature's way can be as cruel and callous as it is caring and divine. This we both understand all too well, my most curious matriarch from far away and beyond. And tinkering and meddling in her set-upon ways is simply what we do as part of our unique and predestined wizardly trade. However, do not be so brash as to think that you can swoop down from afar and effect any manner and means of change without facing the utmost resistance from those that want the present state of conditions to stay and remain! These flocks of yours most certainly did not figure their own course through yon intergalactic portal way! Nor did your herds conjure themselves up from the depths of the underground to join in on this unwarranted and unasked-for raid! Indeed, it was by your hand and with your sway that this most selfish of campaigns was orchestrated and has now gotten underway. Therefore, we too will now intervene in an attempt to reestablish a much more civil manner of existence wherein no such injustices can be so easily initiated and carried through by the likes of malevolent beings such as you!"

A steely concentration was then brought to bear in conjunction with the retaliatory words, invoking both Mathazar and me to set our mental focus on high as we attempted to free ourselves from the rigidly confining snare. Still, it seemed that we could not overcome Aleregeni's abounding psychic fortitude, although we certainly stretched it to well near its limit.

"Do not dare to lecture me on nature and its scheming methods and savage ways, unsubstantially composed wizard of tissue and bone. And do not spew forth callow and childlike threats upon the likes of your blatant superiors, especially not toward those who are willing and oh-so desperate to wage and war in the name of salvaging their kindred species from complete and utter extermination."

"And so now we know the true motivation for this forceful intrusion that is upon us and at hand; it is with effort to deprive the universe of its dictatorial workings and to marginalize its unilaterally imposed laws and ways. But to save one's flock at the expense of consuming another is surely not to be tolerated, at least not in this realm of existence, and certainly not in the presence of its wizardly overseers, who will doubtlessly thwart any such attempts that may occur."

Intensity was then further escalated to an even more powerful degree, as was my tone when it approached the end of my closing decree. And the whole time, Malthazar was persisting with his own brand of mental fervency, which forced our bounding wizardess to extremely high levels of focus and fixation as she struggled to maintain her restrictive grasp. Thus was she caught wholly off guard as my trusted and called-upon Venificus crashed down upon her with a momentum and impetus that could only be described as crushing or eminently hard. Immediately subsequent to the abrupt and most unpredictable turn of events, a valiant and seemingly godlike and superior being imposingly remained atop the smashed and broken-down form, whereupon his towering framework served as a screen to the rearward bombardment of accentuating sunlight. The streaming rays amplified the perimeter of his Herculean silhouette and gave clear view to the pearly robed figure with a stoically aged visage adorned with nicely coiffed bristles and wavy white hair.

"What have I told the two of you about playing nicely with your newfound friends! You beckoned, Prime?" A conciliatory nod followed the rhetorical remark. A quick up and down perusal paused the salutation to a minimal degree, and in that brief period, my cohort and

I managed to free ourselves from our entrapment. "And, Malthazar, I cannot say that you look particularly well … and so it delights me to find you in your usual manner and way!"

"Venificus, my old friend, once and again you are quite the sight for my tense and weary wizardly eyes. I reckoned that you would more than appreciate having a hand in a most exhilarating of campaigns, at the same time taking the opportunity to touch shoulders with our newly initiated and earthly made compeer." The pulverized mass of mangled and mineralized material then suddenly kindled and eagerly stirred as it made an effort to right itself from underneath my superlative fellow wizard's burdensome mold. At once, the imposing figure that was my stalwart companion held up his substantially metallic yet plainly shaped staff, which was previously fastened down against and compressed upon its recently targeted aim. With blurring speed, the sizable and steely shaft was plucked at vigorously, with each motion bringing to pass a more slender and less dense yet equally capable pole. Then, one by one, the sturdy bars were instantaneously and securely arranged any which way and all around Aleregeni's recuperating body, each length of which being used to anchor her deeply and firmly into the bordering ground.

"You don't know the half of it, my age-old acquaintance and prodigious Prime." The words were revealingly spoken as my most senior associate busied himself in an effort to keep down his bound and constricted otherworldly prize.

"We may have some work to do yet before I make acquaintance with our superlative boy; the imminent chore of keeping him safe from vile and debased invaders immediately comes to mind." Venificus's stately crown then turned with a directing gaze as his body and limbs continued with the task of keeping Aleregeni's wiggling form pinned down to the ground. With that, the sky suddenly relinquished its glimmering shade of blue as a dark and overcast shadow befell the entire near and far view. Sparky flares erupted forth silently yet energetically from a profound and newly formed abysmal cloud, soon to be followed by a triumvirate of heavy lightning flashes that paved the way for their thunderous followers to bellow and blast piercingly as though ripping apart and savagely splitting the heavens. A crowd of dark and devilish broad-winged creatures then emerged with a swarm-like arrangement and a malevolent mood, squawking and screeching excitedly as they descended with eagerness and with probing appendages sporting razor-like grapplers and donning a bloodthirsty attitude.

Noxerus was all of a sudden seen to appear, hovering commandingly just outside the portal's ominous egress point, where he took a watchful pause to survey the scene and soak in the widely discernible field of view. A few deep and satiating breaths were drawn in with hardiness and then were almost hesitatingly forced to exude as the brawny and powerfully built chest of the monstrous overlord alternately augmented and then constricted on cue. A lighter and almost colorless tinge painted over the villain's more conventional and deep red shade, giving rise to an almost unbefitting coloration that tended toward a more subtle and gentle pale rose hue.

"Ah, to take in the sweet taste of yellow sun along with its uniquely palatable oxygenated and gaseous brew. Long has it been since I last felt such tingle inside as the water vapor and its fiery deluge circulates and works its way fully and through. Make haste, my slaughterous pets; onward onto your targets with fervency and make quick work of your murderous quest. Spill and drink of the humans' sanguinary nectar before dispatching of them so as to deliver a batch load of passionate souls back unto the waiting excitement of our raging netherworld home!

And as for you, my most capable and vengeful subordinate number one, go forth and seize upon that troublesome and fortuitous boy." The ensuing command was aimed toward Certasus, who had just then sequentially appeared. The directive continued with its sobering mandate as the enormous cyclops went through his own strain of transformation—a similar yet distinctive Earth-acclimatizing ordeal.

"And do not let him get the better of you this time; otherwise, my temperament may not be so tolerant when you should so happen to reappear. Consider it permissible should you come to conclude that either or both he and that supple-skinned enchantress could do well with some time off from cognizance in the nothingness domain, wherein they could more un-distractedly reconsider their disrespectful and treacherous ways."

"Not to worry, master. I will take care of that softish little nuisance and at the same time will teach a lesson to that meddlesome and modestly skilled glorified witch. Her water-inducing wizardry will fall short of its desired effect on this already moistened and saturated vegetation-inspiring earthly tier." Certasus reciprocated the instruction as soon as his physical alteration was finally complete. "I will now leave you to your own pleasurable undertakings, master, which I assume entails the walloping of those three old and unsavory animus-based adversaries down yonder."

"Indeed, my good sycophant, it appears that the matron of all matrons is in desperate need!" And with that, off they went, with Certasus barreling headlong toward the palatial encroachment while riding the momentum of his vigorously heaved club, and with Noxerus heading at breakneck speed toward the rest of us, fuming and frenzied as he was descending, flying exclusively under the power of his own will and control.

Further ahead and still a good distance beyond, Cristofo and Bellatrix were approaching the occasion whereupon their own adventuresome circumstance was unfolding.

"Drop me off in the vicinity of my most excellent dragon, fair mistress. Already he responds to my signaling hail. Alleviate yourself of your burdensome cargo so as to more comfortably partake in the thrashing of this overswarming race. I expect that a good dose of lightning flash would do quite well in curtailing their numbers."

"Indeed it would, my brave young compatriot, and this is very much the time where we drift off and part ways. But first I must stop the incoming deluge before hoping to deal with the onrushing waves. Good luck and Godspeed on this most consequential and meaningful of inaugural campaigns Cristofo, newfound wizard of earth, and remember to make full use of your skillfulness while bringing to bear your newly acquired wizardly powers and ways. Do not underestimate your innermost potential, for I assure you that it is truly extraordinary and beyond what you can expect or hope for. I'm off to dissolve that intruder enabling portal way, leaving you to your own devices so as to make your own decisions, engage in battles at your discretion, and to find and face your own choice of prey."

An abrupt and well-timed release sent Cristofo off and adrift while still at high elevation, where he soared for a mere moment until his remarkable Cimtar cut short the downturn and met him midway.

"Cimtar, my most loyal and splendiferous of beasts! It brings me both amazement and great joy to see you so well and recovered. Now let us ride wild and with pace as we seek to assail and encounter. And have patience, my pet, for our chance for revenge will most certainly come to transpire." The vasculomen swine were on both Cristofo's and Cimtar's minds as the invigorated boy discharged the words while they caught a glimpse of the descending swarm's swooping raid. Few have ever felt the stimulating rush and exhilarating brace that comes with a wizardly impetus as it inundates its called upon aim, but let me tell you straight from the mouth of one who has experienced it firsthand: there is nothing like it. It is most unpredictable, and it spreads rather infectiously unto the companions and creatures that accompany you and share along in your plight.

Cimtar then swiveled and rolled with an effortless grace and jetted back toward the airborne busyness, wherein Somnia and Myrina were still having their way and pressing upon a spate of bomb-dropping turtibrida. Without hesitation, Cristofo leaped upon the frontal part of the first hybrid anomaly that they came to overtake, averting the head of the turtle like chassis in favor of having a look-see into the cockpit of the most bizarre and unfamiliar aerial being. A meager shrivel-skinned operator stared back with bulging and oversized eyes, donning a passionless and almost uncaring demeanor while returning a simple and expressionless gaze. No threat or challenge of any kind was perceived, as the boy wasted no time in commencing with his furious blitzkrieg, taking firm hold of his dependable half-pounder and stabbing sharply into the fringe of the flying device's elliptical and convex-shaped glass-like faceplate. A quick shimmy and hoist cracked open the connection and allowed fingers to effectively grasp and fit through. Then a vigorous upheaval was all that was required as the transparent covering was altogether and utterly heaved and removed.

"Do your stuff, Iggy! And waste no time in reconnecting with us, for your powder bag is once again indispensable in this more customary and terra-molded land." An abrupt plunge was then fluently executed as the fiery wonder swooped headlong into the pith of the strange and extraneous cockpit while the unfaltering boy came to reestablish position upon the back of his mercurial and gracefully winged dragon, who had just then returned from his own brief and decisive fire-breathing and incinerating near-at-hand campaign. Indeed, the action was fleeting and furious on all fronts, including the within of the just recently propped-open airship, where our fulminant and fire-derived creature expanded and intensified in an all-encompassing effort to debilitate the alien bomb-dropping living machine. A violent and raging blaze sprouted instantaneously, satiating the whole of the contraption's smallish interior as accessories and operator alike smoldered, fused, and for the shortest of times suffered the gloom of excruciating and torturous pain until the device's most volatile of cargoes was made to prematurely detonate. An explosive cloud mushroomed outward with zeal as the obliterated portions of both fleshlike and mechanized steel burst forth before plummeting earthward, each piece of which bearing a darkened and smoke-filled lingering trail that etched itself upon the sky to create what looked like a clustering of savage claw marks that ran deep and tore wide.

Iggy then proceeded to rejoin his companion as a casual stream made its way back into the comfort of the golden locket's powder-filled tranquility.

"Well done, boy, but don't get too complacent in your cozy little abode. As you can plainly see by the airship-filled horizon, we have our work cut out for us. And look, there you have Myrina and Somnia hard at work at our fore!" Inasmuch as Cristofo longed for a clear view of his beloved's exquisite face, a faraway view of her dark and captivating twisting and winding mane of hair was sufficient in uplifting his heart and stimulating his overall vigor and vim. Thusly did he make way toward the locality of the busily battling dragon that was at the command of his fencing and jousting flame, being sure to engage upon several randomly encountered turtibrida that both he and Cimtar would come upon sporadically along on their way. Slashing swats of nethersword put an end to a good number of the fluttering buckets of fleshy steel, as did the voracious thrust of dragon's breath, not to mention the occasional dose of Iggy-induced implosions, all of which served to leave a trail of destruction behind as the boy and his magnificent fiery pet and dragon jumped and capered along a profusion of turtibrida, using them as stepping-stones as they prodded toward their busily engaged comates.

Scads of blinding flashes shot out into the heavens as deflected fractional rays of the sunlight's blistering gleam bounced off the princess's rampantly swaying length of royally crafted steel. High-flying hybrid beasts tumbled and swayed to the ground in large numbers as Myrina's well-yielded sword made quick work of the creatures' discontinuation while her tightly bound leg strappings conjoined her to Somnia, whose nimbleness and astonishing pace carried them about and among the almost pitiable bomb-dropping fiends.

"Cristofo!" Her most precious and soon-to-be betrothed then whisked into her line of vision and flooded her with a wave of joy and invigoration that was distracting in the most satisfactory of ways. Words were inconvenient, to say the least, due in principal to the aerial locality and in part to the swooping and swiveling movement and pace. A nimble leap made for quick resolution of the connectivity concern as the agile young champion all at once set down upon his romantic companion's flawlessly postured backside.

"Be careful with that finely sharpened sword, my most exquisite if not over-refined subsidiary queen!" Cristofo's tight embrace brought much elation to the sidetracked princess as a soulful beam overtook her beauteous face while he filled her ear with the flattering yet facetious pitch. "For that feverish swinging and swatting of yours may just cut short your admirer's heartfelt wholeness as well as his thriving affection and unbridled desire."

"Worry not, my most valiant of defenders, for you know full well that my blade is most precise in all of its slashing and sundering endeavors." Myrina gushed forth the words amidst her dragon's twisting and winding movements and veers, for although the majestic beast was indeed content to reconnect with her treasured male sibling and overseeing mate, both she and her like-minded brother favored continuing on with their burning, blighting, wrecking, and decimating rave.

Another swift and agile saltation brought Cristofo around and about the face of his treasured future bride. A firm grasp upon the back of her neck took control of the situation at hand, and a deep, pressing kiss summarized the emotion of the moment before any words could come into play to undermine the gesture and to skew it toward the ineffectual or noticeably more bland.

"Soar along and stay safe with your dragon, my sweetest of thoughts and of dreams. And under no circumstance am I to be followed. Just rest assured that upon the battle's completion, we will once again make full effort to come together and reconvene."

"Be careful, Cristofo! Bring yourself back to me whole and sane so that our love can advance full throttle. And you better be ready for it to be thoroughly declared and proclaimed!" Myrina bellowed forth the words with unclear sureness as to whether or not they were heard since her beloved had already shuffled off and rejoined with his dependable Cimtar. Off they veered in the opposite bearing just as a menacing figure could be detected in the distance, flying headlong toward them with an obvious purpose, while being carried along by the impetus of a large and menacing implement of club-like characteristic and design.

CHAPTER 12

Of Wizards and Warfare

Elseways and meanwhile in the relatively far-off range, our intrepid female compatriot had managed to come upon the once-barren and incongruous but at that moment ridiculously crowded locality that was the Defluous Highlands. A profusion of materials, supplies, equipment, and apparatuses lay spread out and organized in sprawling stations and stockpiles of perfectly symmetrical and meticulous scheme. Fleets of turtibrida were similarly laid out in the approximate whereabouts, wherein a proportionate number would take off on a mission while others would return with depleted payload and come to rest upon the appropriate line. Overall, it was a massive although perfectly coordinated and systematically arranged circumstance that saw an immeasurable number of the charcoal-skinned evacuees accumulating and coalescing along a vast and ever-increasing stretch of the expanse as they gushed forth from their intergalactic underpass and swelled outward with the unbridled profusion of a newly struck oil spring.

All at once, the ground beneath us began to quiver and shake. Noxerus had set down hard at our fore with vehemence, but 'twas not by his thrust that the earth had been incited to tremble and roll. My firm and unflinching colleague Venificus had simultaneously abandoned his effort to keep down his supernatural and age-old wizardly prize. Aleregeni was to be suppressed no longer, for it was she who first recognized the true cause of the artificially concocted subterranean uprise, and up she shot with an unrecognizable howl, making quick work of her reconfiguration to regular shape and fully intact size before recapturing her fine implement and flying off in the direction of the Defluous Highlands.

"Not so fast, my fleshy and most favorable trio of fair-weather friends!" Noxerus had put a quick halt to our attempted pursuit of the wildly onrushing matriarch as an electrified streak of energized matter looped around the three of us with blinding speed and implausible tenacity, chaining us tightly together as he heaved with might and crashed us back down to the proximate surface. "Rushing off so discourteously when being called upon by a visiting acquaintance could easily be interpreted as an intention to offend. Especially when considering that the guest in question has traveled such great distance to see you, and that they in turn are found to be all too hospitable whenever the reciprocal circumstance should so happen to be at hand!"

Well then, as it so happened to transpire, our pursual of the feverishly beset Aleregeni had at least temporarily come to an abrupt halt on account of her devilish coconspirator's meddlesome intrusion, granting a suitable pretext for us to shift our tale back unto the confines of the Defluous Highlands. That's where the epicenter of the ground-trembling upheaval could be found smack-dab in the heart of the busily bustling subterrestrial portal way. Lightning flash made quick work of the disruption and dismantling of the ill-conceived and invasion-enabling thoroughfare as vast sections of boulder and stone crumbled and caved toward the within of the heavily occupied Corbominian transporting vein. The inscrutable whisk and stir of Tempestas summoned up the overpowering salvo of firebolts with ease as Bellatrix choreographed the fulminant production with an overseeing presence and a glazed-over mien. At the behest of her rational and uncompromising mind did the pair of them press on with the eradicating onslaught, sentencing the crowd of portal traversing Corbominians to the most abrupt and inelegant of deaths. At the same time, they were perpetuating the conclusion for the whole of the remaining species that trailed in the background and lingered behind on their disintegrating home world while still waiting in the vast and far-reaching lines of the threshold crossing array.

Ah yes, so goes the course and line of a wizardly burden on the odd occasion and from time to time. A decision is made in defense of the flock toward which one is tasked to protect and to keep safe from harm, inciting a forced disregard with respect to the reason or rhyme that motivates the behavior of the contrary side. In one fell swoop, our co-defender of the vast and prolific animus domain cut off the source of the onrushing invasion, thus sealing the fate of the countless remaining members of the most misfortunate and extraneous Corbominian race. And nearing, yet still a fair distance away, the heart was figuratively ripped from the chest of the matron of all of the now—considerably truncated strain. However, the agonizing wound of loss would have to be held off and constrained until such time as the ongoing devastation could be dealt with, for the lightning strikes continued with their crushing and wrecking consequence, which now pinpointed the widely ranging group of intruders who persisted on the newly arrived upon earthly terrain.

Once again, a most disturbing and never-before-heard yowl filled the near-at-hand sky as Aleregeni's frantic progress brought her within the range of her opening offensive. Her brilliant and bejeweled staff was deliberately yanked and shifted in a flurry of angles and sways while still she soared upon it and continued toward the source of the destructive firebolt spray. Narrow and intense beams of light shot outward in a variety of colors and rays, seeming to originate from or perhaps be deflected by several of the implement's gem-like components as they were discharged with potency and with a surprisingly accurate aim. Lightning bursts fizzled and were no longer whipping and lashing down through the air as Bellatrix perceived the strangely derived onslaught and Tempestas faded and reverted to its more dormant shade of lackluster whitish gray. Annabell was then summarily unsheathed as her exceptional wielder spontaneously swiveled to face the oncoming cannonade.

Blinding streams shot toward her in a multifaceted and colorful display as she scrambled to deflect and divert the assortment of them with an extraordinary effort to turn them all away. Still and even so, a pair of the laser-like gleams from the tail end of the lingering and long-lasting barrage managed to escape her impeccable swordplay, piercing straight through her blade-swinging shoulder and leaving behind two perfectly cylindrical voids, the sizes of which measured about the same diameter as a fully ripened cobnut. The acute high-powered beams carried straight through her meat with a smoldering and bloodless follow-through, leaving an unhealable emptiness of tubular configuration with smooth, clean, and cauterized sides. The blistering pain of her newly acquired vacuities were easily ignored by the weathered and worldly-wise battler, who took strict notice of the menacing and rage-filled presence that the oncoming supernatural being was seen to exude. Without hesitation did she whisk off in a flurry, switching her upholding current into a much more forceful and fleeting cyclonic breeze. For not only did she recognize the laboriousness with which the approaching engagement would most certainly be mired, so too did she surmise that for the moment, her skills would be much better placed zapping and stinging in defense of the human survivors.

So off she hastened back unto the palatial locality from whence Cristofo was just a short while previously left to clashes and confrontations of his own accord. The permanence of her freshly formed wounds hit upon her thoughts as she fully evaluated them while scuttling along on her way, rationalizing the disfigurement as somewhat restitution for the species-eradicating performance that had just been wholeheartedly dispensed. She remained more or less remorseless, justifying her actions because the portal way was in every respect unnatural, as was the incursion itself most unconventional and altogether unconscionable as well. As an aside, there Aleregeni remained, grief-stricken and wallowing in the aftermath of the transcendental gateway's wreckage with thoughts of the masses of her children that were uncaringly left behind. Yet she was satisfied to a smaller degree knowing that the lightning- based onslaught of her fellow Earth-stationed compatriots was summarily halted and also on account of the much-anticipated satisfaction that was due to satiate her pain when she should so happen to come across Bellatrix the executioner once again.

At the same time, in a distant yet interrelated circumstance, a ferocious roar preceded an enormous outburst of blaze and flame as Cimtar touched down upon the battle-riddled terrain just beyond and outward of the besieged palatial wall. Corbominians swung and swayed frantically and freely with their sickle-like blades, dispatching a multitude of the lesser-skilled human defenders as they made way toward their swarmed-upon royal prize. Herein lay the most overrun strain of the courageous yet inadequate and unavailing masses. Persons, proletariats, communities, and crowds were all waging and warring in desperation yet destined to meet with disaster and most likely to be run aground. All save for those near the fire-exuding wonder, the exceptional creature burned up a good number of the charcoal-skinned intruders as he breathed upon them with dragon's breath and aptly cleared scads of them away. Cristofo also brought much consolation to the more-seasoned battlers as well as the plebes, rallying and reviving the lot of them, including all factions in the middle and clans in between. The boy had previously dismounted while still airborne, touching down a distance away from Cimtar, who then proceeded to reverse with his flapping so as to find footing and land himself somewhat astray.

Azrael overindulged in the grainy and granular feast as it sank itself deeply into the dense and compacted mineral-based meat. Slices and wedges were likewise cut off and strewn as the unmatched blade continued to gluttonize on dissected wads of the alien body parts and flayed off portions of charcoal-like skin. The lengthy hunk of meticulously forged netherworld steel proved to be no match for the long-reaching scythes, even as they were further extended by the far-spanning Corbominian windups and their protracted strides. Add Cristofo's unparalleled skillfulness and wizardly zim to the picture and it's not hard to conceive that batches and piles of the dispatched and decimated creatures were accumulating swiftly and aggrandizing with ease. Quite the number of casualties were generated by the dynamic sword-swinging boy, all in the shortest of time frames, and all the while as he kept a keen eye on the previously spotted and soon to arrive, bludgeon-conveying colossus.

A hard and pulverizing thump jarred the surface of the ground just at the forefront of Cristofo's ongoing and free-flowing sword-swaying ballet. The impact resonated with a somewhat muted tonality as busted and smashed Corbominian body parts served to cushion the leviathan's harsh and unmerciful entree. Shattered and crushed sandy particulate gusts flew through the air and dusted our fine young champion's body and hair as Ceratusus's opening deed was swiftly followed by a vigorous and far-sweeping full-circling clubbing spree. A good-sized stretch of space was cleaned and cleared of the pitchy-skinned intruders round and about the menacing cyclops, as was also the case in and around the area of the near-at-hand boy. Iggy had curiously seemed to vitalize and flare as Cristofo inferred a strange modification in the bearing of the enchanting little creature who had up to that point chosen to remain in the luxury of his close to the heart of his master, hollowed-out and golden abode.

"Well then, my paltry little humanoid and his now much-less-imposing fiery little pet!" The intimidating and aggressive goliath sported somewhat of a smile, or perhaps *grimace* should be used to more accurately depict his sentiment, or to convey more properly his confident and bloodthirsty mood. Iggy had just foregone the coziness of the locket-like refuge and had perched himself upon his favorite roosting point—atop the shoulder of his master—where he remained watchful and, as always, ready to engage. A deep scarlet tincture now curiously overspread the tiny little creature. It was a darkened shade of crimson with a subdued radiance, like a blackish hue of cherry with a muted phosphorescent sort of tinge. Moreover, a quivering blur would further describe the comportment of the unpredictable and multifaceted being who then sat there and oscillated to and fro in a most vigorous manner and with a speed that defied even the most concentrated visual strain. Cristofo was fully aware of his sidekick's transmutation and somewhat hyperactive willingness to assail.

In the meantime, Cimtar caught wind of the imminent engagement and began to approach the circumstance with an anxious fervor and an overly enthusiastic zeal. But the boy did not hesitate to hold back the impending interference from his two loyal comrades, for he resolved to take on the menacing giant single-handedly; a one-on-one battle would be most suitable and forthcoming according to his strictly valiant and rigidly self-imposed ideals. He thus conveyed the fact telepathically to both of his closely held companions, stating it unequivocally and making it perfectly evident and clear.

"It is with regret that I find you wholly unsupervised. In fact, it disgusts me to bear witness to such blatant neglect at the hand of the lot of your second-rate wizards and make-believe friends. Oh, how I wish that your womanly comate were still here to tend to your amateurish requirements and needs, for long has it been since last I savored and drank deep of a vanquished opponent of the female persuasion and animus breed. Sweet indeed would be the nectar of that meddlesome and maternally inclined wizardess with her oh-so-flavorful and satisfying brand of sanguineous sap!"

Cristofo stood there silently with a studious posture and an intensified focus, letting the belligerent blowhard ramble on boastfully until such time as both his patience and blathering parlance would be fully exhausted and finally spent.

"All in good time, I suppose, eh, my insignificant little speck? Her time will unquestionably and soon enough come. And perhaps that dragon-riding little vixen of yours in the distance will soothe my thirstiness in the meantime. Oh, how I long to reunite my tongue with that legendary interior liquid of the most refined and feminine flavored humanoid strain."

Maintaining composure became a Herculean task for the ready to scrap and skirmish but patiently waiting and calculating boy who wanted Certasus to strike first so as to properly formulate his next maneuver and fully develop his forthcoming ploy.

"But first I must refocus myself to the task imposed and immediately at hand, as the time has come for me to dispatch of you and to move on to more significant battles with the remainder of your somewhat more worthy yet still animus-tainted band. Oh, and one more thing for you to be sure of before we lingeringly break off and part ways, just a tiny little nugget of circumstance that you can brood over as you embark upon your upcoming journey across and through the empty and timeless terrain ... Your dragon will be next to be slaughtered, for unique and exceptional creatures have no place in the shadow of their more eminent and superior beings of similar vein.

"Afterward, I will move on to your princess and her likewise notable creature, whereupon one of whom I can assure you will be inflicted with the most unnatural and unspeakable of deeds before I continue to forge onward unto the whereabouts of your fair Bellatrix. She shall in turn serve quite well as the consummating component of my torturous and murderous life-ending sortie. Only then will I turn my focus unto the matters that need addressing with respect to the remaining nincompoop three, the lot of which I will most likely humiliate without imposing an excursion off unto the land of the transitorily deceased. Or perhaps they too shall be more permanently dealt with, for I would certainly not be averse to a long-standing break from any and all of the overly annoying and constantly interfering animus wizardly breed. In any event, we shall soon see!"

With that, the mighty Certasus concluded his long-winded tirade and commenced straightaway with his impetuous and overly confident club-swinging foray. *Swoosh* went the first of the forceful and speedy swats that bore down upon the position of the agile and well-prepared boy, who not only sidestepped the whacking with ease but also feigned difficulty in doing so by way of remaining alarmingly close to the walloping breeze. A fabricated stumble and flop to the floor served to strengthen his calculated performance and at the same time succeeded in bolstering and emboldening his opponent's brashness by reconfirming the abundance of confidence that the experienced and capable goliath already sported aplenty, with a profusion stockpiled in store. *Whish* went the second and crosswise-oriented stroke, a turn that was also easily handled by Cristofo as he once again minimized the ease with which he averted the vigorous blow.

"Hold still, you fidgety little insect, so that my club may know the taste of your squishy and nectar-imbrued strain! Succumb to the inevitable and make smooth your transition into the territory of the lasting unease, whereupon you will face the unaccompanied and most lonesome of all deeds!" Impatience with a hint of anger began to take hold of the aggressive and battleful beast, and unfortunately for our youthful wizardly warrior, such a turn when at the hand of an omnipotent creature is usually followed by intensified methods and a more purposeful employment of means.

Swish went the third faster and more fiercely initiated swing, which once again carried intention to cut across the midsection of its agile and acutely skilled aim, but this time the club lengthened itself forward and extended just as it came upon the position of the bouncy and volatile boy's sinewy frame. Only the swiftest and most spirited of efforts granted the young champion reprieve from a dense and conclusive bludgeon-induced end. Furthermore, his wavering was wholly unfeigned as he shot back desperately and came down harshly upon his backside. However, valuable information was spontaneously garnered and gleaned as he executed a barely discernible maneuver just prior to bouncing back up with resilience and with no time to waste before the weapon continued full circle with its subsequent and momentously delivered careen. Strangely enough, it was the young lad's trusted half-pounder that was elusively taken ahold of in lieu of what one would think to be a much more practicable choice, namely his exceptionally long, sharp, airy, and phenomenally well-suited length of netherworld steel.

Whoosh was the sound that echoed through the air as the fastest and most dynamic stroke yet sailed in the direction of Cristofo with a barely visible quickness and a most precarious flair. And this time, as the extraordinary cudgel passed in front of its target, it extended doubly as compared to its previous effort, jutting out to a distance that would be impossible for the boy to avoid in the same manner that he was barely able to muster before. This turn however and instead, an ample and headfirst leap was employed by the never to be underestimated and wizardly suffused battler who feared no manner of contest or challenge and who always performed with the utmost confidence and semblance of relative ease. As his upsurge brought him over the top of the fast-moving bludgeon, he stabbed down and into it with fervor and with a perfectly calculated centrally located aim. An unshakeable clutch held firm as the club's velocious sway wrenched the boy along on its momentum incited circular trajectory around and behind of the never before defeated, indomitable battle crater champion.

Then, at just the right moment, Crostofo unfastened his grasp on the relatively meager yet infinitely valuable earthly forged blade and drew upon his equally precious and more newly banded together with netherworld-spawned Azrael. The twirling club's forceful drive and thrust carried the boy onward and around in midair with just the right measure of illusory positioning and feel so as to disorient the massive behemoth as he swiveled and struggled to keep sight of the evasive young whippersnapper while attempting to follow him along and in stride. The beast's singular and by its nature somewhat imperceptive eye bulged forth with a shocking disposition as if to meet dead-on with Cristofo's focused and fiery gaze just as the boy's far-reaching and effectual blade cut surgically across the creature's thickset yet at that moment exposed and vulnerable nape. And so did the open and agape oculus remain as it rode involuntarily along within its decapitated and inexorably linked housing, a floating and tottering stray that remained somewhat airborne, while its massive and disconnected trunk crashed to the ground in an Earth-jarring and permanently reposing fade.

Two more barely perceptible and lightning-fast strokes came to unfold as the sun's ineludible rays caught hold of the netherworld blade's near invisible trail and touched upon it with a barely perceptible flicker of flash and gleam. One sweep was veered in a crosswise direction, while the other took on a more precise and perpendicular aim, the net effect of which was undeniably the same. A quartered crown concluded the decisive operation and left no shadow of doubt as to which of the two combatants would be whisked along unto the obscurity of the darkest and gloomiest of undesired pathways. The boy's feet touched ground with the same blow as did the quadruplicate portions of springy and squishy eyeball, which were no longer secured within the socket but remained loosely tethered upon their corresponding quadrants of pulpous and glutinous brain. Each of us other Earth-tarrying wizards took deep notice of the spirit-exiling occurrence that hit upon our senses with intensity and forced us into a distraction-induced pause. Astonishment would most accurately describe what was felt by the lot of us as we immediately came to realize that 'twas Cristofo who had not only survived the momentous clash but also managed to dispose of such a formidable opponent who had not come anywhere near to being so competently vanquished at any time ever before.

As it so happened, Bellatrix was indeed near at hand when the development had specifically occurred. In fact, she bore witness to the deed from her aerial standpoint as she caught wind of it while whisking back unto the turmoil of the previously departed-from besieged palatial arena. Her shocked and gawking eyes came across a reciprocal but much less taken aback gaze as Cristofo beamed upon her with calmness and with a newly derived coequal grace. Much was communicated between the pair during that relevant moment which they were both fortunate enough to have shared, and their closeness sprouted and swelled because of the brief interaction in which an assortment of emotions were back and forth declared. Bellatrix had conveyed genuine comfort in the fact that the boy had survived the high-profile foray, further revealing an awestruck incredulity and impressiveness infused with a hint of dissatisfaction and dismay brought to bear by the underlying wizardly predisposition to not frivolously put an end to each other's existential crusades. It was a protocol of particularly high value as viewed in the animus manner and way. Yet still leniency and forgiveness prevailed because of Cristofo's inexperience regarding his newly formed and more elevated state.

A firmer and devoid of atonement glare summarized the freshly invigorated battle champion's attitude that his actions were not only justified but in addition were exceedingly fair given both his newness within the wizardly faction and more importantly considering his opponent's determination to deliver unto him a ruthless crossing into the dimension of uttermost desolation and despair. To be sure, the wordless exchange brought light to the boy's first glimmer of leadership within the animus-hosted brigade as he proceeded to urge Bellatrix along on her way back to the palace with an agreed-upon presumption that she was to carry forward with her lightning-based and intruder-blasting cannonade. For his part, it was off to the factory in defense of his father and his grandfather and all the other benefactors that were to be found in and around the affectionately thought upon and mountainous domain as the brave and unafraid conqueror proceeded in rapid succession to wrench loose and re-holster his firmly stuck throwing knife, scoop a quantity of crushed and pulverized corbominian remains into his satchel, and then mount and maneuver away on his remarkable dragon-composed steed.

And so on and on did the most noteworthy of incursions and battles and blood-shedding campaigns persist and persevere as factions from far-off dimensions and plains intermixed to fight and flare with earthly dwellers and their supernatural defending wayfarers. Rare indeed is the occasion whereupon the lot of animus guardians come together in one single and proximate range, and rarer still is the occurrence upon which they find themselves compelled to do battle with a co-conspiracy of their counterparts from disparate wizardly strains. Dragons and otherwise earthly placed beasts, animus-based mortals as well as those that never cease; sub dwelling and formerly supplanted otherworld originated beings, along with their portal-conveyed counterparts and high-flying bomb-dropping mechanized buckets of meat...all of which warring and intermingling in battle and blusterous foray, swinging and striking and hurling fulminant and fiery sprays. And let us not forget about the legions of winged and devilish creatures of netherworld root, those three-legged demons of brutality and ravenous attribute. Indeed, the flowering and proliferous if not non-interfering Mother Earth was host to a barrage and wide bevy of bombing, blood spilling, and other varieties of crust-scratching and surface-sopping bad-natured pursuits, one such example of which found itself playing out in a near-at-hand circumstance and with a most powerful foursome of sparring and quarrelsome wizardly adventurers.

"Scamper back unto your foul and fiery world, you beguiling and bedeviling, bloodthirsty brute!" Noxerus's energized snare did not serve its full purpose for very long as the three of us invoked firm focus to weaken his tenacity and loosen his intransigent hold. At the first sign of abatement, Maleabar was rearranged into a cylindrical mold which first encircled my torso and then lengthened with swiftness until shielding the entirety of my stately and tallish, animus-based form. The electrified lasso was then obliged to wrap itself around my buffer of miraculous material, leaving me more or less at large and uninhibited within. Before even the briskest of moments could transpire, I flew up from my tubular stronghold and placed myself into an aerial position that elevated me with relation to my stringently concentrated upon prize. A vigorous tug and spiraling swoop then ensued, which whisked away the pair of my cinched and corralled companions, casting them off unto a high far and away bearing and altitude. Airborne did they remain, as I had just previously drawn upon Maleabar and extracted from it a long and linear handle-like offshoot that allowed me to easily wield its hollowed-out circular metallic frame, which I then used to hit down upon Noxerus with the uttermost force and with brutal precision and impeccable aim.

Down into the ground did the robustly shaped being get encapsulated and sequentially hammered as the open end of the velocious device closed upon him and cut into the ground with a puncturing power. The transverse side was refitted to maintain a hardened covering that smacked down over the top of the beast with such impetus so as to bend and buckle the resilient material to the point that it took on the shape of the creature's crushed and semi-implanted outline.

"Dare not assume that all existent dominions encompassed within of all of totality's spheres must bend to your selfish ambitions and succumb to your malevolent whims and your treacherous steers! For once not so long ago, yet perhaps too distant for your fading memory to store, I taught you a valuable lesson as such, a lesson it seems that you now have chosen to altogether ignore." With Maleabar's molded handle still firmly held within my impervious grasp, I remodeled the miraculous material back into its more familiar and most agreeable shape, namely that of my trusty and loyal companion, my formidable pole-shaped staff.

In one fell swoop, a vigorous and crossways blow was delivered with unrelenting momentum and amplified verve, and off flew the still-dazed and disillusioned scoundrel, off into the by and wide distance with the same manner and magnitude as were lofted my two counterparts, but in the direction of the opposite range. My impassioned eyes looked fixedly and followed along with the arcing trajectory of my freshly batted-away foe, and as a consequence of my largely successful counter strike, fulfillment took root and swelled up inside as satisfaction levels blossomed and rose.

Seriousness was once again restored seeing that a subsequent aerial and high-flying figure was spotted whisking flat out in the sun-soaked foreground. Noxerus's stream was altogether ignored by the breakneck barreling body or being, as was the whole of our wizard-wrangled circumstance, while the phenomenon continued in a beeline toward the besieged-upon Nepeshan stronghold where a miscellany of Corbominians, turtibrida, and vasculumen swine were being frizzled, fried, and more or less handled by our fair Bellatrix, who with no uncertainty represented the ambition of the hurtling trajectory; indeed, she was Aleregeni's singular focus and aim.

Yes, 'twas for certain that our valiant and most capable female collaborator was to be met with a thrust of the most powerful of onslaughts, namely the type that is incited by the fuel of vengeance and fanned with the quavering pulsation of hate. And thus and so was the mighty Bellatrix once again distracted from her enraptured wielding of the stone of Tempestas, only to be alerted of the forthcoming danger thanks to a sense that is not only invaluable but also unconditionally innate. At once, the lightning-based salvo was halted as she swiveled around with a twirl of her subservient air currents just in time to catch sight of another oncoming barrage of Aleregeni's lethal and laser-like spray. Annabell was spontaneously drawn upon and utilized with its usual deflecting sway, but this time the slightly taken aback wizardess had the good foresight to whisk herself back in a flurry, straight into the moderately dense cluster of vasculumen savages with which she had just previously been engaged.

A myriad of acute lightning-fast beams shot toward and were showered upon the crowded circumstance, fanning out and dispersing to a degree because of their approach from relative distance. For this reason only, Bellatrix was just barely successful in diverting and veering away the potentially impacting portion of the incinerating rays. Although much benefit was garnered through the collateral damage inflicted onto the surrounding mesh of netherworld-spawned demon beasts, little did the obstructing multitudes help by way of shielding, blocking, or even slowing down the remarkably potent and efficient offshoots. Gratification permeated through and through to the core of our seasoned and battle-scarred wizardess as she bore witness to scores of her unsightly adversaries faltering and dropping heavily downward en route to the body-crushing impact of ground. A rearward pair of turtibrida were struck down in like manner and with likewise consequence, or so it had seemed to the adamant and iron-willed warrior who would this time not even consider the option of fleeing or otherwise deferring from the oncoming and fast-approaching threat.

Instead, she braced and prepared herself, as the tail end of the deadly and colorful cannonade had completed its virulent pass, and now, from a much more proximate vicinity, the stalwart wizardess was able to survey and scrutinize the intruder's stone-cold and determined charcoal- resembling face. It revealed to her with inevitability that another decimating discharge was forthcoming, and this time, unfortunately for her, from much closer range. An electrified lightning ball was immediately conjured from Bellatrix's fingertips and kneaded with urgency to amplify and swell. Yet even as it grew to beyond her full stature, there was still a great deal of uncertainty with regard to whether or not the configuration would serve the purpose of either stopping Aleregeni or blocking her fiery and glittering spread. The query would be destined to go unanswered, as Candilux and I had unanticipatedly swooped in on the scene at that moment.

Although a little behind in the time frame, there was no way that I would allow Bellatrix to face the maddened and mightily enabled matron single-handedly. And so my previously called upon and most majestic of dragons sailed fluently into the crowded circumstance while bulldozing her way through a spattering of vasculomen interlopers, only to arrive at a lingering halt just to the fore of our staunch and steadied female compatriot. With no time to spare, Aleregeni's deadly yet luminous sprinkle came to an abrupt impact against Candilux's equally lustrous and shimmery scales, whereupon they were deflected with effortlessness and with an almost unnatural ease. Indeed, it was I too who had contributed to the ricocheting blockade, I must confess, seeing as how an age-old enchantment was implemented in order to further buttress my loyal ride's impervious coating while also amplifying its irradiant burnish and making impenetrable its polished and steel-like dragon skin vest.

In the subsequent moment, Aleregeni's fury was forced into a sudden and sobering state of outright decline as Candilux's true potency and fortitude was put on display when the magnificent creature roared with ferocity while simultaneously executing a violent tailspin that essentially slapped the invading wizardess with vehemence and effectively sent her soaring a far-removed distance away. A satisfied look summarized Bellatrix's frame of mind as both relief and contentment overcame her, not only because of Aleregeni's abrupt and substantial thwarting but also due to the increasing number of long-winged and three-legged monsters that were shot out of the air by the deflected beams' residual spray. In addition to this, Veneficus and Malthazar were spotted on an immediate course to reassemble and forgather, whereupon they would unite and join forces and continue along in the fight against the invading barrage of otherworldly attackers.

"Remain together at all cost! Dispatch with as many adversaries as possible but be vigilant and stay on alert for our omnipotent alien opposer's imminent and inevitable return! I will take leave of you now, as I am most certainly needed elsewhere, for it is no mere happy accident that keeps away our more familiar and devilish netherworld-based compeer." To that end, off I flew with eagerness and with a sense of urgency nipping at my heels in view of the fact that Noxerus's absence from the near-at-hand circumstance could only foretell of one singular and surefire thing: he was away in pursuit of our newly brought-in wizardly champion, off to Christofo's inevitable whereabouts. Off to the mountainous domain of the all-important Nepeshan factory would he definitely be straightaway bounden and set.

Cristofo's aerial approach toward his most valuable and familial enterprise was fleeting and fast paced, to say the absolute least, and although he was understandably quite unsettled with regard to the safety of his irreplaceable kinsmen and friends, soon enough he set eyes upon a flock of hovering and infiltrating vascolumen monstrosities. Just like that, his apprehensiveness dwindled and more or less completely gave way as adrenaline took over the principal charge of things and exceptionalism sequentially kicked in. A resounding and protracted outcry was subdued in favor of stealthiness, yet from the voiceless and fiery furnaces of within, it barreled forth with the strength of a hundred roars as the ready-to-engage young warrior dug his heels into the flank of his equally riled and revenge-thirsty dragon. He drew upon his exorbitant length of netherworld steel, thus signaling preparedness and inciting a furtherance of the wondrous creature's already incredulous speed.

"Get me as close as you can to as many as possible, my good Cimtar, and feel free to set teeth upon them and tear apart as many as you please. And as for you, my fiery little wonder, fear not, for I too caught wind of your recently transpired and strangely befitting, vigorous little uprise and stir."

With that, the magnificent boy and his equally impressive and outstanding supernatural companions had set upon the multitudinous members of the winged and three-legged razor-clawed brood. The first in line felt but a tickle on its wing tips as Cimtar's swift and stealth-like swoon was consummated with a ferocious and decapitating chew. Azrael was next to carry on with the performance as Cristofo leaped from his lofty standpoint and came down upon another unsuspecting demon with a perfectly centered sword swat, which cut downward and split its ill-fated target lengthwise and uniformly in two. A half dozen or so swift and nimble strokes were executed fluently and in sequence upon another small number of the flying monstrosities before the boy returned to his position atop his loyal ride's reappearing backside—a station that presented itself conveniently and with a predictability that he took for granted and about which he undoubtedly felt most assured.

Foggy bursts came to follow in the aftermath of those non-fatally administered blows that saw various vasculomen limbs and body parts floating loosely asunder while the regenerative hellions transported themselves to a location of safety to refit themselves before reentering the sky-high foray. A second and similarly laid-out assault was successively and immediately delivered, taking to task a further number of the alerted and more cognizant near-at-hand beasts just as a more sizable collection of them caught wind of the sly and skillful incursion. They managed to shift and face the rearward offensive while posturing themselves for an appropriate counterstrike that would necessarily be forthcoming and eagerly transmitted in turn. Intensely focused and deep red laser-like beams were shot toward the boy and his swooping ride, as a scattering of the invading creatures had initiated a counteroffensive while prudently remaining at a safe interval from flailing netherworld steel and tearing and cleaving dragon's teeth.

Yet even still, the comfort of distance was soon to fade and dwindle away as the boy and his dragon surged onward while Azrael was expertly used to deflect several the incoming rays and others still were outmatched by Cimtar's extraordinary agility and evasive sway. In the blink of an eye, Cristofo's eloquent swordplay would once again come upon the laser-emitting beasts, effectively putting an end to a good portion of the advancing and incinerating gleams. At the same time, sharp and bony cuspids would further contribute to the cessation of the intensely shooting discharges as Cimtar took a decidedly more savage approach to resolving whatever offshoots would stubbornly linger and attempt to remain. Nevertheless, more and more of the rubber-skinned and skeletal framed fiends became distracted from their advancement against the factory and its grossly outmatched but steadfast and tenacious human defenders, who did what they could by way of artillery-based bomb flinging and far-reaching launches of Cloud Cutter shells.

"It's your turn now, Iggy. Take care of the lot of these foul-minded monsters, my irrepressible champion and fire-made friend!" A quick reach into his satchel rendered a chunk of the recently crushed Corbominian framework in hand, and with the simplest of maneuvers, it was fed to the fiery wonder who in turn absorbed it with a vigorous guzzle as though an eagerly hungry recipient, an anxiously ravenous pet. At once, fire burnished, gleamed, and became dynamically aglow, and what we have by now discovered to be the most extraordinary of creatures vibrated vigorously and reverberated energetically with a nearly hypersonic and speed-blurring to and fro. Indeed, it was quite the privilege to bear witness to our fiery phenomenon's propensity to metamorphose vigorously yet again. Although this time the transformation was visibly different, an obvious evolvement of potency and power was blatantly evident, as was previously demonstrated during the recently transpired netherworld exposure.

"Unbelievable, my little wonder! Your abilities have never ceased to amaze me, and now it seems that we have found you a much more fitting and exponentially more efficient manner of fuel!" The Corbominian morsel showed itself to remain a silhouette of consistent stature as it lingered within Iggy's somewhat see-through and combustible frame even as the creature was expending exorbitant amounts of energy, bouncing around in midair like a dancing and deviating fireball that would catch hold of every vasculomen laser launch with fluency, returning the discharges with beams of increased potency and with a precise reciprocal bearing that ricocheted them back unto the direction from which they had been hurled.

"Stay back and have at these demon seeds, Iggy. We must part ways for a limited interval while I swoop down unto the factory's opening and take part in the ground-based invasion that advances with vigor and also permeates profoundly within." With that, the irrepressible young champion veered downward with a beeline course aimed directly at the manufactory's monumental and Corbominian-riddled entryway.

"You are also to hang back Cimtar; do what you can to help and defend our stand while I make my way toward the factory's inside so as to see what turmoil and troubles lie waiting for me to contend with among its numerous passages and chambers and all throughout its interior range." A vehement and flaming blast of dragon's breath responded with perceptivity and served to clear away a landing pad amidst the crowded and overly aggressive, advancing otherworldly herd. Cristofo dismounted with swagger and stood there momentarily with focused and fervent eyeballs that emitted an almost devilish and bloodthirsty type of gleam as he scoured and scrutinized the immediate surround. In the background, the mighty dragon initiated its flaring, slashing, chomping, and mangling campaign as Candilux and I swooped into the field of vision just in time to catch wind of Noxerus's more immediate approach as he came to arrive upon the mountainous arrangement from a more perpendicular angle and steer.

Without hesitation, our diabolical and netherworld-based compeer took aim upon the invigorated young champion's position from his rearward and rapidly approaching trajectory, and due in part to his strictly placed focus on Cristofo, a simple cloaking spell was sufficient to ensure that he remained completely unaware of me and my stupendous dragon's fleeting and furious oncoming course. I fastened and braced myself for the substantial impact as Candilux smacked upon Noxerus and hammered him against the near-at-hand mountainside, pounding him straight into its rigid exterior and leaving him implanted there, a stupefied and semi-oblivious victim of the vehement and dizzying percuss.

"You didn't think that our discussion was done and completed, did you, my self-centered colleague and stubborn yet very old "friend'?" Little time had transpired before the uncontainable and abundantly resilient beast began to recapture his senses and before his devilish eyeballs glimmered with fierceness and readiness as he became decidedly more aware of his disadvantageous position and newly established vulnerable state.

"Calm that fierce and fiery rage, my overly anxious and excessively heated Prime!" A cold, slushy, and showery breeze lambasted my revitalizing adversary just as he had started to break free from his rockbound placement. Candilux's robust and vigorous discharge was once again touched by my ever-useful staff, which delivered unto it my wizardly bequest for an evidently radical yet elementally miniscule change, thus transforming it from a fiery missile blast into a frozen and virulent stream. In an instant, an icy and encrusted glaze was set upon Noxerus's cliffside roost, burying and solidifying him in place for at least a fractional period.

"Get on with it, boy. Onward and into the factory's interior and to the aid of your kinsmen and relatives and friends." Cristofo had spotted our skirmish from a good distance away, and although he did not physically harken my insistent plea, he did indeed catch wind of it due to my communicative gesture and my telepathic transmittal of the reassuring decree. Even though there was definitely a bit of hesitation and uncertainty felt on the part of the loyalty-inclined young champion, I managed to convey to him the impression that I had the situation under control to a sufficient enough degree. For this reason, coupled with worriment regarding his father and grandfather, Cristofo proceeded into the tumultuous mouth of the factory enclave with sword flailing in hand and with the sole objective of setting eyes upon his blood relations as he pressed his way into the cavernous interior expanse. In the almost immediate subsequence, Noxerus unfastened himself from his mountainous confinement pad and managed to turbulently surge forth and break free.

"Come on then, you charcoal-made beasts, you relentless and unmerciful murderous fiends! Just a little farther along now ..." Elsewhere and aside, deep within the bowels in the midst of the Nepeshan factory's twisting and winding array of tunnels and interlacing access ways, a softish and weathered voice whispered aloud as my feisty and fiery-souled old acquaintance huddled stealthily against an arbitrary nook. Indeed, the magister had placed himself there, alone and in a far-removed circumstance, where he had managed for yet a successive time to break off from the more crowded and fervent clashes and confrontations that permeated throughout the great factory's innards and succeeded in leading along a small-numbered crew of the systematically invading foreigners. Under the guise of frightened and fleeing prey, the conniving combatant duped and drew in his victims so as to unleash upon them a violent and vicious body-crushing affray.

"Have at the guts of the mountain, then, and let's just see just how well you fare with your highly sharpened weapons and your blood-shedding and butchering aptitude!" A simple yank was all that occurred as Cristofo's far from ineffectual grandfather leaped into the oncoming field of view with a previously arranged rock wall–mounted and camouflaged rope held securely in hand. The nearby noise from a pair of terse and fierce simultaneous blasts barreled through the tubular setting with an ear-shattering and resounding echo. It stunned the quintet of unsuspecting Corbominian raiders, who hadn't a moment to react before a bounteous volume of bedrock and boulders came crashing down upon them from a highly placed angle and from a previously set in place load.

"And there we have it, *cough cough*, and so it seems, *cough cough*. The hunted turns out to be the hunter, *cough cough*, and the victim reverses the deed!" The magister wagged and waved his hand with vigor in an effort to clear up the post-rockslide's powdery murk and dusty veil.

"And there's plenty more where that came from! It will be no easy chore to overtake and make yours this long-held and vigorously worked-upon inheritable store, a cautionary note of little value to the lot of you at this point, and likewise of no use to the next batch of the soon-to-be had upon members of your similarly deserving breed!" The magister made way toward the heaping mishmash of rock and stone, crushing and extruding body parts intermixed with broken hunks of calcified and mineral made bones. A spasmodically lurching and oscillating neck managed to somewhat jostle and sway its protruding and charcoal-like crown, catching the eye of the oncoming defender as he reached the foot of his handiwork-generated mound.

Hard thwacks reverberated in turn just as the post–rock tumble dusting concluded with a drizzling and sprinkling wane, giving rise to the more distinctive sound of rock being chopped at with the edge of sword made from exceptionally well-forged steel. Once, twice, thrice did the feisty old scrapper hack with a full head of steam until finally managing to cleave the orbicular appendage and force it to conclusively yield as it toppled and rolled farther along down the indurated tunnelway floor. The wholly unnecessary act was undertaken more so to satisfy his own animosity and frustration than for any other legitimate reason or under any alternative, plausible guise. Onward he climbed, up and over top of the perfectly quantified volume of rubble, which left just enough room to accommodate and allow passage to a person of his volume and stature—a human specimen of average proportion and size.

Meanwhile, back at the vast and wide-ranging factory entrance hall, scores of distinct and disparate battles and skirmishes of diversified classes and kinds raged on with a disorienting turbulence and spewed forth with a boisterous ear-shattering grind. Explosive blasts erupted with regularity as the Nepeshan troops and company men took full advantage of their ready-made devices of smaller and more convenient packaging, launching them without restriction and with every opportunity, wherein their attackers were clustered together with little risk of their fellow battlers becoming hit by residual spray or shrapnel of any significant size. Yet still the concise and powerful blows would impact a number of human casualties, and in consequence, a proportion would invariably fall. But regardless of this, desperation led the charge forward and frenziedly as long-reaching swinging and slashing sickle-like blades would otherwise bring forward a multitude of suffering and thwartings, the alternative effect of which being a much more voluminous quantity of fatalities with resulting reactions of a much less inspiring and moreover disheartening kind.

In his own little corner of the space, just inward of the equally bustling turmoil of the exterior open air and not far beyond its entranceway's widely accessible gate, Cristofo hacked and slashed away in his usual flawless manner as he moved forward while engaging with and disposing of an increasing number of the methodically advancing and systematically flailing sediment-made beasts.

"Father!" The heartfelt wail went largely unheard as it fell well short of its intended aim, losing itself and becoming suffocated among the myriad of other undulating cacophonies and bursting forth, aimlessly wandering sound waves. It was a truly genuine pronouncement that dissipated to nothingness along with all the other audible casualties and vociferous outbursts that were necessarily spawned because of the ongoing and uproarious war, a collection of phonetic soldiers that subsisted beyond the usual recognition but nonetheless existed on some alternate level or largely unsimilar plane.

Urgency then set in as Cristofo's sighting of his admired forbearer invoked him to scuttle and scramble as he slashed his course onward while making way toward his father's not-too-distant position, where the more than proficient commander appeared to be doing surprisingly well in leading a squad of men against a decent proportion of the tallish and tactical calcified beings. Suddenly, a resounding detonation was brought to bear and was just barely heard as it came to burst upon the small number of Corbominian battlers with whom our exceptional protagonist was actively engaged, destroying and damaging a few of the interlopers while also serving to floor and daze our unrelenting wizardly defender. A foggy vagueness overwhelmed the youthful champion as he fought hard and feverishly to restore his senses to a more agreeable grade, knowing that an onrush of otherworldly advancers would almost immediately be upon him with a singular and bloodthirsty aim. Just then, the morsel of Maleabar was promptly called upon and fashioned into a thin yet sufficiently broad and practical shield that at once absorbed the brunt of a sickle-induced impact. It then deflected the long-winding stroke of another similarly placed wallop before proceeding to protect him further from yet another bevy of barbaric and ill-contrived slashes and lunges from the onrushing horde.

Azrael was almost instinctively drawn and waved about in a not-so-decisive but more so in a deterrent-aimed manner as the fierce young warrior struggled to intensify and reinstate his much-needed stronghold of pure and unmitigated mental focus. A shadowy aura manifested itself in and around as well as within the mind of the boy as a consistent flow of the Corbominian raiders advanced in numbers and enclosed upon his position with an increasing unleashment of steady and persistent percusses and blows. Just as Cristofo managed to regain a modest degree of clarity, a sufficient amount to allow him to set eyes upon an oncoming sickle swipe that had been initiated from a high overhead position as he began to rise to his knees, a familiarly made sword tip materialized right in front of his face. It burst forward through the head of the imminent attacker and stopped inches away from affecting him while still scattering forth a considerable portion of rubble-like particles, sediment-based fragments, and scree.

Several of the tall and imposing invaders were still more or less right on top of Cristofo's rising and now almost fully repositioned frame as the boy caught wind of the furiously advancing figure who was the catalyst behind the sword launching's conclusive and impeccable aim. Indeed, it was his venerated father who had come to his rescue—his highly esteemed procreator who had unanticipatedly come to respond. And just in time, I might add, for a few moments were furthermore required until the young wizard was to be fully and outright restored.

A feverish outcry was much too near at hand for it not to be heard as Cristofo listened to it with utter engrossment while bearing witness to his father's mounting of another imminently pouncing interloper. An overly nimble surging and saltating maneuver served to bring the exhilarated commander high upon his ambition's backside, whereupon he instantaneously followed through with a series of savagely delivered dagger thrusts that didn't take long to chip and chisel away at the charcoal-based monstrosity's invariably rigid yet still undeniably shatterable crown.

"Welcome back to the sum and substance of the scintillating scuffle, my good progeny!" A firm yet short-lived grasp by the arm served to greet and fully revivify Cristofo as his aggressively engaged father lost little momentum in his thrashing and thwarting campaign, continuing on to the next near-at-hand assailant, where he drew himself closely within and away from the range of an overly drawn-out sickle-induced sway. Without missing a step, the prior-generation champion shot upward with a blur and made no mistake of punching his fist straight through the open and actively shrieking gritty and granular mouth of the Corbominian bane, at which point he skillfully proceeded to jam in a small and convenient explosively constructed prize. A graceful wielding of his circular and back-mounted buffer made it seem effortless as he turned to his backside and carried through with a meticulous safeguarding of both his and Cristofo's considerable frames. Powdery and particulate rain then fell upon the upwardly held shield, along with a variegated scattering of lumpish-shaped morsels and a sprinkling of larger-sized grains.

As soon as the sandy and crumbly spray was concluded, father and son pressed on in a completely proactive and dynamically predisposed manner, whereupon Cristoforo repositioned himself while once again flawlessly brandishing Azrael. His more-seasoned begetter strode purposefully forward to take hold of his previously flung sword. A rigidly placed foot was used to apply the appropriate amount of bracing pressure required as the commendable director proceeded to extricate his rocklike skull-embedded length of expertly forged steel that emitted a quavering and grinding squeal as it pulled away from the oily and ooze-infested head of its lifeless and hard-bodied claim. The two exceedingly capable descendants then converged in a back-to-back stance as they continued along with their trouncing and flailing, while the commander's expertly led squadron fought its way closer toward them on a vigorously worked upon and hard-fought approach.

"And what of Grandfather? Do you know his whereabouts, Father?" The words were spoken in a conspicuously casual manner considering the tumultuous nature of the ongoing circumstance, also taking into account the fact that the morsel of Maleabar was concurrently being wielded in a most notable manner in the form of a razor-thin sharp and circular blade that whizzed about the immediate vicinity. It took aim upon and cleaved the heads off a considerable number of the teeming and besieging off-putting beasts.

"He's wandered off somewhere into the bowels of his precious home away from home, taking to the uncounted passages and tunnelways like a badger that saunters and tarries about its multitude of setts. I too fear for his safety, my son, yet waste not your worry on that surprisingly capable relation of ours, for I have learned long ago not to underestimate his abilities or to sell short his resolve."

"I certainly hope that his tricks and traps serve him faithfully and without flaw, my dear father, for legions upon legions of these far-from-hospitable beasts are surging and swelling upward from the depths of our mountainous enterprise's underbelly; believe me, for I have seen their numbers with my own eyes and I aim not to exaggerate. Carry on with your warring and drudgery for the time being while I take my leave of this battlefront, for there is no escaping or hiding in safety in this endless parade of advancement and duress. Only with wizardly backing can we end this most harrowing of infiltrating campaigns, so off to the exterior plains shall I proceed, off to take care of this plague-like overswarming in the most feasible of manners and means. Off I go to cut off the head of the hostile race's rigid and merciless queen!"

"Well, go then and make haste with it, son. Make no mistake in the fact that we will hold for as long as those of divine godliness may require us to, or for as long as they otherwise determine and destine!"

Cristofo broke away from his battles and left the fighting and skirmishing to others of lesser abilities but still very capable means, whisking himself forward with an uncanny impetus, a momentum driven by wizardly potency and induced by subliminal powers that he had not yet even begun to fully garner or glean. Indeed, he leaped onward with a stride that was akin to near flight as the miniaturized proportion of Maleabar cut clear a path at his foreground and Azrael kept the others at bay by preventing them from coming in tight. Within a fleeting moment or two, the inspirited boy was back out into the open air, where still the battles were crowded and cramped but nowhere near as brimming as the elbow-to-elbow fracases that were occurring inside the mountainous and more compacted interior range.

A deep breath fed and firmly established the boy's vitality and also his unrestrained sense of freedom as he took a miniscule part of a moment to survey and scrutinize the newly returned upon exterior grounds. Wave upon relentless wave of the Corbominian intruders continued to advance upon the steadily and surely diminishing multitude of human defenders, providing Cristofo with a glimpse of the imminent and inevitable overtaking that was sure to progress unless something drastic was to be otherwise forthcoming or some momentous deed alternatively done.

Cimtar turned at once to set eyes upon his freshly emerged master, breaking away from his aggressively ongoing and intruder slaying campaign to return to the side of, and be at the ready for his venerated rider. His most treasured owner and commander who was also considered a lifelong companion as well as someone with whom the exceptional creature shared camaraderie and adventure and a friendship that was held very dear. Iggy caught wind of Cristofo's appearance in a likewise manner, reporting back to his doted-upon comate after having dispatched an exceptional number of the overly destructive and hideous members of the besieging violators of vascolumen strain.

And still a more or less unchanged quantity, or at any rate at least a barely diminished volume of Corbominian material remained nourishingly within the fiery wonder as he sailed back into his cozy little hideaway as though nothing of significance had transpired, nustling into the gold-composed resting ground which gently jostled and swayed against the heart of his bonded with human counterpart, his one and only accomplice and compeer.

"I know, Iggy. I can see and sense the same thing as well. As much as it pains me to do so, we must abandon the current and harrowing circumstance in order to put an end to this rampant and unabated mimicry of hell. Carry us forward at once to the not-so-distant mountainside, Cimtar, for Alterius must be aided with his one-on-one battle match, as there is little time to waste on our principal adversary's glorified minion. Onward must we proceed to the matron of all matrons; to our ultimate confrontation must the lot of us inevitably speed.

Now let us veer back for a fractional moment, back to a previous period in our fabulously recounted tale. To be more specific, back to the precise moment when Cristofo somewhat reluctantly turned away from my clash with Noxerus and set foot into the boisterous factory entrance hall. In retrospect, perhaps I did indeed overstate my control over the severe and significant confrontation, but in any event, I was certainly not going to hold the boy back from his forbearer-finding campaign. Furthermore, a no-holds-barred contest against my otherworldly nemesis was a long time coming and unquestionably well overdue. To that end, Noxerus proceeded to break free from his icy hold with a forceful and vigorous thrust that effectively smashed his rigid and shivery coating to smithereens and lambasted both Candilux and me with a splintered and slivered icicle-laced cannonade.

"So, here we have it, eh, my high and mighty windbag and lecture-spewing old friend? It seems that my moment of revenge has been gifted with time to spare—my hunger for vengeance to be satisfied sooner than expected in light of your animus-induced meddlesome and interfering flair."

"Bring on your best, then, you barbaric and blusterous old fool. I suppose that I needn't remind you of the outcome from our last earthbound confrontation, whereupon your trouncing not only off-put you from returning to this land for centuries so as to not awaken the bitter memories of that harsh and conclusive thwarting, but also saw you squander away your cherished stockpile of precious material, a turn of events that just so happened to enrich me with potency and companionship beyond any measure of likeness or compare. And now in a glorious wisp of irony, that same prized possession will be used against its previous master by way of dispensing yet another walloping and thrashing—another doozy of a defeat filled solely with detriment and imbued with a heavy-handed splash of despair."

Maleabar was then forcefully and concurrently hurled, heaved with a vigor and vehemence the likes of which I had never mustered prior nor managed to equal heretofore. Noxerus braced for impact by making himself impenetrable and invariably hard, for he knowingly would not have the ability to otherwise manipulate or steer away the wholly obedient fabric. Just prior to contact, I altered my previously executed command and brought to bear one that carried forward a different and more distinctive exertion of my will as my pole-shaped bludgeon was compelled to branch off into a multitude of filament-like fibers and steely, fibrous strings.

At once, the rigid and resilient tendrils laced and lashed about the demonic being's powerful and hulking frame, strapping him securely in place as though victimized by the spider's silken binding, a cocoon-like and wholly smothering embrace. Without hesitation, a conjured and shock wave–like blast sent the constrained figure reeling back into harsh contact with his recently escaped from and rockbound mountainside hold, while at the same time, Candilux followed through with a massive blasting and bursting forth inferno, a much more grandiose display compared to the more typical dragon-induced and flamethrower-resembling regurgitation.

At the end of the rather lengthy and scalding stream of blaze, a charred and blackened face with a piercing gaze remained there with a stubborn resilience as though its blatant seriousness was a mere mask to the mocking and almost delightfully entertained tone that flew in the face of its opponent's laborious efforts, leaving it damaged and ingrained into the crust of the mountain's nearly impervious stone.

"And with this you expect to foil the efforts of Noxerus the ultimate of Primes?" No sarcastic smile or berated chuckle followed in the wind of the derisive query. "If this be the best of your trouncing and triumphing endeavors, then it is merely a whisper of time longer that I need suffer the uncomfortableness of this murky, mud-stained, meadowy, and tree-infested land. I shall return home forthwith with your precious little prodigy in tow—or perhaps with him otherwise disposed unto an indeterminate passage through the most isolated and unattended of hollows. What's more, my homeland and all of its tiers and arenas alike will be brimming with human participants wherein there will be no lack for frenzied and tumultuous battles. There will be no end to the joy of witnessing the eradication and extermination of soul upon willful and non-conceding soul and no limit to the bounteous fortune that will be generated by the creatures' delicious and delectable inner liquid that will assuredly and unequivocally flow!"

In a raw and unabated display of strength, the muscle-bound demon roared and carried forward with an unprecedented exertion of force that blasted him free from his steely shackles with a glorious and invigorating outcry. Maleabar indifferently reassembled and returned to the hand of its master while Noxerus proceeded to follow through with his heavy-handed and counterattacking foray, which saw a barrage of wizardly conjured energy bursts concurrently being hurled back and forth in an alternating seesaw-like sway. Finally, the devilish fiend got the better of me, or at least so it seemed to appear. The demon's strained and held out hand served to consummate the bombardment of his potent attacks, acting as a more than sufficient conduit in conveying a powerful wave of dynamism that spontaneously overtook and made immobile the whole of my relatively more modest yet still somewhat substantial frame.

"This may indeed prove to be too easy for me to fully enjoy and take pleasure in, I must in all honesty concede ..." The hulking beast wallowed in his own prominence and reveled in his typically brash and overly confident manner and way as his other hand was impelled to sway sideward in like fashion. Candilux was immediately set upon with a similarly conjured beam of fortitude that jostled him free from his passenger and whisked him along with a velocity that sent him reeling a considerable distance astray.

"Hmm. Now what to do with you is the question my age-old adversary. How do I deal with you in the most compelling and poignant of displays? It seems to me that true fairness can only be established in a singular mode and manner, seeing as how my principal subordinate has been taken from me in the most selfish and invariably long lasting of ways. What's more, yonder in the distance, I see my co-conspirator on approach and speedily drawing near. Indeed, it is the matron of all matrons who thrusts and drives forward with a frantic and furious veer, followed, of course, by your less than effectual counterparts. They desperately and clumsily follow and hurl strikes and attacks against her in a futile effort to block her advancement and to thwart the invasion of this petty little world about which, for some reason, you seem to feign caring and actually expect me to believe that you hold quite dear. As if that is not audience enough, hitherto we see drawing near your precocious yet reckless apprentice. Onward does the little bug fly straight into the awaiting predator's trap, where he will find himself bearing witness to the slaying of his newfound mentor before being spun around in a tangle of aggressiveness that will leave him bruised, battered, and more or less muted and constrained. Basically, seized upon like the inefficient creature that he truly exemplifies and invariably is!"

"Do your worst, then, you malicious scoundrel."

Indeed, my body was more or less paralyzed as though caught in the force field of a powerful magnetic array, and therefore I lay wholly susceptible to any oncoming and significant form of physical violation or raid. However, little did my conceited adversary realize that my tangible defenses were purposely cast aside and that the lot of my inherent energy stores were refocused into my psychological marrow, my innermost spiritual vein.

"Oh, and by the by, my petty little opposer and soon-to-be vanquished speck of a friend, have I ever shared with you the presupposition of Fingo, which contends that any amassment of miraculous material will automatically return to its former master at the exact moment when its current controller comes to a conclusive and clearly defined end? Well although never proven, one should definitely concede the possibility based solely on the magical little forger's reputation and knowledge base, which, as you are well aware, is vast and exceptional near to the point of no end!"

With that, a sharpened and satiny staff was drawn from the demonic beast's backside—not his recently shattered former and formidable principal pole but one of a multitude that could be considered equally powerful and readily found within his limitless stockpile. Blackened and beady eyes zeroed in on their target as the spiraling weapon was launched with a craft and precision that left nothing to chance as it wisped the missile-like projectile soundly forward to effortlessly cut through the air. Not a hint of resistance ensued as the knife-edged pike entered into and forced itself full through my substantial yet unprotected center mass. Strange indeed was the painless sensation that followed and the heightened awareness that was made to exude as the piercing shaft bore into the gist of my heart before proceeding to shatter a number of vertebrae while exiting out from my backside, where it remained and came to protrude. Every inner morsel and moiety—those devastated, damaged, and unblemished alike—was seen and felt with the most unusual clarity as an accentuated focus came to bear and all but mitigated the physical trauma of the otherwise cognizance-ending circumstance. Almost to the point of ecstasy, elation was discerned with pinpoint accuracy as I glanced upon Noxerus's satisfied and glazed-over eyes. Contrarily, Cristofo's reaction brought a sweet and melancholy type of sorrow as the boy looked on in disbelief before slowing significantly in his forward advancement and becoming imbued with a most genuine type of sadness that bordered on a wholehearted runover of despair.

As it so happened, the boy's mournfulness was short-lived, as was the crude and callous gratification of my principal foe, for I had foreseen the whole of the freshly developed happenstance on account of my mind's heightened intensity and as it was revealed with the utmost certainty in the marrow of my newly enkindled all-seeing eye. A vigorous grasp with both of my hands then remarkably and unexpectedly ensued as my shocked and disbelieving audience was sent reeling into a slow-motion type of energy wave that inundated them as they looked on while I proceeded to yank on the terminal end of the firmly stuck pole. But 'twas in truth the circumstance itself that was soundly wielded and played out with a tightly held measure of control as a terse yet exceedingly challenging reversal in time was successfully carried out to perfection—one of the rarest and most difficult of wizardly conjurings performed with precision and consummated in a glorious, openly observed, and incontestable display.

For you see, time is a mere tool to those of us who dare to make use of it—a highly effective yet uncontrollable instrument that can cede only the slightest and most subtle of sways. Yes, indeed, 'tis a perilous and oftentimes ill-advised weapon, but still it remains one that can prove to be of the utmost effectiveness when tampered with and carried forth in the properly executed manner and way. Therefore, the would-be instrument of my downfall was extricated and let drop downward as though never having any impacting influence at all. At that point, it was a simple matter to transform and wield my most reliable and unfailing amassment of remarkable material so as to send it sailing straight through the shoulder of my exasperated and still somewhat astounded adversary.

In and around the brute's strapping and muscle-bound form did Maleabar then circle, swivel, and furiously swirl until finally tightening and compressing once reaching the point that enough rotations were completed, thusly allowing it to fully fasten and secure its netherworld-based prey. Pain and solid anchoring were the principal considerations when targeting the flank of my age-old rival, not to mention his fatality, the avoidance of which I thought to be unnecessary but still more appropriate in that it showed a more elevated standpoint and proved that I was the greater potentate, the utterly superior and vastly more prominent of Primes! A vivid burst of mental energy then overwhelmed me as Cristofo was felt and seen to draw ever so near. In the same instant, my newly initiated protégé orchestrated and telepathically communicated a combined plan of action that both invoked me into compliance and impressed upon me a newly developed level of power and capacity that he would be able to draw from and act upon as he chose and saw fit.

"Now, Altarius! Drive him into the ground while his senses are still somewhat frazzled and waned!" Both of us furthermore discerned a sense of urgency, as Aleregeni had effectively shaken off the temporal shock wave's briefly set debility and had begun a furious advancement with a trajectory of pinpoint aim and design. Little did I realize at the time that the boy's reinforcing influence would take on the form that it had intended and toward which it was ultimately inclined. Although I was under the impression that he would contribute to a more thrustful and forceful strike of impact, imagine my surprise when I extricated a handle-like apparatus from Maleabar's hide and swung down with vehemence in expectation of sending my opponent on a crushing and sledgehammer-resembling ride, only to see him plow into the hardened earth with an atypical and burrowing type of perpetuated downward glide. Just like that, he was gone, wrenched away from the throws of the existing circumstance like a tiny little morsel tossed into the mouth of the indurated groundwork and swallowed down into the depths of wherever such a figurative food scrap would invariably disappear to or go.

Indeed 'twas back unto the netherworld that our nemesis was suddenly and unwittingly thrown, forced in through the opening of a wormhole-like portal and sucked away with little choice in the matter and even less of a chance of reentering from the opposite pole. Never before had an interdimensional gateway been conjured and created in such a way. Up to that point, they had always been preexistent apertures that seemed to call upon and accommodate those of the wizardly vocation; moreover, they were catered to each one's individual perception as they followed them along in accordance with the signals and scenery toward which they tended to be more favorably predisposed. Once again, our newly established and proving to be quite exceptional and outstanding wizardly boy had evoked a sensation of shock and awe among the entire assembly of his near-at-hand and closely observing supernatural peers. None were more surprised than yours truly, for never had one so freshly emboldened and recently interfused demonstrated such an effective combination of confidence, firmness, and fortitude. The resulting conclusion served to vanquish the most formidable of foes, a difficult enough task for one or even a small number of the infinitely more seasoned and exceedingly more qualified carriers of the wizardly banner and bearers of the boundlessly modified soul.

At that point, attention was fiercely and forcibly shifted toward the crux of our ongoing conflict and with respect to our supereminent invader, our by far most predominant of opponents and orchestrator of the entire ill-contrived attempted overthrow. And nothing was going to stop her steadfast momentum as Aleregeni the iron-willed matron swept down upon me with a vengeance and swatted at me with a wallop that sent me reeling away in a tizzy on account of the business end of her glittering and mystical pole. Pain once again materialized. No longer was my temporal maneuver actuated, and therefore no longer did it grant me any sought-after reprise from the searing throb of a gashing wound, nor from the burning pang of shredding blow. The embedded fragments of jewellike stones were somehow lengthened and sharpened before coming to impact and lacerate a number of places on my body as they were spontaneously extended.

"The moment has come, foul creature, for you to have a taste of just what it means to take on the whole of the animus crew!" Venificus, as usual, was the first to arrive and draw upon his trusted and most favorable sword, just in time to distract Aleregeni as she was turning her attention toward and beginning to establish a Cristofo-aimed onslaught. Sparks flashed and flied and then flickered and died in a tumultuous hail of offshoot as netherworld-forged steel clashed and clanged with the yet unexplored efficacy of the otherworldly matron's bizarrely capable and multifunctional pikestaff. Strokes and swats jetted and flew with a speed-induced blur as both combatants demonstrated a level of agility and expertness that was most difficult to observe, let alone fathom. A brash and robustious bolt of lightning then shot itself onto the scene, a Bellatrix- induced creation that targeted Aleregeni and carried the intention of blasting and electrocuting the Corbominian-made queen.

Alas, the age-old wizardess's speed was implausible, as was her adroitness and overabundance of prowess and skill, for she made it look effortless while using her pole to catch and redirect the Tempestas-derived firebolt so as to effectively divert its rush of power down through the shaft of her bejeweled and conduit-resembling staff and straight into the pith of Venificus's massive and full-figured frame. All the while, she didn't miss a beat in her baton-wielding frenzy, which at minimum met and matched her opponent's spectacular sword-swinging display, at least for a stretch, until Bellatrix's intensely forged fulmination was redirected to touch upon his person. The overachieving warrior was shocked stagnant, became listless, and proceeded to simply drop down and drift away.

Aleregeni's mystical conductor continued to sustain the dynamic and forceful electrical blast somehow, a deadly flickering beam that she somehow harnessed and then veered toward a more near-at-hand Cristofo, who was next in position to carry forward with an all-out attack. So too did we expect our up-and-coming apprentice to falter upon impact with the violent bolt, but lo and behold, if it wasn't our endlessly unpredictable little fireball who suddenly burst to the forefront in response and yet again, energizing and aggrandizing so as to encompass the whole of the boy as well as his exceptional dragon-framed ride. And unwavering did Iggy's fiery outer coating remain as it absorbed the lightning shot's impact with a seemingly effortless ease, leaving Cimtar as well as Cristofo sheltered and completely unscathed. It was a protection similar to the one carried out back in the throes of the boy's netherworld clash with Noxerus, but this time there was a difference that was apparently subtle yet blatantly felt and perceived. It was as though the boy was part of the blazingly shimmering creature, encompassed by it to a certain degree but still separately functioning. He was an active and able-bodied participant who bore the shielding dynamism like a magnificent cloak, as opposed to a helpless and incapacitated rider that was involuntarily swallowed and carried along like an infant smothered in the comfort of its mother's blanketing tote.

A mere moment transpired as the lightning blast dissipated and completely relinquished its hold on Iggy's all-encompassing and overly resistant veneer. In the exact instant that followed, Cimtar was disengaged from the protective coating and was cast forth and urged unto the nearby more suitable battles. He would be much more effective in thwarting the Corbominian invaders and be more valuable to the survival of the multitude of Nepeshan fighters and defenders, both the skilled soldiers as well as the less capable plebes. The creature's aerial aptitude was no longer required, for Iggy's burning vitality was more than sufficient in keeping Cristofo airborne. In fact, the fiery wonder was abundantly lively and replete of stamina, maneuverability, and exceptional speed.

All of a sudden, in swooped Bellatrix on the heels of a vigorous and cyclonic breeze, clashing with and engaging mano a mano with the vehement and furiously determined otherworldly being. Indeed, it was a close-at-hand battle that left no room for Cristofo to meddle or in any way intervene, so he bided his time with a nearby hover and watched intently as Annabell clashed headlong with the mystical pole. Body blows were exchanged intermittently and forcefully to and fro. As with Venificus, it seemed to be a more or less evenly matched battle, yet there remained a proclivity toward Aleregeni's superiority, a perception that she could easily handle her opponent's aggression with marginal effort and all the while exhibit a posture and overall comportment that yielded no lack for disdain. Still, the back-and-forth onslaught lingered and tended to remain, with both wizardesses too distracted to notice what Cristofo had quite easily come to observe and ascertain. 'Twas a tiny gnat-like creature stealthily and silently fluttering and flying in and around the violent, ongoing, and for the most part uncontrollable melee.

It was Malthazar who now took up his turn in the all-out foray, taking on the form of a barely noticeable little insect and veering straight into Aleregeni's hooded top part, wherein a tubular and earlike opening was smoothly and effortlessly located, entered into and landed upon without any trace of suspicion or sound. The tumultuous rhythm and stroke of swordplay served well to distract the overly capable and carbon-based queen as the tiniest load of munitions was planted within her gritty and granular ear canal. They ignited with a somewhat muted but still loudly erupting and bursting forth pounding. A shrill screech was uncontrollably emitted as though an ode to the pain and suffering of a wounded beast, while miniscule pieces and portions from the side of the invading wizardess's face and head exploded outward and into her burlap-like cowl just an instant after Malthazar transmogrified on the heels of the outburst and was forced to exit from the opening while being impelled to return to his more familiar and human-resembling shape, form, and size.

Bellatrix was momentarily bewildered and taken aback as both the modest yet near-at-hand explosion as well as the sudden outflow of her unexpectedly appearing comate were thrown upon her with an abrupt and nerve-racking jar. Small amounts of charcoal-colored scree and bits and hunks of Corbominian-made debris also fell down upon the chest piece and brow of the now silently simmering and boiling over matriarch, who remained hovering menacingly, forebodingly, and relatively unstirred as she unhurriedly peeled back her overly broad, tattered, and torn-apart headgear. What a sight it was that came to be revealed, as the concealing covering was no longer masking the creature's features, facets, overall mysterious semblance, and feel.

Deeply socketed eyes briskly declared themselves as though awakened by the irrepressible throes of a furious rage; fiery and red-hot embers that were ignited and came to the forefront with a shimmering and devilishly sinister glow that intensified vigorously as they pushed forward toward the cusp of their rooted cavern-resembling hollows. Fault lines and fractures cascaded down from the queen's age-old and seemingly petrified crown. They were streaks and striations more akin to weathering and wear as opposed to damage or permanently blemishing wound—save, of course, for her now–blown apart profile, which imparted a blatant asymmetry and rendered her spherical head congruous in stature when compared with her previous homeland and its damaged and devastated asteroid-percussed side.

Horns were made out to be subtle yet plainly visible, short and stout outthrusts with a rough and bark-like surface that curled back and descended toward their skullcap, whereupon an ample tapering brought each of the two thinly rounded ends to a pinnacle that spread slightly as they firmly touched down. And within the arched and teardrop-shaped apertures that delineated the consolidation of horn and cranium, a fibrous and crystalline marrow was made to exude—coarse and wiry, jewellike, and semi opaque windows that glowed and glimmered as they carried forward a current of activized matter back and forth and betwixt each of the two. A self-sustained power station of sorts with unknown origin and flowing with an unexplained drive save for the theoretical deduction that it remained fueled by what would appear to be a biomass strain of energy generated spontaneously and by the within of the unusual and extraneous omnipotent being. In any event, it remained a most intimidating characteristic, one that imparted power and potency of an extremely high level, the limit of which seemed impossible to determine, let alone even remotely consider, guess at, or otherwise ascertain.

Now we have arrived at a most epical point in our spellbinding tale, a climactic and breathtaking moment whereupon the true antagonist and principal moral opposer conjures up and sets forward with an immediate and intense thrust of energy that barrels outward in a most powerful burst of aggressiveness and wreaks havoc about the far-reaching circumstance. It brings wrath upon all manner of creature within a wide-sweeping radius, including and encompassing all beasts, animals, demons, wizards, Corbominians—both the extraterrestrial and subterranean strain alike—and most of all its preeminent target: the native and earthbound creatures, namely the women and children and legions of men. Indeed, you have hearkened correctly. Even those of her own flock and breed had become caught in the throes of a massive, destructive, and incapacitating blast that continued to emanate and flow with persistency and vehemence while indiscriminately paralyzing and immobilizing all in the scope of its wide-reaching flash.

Humans, animus-made animals, and beasts alike were first to fall victim to the magnetic allure of Alleregeni's destructive, all-powerful, and unconscionable strum. With no time to react, a sharp and biting pain pervaded each of our bodies as though ignited from the core and torturously making way outward through marrow and meat before continuing to exit beyond the outermost layer of skin where bubbles swelled and accrued. A profusion of tiny pus-imbued pockets fought with every effort and means in a desperate attempt to maintain the shielding coating's integrity and overall vigor and vim. But it was to no avail, for blood and otherwise liquid-like interior fluids could no longer be contained as they pulled apart and blasted away with a spouting and boiling-over teem. An abundance of the weaker and of those less hearty in spirit and mind were blown apart forthwith as though dandelion fluff whisked and carried adrift by the forceful yet fluent thrust of a semi-violent midsummer's breeze. However, others persisted for a while as they brought to bear their iron-willed manner and vigorous fortitude, which afforded them the ability to momentarily muster through the utterly painful and pervasive misdeed.

Vasculomen swine followed swiftly behind in the suffering, as did Aleregeni's own conglomeration of both earth dwelling and portal-jumping Corbominian-made peers. Screeches and squeals echoed resoundingly and with a recurrent and overlapping zeal as the netherworld-originated demons were next to succumb to the devastating and far-reaching siege. At first, the bevy of Noxerus's most resilient subservients seemed to display a more concerted endurance with regard to withstanding the lethally discharging array. However, in the end, their resistance was short-lived, for at a certain point of magnitude within the pulsating, undulating, and outbreaking flux, the lot of them collectively broke down in a writhing, convulsing, and desperately volatile state. This culminated in a bursting and shattering firework-like display that saw the near-at-hand sky intersprinkled and bestrewn with their broken-apart portions of rubbery, sinewy, and otherwise viscous, somewhat gooey, and glutinous spatter and spray.

Likewise did the maddened queen's charcoal-based subjects yield in response to the ominously discharged and indiscriminately cast forth eradicating array as grist and granule and grainy morsels alike disassembled from their rigid bodies. The out-bursting particles flitted, fluttered, and danced near and away and throughout the proximate range in an all-encompassing swirl that brought forth a gloomy undertone as it congested and shadowed the sun's brilliantly glimmering rays. It was indeed a delirious and irrational psychotic furor that drove Aleregeni forward to the point of destroying and disseminating her own brand of beings, those very offshoots and progeny about which she labored with such unyielding tenacity and toiled over for centuries. Nay, more like an age, all in an effort to salvage what remained of her race and bring them to safety with some hope of fruition and a glimmer of faith. It seemed all for naught on that fateful and direful ruinous day whereupon such death and devastation reared its ugly head by way of she who was supposed to represent the oldest and most superior member of our exceptionally well-advised and highly talented band, the most preeminent and high-ranking wizardly sage.

In retrospect, one could only assume that the matron of all matrons had originally carried forward with her overly ambitious scheme with good yet misguided intentions and that it was her substantial head injury that put an end to any reasonable logic. It sent her into a dispassionate tizzy that left her loyal and doted-upon offshoots more or less abandoned, at a loss, and altogether betrayed. In any event, it looked as though nothing would have been able to separate Aleregeni from that fierce and indiscriminate rage that continued with calamitous consequence and endured for mere moments that seemed like an age. A handful of similarly graced and mightily endowed beings still attended the space and would wholeheartedly continue to fight in defense of their congregation and battle to the finish until either the eradication was stopped or their physical presence was laid to waste.

Cimtar, for one, would refuse to concede to the do-nothing way, instead opting to battle onward with a determined and stronghearted display, pressing his way painstakingly forward toward the all-powerful being while fighting through the agonizing discomfort in an attempt to inch his way to within an attackable range. Indeed, it was a most excellent and commendable effort that saw the valiant creature stay the course even as scales tautened and obtruded substantially outward and inner juices were alluringly drawn and pulled outward to the point that they began to secrete and transude. But in the end, nary a stroke of his magnificent wings could beget flutter nor blistering fire could his mighty dragon's breath cough up or stir. At a standstill did the glorious dragon more or less hover, not quite bent for attacking yet still managing to persist and endure.

As for we battle-scarred veterans who boast talent and aptitude of a wizardly made strength and degree, not any of us could take charge of the circumstance and make headway toward our delirious and disarranged adversary. Indeed, we fought hard and with all of our might, but in the end, our efforts could only muster sufficient resistance to keep our bodies from bursting apart amidst the annihilative array. And so stuck in limbo did the four of us animus-based guardians reluctantly remain, unable to act in support of our earthly compatriots as Aleregeni's virulent outburst continued to flourish and expand outward unto the multitudes that helplessly and progressively succumbed to the onslaught and relinquished their lives in the most violent and unbearable of ways. The debilitating and lethally pulsating onset of waves now encompassed even the scattering of remaining high-flying turtibrida, whose ordnance-carrying housings exploded forth with a mechanically dominated dispersion of their frameworks along with other miscellaneous contents. Unfortunately for their unearthly operators, this included a flurry of variegated body parts intermixed with a crude and vulgar medley of outward spurting viscera and streaming entrails.

Only Cristofo would remain to be spoken of; our unfailing principal protagonist's forthcoming actions will at this moment be my great privilege to convey. For although some may have misconstrued the boy's short-lived interval of non-reaction as a stunned and somewhat petrified entrapment, rest assured that this was nowhere near the case. A fierce and sharp-minded analysis was immediately initiated at the onset of Aleregeni's energy blast, with the corresponding plan of action concurrently established and soon thereafter evolved into a well-thought-out strategy that was ready to be called upon and gotten underway. He knew that precious time spoke to the suffering and dissolution of soul upon defenseless and unsuspecting soul. Yet still the earthly made champion recognized that in such a situation, a moment's pause is an asset of inestimable value, whereas impetuousness only promotes a tendency toward miscalculation and results in errors of execution with a corresponding failure to make the circumstance come together according to your intended manner and way. A one-time solution had long been the boy's favored approach, and a simple interval for analysis would go a long way in helping to increase his odds toward a more favorable end and result.

The magnificent boy edged his way ever so close, using Iggy's flaring coating as a shielding membrane to absorb the brunt of the destructive and onrushing waves. Indeed, the two beings were as one, as they shared a good portion of both body and mind in this newly evolved partnership and freshly come upon ability to meld into a combined capacity and state. A compulsion to work together propelled the dynamic duo forward with a fluid harmony, even though there still existed an underlying conflict as each individual spirit held intention and propensity to act according to its own disposition, method, and sway. By then, Cristofo had actualized a slight yet intrinsic similarity betwixt the attacking matron's self-sustained energized current that irradiated her head top as it flowed amidst horns and his fiery sidekick's combustible protoplasm. The vitalized elemental matter was very much comparable, as was its unique and peculiar coloration and visual tone. Furthermore, a more subtle yet deep-rooted connection was inferred and presumed to be true. Indeed, a genealogical link would have to be contended with, a stringently drawn tie between the two disparate yet uniquely powerful beings that the boy would undoubtedly and somehow have to overcome and undo.

Attention was now strictly focused on Aleregeni as Cristofo scrutinized her manner and bearing with such detail so as to make one think that he had managed to act within the scope of a slow-motion version of time. The vehemently bombarding creature was wantonly expending such a vast amount of energy, so much so that her outstretched arms were wholly occupied with the task of harnessing and refocusing the deadly and outreaching spray. A vibrant and dynamic brightness clustered about the being's power station–like head top as energy levels approached an indescribable potency and level of gain, almost as though a lightning bolt had been captured, sustained, and channeled into some sort of rippling and surging formation consisting of destructive waves that spread out to strike against the called-upon targets with a most devastating and hardhanded weight. By necessity, it was a most intense focus of the mind that fueled the powerful and unrelenting attack, leaving the matron of all matrons with little by way of defense and deterrence against any methods of attack that could possibly manage to penetrate the intensely irradiating and all-powerful spate.

As it so happened, our most newly found and remarkable young champion was the remaining combatant left to spearhead humanity's last-chance effort against the ominous and pulsating malevolently onrushing waves. Ultimately, it would be he who was tasked with the chore of battling head-on against Aleregeni, thereby playing the decidedly relevant role in determining her imminent and immediate fate. No better alternative could realistically have been conjured or fathomed, no other hope was to be found near and at hand, nor would any be found or otherwise brought to the fray.

With slow but steady progress, the young whippersnapper initiated his convergent pace, with Iggy still absorbing the brunt of the radiating diffusion. Iggy's exposure to the virulent blast was indeed a required sacrifice in the execution of the boy's ultimate plan, the crucial component of which entailed preoccupying the mind of his blistering companion, whose advancement necessitated the need to expend more and more energy in an effort to bolster his outermost surface and shield. There was a significant sense of resistance emanating from the underconsciousness of the boy's fiery wonder and most loyal and loving of friends, an undertone that hinted toward full knowledge of his master's true intentions and a resulting dissatisfaction that carried with it a propensity toward rebellion of the utmost degree.

Cristofo knew with certainty that he could not have allowed himself to be held back in any way, shape, or form while engaged in the furious heat and fierceness of battle. Therefore, little by way of regret or dismay was suffered as the boy pushed forward unto the point that Iggy's outer veneer touched down upon the perimeter of his violently irradiating adversary, causing an immediate and immeasurable flare-up of energized matter that burst outward with unbounded intensity. It blinded all onlookers that could muster a glance upon the blistering phenomenon, including all creatures both near and away. An explosive discharge of resplendent flare manifested itself as the two incomprehensibly powerful reactionary powers met and intertwined in a clashing and unmixable grazing of currents, circuits, and unexplainable elemental entanglements and fields, instantaneously thereafter fizzling out and deadening as a result of the blown-apart structural workings and total collapse of the harmoniously flowing surges and streams.

Mere moments presented themselves to our glorious defender, who long before had prepared himself to act with steadfast quickness to capitalize on his one-shot attempt to strike with uncompromised fortitude. He mobilized and soared upward with a wholly individualized propulsion and with a momentum that came to fruition just at that instant when his wizardly induced capacity was enkindled by pure thought and then carried forward with the clearest of aims. He broke free from Iggy's melding and enrapturing hold, freeing himself at the precise juncture where Aleregeni's energy field was touched upon by the flaming phenomenon's scintillating surface, thereby forcing it to instantly weaken and then altogether fail. Even though the fiery little creature was more or less depleted and absent of wonder, still there was an inherent attempt to hold off his decidedly aggressing master. However, the obstructive effort was to no avail, as Azrael was fluently and decisively drawn out and flailed. From a higher-up standpoint was the airy yet extensive length of nethersteel forced downward with precision as it sported a speed-induced vertical trail. Straight through the top of the Corbominian queen's headpiece did the implement plant itself firmly and continue to sail until stopped by the impact of the hilt piece as it percussed against the no longer energized skullcap with an echoing and loud sounding wail.

A sudden silence and somewhat surrealistic ambiance materialized and came to ensue as Cristofo proceeded to wrench and twist with a surgical precision that split apart the sediment-based framework with a heavy-handed and consummating follow-through. The short-lived quietude then succumbed to the resounding crack that provided an overture to the performance-ending victory that also served to revitalize the masses of still-alive creatures and beings who were at last liberated from their painful and debilitating hold. My wizardly companions and I gazed upon the circumstance with both a hesitant reverence and an unsettling disbelief as the oldest and most high-ranking member of our exclusive and privileged clan's dissevered and symmetrical portions slumped downward and clumsily drifted to the ground. Granular coarse-grained goo exuded and stagnated for a moment before proceeding to join each and both of its split-apart segments of housing as it caught up to and splattered upon them where they lay shattered and broken apart on their ultimate and earthbound resting place.

All at once, the sky cleared and the sun's soft yet all-powerful and yellowish waves permeated throughout the far and wide circumstance, bathing every creature and corner with a warm comfort that universally soothed and brought solace to all beings, creatures, and planes. It was as though the mightiest of adjudicators had stepped in to signal the end of the free-for-all and to compel all participants to cease and dissuade. Every soul acquiesced in acknowledgment to the fact that the earth's current occupants would unequivocally remain and be saved. Cristofo sheathed his prized sword as he nimbly surged to the ground at the foot of his fallen and broken-apart adversary, whereupon he almost immediately turned his back on the happenstance and simply continued along on his way.

Elsewhere and farther along, the ongoing battles were collectively halted. The large number of remaining Corbominian raiders relinquished hold of all weapons and implements before initiating a species-wide systematic and steady march into the factory's mountainous entryway, their final portal-crossing endeavor before following after and joining up with their similarly progressing Earth-based and subterranean counterparts. Humans of all classes and varieties began to pick themselves up and clean and carry along without any elaboration in the aftermath of the devastating wave of destruction. It was as though some divine force had finally grown weary of the commotion and turmoil, only to take it upon itself to intervene and neatly whisk all parties and participants away.

The few remaining turtibrida coalesced and set themselves aground some fair distance away, where they, along with their listless and intrinsically linked operators, made up their own plans and protocols before venturing off on their own unfamiliar campaigns. Even the small handful of surviving vasculomen demons seemed to be included in the all-encompassing, dissolving, and dismantling deed as they scampered off into a small and far-off cloud's obscurity, where a convenient gateway back to the nether was improbably yet somehow conveyed.

As for my long-serving wizardly concomitants and me, you might ask? Well, we merely remained, quite candidly awestruck to a degree and that is no slight matter for a small and all-powerful grouping that has seen almost everything imaginable, even including that which is unpredictable and totally unforeseen. Yet still we stood there silently as we stared at our approaching newcomer, who seemed to be carelessly chirping and whistling away as though not a thing of consequence had taken place or transpired. His blazing little pet then swooped in like a miniaturized fireball until setting down upon his companion's shoulder top, while at the same time, his loyal and splendiferous dragon furthermore converged.

"Maleabar, I return you to your master!" was the boy's singular and solitary phrase as the miraculous morsel conjoined with its staff-shaped plurality and Cristofo proceeded to grasp my arm with affection before withdrawing from proximity. He mounted the magnificent Cimtar, whereupon the three magnificent creatures immediately blasted off with an enthusiastic disposition and with thoughts of their loved ones wholeheartedly ingrained.

EPILOGUE

A warm breeze blanketed Cristofo and his playful younger siblings as they pranced and rollicked carelessly and with the lightest of hearts. A far-removed corner of their manor's luxurious and well-manicured lawn was the backdrop for the post-festivity kerfuffle that saw the pair of rambunctious twins reconnect with their treasured and highly regarded older brother after their return from a modestly long tarriance some distance away. It was a consequence based more on its relatively remote location as opposed to a mere twist of fate that saw the extensive residence and its sprawling parcel of land remain for the most part untouched by the recently transpired and widespread attempted invasion.

"Go on, you little brats, off to make merry and wreak havoc upon the other little rascals your age!" The jovial remark struggled to maintain coherence amid the diversified clamor of numerous giggles and snickers and other tickle-based chimes and rings. And there Cristofo decidedly remained, comfortably sprawled among the velvety blades of grass as he perused the diverse range of interactions and minglings that resulted in the aftermath of the belated yet much anticipated feast in honor of his grandfather's magnanimous guest; a great wizard of age who just then broke off from his conversational entanglements and began to converge on the circumstance with a modestly quickened pace.

"Well, well, what have we here? If it isn't a bevy of younglings that have seemed to escape from the comfort of their outbuildings and sheds! Ha, perhaps it is best that I corral the lot of you so your parents don't have to fret about your running off, getting lost, or being misled." Enthusiastic eyes brightened with bewilderment as flashy and glittering fence-like barricades were suddenly conjured and displayed in a boisterous effort to cut off and redirect the high-spirited scampering and scuttling that was already well underway in the typically energy-filled and haphazardly orchestrated childlike way. Cristofo looked on with a satisfied grin as the toddlers, youngsters, and juveniles alike succumbed to my habitual and ever-present charm.

"Ha ha! All right then, off you go now, you little rapscallions. Begone! Back to the gallery with the lot of you, where I think you will find a table of treats and deserts that has been at long last arranged."

A jovial smile was reciprocated by my pleasantly occupied young protégé, who seemed both amused and contented as the gathering of children quickly dispersed and headed back to the imposing estate in a frantic and beeline manner. I infringed upon his short-lived solitude by nuzzling up to his tethered and near-at-hand carelessly munching gorallion.

"Alas, 'tis indeed a most delightful and satisfying of breeds. Isn't that so, eh, Brunella? Yes, such a good girl … Enjoy your snack and listen to our discourse as you pervade us with your unabated aura of kindheartedness and ease." A suitable pause followed the favorable remarks as I resituated myself on an adjacent lawn seat. At the same time, Cristofo ascended from his stretched-out position and parked himself beside me with a more relaxed and semi-elevated pose.

"Well, don't keep me in suspense any longer, Altarius. What did you think about the wild barb-fanged boar?"

"Ah, even to this point I appreciate its savory medley as it continues to enchant me with its spell while still simmering and suffused in the confines of my overly satisfied belly. My compliments to the chef for his precisely calculated aging as well as his uncanny ability toward roasting—with no small credit due to the huntsman and his unarguable expertise, of course, I might add."

"I am quite glad that you enjoyed it, and thank you for the complimentary remark," Cristofo reciprocated with a cordiality that was meant to wrap up the idle chatter with the aim of moving on to the more nitty-gritty substance of the forthcoming exchange. "So tell me, Altarius, what is next for us? What challenges and adventures yet remain?"

"Ah, the impetuousness of youth … Enjoy these peaceful moments, my young apprentice, for they are the ones that will snag upon your memory like a firmly embedded fisherman's hook. The adventures will come and go for the likes of us wizards and wayfarers, but do not overlook the most pleasurable of undertakings that are oftentimes discernible and right under your nose." A directed glance toward the not-too-far-away distance steered Cristofo along as the two of us then proceeded to share in a favorable view. Princess Myrina glistened with a radiant air as she marched along on a casual promenade that saw her flanked by her mother the queen on one side and by her forthcoming mother-in-law, Cristofo's cherished progenitor, on the other.

"I do envy you to a degree, boy, for although the details of my initial familial relationship have long become faded and for the most part substantially obscured, that beguiling stare that your fair princess now brings to bear upon you kindles the heartwarming sentiment that lives on in the core of my being and lights me up with an inner radiance that is without a doubt beyond compare. So worry not about the next crisis or calamity, as you will find that there is no shortage of them to be certain—nay, conversely they will always exist and be there. But a true love's most beauteous ensnarement … Well now, that is a genuine commodity the likes of which are found to be exorbitantly rare. Besides, your engagement is freshly announced! A princely vocation is part of your destiny, so it seems, as is a wizardly one as well. Enjoy and be light-minded, my boy. Carry on enthusiastically and with thoughts that are untroubled and carefree!"

"By all means, Altarius. As is to be expected, you are correct to a significant degree. But how long do I have to wait until our next exploit? Surely you can foresee it to within a reasonable preciseness, can you not?"

"Tomorrow, perhaps, or maybe in an age. Such things are not meant to be quantifiable, my dear boy, especially when considering that your notion of a time frame is no longer viable, nor is it relevant given your newfound longevity. So expect nothing except the eventuality itself ... and let us agree that enough has been said about that!"

Once again, a brief quietude fittingly presented itself within the exchange, and then a firm yet endearing pat on the back jostled Cristofo free from his pensive reflection.

"Cheer up, my good companion, and fear not, for I assure you that the forthcoming adventures will be diverse and aplenty! In the meantime, there is a lot of matter and meaning for you to digest and absorb, so by all means take some time to collect your bearing and compose yourself. And for the love of all that is holy, focus on what is right in front of your face, namely your delightful and most beautiful prize!"

A surrendering smile crept its way onto the fledgling young wizard's pleasantly constituted yet nonetheless contemplative face. "What would I do without your wise words to guide me, Altarius?" The boy was reciprocating with only the mildest measure of sarcasm as he took hold of a stored-away object still hidden within the confines of his trousers' inconspicuous waist pocket. "But answer me just one last thing: whose tooth is this, exactly?"

"Ha, well played, my boy! When did you first realize that you had no need for it?"

"No need? Oh, don't you worry, my infinitely wise collaborator. I assure you that I will find a purpose for it yet!" Cristofo ascended from his seated position as he blurted forth the words while returning the decayed and discolored tooth back into its comfortable and secure hiding place. "Farewell for the time being, Altarius the Prime and exalted wizard of age. I will heed your advice for the moment as I snatch and make off with the princess Myrina, who signals her eagerness toward a good-natured ramble and jaunt."

At that time, I proceeded to hoist my lanky and overly satiated frame that concurrently was hit by a glimmering flash from the boy's swinging and swaying locket, signaling Iggy's wholehearted salutation in turn. Cristofo, along with his beaming companion, mounted the trusty gorallion and made way toward the promenading trio of elegant high-ranking dames.

As for my part, the occasion presented itself as the perfect termination point for our tale of the moment. Maleabar was took hold of and struck downward with force and with goal as a beckoning toward my remarkable dragon was sent forth with a soon-to-be answered signal and toll. All was good and well in the aftermath of outrageous adventure as I soaked up the ambiance of the whimsical circumstance while awaiting my gargantuan and glorious ride.